If your heart is in the highlands ...

Tall, Dark and Kilted

by

Lizzie Lamb

A humorously-ever-after contemporary romance

http://www.lizzielamb.co.uk

ISBN 978-0-9573985-0-4

For Dave
aka Bongo Man
who came out from under his camper van to
bring me coffee and biscuits.

And for Jasper,
who helped eat the biscuits

Chapter One

The music hit Fliss as she rounded the corner of Elgin Crescent, Notting Hill.

The sugared almond pink and yellow houses were almost vibrating in the late May evening as *I Predict a Riot* blasted out from an open window half way down the street. Her stomach flipped over with a mixture of excitement and nerves as she acknowledged the Kaiser Chiefs were bang on message.

It was going to be that kind of night.

That kind of party.

She gazed wide-eyed at the grand houses and the expensive cars parked in front of them. It wasn't every day she was invited to this exclusive postcode. In fact, she was more likely to be found passively inhaling her friends' cigarette smoke over shared laughter, gossip and Mojitos outside her favourite pub in Pimlico than hanging with the Notting Hill set.

But, tonight was different.

If she read Isla Urquhart's invitation correctly, she was about to be made an offer she couldn't refuse. One which would whisk her away from her poorly paid job at *Pimlico Pamperers* therapy centre and propel her towards . . . well, if not stardom exactly, then something more promising than the long hours and low wages which were currently her lot.

She drew near the Urquharts' house where Isla was holding court at the top of the stone steps. Ranged below her on the pavement were two Police Community Support Officers and a group of angry neighbours. The butterflies which had been performing loop the loops in her stomach all the way up from the station, slipped on black opaque tights and hard shoes and broke into Riverdance.

'We won't ask you again Miss, turn that music down.'

Isla insolently flicked cigarette ash in the PCSO's direction, but in spite of her defiant stance she looked openly relieved to see Fliss coming along the street. 'You tell them Fliss. They won't listen to me.'

'Tell them what exactly?' Sensing a Mexican standoff developing, Fliss readied herself to push through the cordon of police and neighbours, bundle Isla indoors and get down to the serious matter of discussing the proposal Isla had mentioned a couple of days earlier

'About Mumma - Being - In - India.' Isla enunciated slowly, putting an exaggerated stress on each word.

Quickly realising what was required of her, Fliss said smoothly, 'She's at an ashram in India, officer - Jaipur to be precise - having her chakras freed. Won't be home for weeks. Would you like the number?' With all the aplomb of an Oscar winning actress she slipped easily into role, scrolling through her mobile phone and then pausing. 'But, with the time difference and various treatments I *really* can't see her coming to the phone.'

Clearly she'd said the right thing because she was summoned to stand on the top step. And for a moment she felt chosen, special and it didn't seem to matter that she was a poorly paid holistic therapist and Isla a Notting Hill trustafarian with money to burn. They were friends, in this together and that's all that mattered.

'She's probably posted a notice on Facebook. The Crescent will be swamped with rioters and the gardens trashed by hoodies,' one neighbour persisted, clearly underwhelmed by the PCSO's performance.

At that moment, the Ministry of Sound medley blaring through the open window came to an end and a blissful silence descended on Elgin Crescent. Everyone drew breath, the policemen and neighbours made as if to walk away - then the music resumed and Johnny Rotten informed everyone he was an anarchist.

This, apparently, was a groove too far for Isla's neighbour.

'That's it; I'm calling your brother . . .'

For a moment, Isla's poise wavered and the colour drained from her cheeks. Fliss wondered what kind of man had the power to dent the thick armour of her self-belief where a visit from the police had no effect. But she wasn't allowed time for further reflection because Isla was back with a vengeance.

'Ruairi's too busy to bother himself with the likes of you. Anyway, chillax - we're moving into the communal gardens.' She waved a queenly hand at them.

'Those gardens are for residents!' a second neighbour spluttered.

'And the Urquharts have lived here longer than any of *you*,' she said, looking down her aristocratic nose at them. The police officers exchanged a let's-get-this-over-with look and moved in.

'Right. That's enough! You,' the elder officer addressed Fliss, 'take her indoors. Close the window and turn down the music. Or this party will be over quicker than you can say: *injunction.*'

Seizing the Get Out of Jail Free card, Fliss dragged Isla over the threshold and slammed the front door behind her. She stood with her back pressed against its reassuring solidity as Isla, predictably without a word of thanks, sauntered off towards the back of the house where – judging by the noise, the party was in full swing.

At that moment, Fliss remembered her best friend and fellow therapist at *Pimlico Pamperers* had nicknamed Isla and her sister Cat: *The Spawn of Satan,* and resolved to proceed with caution. Longing for a quiet place to marshal her thoughts and make some sense of why she'd been invited here tonight, Fliss made her way towards the cloakroom.

As she did so, the motto on a t-shirt she'd seen at Camden Locks Market flashed into mind: *If you can't run with the big dogs, stay on the porch.* Maybe that was the point of her being here - to determine if she was poodle or Rottweiler; worthy of inclusion in Isla's posse, or not. She knew Isla collected friends irrespective of class or upbringing, provided they were amusing - or, as she suspected was more likely in *her* case - could be of use to her.

Although just what service she could render the honourable Miss Isla

Urquhart wasn't immediately obvious.

She tried to shake off the feeling of disquiet, of being out of her comfort zone that accompanied her along the shadowy hallway. How could she fit into Cat and Isla's world? They had a trust fund to smooth their path and make life pleasant, whereas all she had to look forward to for the next forty years was **work, work, and more work.**

The very thought made her head ache.

But just for tonight, she was going to allow herself to imagine what might happen if Fate - maybe in the unlikely form of Isla Urquhart - intervened and sent some good karma her way. She pulled a face and took a reality check - there was little hope of that happening. Hard work would get her out of her rented flat in Pimlico; not Fate, karma or a knight in shining Armani. And, for the record, knights in armour - designer or otherwise - had been thin on the ground of late.

She headed towards a door screened by a thick curtain embroidered with appliquéd elephants and tiny, tarnished silver mirrors. She tried the door, but it was locked. One of Isla's friends was probably in there snorting illegal substances, she thought annoyed, while she was standing cross-legged, desperate to use the loo. She gave the door a kick and rapped on it with her knuckles in an attempt to hurry up the occupant.

'Give us a minute, will ya?' came back a voice that was more Chelmsford than Chelsea.

This was followed by a thump, the sound of breaking glass and hyena-like laughter. The key turned, the curtain was pulled back and peering round the door with a broken mirror in her hand and looking guilty as hell, was her best friend Becky Casterton.

Chapter Two

'Bex - What are you doing here?' Fliss asked after a stunned silence.

'Fliss, babe. Thank God it's you. I thought it might have been one of the Urquharts.' Becky gazed round like a child who'd been invited to a maiden aunt's house and warned not to touch anything. 'Quite a gaff, ain't it?' She pulled back the mirrored curtain to reveal a Victorian lavatory in all its glory, complete with cistern, dangling chain and flower transferred toilet bowl. 'Gross,' was her considered opinion.

Fliss laughed at her expression. 'And did you clock the art work while you were in there?' She pointed to a group of framed erotic prints under a tarnished picture light and Becky twisted her head to check out the graphic sexual positions. 'Fifty shades of grey. Or should that be *tartan*?'

'Yeah. What's that all about?' she asked, plainly taken aback to find erotica next to the Andrex and air freshener.

'They're nineteenth century prints of the Kama Sutra and highly collectable - if you're into that sort of thing,' Fliss shouted through the door as she used the loo and then washed her hands.

'Posh porn - I get it! Hey, do you think that's what Cat and Isla get up to after hours? God, I pity any blokes those two drag back here. They probably eat them alive and spit the bits out for breakfast. Bit of a dump though. You'd think - with all their dosh - they'd give the place a makeover.' Fliss re-joined Becky who was giving the Urquhart's eclectic collection of antique furniture and artefacts a second look over. 'Ain't they heard of IKEA?'

'The look's called shabby chic, sweetie. It means that you inherited your furniture from Granny and didn't buy it in Furniture Land.' Unlike

5

Becky, she wasn't fazed by the surroundings because she'd visited the house several times to give Cat and Isla treatments. And last March had organised a Girls' Night In party where she'd given free demonstrations to the sisters and their girlfriends in return for a large donation to Comic Relief.

'It's the haunted house from Scooby Doo crossed with the Addams' Family mansion. If you ask me.' Becky shuddered as Fliss took the broken mirror from her and carefully placed it on the pier table next to a retro Bakelite telephone.

How was she going to account for Becky's presence here tonight - let alone the broken heirloom, she wondered? Her arrival was an unforeseen complication and couldn't have been worse timed. Shrugging off the thought she went on to explain why the house looked so unloved.

'Apparently, the house hasn't been touched in years - not since the death of Ruairi Urquhart's mother.' She looked two floors above them where a cupola let summer light into the dark hall, half expecting to see the ghost of the late Lady Urquhart materialise and float down towards them. 'From what I've heard, he won't be too pleased to learn Cat and Isla have organised a party, alienated their neighbours and received a verbal warning from the police.'

'Guess they're in deep dung, huh?' Becky's concerned expression was at odds with the hopeful inflexion in her voice. She disliked the sisters and didn't bother to hide it.

'Up to their necks,' Fliss confirmed, hoping that was enough to distract Becky from asking why *she* was the only therapist from Pimlico Pamperers Isla had invited to the party.

Actually, it was a question she wouldn't mind having answered herself. Had she read too much into Isla's throw away remark - *arrive for ten there's something I want to run past you*? Knowing Isla that could simply mean that she wanted a split nail filed before her boyfriend arrived. Or was about to offer Fliss a room to rent in this large house because she knew how cash- strapped Fliss was - and how much she hated her mouldering flat in Pimlico.

'I didn't know they had a brother,' Becky said, suitably distracted.

'Stepbrother. It appears that he's the laird of some vast estate in the highlands of Scotland. Cat and Isla call him The Wolf.' She shivered, imagining a highlander - tall, dark, and kilted - silhouetted against a full moon, striding romantically along a mountain ridge. 'I get the impression he's not the kind of man you mess with.'

'He sounds well bad. A bit like the bloke in Being Human? Except he's a vampire - and Irish, - I think.' Fliss watched as Becky struggled to reconcile conflicting images of bad boys, vampires and lairds.

'Forget about him, Bex. He's out of our league; probably eats therapists like us for breakfast.'

'Mind you, I do love a bad boy.' Becky smoothed down her top. 'Even if his house needs a serious make over and is a *whatshisname* to his mum.'

'A shrine,' Fliss supplied.

'This house reminds me of the one in the movie we watched last year. You know; the one with the scary housekeeper.'

'Rebecca . . .'

'Yeah - Creeped me out, just like this house.'

'This must be one of the few houses in Notting Hill that has all its rooms intact and hasn't got a swimming pool in the basement.' Fliss was glad that she wasn't the only one who felt the weight of unhappiness and bereavement in the air. 'Most of the other houses I've been in have been knocked right through to the gardens. Or turned into swanky apartments.'

Becky did a double take. 'Hang on a minute, girlfriend; other houses? Oh, I geddit - you've been moonlighting again. You know what'll happen if you're found out.' She left the phrase hanging as concern for Fliss's welfare drove scary housekeepers, wolfish lairds and bad boys from her mind.

Fliss knew *exactly* what would happen. She'd be sacked on the spot. Dismissed without a reference - like the governess in a gothic novel caught in flagrante with the master of the house. But she could earn more moonlighting in the evening than in a whole day at the salon, and that made it worth the risk.

And needs must . . .

The extra money helped to pay the rent and utilities on her flat; it filled the fridge and bought a few luxuries. Anything left over at the end of the month went straight into the building society to fund her dream of managing her own therapy business.

'Well, I'd better make sure that she doesn't find out, then,' she said with considerably more bravado than she felt.

'You don't need to worry about Mrs Morris. Cat and Isla Urquhart will get you into plenty of trouble.' Becky folded her arms across her breasts to underline her point. 'I don't get what you see in them, Fliss. They're nothing but a pair of stupid tarts. They'll use you and then spit you out - see if they don't.'

'I know *The Spawn of Satan* - you've said.' She tried to make light of Becky's fears but conceded that she had a point. However, Fliss knew Cat and Isla were only dangerous in the sense that they came from a different universe and could take her away from everything she and Becky had shared since childhood. That was the root of Becky's dislike and distrust of them. 'Okay . . . moving on - how did you get in here tonight? I overheard several of my clients bemoaning the fact that Isla was being very stingy with her invitations. Keeping out the riff-raff, as she put it.'

'I just walked up to the front door along with all the other posh totty and blended right in.'

Fliss gave Becky's thigh-skimming skirt, killer heels, low cut top, jacked up breasts and fake Mulberry handbag a doubtful look. 'I'd have said that your look owed more to Katie Price than Kate Middleton.'

'Think you're soooo funny. Don't cha?'

'Knicker-wettingly amusing, most people say.'

'Well, I'm not most people,' Becky responded, giving her a playful shove.

This banter was a well-established routine and the very essence of their friendship which went back to the first day in nursery school. They'd pretty much lived as sisters since the death of Fliss's parents six years earlier when Becky's parents had assumed legal responsibility for her until she reached eighteen. And, much as she owed them a debt of gratitude, Fliss knew it was time for her to leave Pimlico and make something of her life.

There was a fundamental difference - of ambition and aspiration, mainly - that marked her out from Becky and the other therapists at the salon. She guessed the Urquhart sisters had noticed it, too, and that's why they'd asked her along tonight. She needed a passport out of Pimlico, the chance of something better in life; maybe the sisters and their circle of upper class girlfriends could provide it.

'Come on, let's touch up our war paint and hit the party,' she suggested.

Becky was only too happy to oblige. She made room so they could share the mirror above the pier table, sprayed a throat clogging mist of perfume around them and arranged her blonde hair extensions to best advantage. Fliss regarded her own reflection with some dissatisfaction. Her grey-flecked green eyes beneath a straight cut fringe held a whimsical, far-away look, but her lips were set in a firm line. Maybe it was this combination of vulnerability and determination that attracted men in the first instance, but scared them off when they encountered her stubborn streak and independent nature. Whatever the reason, she hadn't been out on a second date in a long time or had a serious relationship in years.

Perhaps all that would change tonight.

'You, okay?' Becky asked, clearly sensing Fliss's anxiety but misinterpreting the cause of it. 'You look drop dead gaw - jus and you don't need me to tell you that.' Reaching out, she fluffed up Fliss's shoulder length auburn hair and tenderly straightened her floaty top.

'I'm a little tired, that's all . . .' Fliss felt a pang at keeping secrets from Becky, but much as she loved her, she couldn't allow Becky's unscheduled arrival to jeopardise her chances tonight. However, she needn't have worried, because Becky had already moved on to her favourite subject: *Men*.

'Let's go and find those two fit blokes I clocked earlier. I told them to wait in the kitchen for us. Blokes on tap! Save us a lot of time - how cool is that?'

'Decidedly un-cool. You're complete rubbish when it comes to finding me a decent man. I'm not interested, Bex - even if they're a cross between Johnny Depp and Brad Pitt, with Lady Gaga for a mother.'

'You're way too picky, know that? Come on, lighten up and get laid, girlfriend. You're only young once. We'll probably never get invited to another party like this.'

'*We*?' Fliss gave her a severe look.

'Okay, me. Where's the harm?' Becky asked and then skidded to a halt in front of a brass Buddha sitting in the lotus position on a pier table. The scent from joss sticks stuck into the pierced fretwork of his robes didn't quite mask the pungent sweetness of cannabis permeating the house.

'Now what?'

'Skunk!' She sniffed the air knowledgeably. 'I might not know about shabby chic and posh porn, but I recognise Moroccan Woodbines when I smell them. Bring it on, baby.' She rubbed her hands together. 'This is definitely my kind of party - and Cat and Isla have just become my new best friends.'

Fliss groaned. Now she'd have to keep an eye on her all night and make sure she stayed out of trouble. That would seriously derail her plans for a one-to-one with Isla. She sighed resignedly; nothing was going according to plan. The words of the horoscope she'd downloaded onto her mobile that morning now seemed doubly prophetic: *Friends will make or break your weekend. Have an escape plan at the ready.*

But which friends was the horoscope referring to, and how was she supposed to come up with an escape plan when she had no idea what - or who - she'd be escaping from? Touching Buddha for good karma, she guided Becky towards the back of the house where screams, the sound of crockery being smashed and the insistent thump, thump of garage music announced that the party was well under way.

Chapter Three

They entered the kitchen in the middle of a food fight. Cat Urquhart hurtled past them with an armful of tomatoes, cannoned into a Welsh dresser and then straight into the kitchen table.

'Oops,' she giggled as Fliss reached out to steady her. 'That could've been expensive. Mitzi - our Mumma, loves this junk.' She nodded towards a collection of Emma Bridgewater pottery on the dresser as she lobbed tomatoes at her friends. Her eyes were crossed like a Siamese's - the effect of too much drink or drugs, Fliss assumed - and the tomatoes missed their mark, splattering the walls and kitchen cupboards instead.

'You guys wanna a drink?' she slurred, waving towards an ice filled Belfast sink where a spectacular range of booze was chilling.

'Thanks, we'll help ourselves,' Fliss remarked, doubting Cat's ability to pour wine into a glass. Ducking to avoid some low flying bread rolls, Fliss walked over to the draining board where monogrammed napkins and solid silver cutlery had been dumped next to antique Waterford goblets. She poured two glasses of Pimms from a heavy jug that looked remarkably like one she'd seen on Cash in the Attic recently - a Lalique worth several thousand pounds.

As if suddenly remembering her duties as hostess, Cat gestured towards the buffet abandoned on the table like supper on the Marie Celeste. 'Help yourselves, guys,' she hiccupped. Then someone shook a bottle of champagne and sprayed it over her, like it was the end of the Grand Prix. 'Hey - mind me bleedin' cloves, will ya?' she squawked in a faux cockney accent.

The forsaken buffet and the casualness with which the sisters treated family heirlooms was a testament to their belief that life was

11

too short to spend it stuffing mushrooms. Ever practical, Fliss thought of the mammoth cleaning operation that would be required when the party was over. Then a sobering thought struck her - what if she'd been invited to the party to take charge of their shambolic attempt at entertaining? Would Isla march through the door, give her a pair of Marigolds and tell her to get down to it, lickety-spit. Like a latter day Mary Poppins?

If so, then she'd be told *exactly* where to stick her Marigolds.

As Becky said, it was time she chilled, forgot the day-to-day struggle and lived for the moment. Then she reminded herself that she wasn't free to act like Cat and Isla, she lacked the necessary clout, connections and money to get out of trouble. When the brown stuff hit the fan, girls like her had to rely on nous, a fast pair of heels and a bomb proof exit strategy.

A death-like groan drew her back to Cat who was bent over the edge of the Belfast sink and had turned a nasty shade of green. Acting instinctively, Fliss put down the two glasses of Pimms she'd just poured and dragged Cat into the garden where she was violently sick in a flowerbed.

'My bloody shoes,' a woman complained as her black suede high heels took a light splattering of vomit. 'They're fucking Laboutins,' she shrieked in a voice capable of waking all the dogs in the Royal Borough of Kensington and Chelsea.

'That'd be Charlie Laboutin, would it?' Isla strolled up to inspect the shoes and her drunken sister. 'They're fakes darling,' she pronounced with obvious satisfaction.

'They're soooo not fakes . . . they've got red soles; and cost me over five hundred pounds in Harvey Nick's,' she said, disappearing indoors to clean them.

Isla bent down until she was level with her sister's pallid face and gave her a vigorous shake. 'Snap out of it, Cat, you're spoiling Fliss's fun. No one's going to spend the whole night looking after you.' Fliss took that to mean that *she* wasn't, but hoped that Fliss might. Cat gave another groan, her head rolled sideways and she was sick again. Feeling rather sorry for her, Fliss helped Cat to her feet and then wiped her face with a tissue she'd found in her jeans pocket.

'You appear to have it all under control, Fliss,' Isla said with the brisk air of a WRVS organiser sending out troops to a battle zone. 'You'll look after her, won't you? You've been trained for this sort of thing, after all.' Fliss wondered how on earth Isla had made the giant leap from her being a member of St John's Ambulance Brigade (lapsed), to ward sister at Holby General.

'I think you'd be a better choice. But shouldn't we call a doctor?'

'No. No, she'll be fine. Besides, we don't want the Plods sniffing round, do we? There's a padded couch in the summerhouse, put her in there. Let her sleep it off. Yeah? Oh, hang on - better check her pockets.' She rummaged through Cat's skirt and found an iPhone, a half-smoked spliff and a wrap of cocaine. She gave the phone and the drugs to Fliss. 'I thought as much . . . cheeky little cow's been at my stash.'

'What am I supposed to do with them?' Fliss had no intention of spending the party in possession of class A drugs or playing Super Nanny to Cat Urquhart.

'Keep them, for helping,' Isla said magnanimously. 'Yeah? There's plenty more where they came from. Although, not the iPhone. Obviously.'

'Obviously.' But Fliss's sarcasm went right over Isla's head.

'Hey, you guys . . .' Isla shouted at some friends who'd draped a life-sized statue of Venus de Milo in next door's garden in what appeared to be her best Agent Provocateur underwear. Shaking Fliss off, she signalled for the music to be jacked up to ear bleeding level and went over to join them.

'I'll look after your sister then, shall I? No, of course it's not too much trouble, Thanks for asking.' But Isla had already disappeared into the May twilight and Fliss's ironic curtsey went unnoticed.

Resigned to her role as babysitter, Fliss wondered briefly where Becky was and then headed towards an Edwardian summerhouse framed in fairy lights. Guiding Cat onto a padded couch, she put her into the recovery position with a pillow at her back and left her to sleep off her excesses. Looking round the summerhouse, with its broken toy box and old doll's house crammed in the corner, she could imagine the sisters playing here in more innocent times.

Then she glanced down at the drugs in her hand and serious second thoughts began to crowd in. Was it wise to hitch her wagon to Isla's wayward star? Stake everything on a vague promise which she'd most probably forgotten? Feeling disenchanted with the evening Fliss slipped the drugs and iPhone into her pocket. She checked on Cat one last time and then walked further into the garden where the air was sweet with the scent of tobacco plants and regale lilies.

Lights in the shape of red chilli peppers had been threaded through the branches of old fruit trees to mark the boundary. And citronella flares - lit to keep the bugs at bay, mingled with the smell of crushed grass, creating a heady cocktail which was balm to her senses. She shivered despite the warmth of the evening and wrapped her arms around herself, beset by restlessness, a longing for something just out of reach. Something she wanted but couldn't give a name to, a feeling that she couldn't express in words.

Isla's friends, obviously tiring of the food fight in the kitchen, spilled onto the lawn and started dancing to a Ministry of Sound track like this was a beach in Ibiza, not a garden in W11. They were soon joined by Isla and her posse of girlfriends and Fliss's whimsical mood was killed, stone dead.

'Buggery bollocks; bloody neighbours. Turn off the music,' Isla ordered. 'We've had another visit from Mr and Mrs Plod and they've issued a formal warning. Jeez-us, you'd think they'd have something better to do on a Saturday night than break up a harmless little farewell party - wouldn't you? Isn't it punishment enough that *Himself's* ordered us home to fuckin' Scotland to die from an overdose of tartan, Gaelic and midges?'

Fliss was startled to realise that Isla was addressing her - like they were best friends or something. Clearly, Isla *did* want something from her. Fliss eyed her suspiciously; best friends? She hardly thought so . . . the contrast between them as they faced each other in the flickering light of the citronella flares couldn't have been more marked. Her Top

Shop combo of white skinny jeans, filmy kaftan and gladiator sandals when measured against Isla's vintage Indian waistcoat, voile shorts, ripped fishnets and leather biker boots - made it clear that she came from a galaxy far, far away.

Far away from Notting Hill, that is.

'Well, I'm going to make this a night to remember,' Isla assured her. 'Come on guys; grab a couple of bottles each - we're moving into the garden square. Party on, dudes; woo - hoo.'

The stirring speech reawakened the restiveness in Fliss. She looked longingly towards the well-tended communal garden beyond the archway of roses, then back at the kitchen door. The window of opportunity for finding Becky and leaving before the real trouble kicked off was disappearing - fast. Then she thought - why not? She might never get another chance to walk in this exclusive communal garden and gaze into the million pound properties that surrounded it. How many Brazilians, eyebrow threading and reflexology sessions would it take to earn that kind of money, she wondered?

She took a glass of champagne from one of the trays being passed round and walked through the gates. She drained the glass in several thirsty gulps and her eyes widened - this wasn't the usual cheap prosecco on offer at Tesco's, but something rarer. Vintage Krug, perhaps; not that she knew what Krug tasted like, but she'd read about it in salon copies of Tatler and Vogue. She held her glass out for a top up, but this time she sipped the champagne more slowly and savoured the taste.

As she walked round exploring the garden square, a brass plaque on the back of a teak bench gleamed dully beneath the security light and caught her attention. Moving closer, she read the inscription using her mobile phone's display as a torch.

For Mairi Urquhart who loved this garden.
Erected in her memory by Hamish and Rhuairidh,
who loved her.

Fliss had heard stories of Lady Urquhart who'd died shortly before her thirty fifth birthday and how her husband, Hamish, had married soon after. Too quickly and too conveniently some said, with Isla being born six months after the honeymoon and Cat two years later. Now, having the seen this poignant inscription, Fliss wished she'd listened more attentively when Isla had talked about her family whilst on the therapy couch. She was curious to learn more about Ruairi Urquhart; how he'd coped with an estate encumbered by death duties. His reaction when he'd been forced to abandon his university studies, take over the lairdship of his estate and responsibility for two wayward stepsisters and an eccentric stepmother.

But, most of all - how he'd come by his nickname: The Wolf.

Running her fingers over the tarnished plaque, Fliss was drawn back to her recent bereavement and felt an immediate connection with him. She knew how it felt to lose the people one loved. She took another sip of the champagne and this time a real buzz of pleasure reverberated through her. She smiled at her foolishness when she realised that the buzz was coming from Cat's iPhone in her pocket. She drew it out, read the caller display and her smile faded, replaced by a chill of presentiment.

Call it Fate, synchronicity or a moment of pure happenstance. But, one thing was indisputable . . . Ruairi Urquhart, The Wolf of the Highlands was phoning home.

Chapter Four

She dropped the phone on the bench as if it was too hot to handle and watched it vibrate and turn through one hundred and eighty degrees - like an angry beetle flipped on its back. She reached out for it and then drew her hand back - much better to let it ring until the battery went flat or Urquhart hung up. If he wanted to know what was happening in his house and what his sisters were up to, he'd have to find out from someone else.

Glancing back at the phone she noticed that ringtone and vibrating had stopped. She let out a sigh of relief, blew her fringe out of her eyes and pressed the back of her hand against her hot cheek. Her relief was short lived, however, as the phone burst into noisy life again. She had no intention of answering it - she really didn't - but then her conscience and her vivid imagination kicked in.

What if there was a genuine emergency and he was stranded half way up a rock face in Wester Ross calling for help? Help that only *she* could summon. She pictured the mountain rescue helicopter hovering over a precipice, the paramedic being winched down to rescue him. Being interviewed on the Ten O'clock News. The family thanking her for saving his life.

She answered the call.

'Hello . . .'

'Catriona . . .'

That was the last word she understood. The rest of the conversation appeared to be conducted in Klingon. Or some other language she hadn't studied at school or picked up on holiday in Ayia Napa last summer with Becky and the girls from *Pimlico Pamperers.* Unaware that she'd actually said *Klingon, she* gave a start when Ruairi Urquhart repeated it.

'*Klingon*? What the f-. Who is this?' His voice poured into her ear like posh treacle - deep, well-modulated and with a faint trace of an unfamiliar accent. It made a shiver run down her spine, in spite of it being the hottest day of the summer.

'A friend of Cat and Isla's,' she said, thinking fast.

'Okay, *friend of Cat and Isla,* why are you answering my sister's phone?'

'Because . . . she's busy.'

'That'll be a first.' He laughed sarcastically as if the idea of Cat doing anything useful was extremely unlikely. 'Busy doing what?' His peremptory tone dissipated Fliss's pleasant champagne buzz. 'Hello, are you still there?'

'Y- es,' she responded after a long pause. 'Cat's - well, she's busy doing - stuff, you know?'

'Stuff?' he repeated as though talking to a half-wit. 'No, strangely enough, I don't know what constitutes *stuff* in the surreal world you and my sisters inhabit. I don't know who you are and I care even less, but there's a party going on in my house and I want to know who's responsible for it. Take Cat's phone to her - immediately - and tell Isla to switch hers on.' His barked instructions made it clear he was used to issuing orders and having them obeyed.

'I really don't think . . .'

'You aren't required to think,' he said, as though that was beyond her capabilities. 'Just put one foot in front of the other, repeat the action several times and take this phone to one of my sisters. You *can* do that - walk, I mean? You aren't so drunk that you can't stand up, for example?'

'Of course I'm not drunk, but . . .'

'Can't you do anything without arguing about it first? I've just been woken up by my next door neighbour Mr Shipstone, and I'm not best pleased. So I'll make this easy for you. Take. The. Phone. To. Cat.'

'Just woken up? But it's only eleven o'clock.'

Who in their right mind drew the curtains and went to bed on a glorious evening like this? Just how old was this stepbrother of theirs?

He sounded about a hundred and ten and dry as dust.

'Not that it's any business of yours, I'm in Hong Kong where it's six o'clock in the morning. I'm jet lagged, got an important meeting in a couple of hours and really don't appreciate exchanging inanities with one of my sisters' idiot friends. So, if you wouldn't mind?'

She did mind; she minded very much that he thought he could talk to her like . . . like she was a minion and he was the master.

'Hong Kong? I thought you were in Scotland . . . was that Mandarin you were speaking earlier? No wonder I couldn't understand a word.' She was curious and wanted to find out more about him. Needed to see if he was as she'd pictured him: tall, dark - and as it now turned out - *bad tempered.* Or if he was some middle aged man who needed his full eight hours of sleep. She heard his jaw splitting yawn and knew she should hang up. But a devil of mischief made her want to her drag out the conversation long enough to make her point that no man had mastery over her.

'Look. I don't know who you are. Why you've got Catriona's phone or why - for one minute - you'd think I'd be speaking Mandarin or any other Chinese dialect to my sister. I was speaking Gaelic, if you must know; Scots Gaelic. You're clearly out of your mind on drugs so I'll make this easy for you: *tell - Isla - to - ring - me.* And if you have any sense of what's good for you, you'll get out of my house, PDQ.' He paused as if he was going to say more but had changed his mind. 'Is that in plain enough English for you?' and with that, he hung up

Fliss put the phone back in her pocket - the nerve of the man! He'd completely shattered her chilled out mood and been damned rude into the bargain. She had the feeling he'd be ringing back within the next five minutes to check if she'd done as he'd commanded. But she felt in no hurry to pass on his message. She'd hand the phone over to Cat or Isla as and when she caught up with them and they could field the calls from their obnoxious stepbrother.

Getting to her feet, she rubbed the small of her back where the tarnished plaque had dug through her flimsy top, touched the inscription and read its poignant message again.

> For Mairi Urquhart who loved this garden.
>
> Erected in her memory by Hamish and Rhuairidh,
>
> who loved her.

Her earlier empathy for the young, bereaved Ruairi Urquhart now seemed misplaced. True, like her he'd lost his parents; but unlike her, he had a ready-made second family to help him over the worst of times. Not to mention property and thousands of acres in Wester Ross to keep him off the bread line.

What a brute, she fumed! Small wonder the sisters had nicknamed him The Wolf. She was suddenly grateful he had no idea who she was and that Notting Hill and Hong Kong were half a world apart.

'I'm not leaving the party, your Lairdship - is that in plain enough English for *you*?' It gave her great satisfaction to shout her defiance at the garden and do the exact opposite of what he'd ordered. She only wished that Urquhart could hear her in his hotel room in Hong Kong.

There was a great thrashing in the undergrowth as Becky - dragging Cat Urquhart behind her, burst through the bushes and into the garden. She pulled laurel leaves out of her hair extensions and then plonked Cat down on the bench next to her stepbrother's dedication.

'Hey Fliss! I've promised Cat we'd show her our matching tattoos.' Becky rolled down the waistband of her skirt to where the legend *Carpe Diem* was tattooed on the creamy curve of her hip. 'C'mon, Fliss, be a sport.'

'Seize the day,' Fliss translated automatically, her mind still on her coruscating conversation with Urquhart. Then she snapped out of her introspection and focused on Becky and Cat. 'Or, in our case - the *night*. Time to party, ladies. Woo hoo!'

'We've watched that movie a hundred times on DVD, ain't we Fliss?' Becky put in, returning to their tattoos. 'It's dead sad; Robin Williams is dead good in it. All the boys are drop dead gorgeous,' she prattled on. The result, Fliss guessed, of too much vodka being mixed with too little Red Bull - and God knows what else she'd had access to, courtesy of Cat, Isla and their posh friends.

'All those *deads*, yeah?' Cat pronounced with a flash of apparent insight. 'Guess that's why they called the film Dead Poets' Society, huh?' Apart from looking like an extra from Twilight, she'd made a quick recovery and plainly had more tenacity than Fliss had given her credit for.

'Yeah. R- ight.' Fliss regarded them with wry humour. One had attended a comprehensive in Walthamstow, the other an expensive boarding school in the Home Counties, yet both seemed to have attained exactly the same level of education. The government would be very pleased with that result.

'God, I'd love a tattoo,' Cat said with open admiration. 'You two are so lucky, but Ruairi would kill me.' Fliss didn't doubt it for a second. A two-minute conversation had been long enough for her to deduce that he expected his stepsisters to come to heel after one yank of the choke chain.

And everyone else, too - apparently.

'We got them when we were seventeen and under age,' Fliss said, returning to the here and now. She undid the fly on her white jeans, pulled down the waistband and showed off her tattoo to Cat. 'Not that the tattooist minded as long as we paid up front and didn't faint.'

'My dad still doesn't know about it.' Becky said. 'It's our little secret. But, then, there are lots of things about me - and Fliss - that my Dad doesn't know. And doesn't need to know. Eh, Fliss?' It took considerable effort, but she managed to tap the side of her nose with her forefinger. Cat looked at Fliss wide-eyed and she guessed that her reputation - *practical, hardworking, down to earth Fliss,* was being re-written tonight.

But she was given little time to ponder the fact because the statue of Venus de Milo - which had earlier been draped in Isla's underwear - toppled over on the patio and lost its head as well as its arms. Glancing across the gardens, Fliss saw Cat's next-door neighbour - presumably, the one who'd disturbed Urquhart's beauty sleep - observing them through nautical binoculars mounted on a brass stand. His wife was by his side and it looked like she was writing something in a notebook.

They had a perfect view because Isla's friends were dancing round the garden like demented fairies and setting off the security lights on all the surrounding houses.

'Hey. Get a load of that old perv over there. Seen enough?' Becky demanded and mooned him.

'OK. Hold it there tiger,' Fliss hoisted up Becky's skirt. 'Isla's in enough trouble; we don't want to aggravate her neighbours any further.'

'Oh, come on Fliss. I've seen you do a lot worse. Remember last summer in Crete? Don't be such a party pooper - anyway, it's done the trick; he's gone back to his cocoa.' She rearranged her clothing, pulling down her light summer top where it had ridden up over her tanned midriff. 'So, whassup? I came looking for you and found Cat staggering round the garden.'

'It's the neighbours, Old Man Shipstone and his missus,' Cat butted in, coming back from the dead. 'He's a *grande fromage* in the Home Office and practically has the local police doing his weekly Waitrose shop for him. His wife's an Hon, some viscount's daughter, as if we're *ever* allowed to forget it. They know the great and the good; whereas, we only know the groooo-vy and the bad.'

'Blimey, girlfriend. That's quite a speech considering how shit-faced you were half an hour ago.' Becky gave Cat a long look before continuing. 'You ain't a stuck up cow like your sister, are ya?'

'Oh yeah, Isla's a piece of work. No doubt about it,' she confirmed with a great lack of sisterly loyalty. 'She's always bossing people about and likes everything done her way.'

'Must be a family characteristic,' Fliss said half to herself as she remembered the phone conversation.

As Becky and Cat prattled on, she zoned out and tried to shrug off the feeling of unease which had dogged her since leaving the kitchen. Despite the shouts and screams coming from the outer reaches of the garden where the head of Venus de Milo was being passed around like a rugger ball, the party felt over.

She turned her back on Cat, gave up on her quest to find Isla and dismissed the conversation with Ruairi from her mind. She'd had enough of the Urquharts for one night and wanted to head back to Pimlico, dragging Becky with her by force if necessary. If their luck was in, their friends would still be drinking in the gardens of their favourite pub well into the warm summer night.

She retrieved the iPhone from her pocket and handed it over to Cat. She was about to leave when Cat grabbed her by the arm, like a younger, hipper version of the Ancient Mariner.

'I'm in deep shit, Fliss. School's been trying to get in contact with Mumma. She really is in India, you know, at an ashram - cum - spa. How am I going to explain to Ruairi that school doesn't want me back for the Upper Sixth? He's gonna go ape-shit; ballistic.'

Fliss didn't doubt that for a second!

'Might as well have the tattoo, then; slip it in under the radar while he's bollocking you for other things. Wot?' Becky asked, as Fliss sent her a chastising head prefect look. 'Wot!'

'Becky - shut up. You're not helping,' Fliss steeled herself for another flippant remark but it never came.

Street-wise, and with an instinct born from years of living in Walthamstow, Becky was standing as still and alert as a meerkat, watching the patrol car that had pulled up level with the Ladbroke Grove entrance of the communal garden. It had slid up without sirens or flashing blue lights, giving the two officers inside plenty of time to assess the scene.

'Bloody hell, Rozzers,' Fliss swore softly and then turned on her heel, prepared to take flight. Becky and Cat were momentarily transfixed as the patrol car's blue light was switched on and the siren gave a long warning yowl before dying away.

'Holy cr- aaap!' A broad Glaswegian accent shattered the following silence as Isla, obviously making a quick assessment of the situation, realised they were about to be rounded up. 'It's the Po-liss. We're busted, Puss Cat.'

Two police wagons, their mesh riot shields raised above the windscreens, appeared alongside the fence and Fliss knew the game was up. Thinking only of herself and Becky, Fliss grabbed her best friend by the arm. 'Don't just stand there . . . Run!'

Chapter Five

F liss tried to shake Cat off, but she clung to her arm as though her life depended on it.

'They won't arrest us, will they?' she whimpered as two officers unlocked the main gate and entered the garden square. Isla's half-stoned friends began running in all directions, careering into each other as they headed for freedom in Elgin Crescent.

'Didn't you hear me?' Fliss turned to Becky. 'We've got to get out of here!'

Fliss took command, dragging Cat and Becky along with her as she headed for the Rosmead Road entrance, her breath catching in her throat and her heart pumping. She removed her high-heeled shoes and threw them into the street, closely followed by her handbag, grabbed hold of the hooped tops of the fence and tried to pull herself up and over.

'Give us your hand, Fliss,' Becky encouraged as she effortlessly shinned up the iron palings and over into Rosmead Road. Fliss reached up to grasp Becky's hand but hers was slippery with perspiration and slid out of Becky's fingers. She looked for a foothold knowing that lacking Becky's long legs and athletic build, climbing the fence would be a challenge for her. She attempted to scramble up the railings for a second time but lost her grip and landed on her back in the soft mud.

'Oof.' She lay on the ground winded, her top ripped where it had caught on the railings. Damp soil seeped through her new white jeans and her eyes stung as sweat sent rivulets of mascara trickling down her cheeks.

'Fliss. Fliss, are you OK?'

Becky peered through the railings like they were prison bars, her face white and anxious in the dusk. Fliss got to her feet and blinked away the black spots in front of her eyes. Taking a shuddering breath she tried to appear cool and in control. She knew Becky would never willingly leave her in the lurch - looking out for each other was their unwritten rule - but this time she had no choice. While the thought of being carted off to the nearest police station filled Fliss with trepidation, she knew it made sense for Becky to hightail it out of there.

'There's no way I'm getting over that fence, Bex. You go. There's little point in both of us getting arrested. Besides,' she tried a feeble joke to make light of her dilemma, 'if they arrest you, who's going to bake me a cake with a file in it. Go on; get out of here.'

In a moment of Thelma and Louise solidarity they held hands, then Becky passed Fliss's handbag back to her and melted into the darkness. Fliss looked helplessly towards her new shoes languishing in the middle of Rosmead Road - but she could hardly call Becky back, so she was going to have to do without them. Turning round, she saw Cat biting her worn down nails to the quick and looking very young and frightened - in spite of her Goth makeup and multiple face piercings. The adrenalin rush brought on by the arrival of the police appeared to have had a de-toxing effect on her and the last vestiges of her drink/drugs binge vanished. Fliss guessed that tonight's events would put being expelled from her posh boarding school into perspective.

'Come on.' She led an unresisting Cat away from the fence. 'Don't worry. We've done nothing wrong.' She crossed her fingers behind her back but phrases like: *creating a disturbance and breech of the peace* crept into mind. Crazily, the words - Keep Calm and Carry On, she'd seen on mugs and posters danced before her eyes. Maybe, if she kept her nerve - everything *would* turn out right.

She skirted past Isla who was giving a young WPC a hard time, asking in a supercilious tone: 'Aren't you supposed to say: *you're nicked*? To which I reply, *it's a fair cop*?'

'I think you've been watching too many re-runs of The Sweeney, Miss,' the officer replied, patently not amused by Isla's flippant tone. Or the way she held her upturned wrists towards another officer, inviting him to handcuff her.

Fliss could cheerfully have throttled her, it looked like they were about to be taken into custody and she was treating the whole thing like a huge joke. Evidently, the rule of law and those who enforced it held no terrors for Isla Urquhart. Eight hundred years of unbroken lineage, a castle in Wester Ross, thousands of acres of hill, forest, loch, farmland and the deference of all those who worked on the Urquhart estate - had clearly given her an exaggerated sense of her own importance.

'Well, am I to be arrested or not?' she demanded.

'Shut up, Isla,' Fliss hissed.

Being born and brought up in Walthamstow by parents who had worked in the local B and Q had given her an appreciation of how things worked for girls like *her*. She considered - briefly, dragging Isla away from the scene but resisted the impulse. There was no saying what she might do if she was denied her fifteen minutes of infamy. It almost seemed as if she *wanted* to be arrested.

'No one's been arrested. *Yet.*' The WPC was momentarily distracted as someone communicated with her through her earpiece.

'If you're ordering pizza, I like mine without anchovies,' Isla said with evident relish before turning to another officer. 'What's all the fuss about? I'm entitled to use these gardens and to invite my friends to use them, too.'

'Yes, you are. But this is the third time this week you and your friends have created a disturbance in these gardens. And your neighbours want an end to it.' Isla lounged insolently against her garden gate, as if she considered being taken into custody a badge of honour, a viable alternative to being imprisoned in the Scottish highlands under the eagle eye of their stepbrother.

Fliss knew that given the choice, *she* would settle for the overdose of tartan, shortbread, Gaelic and midges. Anything was preferable to spending a night in the cells. But, in a moment of clarity, she understood that Isla's posturing was her way of letting Ruairi Urquhart know that while she and Cat were returning home, they weren't going down without a fight.

She experienced a sudden flare of anger. Perhaps she should point out to Isla that all her rebelliousness was just window dressing - everyone knew her family connections would get her out of trouble. But for *her* - a beauty therapist living on her own and with no safety net to cushion her fall to earth, the threat of arrest wasn't something she took lightly.

Cautious but determined, she edged towards the shadowy margins of the garden square and tried to blend into the shrubbery. Somehow she couldn't *quite* see clients booking treatments with a therapist who'd spent a night in the cells. No job, no money. Without an income, she'd have to give up her flat and move back in with Becky's family. And there was *no way* she was going to let that happen.

'My family will be making an official complaint about police harassment,' Isla drawled. 'Our stepbrother knows the Chief Commissioner, personally.'

'Good! Then he'll have no trouble finding his way to the station when he comes to collect you. I'm arresting you because a breach of the peace has been committed and I have reasonable grounds to believe that it will be renewed in the immediate future. Your taxi, ladies,' she gestured towards the police wagon. 'This officer will read you your rights. The party's over, but the night is just beginning.'

A few minutes later, Fliss followed the others into the police wagon and sat down opposite Isla and Cat. By now, mud had seeped through her jeans, her bare feet looked like she'd been potato picking and her voile top was ripped, revealing a less than pristine lacy bra. She reached up and removed clods of earth from her hair while the girl beside her muttered: *ohmigod, ohmigod, ohmigod,* and rocked back and forth.

'Shut it, will you?' Isla snapped, 'cool, calm and collected is the way to go. Take more than a little trip to Ladbroke Grove to rattle us. Eh, Fliss?'

'You don't understand.' The girl seized Fliss's arm, clearly hoping for a more sympathetic hearing from her. 'What if the paps are waiting when the doors open? The publicity . . . My father's career.'

Isla gave an incredulous snort. 'Look around you darling,' she indicated the daughters of some of the most prominent families in

London. 'If the paps are photographing anyone, it won't be you.'

Sitting among them, like a cuckoo in an up-market nest, Fliss cheered herself with the thought that there was nothing newsworthy about her. One of the advantages, she guessed, of belonging to one of the *least* significant families in Britain. Maybe she could just blend into the background and no one would notice her.

'Don't worry, I'll sort things out at the station, I'm well known to the duty sergeant.' Somehow that thought didn't make Fliss feel any better. 'Any problems and I'm phoning my godfather. He's a silk - they'll listen to *him*!' Isla said confidently.

'Or,' another girl commented, 'what about that gorgeous stepbrother of yours. Maybe he'll come over the hills like Mel Gibson in *Braveheart* and rescue us. I Googled him and read all about his wild life conservation scheme. Mind you,' she giggled and rolled her eyes, 'I couldn't decide whether to fancy him or be terrified of him.' She gave a delicious shiver, as if conjuring up an image of Ruairi Urquhart sorting her out in an entirely different set of circumstances. 'Impressive. I can see why you call him The Wolf. Tall, dark, verging on ruthless - very sexy. Just my type.'

'Well, you're so not his type.' Isla's look intimated that he was out of her league. Out of all their leagues. 'Not that it's any of your business, but *Wolf* is short for *Big Bad Wolf*. We call him that because we're not afraid of him. Like in the nursery rhyme? Geddit?' she snapped. This was her moment and clearly she didn't appreciate it being ruined by their comments.

'He can be very . . .' Cat butted in, and then words failed her. Plainly, the thought of Ruairi's reaction to their latest escapade filled her with dread. 'We're going to be grounded for life - allowances stopped, mobiles confiscated, put to work on the estate beating for grouse and schlepping picnics out to the guns for the *whole* summer. And that's if he's in a good mood,' she concluded. Seconds later Isla's phone rang and their stepbrother's voice echoed in the close confines of the police van.

'Don't even think about hanging up, Isla.' His tone brooked no defiance and even Isla didn't have the nerve to cut him off.

'Ruairi. How are you? There's nothing wrong with my phone. I didn't hear it ring . . . cut off you say? Probably a signal black spot.' She banged the phone several times on the side of the van and made a sound like a demented cappuccino machine. 'See what I mean. Maybe, the battery's flat. You know me.' After a few seconds, everyone was under no illusions just how well Ruairi Urquhart knew his stepsister!

'Isla, please,' Cat pleaded, 'don't make things worse.'

'I'm in a taxi if you must know - on my way to Boujis . . . yes, Cat's here.' She passed the phone to her sister.

'Hi, Ruairi,' Cat sounded as though her throat was suddenly dry and her vocal cords constricted with nerves. 'No. Well, yes I suppose so. Yes. Sorry, sorry.' Isla snatched the phone off Cat and mouthed *"wuss"* at her.

'Still there Ruairi? No - no, I don't think it's funny. Not funny at all. Yes, I know you ordered me home - but something came up and . . . I've decided to have a highland fling of my own.'

Words such as: *unreliable, immature and feckless* bounced round the wagon as Ruairi Urquhart ripped into Isla. One or two girlfriends exchanged looks of schaudenfreud, openly enjoying Isla's discomfiture. She was a bit like Marmite Fliss decided, you could love her one minute and hate her the next. She'd stolen their boyfriends, acted high-handedly towards them, made sarcastic remarks about their clothes and played on their neuroses about their weight. Now it was payback time and her girlfriends looked like they were enjoying every moment it.

'I didn't ask bloody old Shipstone to ring you, did I? I don't care if it was his third phone call this evening - the man's clearly obsessed. His wife keeps a log on us, can you believe that?' Fliss noticed that Isla's faux Estuary English had become perceptibly more upper-class as the conversation progressed.

'*Bugger*! Ruairi wasn't supposed to find out about that,' Cat explained unnecessarily as they reached their destination and Isla killed the call. A young officer opened the doors and was greeted by a loud *woo - hoo* and appreciative applause, as if this was a hen party, the police van a stretch limo and he was the strippergram.

'Take them into the station, Collins. And you lot . . . keep the noise down,' a more mature officer snarled at them. 'You are in serious trouble.'

Fliss suddenly remembered the wrap of cocaine in her pocket and anxiety scoured her intestines like battery acid. She thought was going to be physically sick. Being arrested was bad enough - but being in possession of a Class A drug was much worse. She doubted that saying she was looking after them for a friend would cut much ice with the judge. Subdued, she followed the others into Ladbroke Grove Police Station where they were brought before a tired looking duty sergeant. At the sight of the Urquhart sisters, he glanced at his watch and sighed, giving the impression it was going to be a long night.

'*Darling* Sergeant Chapman,' Cat and Isla said in unison, exchanging relieved looks as they rushed up to the desk. Clearly, this wasn't the first time they'd been brought before him.

'We'll soon have this little misunderstanding sorted out with *you* in charge,' Isla schmoozed.

'Sorted out, eh? Well, I don't know about that Miss Urquhart. Let's see.' He consulted the charge sheet, and then looked over the top of his glasses at her. 'We've had complaints of drugs, underage drinking, sex, nudity and trespass in the communal gardens. Your guests using designated parking spaces. Your neighbour asked you several times to turn down the music and you were abusive to him.'

'He was abusive to *me*, actually,' Isla began belligerently, then obviously thought better of it. She dragged Fliss forward, 'My friend here *is very sensible* and can tell you *exactly* what happened.'

'Can you, Miss?' Sergeant Chapman's expression wavered as he took in Fliss's ripped and stained clothing, her mascara-streaked face. His lips twitched, briefly, and then his professional persona dropped into place. 'Name?'

'Felicity Bagshawe,' Isla answered for her, openly relieved that the heat was now on someone else. Fliss gave her a thanks-for-nothing look.

31

'There was no nudity; it was just my friend showing us her tattoo.' She was surprised to find how steady her voice was. Evidently, keeping company with Isla the Blagmeister had taught her a thing or two about lying through her teeth

'Go on,' he urged, making notes on a large pad.

'As for drugs . . .' She managed a casual shrug that suggested drugs were evident at every party these days and tried to forget the wrap of cocaine in her pocket. 'It was just a little party that got out of hand,' she explained, pulling her ripped top further down over her jeans, hoping that Sergeant Chapman didn't have x-ray vision. Surreptitiously, she stuck her thumb in her jeans pocket and splayed her fingers over the drugs packet to conceal it.

'And the underage drinking?' he moved on.

'Well, I may have had a very small alcopop,' Cat admitted, conveniently forgetting that she'd vomited over someone's Laboutins less than an hour ago.

'And what about this lot?' he asked, indicating their friends who were banging on about human rights abuse - as if this was Guantanamo Bay, not West London. Fliss's frantic heartbeat slowed down as his attention was diverted away from her. 'I suppose that's all a big mistake, too? Just high jinks? Broken-hearted at the thought of you two returning to Scotland? Oh, yes, I know all about your farewell party. As does most of Notting Hill - you're very lucky it wasn't gate-crashed by undesirables.' His expression told them exactly what he thought of farewell parties that got out of hand.

'High jinks, that's it exactly! The Crescent hasn't been the same since Shipstone and his wife moved in. I bet they phone you twice a day to let you know that the dustbin hasn't been emptied or that a pigeon has pooped on his BMW. And you so busy fighting crime and arresting *real* criminals.' Isla looked up through her thick black eyelashes with guileless blue eyes at the sergeant.

The Sergeant and the WPC exchanged a look that suggested Isla was bang on message. It was Shipstone's position in the Home Office, his widely expressed views on Law and Order and his friendship with the power brokers in parliament that had warranted the police busting their party this evening. By clearing the gardens, the police had maintained law and order *and* kept Shipstone and the other residents happy.

Evidently hoping to draw things to a conclusion, Sergeant Chapman banged his desk with an empty coffee mug. 'You lot,' he gave them a stern once over, 'Have upset a number of residents on several occasions this week alone. And you, Miss Urquhart,' he gave Isla a more censuring look, 'don't need to get into more trouble. Do you?'

'No Sergeant,' she said with convincing meekness, evidently having the sense not to push her luck. She stood with her eyes downcast, giving the impression that she spent her spare time painting watercolours and embroidering handkerchiefs - not living the vida loca.

'Right,' he threw his pencil down on the desk. 'I want each of you to ring your parents, using the station phone. Or, a responsible adult prepared to vouch for your character and guarantee your good behaviour. The desk clerk will take your names and addresses; once that has been done and you have made your phone call, your parents, or whoever, can collect you and take you home.'

'Yay!' One of Isla's friends punched the air triumphantly, earning a censorious look from the officers on duty.

'But,' he gave them a quelling look, 'I have a good memory and the law has a long arm. If any of you comes before me again this summer, you'll be dealt with more severely.' He signalled his clerk to come forward and the subdued revellers made an orderly queue to give their names and make their phone call.

The phone on his desk rang and he picked it up.

'Sir Ruairi,' Sergeant Chapman greeted affably. On hearing his name, every nerve in Fliss's body went into hyper-drive, he was fast becoming her nemesis; why couldn't he leave the police to sort out his sisters? His interference would only complicate matters.

Obviously of the same opinion Isla slapped her forehead with the palm of her hand. 'Oh, give me a break,' she complained.

'Yes, they're both here. There aren't any charges - as yet. Certainly. Isla,' he held the phone towards her. She took it, holding it as though it were wired to the national grid and was about to deliver ten thousand volts down her arm.

'Okay. So we weren't in a taxi. But you knew that, didn't you? You are an absolute *pig,* Ruairi.' She handed the phone back to Sergeant Chapman, leaving Fliss feeling as if she was a character in some mashed up Sunday night serial . . . *Notting Hill Meets Monarch of the Glen.* It was obvious that the Sergeant knew Ruairi Urquhart quite well and she wondered how many times he'd been summoned to this police station to get his stepsisters out of trouble.

'I believe your sisters are returning to Scotland? And you're returning home, too? Yes, I'm sure there are matters you must attend to.' Isla leaned against the desk, arms folded like a sulky teenager. 'If you can guarantee their good behaviour, then . . . fine.' Sergeant Chapman concluded the conversation, tapped Isla on the shoulder and handed the phone to her.

'Yeah. I heard. Whatever. No, don't send Murdo to meet us. We'll get a bloody taxi. I don't care how much it costs . . . anyway, he won't turn out on the Sabbath; you know he won't . . . not even for you. Oh, I see, he will for his lord and master, will he? Yeah. Yeah. Sure. Whatever the *Laird* says,' she added, and mimed a sarcastic little curtsey before returning the phone to Sergeant Chapman. She turned to her sister, seething. 'He's sending bloody Murdo Gordon to meet us at the airport. Armed escort all the way to Kinloch Mara in case we do a runner. Kilts at dawn; bagpipes playing, banners flying. Too bloody feudal for words.'

'Okay. That's you two dealt with.' Sergeant Chapman was clearly unmoved, by her tirade; in fact, he looked quite relieved to have her and Cat off his hands. 'Now. What about you, Miss?' he turned his attention back to Fliss. 'If you have anyone who can vouch for your good character you'll be free to go.'

It was a lifeline and Fliss grabbed it with both hands.

But, who could she ring?

The station emptied as Fliss thought long and hard about who could act as a character witness for her. She turned to Isla and Cat for some advice but they'd headed home without as much as a backward glance in her direction. She'd never felt so alone and wished that she had an autocratic stepbrother who cared enough to abandon his plans, drop everything and return to Scotland on her behalf.

'Your parents?' Sergeant Chapman suggested.

'My parents are -' Fliss stopped. She didn't want to come across as Little Orphan Annie; she had to maintain some shred of dignity. She considered ringing Becky's parents but she didn't want to bring trouble to their door, considering how good they'd been to her since her parents' death.

There was no one - except . . .

'There is my employer. But . . .' she bit her lip, reluctant to make the call.

She might have almost doubled the salon's takings since joining *Pimlico Pamperers*, but that didn't make her employee of the month where Mrs Morris was concerned. In fact she had already voiced her suspicions about her moonlighting and had hinted that it was just a matter of time before Fliss moved on, taking her clients with her.

With Sergeant Chapman's permission, Fliss scrolled through her mobile phone for Mrs Morris's number and rang her on the station phone. She pictured her getting out of bed, rubbing the sleep from her eyes and imagining the worst. Who in their right mind rang people in the early hours of the morning?

Only the Police or the local A and E with bad news.

'Hello. Who is this?' was the worried but terse response from the owner of *Pimlico Pamperers*.

'It's Fliss Bagshawe. I'm sorry to wake you at this time of night, Mrs Morris - but I have an enormous favour to ask.' She took a deep breath, ploughed straight into the story, knowing that after tonight she would be looking for a new job

Chapter Six

Next morning, after a sleepless night, Fliss paced the narrow patio of her ground floor flat.

'Don't think of ringing up for a reference,' had been Mrs Morris's parting shot as she'd swept out of the police station. 'No one will employ you to fold towels when word of this gets round the beauty circuit.' Then she'd paused, turned on her heel and, with a swirl of her fawn cashmere serape, delivered one last jibe: 'I'll make it my business to ensure that you never wax legs in Pimlico again!'

And that was it . . .

Three years of college, plus another three spent building up her client base. Pouf! Gone without a trace. All she had left were some framed diplomas attesting that she was competent in a range of therapies, a rose bowl naming her *salon based beauty therapist of the year* - and a stack of broken dreams. Unlike the failed candidate on The Apprentice she wouldn't be given the chance to explain herself on BBC Breakfast the next morning.

Mrs Morris was right, without a reference she'd be lucky to get a job sweeping up nail clippings in a poodle parlour. She let out a despondent sigh and imagined Isla's friends this morning, snuggled down in their 400 thread count Egyptian cotton sheets while breakfast was prepared for them. Downcast, she traced the cracks in the patio with her bare toe. The shade of nail varnish she'd applied with such optimism last night - *I'm Not Really a Waitress* - now seemed prophetic. The way things were panning out, waiting tables in some greasy spoon might be the only career choice open to her.

Bright sunlight and bird song temporarily lifted her spirits, but she couldn't quite dismiss the image of the utility bills and rent book sprouting legs and advancing towards her, all demanding to be paid. She stared blindly into the garden where brambles entwined an old bike, a bath, discarded toilet and rusting lawnmower. Were her hopes and dreams buried there, too?

Her introspection was interrupted by a sound like an animal in pain. Spinning round, she found Becky shivering on the threshold of the kitchen door, her eyes ringed with last night's make-up.

'It's bloody freezing out here.' She raised a hand to shield her eyes and her stomach gave a hungry rumble. 'Any coffee left, Flissikins? Hey,' she continued with forced jollity, 'let's go to the greasy spoon for a fry up?'

'A fry up. Sounds great. I need to build my strength up for what I have in mind this morning,' Fliss replied grim-faced.

'Don't tell me you're going to ask old Ma Morris for your job back!'

'Yeah . . . and a pay rise while I'm at it.'

'A pay rise?' It was a few seconds before Becky registered Fliss's ironic tone. 'So, where *are* you going?'

'I've got something to return to Isla Urquhart,' Fliss explained, thinking of the drugs she'd transferred to her handbag in the taxi on the way home. It was no thanks to Isla that she hadn't been stripped searched and charged with possession by the police. 'I can't believe they just walked out of Ladbroke Grove, leaving me in the lurch.'

'Well, I can,' Becky put in. 'If it hadn't have been for Isla's *stupid* invitation, you wouldn't be looking for a new job. Would you?'

Fliss zoned out and Becky's voice merged with the sound of traffic and the wind in the trees. Her mind was on other things - like Isla's proposition, the reason she'd gone to the party in the first place. She would get dressed, march round to Elgin Crescent and demand to know exactly what was going on. If it turned out that Isla had been playing games, or having a laugh at her expense, she wouldn't be responsible for her actions. But one thing was certain, by the time she left Elgin Crescent the Urquharts would be under no illusion *exactly* what she thought of them.

'. . . lowdown slappers,' Becky finished her character assassination of the sisters as Fliss zoned back in.

'I was an idiot for thinking I could hang with Cat and Isla. You were right, Bex, they *are* The Spawn of Satan.' As far as she was concerned, they'd broken an unwritten code. Mates looked out for each other; they didn't save their own skins and a leave you up the creek without a paddle. Becky followed her into the kitchen, looking for once as though it gave her no pleasure to be right about the Urquharts.

'Fliss - Babe . . .'

'No,' Fliss held up her hand as Becky tried to comfort her. 'The signs were there and I ignored them. I should have heeded my horoscope. *Saturn in retrograde . . . friends will make or break your weekend . . . have an escape plan ready . . .* yada, yada, yada. Fate did everything but draw me a diagram.'

'Fliss, they're the idiots, not you babe.' Becky joined her by the kitchen sink, plainly searching for the words to make her feel better.

Fliss let her rattle on and washed up last night's dishes. As the pile diminished some of her spirit returned and she became stronger, more determined, less accepting of the hand Fate had dealt her. When she banged on the Urquharts door later this morning, everything would be different. She would no longer be the hired hand and they the master. Last night had altered their relationship - forever.

'The Urquharts owe you, no mistake.' Becky leaned against the kitchen table grim-faced and folded her arms across her chest. Fliss knew that Becky would love nothing better than to go to Elgin Crescent and give them a piece of her mind. She loved her for it, but knew that this was something she had to do on her own. 'I told you, didn't I?'

'Yes, you did.'

'Silly tarts. Time they deserve a good slapping from that . . . that *wolfy* brother of theirs.'

'Don't think that's going to happen, Bex, the upper classes don't smack their children. They leave it to the nanny to discipline them. But I hope he's got some suitable punishment lined up for when they fly home on . . .'

'. . . their broomsticks?'

'Nimbus 2000's,' Fliss managed a feeble joke before moving the conversation along. 'I'm going to get showered and dressed.' Leaving Becky in the kitchen, she walked through to the bathroom and closed the door behind her. She needed time on her own to sort out the sorry mess that was her life.

She stood under the running shower for several minutes, her forehead pressed against the cracked white wall tiles, hoping her problems would disappear down the drain along with the suds. But when she raised her head and opened her eyes nothing had changed; if anything her worries had grown in magnification. She stepped out of the shower and wrapped herself in a large bath sheet.

How *was* she going to pay the bills?

The thought of her hard-earned savings haemorrhaging away until she got another job made her feel sick. She knew that she could give up her flat and move back in with Becky's family until her prospects improved. But, much as she loved the Castertons, returning to live with them would be a backward step. She'd had the flat for less than a year and it represented her first, tentative steps towards independence. Now it looked as if she was back to square one.

She glanced around her precious, if shabby, bedroom. Old salon copies of Vogue, Tatler and Harpers were stacked neatly by her bed. The folding screen had cuttings of dresses and shoes and some of her sketches pinned to it. The vintage clothes she'd sourced in the charity shops in Notting Hill, Chelsea and Fulham hung on wire hangers from the chipped picture rail. The room was a testament to the career in fashion she would have pursued, given the choice. But, feeling that she couldn't ask the Castertons to support her through a four year degree at St Martins she'd turned to beauty therapy instead.

Her three-year course had come with a small bursary which had made it feasible for her to qualify as a holistic beauty therapist. She'd come top of the class in almost every subject. That didn't make her feel any happier; it simply helped to underline that she was capable of more, so much more.

'You all right, Flissy?' Becky called as she entered the room and placed a mug of tea and two slices of toast on the dressing table. 'Eat - You'll need all your strength if you're going round to the Urquharts. Laters?'

'Sure. Laters. I might also check out if my new shoes are still in the middle of Rosmead Road. They were Ferragamos, I practically had to arm wrestle a woman for them at a second-hand stall in Camden Market.' She tried to make light of the loss and last night's debacle.

'Sure, babe.' Becky gave her a hug before squirting herself with Fliss's perfume and taking her leave.

Once she'd gone, Fliss's shoulders slumped. She picked up a framed photograph of her parents and cradled it in her palm. She raked her fingers through her tangled auburn hair, so like her mother's, and tried to remember happier times. But her memories, like the old photograph, were blurred round the edges and starting to fade.

It was at times like this when she realised how alone she was. The thought brought with it a fresh pang of loss although it was now several years since her parents had died. It'd had been a tough time but she'd got through it, just as she was going to survive this setback and come out smiling on the other side.

She gazed at her reflection in the mirror and read the determination in her grey-green eyes. This was *her* problem and she'd find a solution. Placing the photograph back on the scratched dressing table she drank her tea and chewed at the congealing toast as a plan began to take shape in her mind.

She knew exactly what she had to do.

She'd find work - in bars, restaurants, shops - wherever, and get enough money together to buy a cheap car or van. She'd phone round her friends, call in favours - starting with Cat and Isla. She'd build up her client base . . . carry out treatments in her clients' homes and undercut the salons. It'd take time and it wouldn't be the business she dreamed of owning. But at least she'd be doing what she loved, the job she'd trained for.

That would keep the wolf from her door.

This was her flat. Her life. And she wasn't giving up either without a fight.

Chapter Seven

An hour later Fliss was outside the Urquhart's house, pressing the doorbell in short, sharp bursts. When it remained unanswered, she peered through the drawing room window where the fallout from last night's party was clearly visible. Ripped cushions, empty bottles, overturned tables and a large red wine stain on a Chinese rug were all going to take some explaining to Ruairi Urquhart, given his regard for his mother's house and its contents.

She wondered where Cat and Isla were and what were they up to. Being busted and then released from the local police station with a caution wouldn't have dampened their enthusiasm for life. In fact, she'd lay even money on it having whetted their appetite for more mischief. The thought made her give the bell one last defiant jab. She had drugs to return and a blistering lecture to deliver on the etiquette of abandoning friends in a police station. Friends who had stood by them and had lost their job as a consequence.

Just as she was leaving, Cat and Isla rounded the corner, sashaying down the street without a care in the world - looking as if they'd just attended a clan gathering in some parallel universe.

Isla was wearing a kilt that plainly belonged to some male relative over six feet tall, while Cat had squeezed into a kilt that was *good morning your honour* obscenely short. Both wore long sleeved white blouses with ruffled jabots and had matching plaids in the Urquhart tartan over their shoulder. Cat's balmoral - the archetypal highlander's hat - was set at a jaunty angle, while Isla clumped along beside her in hiking boots just visible below her outsized kilt.

Now what? She was in no mood for their infantile antics this morning.

41

'Fliss! What are you doing here?' Cat asked as if they hadn't abandoned her in Ladbroke Grove police station hours earlier. 'Have you come to visit us?'

'You could say that,' Fliss managed through clenched teeth, her blood pressure reaching way above her normal 100/80.

'Hoots mon. Och aye the noo, bonnie lassie - an' all that jazz.' Oblivious to Fliss's curt greeting, Isla handed her a portable CD player to hold while she rooted in a large badger pelt sporran for the front door key.

'Hey Fliss. Wait'll you see this.' Cat held up a tiny camcorder, watching the playback on its flipped-out screen.

'Not here,' hissed Isla and gestured towards Shipstone's house. 'You never know; he could have MI5 watching us. By satellite . . . courtesy of GCHQ. Scanning the airwaves for *chatter*.'

'In Gaelic,' Cat put in. 'More *hoots*, than Spooks - you could say.' That set off another fit of the giggles. Isla tripped over the long hem of her kilt, fell across the threshold and two brass fire pokers dropped out of her rucksack and landed at Fliss's feet.

So far - so predictable she thought as annoyance fizzed through her. It took all of her effort to remain outwardly calm and smiling, knowing that while she'd spent the morning stressing over her future they'd been up to some lark involving kilts, a camcorder and two brass pokers. It was as if in their world, yesterday's brush with the law had never happened.

'Coffee?' Cat asked as they stepped over the pokers and squeezed past Isla to enter the house. She led the way to the kitchen, unaware of the murderous thoughts running through Fliss's mind.

'Sure. Why not?' Fliss shrugged, picking her moment to deliver the scorching dressing down she'd rehearsed on her way over from the Tube. She glanced round the kitchen at the detritus from last night, if they thought for a nanosecond that she'd be helping them clear up they would be sorely disappointed. She was on a mission for survival and everything else was peripheral.

Isla removed her rucksack and placed the pokers on the draining board. With a surprising show of domesticity she switched on the cappuccino machine, fed bread into the toaster and then rooted in the fridge for butter and marmalade. Congealing party food was pushed to one side as she set three places for breakfast and gestured for Fliss to sit down. Fliss watched, irked but fascinated, as the undomesticated goddess whipped up three cappuccinos, sprinkled them with chocolate and tended to the Dualit toaster.

Cat walked over to the dresser and pressed the button on the winking answer machine.

'Cat. Isla - Ruairi. Ring the estate office to book tickets for your flight home. Check your email for the flight number. Print off the details. Take some form of identification. Passports preferably. Murdo will meet you at the airport. Make sure the house doesn't look like a squat before you leave, remember to set the burglar alarm and to shut the bloody windows. And think up some original excuses to explain your behaviour - you really have outdone yourselves this time.'

The machine gave a long loud bleep as the message ended.

'I wish he'd get off our case and stop phoning us every five minutes,' Isla said with an injured air. 'New excuses! Oh, we'll give him new excuses alright!' she plonked herself down onto the pine chair and started curling her dark hair round her finger. 'Trust him to leave a message - he'll have made a note of what time he called and want to know where we were, what we were doing. *And* who we were doing it with!'

'He'll find out soon enough.' Cat pressed the delete button on the answer machine and then gestured towards the camcorder and shot Isla a conspiratorial look.

Isla then turned towards Fliss. 'Anyhoo, bring us up to date. What happened after we left the station?' She spread her toast with butter and Frank Cooper's finest and crunched into it with straight, white teeth.

'I was bailed by my boss. Then sacked.' Fliss waited for their reaction.

'Cool. Now you can enjoy the summer. Catch some rays; maybe go abroad.' Clearly, the concept of paying the rent and utilities on Job

Seekers' Allowance was alien to Isla Urquhart.

'Not cool, as it turns out.' Outwardly, Fliss appeared calm and unruffled, but she was gearing herself up for her big speech and preparing to slam the wrap of cocaine on the table next to the marmalade.

'I know - I simply meant that you could take some time out. *Have a change of direction, maybe*?' She raised her eyebrow in a gesture Roger Moore would have been proud of and exchanged another look with Cat. Fliss found their sisterly telepathy quite unnerving, but had little time to ponder the significance of the look as she continued. 'Here's an idea. Why don't you come up to Scotland with us? If you're at a loose end?'

'Loose end?' She was just about to explain how she needed a job and what life was like in the real world when she was stopped mid speech.

'Here's the thing. Mumma owns a therapy centre in Kinloch Mara. She's having trouble recruiting someone to manage it for her. You could help out until she finds someone suitable.'

Fliss did a double take. Was this some kind of *job interview*?

'That's what I wanted to discuss with you last night. But every time I turned round, you'd gone.' Isla tutted at Fliss's lack of consideration.

'Selfish and inconsiderate of me, I know. Sorreee,' Fliss responded with heavy irony.

'Then the shit hit the fan? Remember?' Cat added, giggling.

'I think I do; vaguely.' Last night was hardly something she'd forget in a hurry. 'Of course, I was a little distracted at the time . . . taking care of *you*,' she said pointedly. But she could tell that her words sailed right over their heads.

'She's advertised in The Lady and all the usual places,' Isla continued. 'Kinloch Mara's quite remote and apparently no one wants to work there. Or, they've got boyfriends and the hassle of travelling backwards and forwards from London puts them off. But I noticed, you don't have a boyfriend, do you?'

Thanks for that, Fliss thought, but held her peace. There were more important issues at stake here than Isla's monumental lack of tact. Could Mitzi Urquhart be the answer to her prayers? A way out of her quandary?

'Is your mother into holistic therapy?' she hardly dared frame the question.

'Mumma's had every therapy known to man,' Cat laughed and rolled her eyes, 'and then some. It's not that she, personally, wants to give massages and such. The point is she feels out of the loop because her girlfriends run . . .'

'. . . exclusive bed and breakfasts, cashmere companies, boutique hotels. Dinner with the laird in an ancient house - complete with chain rattling ghost - set in sub-tropical gardens. Or they open their house up for visitors for the summer,' Isla elaborated.

'Mumma wants something to boast about when they meet up for girly lunches to discuss their business empires,' Cat said.

'She spends hours watching *The Apprentice* - dreaming of the day when Lord Sugar presents her with Businesswoman of the Year Award and congratulates her on the success of the Kinloch Mara Holistic Therapy Centre.'

'Ruairi refers to it as her *playing shop*,' Cat butted in. 'The therapy centre was our idea, initially. Honestly, there's nowhere to get a decent pedicure or a Brazilian in our corner of Wester Ross. Sometimes I feel hairier than this sporran. Not,' she pulled a face, 'that there are any men up there worth going to the trouble of making yourself look beautiful for. . .'

Unbidden, the fanciful image Fliss had of a highlander - *tall, dark, and kilted - silhouetted against the full moon, romantically striding along some remote mountain ridge* flashed into her mind. Now she knew the highlander in question was Ruairi Urquhart the picture didn't seem quite so appealing. She shook her head free of the image and concentrated instead on what Cat was saying.

'Of course she'll get bored with the project; she always does.'

'Since Papa died, she's had nothing to occupy her. Ruairi's hatchet man, Murdo *bloody* Gordon runs the estate. Ruairi's fond of Mumma but he thinks she's a total airhead, incapable of organising the weekly shop and drop let alone help with the running of Kinloch Mara.'

Fliss saw a flash of pain cross Isla's face at the mention of their father. Bereavement had left a gaping hole in *her* life and she didn't need a psychology degree to figure out that the sisters' behaviour, Lady Urquhart's lack of direction and Ruairi's need for control were manifestations of *their* bereavement. Symptoms of loss and grief that hadn't yet been confronted and dealt with. But it wasn't long before the moment had passed and their usual irreverent banter continued.

'Isla's right, Ruairi's been a pain about Mumma opening the house to visitors. He said he'd rather eat supper with the dogs in the kennels than be dressed up and paraded in front of paying guests like a tartan clad toy poodle. That's why she hit upon the idea of setting up the therapy centre in the Dower House. That's where the Laird's widow is supposed to live after his death, but Mumma doesn't at the moment . . . Anyway, Ruairi has less control over what goes on down there.'

Fliss was in a flat spin and only took in a fraction of what they were saying. She wasn't given time for further questions, however, because Isla reached out across the table and grabbed her by the arm.

'You'd be helping us out, *and* doing yourself a favour into the bargain. If Mumma's busy, she'll save a fortune in cognitive therapists' bills. That'll please Ruairi - which in turn will make our lives easier. And, in any case, it would only be until late autumn; or, until you can recruit a permanent manageress. I mean, you don't strike me as the kind of girl who'd want to bury herself in Argyllshire, not when you're a Londoner, born and bred.' She got up to make another cappuccino.

'Summer and autumn are the very *best* time to be in the Highlands,' Cat added, conveniently forgetting all that'd been said previously about tartan overload and shortbread tin scenery. 'Apart from the midges,' she pointed out, seemingly in an effort to be scrupulously honest.

'Apart from the midges,' Isla agreed.

'It sounds intriguing,' Fliss responded coolly. She didn't want to appear too enthusiastic in case they changed their mind. She was holding all the cards and intended to play this hand poker-faced and to her advantage.

'Shall I ring Mumma?' Isla persisted. 'She's at the ashram in India, but always leaves her mobile switched on. It really pisses off the other guests who are meditating.' I bet, Fliss thought as Isla left to make the call from another room, returning several minutes later. 'Mumma's ecstatic at the thought of the therapy centre finally taking off and can't wait to meet you. I haven't heard her sound so upbeat in months. She mentioned the salary.' She handed a piece of paper to Fliss who did a double take when she read the amount scribbled there.

It was almost *double* what Mrs Morris had paid her. Her innate sense of honesty wouldn't allow her to take advantage of the family - no matter how desperate she was, nor how generous Mitzi Urquhart appeared to be.

'I couldn't possibly,' she began, full of regret at the thought of this perfect opportunity slipping through her fingers. Although she felt she was owed *some* recompense for losing her job.

'Isn't it enough?' Isla frowned, apparently sensing her hesitation. 'She has no idea what to pay you. I just guessed at a ballpark figure and said you'd let her know if she should pay you more.'

'No, it's not that,' Fliss swallowed her reservations, knowing this was a dream opportunity. But was it sensible to become further involved with the Urquharts? So far, they'd brought her nothing but trouble. 'I simply meant that it's too much,' she explained.

'Oh, no worries on that score,' Isla brushed away her concerns. 'Mumma's bankrolled by Aberdeen Angus - one of her love-struck, ancient boyfriends - all of whom are desperate to be the next Mr Mitzi Urquhart.'

'*Hims ancient and modern*, we call them,' Cat added, heaping sugar into her coffee.

'I'd take too long to explain everything. But don't worry; it'll all make complete sense once you're in Kinloch Mara. Anyway,' Isla continued, surprising Fliss by being suddenly practical, 'You'll need a decent salary if you're going to sub-let your flat . . . or keep it on. To return to? In case things don't work out? You might not like Mumma - or she might not -'

'Isla, stop - or Fliss will change her mind,' Cat laughed.

Fliss took a deep breath knowing that she'd do well to give her answer right away. Isla's attention span was notoriously short and she might move onto another topic - or even another candidate - while she dithered at the kitchen table. Curling her fingers round the scrap of paper, she let out a long breath.

'Very well. Scotland here I come.'

'Yay!' Cat and Isla performed a mini Mexican Wave.

'Will you be going home to Wester Ross soon? I'm anxious to make a start if we're to capitalise on the summer visitors and . . .'

'Oh there's no rush; a couple of weeks, maybe?'

'A couple of weeks?' Fliss protested, frustrated by the vagueness of Isla's reply. 'But, that'll take us to the middle of June and . . .'

'No one returns to the highlands until then - and often not until after Wimbledon,' Cat was quick to reassure her. 'You'll love it in Wester Ross. During high summer the days last forever, and at night is barely gets dark. Then there are the highland gatherings in the autumn. You'll be there for the Urquhart Ball in late September. And,' her voice dropped to a reverential whisper,' if you're really lucky, you'll see the northern lights shimmer across the loch.' For a brief moment Fliss allowed herself to picture the romantic scene before continuing more prosaically.

'Won't you have to run this past your stepbrother, first?' She didn't want to look in a gift horse's mouth, but - wasn't there a saying that if something sounded too good to be true, it generally was? She wondered briefly about the advisability of bearding the lion - or in this case, the wolf - in his den.

'Oh, don't worry about that. You won't see much of Ruairi. He's hardly been home since he was dumped by his fiancée a year last Christmas,' Cat said, and another telepathic exchange passed between the sisters.

'One thing you need to know about Ruairi,' Isla explained further, as if reading her mind, 'is that you could go mad trying to second-guess what he will - or will not - approve of. Don't stress over it. We don't jump every time he barks. Besides - he'll be abroad until the end of the summer. By the time he returns home you'll have the centre up and running and we can present him with a fait accompli.'

'Fait accompli,' Cat echoed. 'Besides, Mumma won't be back from India before the end of June, either.'

'Well . . .' Fliss pushed all her reservations aside. Probably when she met Ruairi Urquhart, he would turn out to be as fluffy and adorable as the Andrex puppy. Nothing like the big bad wolf his stepsisters made him out to be.

'Good. I'll ring up the estate office and ask them to book another seat,' Isla rushed on, clearly thinking that she might change her mind if given too long to think about it.

'How much will the airline ticket cost?' Fliss asked, calculating if she actually could afford to fly up with them or would be following later, courtesy of National Express.

'Sweetie - you're doing *us* a favour so it won't cost you a bean.'

It seemed like she'd been presented with a fait accompli, too. With nothing more to say, Fliss took the packet of drugs out of her handbag and left it on the table along with her well-rehearsed speech.

'Better be on my way. Things to do. People to see. You know?' She gave her most casual shrug as mixed metaphors about beggars having little choice but to grab luck by the throat played through her mind.

'It'll be great fun, you coming to deepest, darkest Wester Ross. We'll be able to hang out together.' Cat surprised Fliss by walking her to the front door and giving her a quick kiss on both cheeks before closing it behind her.

Standing on the top of the flight of steps that led down to the pavement, Fliss acknowledged that she'd achieved everything she'd set out to accomplish that morning - and more. Okay, so she hadn't given the sisters a piece of her mind, not to mention a lecture on loyalty - but she was in paid employment and the manageress of a holistic therapy centre.

She'd been given her passport out of Pimlico.

Now all she had to do was break the news to Becky.

Simples.

Chapter Eight

Three weeks later the flight from Gatwick to Inverness began its final descent. Fliss could hardly contain her excitement at the thought of finally seeing Kinloch Mara and the unfinished therapy centre, having dreamed of little else. She glanced across the aisle at Cat and Isla, hoping to share the moment with them, but they were squabbling over elbow room and the remains of a large bag of M&M's. In fact, they'd been crabby for most of the short flight, seemingly put out at being summoned home by their stepbrother and the reckoning that lay ahead. To add to their sense of injury, a large contingent of their friends was headed to Ibiza for the summer - arriving roughly about the time they were due to touch down in Scotland.

The hydraulics whirred beneath Fliss's feet as the undercarriage was lowered. As the *fasten your seat belts* sign was illuminated, she ran through the events of the previous hectic three weeks and ticked them off in her mind in an orderly fashion.

Flat sublet [tick], new therapy equipment following by carrier [tick], bank account more or less intact [tick]. Old life left behind and fully committed to making the therapy centre a success? Yes!

The engines slammed into reverse, and as the rubber wheels smoked on touch down she felt as if she was being propelled forward towards a new life - a new beginning. Fancifully, she imagined the wheels' skid marks forming big black letters on the runway: **NO TURNING BACK**

Not that she wanted to turn back. She wanted to go forward, make a success of her life and break free of the image people had of her. Sensible, hardworking Fliss - the girl who didn't take risks; who always looked before she leaped. She didn't know what she was capable of, but she knew it was considerably more than she'd achieved so far. This move to Scotland symbolised a new chapter in her life - who knew where it would lead?

Her heart gave a joyous little leap and she pushed away any doubts that had travelled north with her. Slipping her hand into her bag, she curled her fingers round the rolled up contract and business plan which had received Angus Gordon's approval a week earlier. Her first task upon arrival at Kinloch Mara would be to thank him and Mitzi for giving her this chance. Then they could go over the plan in greater detail and draw up a timetable for what needed to be done to get the centre up and running. When they'd talked via SKYPE, Angus and Mitzi had been so enthusiastic over her plans for the centre that she'd liked them immediately and she gained the impression they felt the same way about her . . .

'Get off my toes, Cat. I've probably developed deep vein thrombosis because you've hogged all the room,' Isla whined, breaking into Fliss's reverie. Since entering Scottish airspace she'd become increasingly argumentative and sullen, as though she'd left her real self behind in London and taken on a new persona. One that didn't sit easily with her - *laird's sister, brought home to be grounded.*

She and Cat had overdone the whole Goth look with pale faces, spiky black hair, kohl-rimmed eyes and multiple face piercings. Twin versions of the Girl with the Dragon Tattoo in matching biker jackets, skinny black jeans and studded belts. Fliss glanced down at her summery Capri pants, t-shirt and sandals - guess that left her to play Flora MacDonald, then!

'You great greedy pig - you've had more than your fair share of the room all the way from London, and eaten all the M&M's,' was Cat's response. 'Shudd*up.*'

Fliss sighed. She hoped things would settle down once they reached Kinloch Mara; she didn't think she could take much more of their bickering without saying something she might later regret. The thought encapsulated her last niggling doubt . . . where exactly did she stand in the Kinloch Mara hierarchy? Was she a friend of Cat and Isla's who was helping out for the summer to get Mitzi's centre up and running? Or was she an employee of the Kinloch Mara estate - albeit it on Angus Gordon's payroll?

Used to fighting her own corner, she didn't want to lose control over any aspect of her life. The arrangement, as it stood, left her feeling a little uneasy, given what she'd learned of Mitzi Urquhart's capricious nature. What if she lost interest in the therapy centre before it was even up and running? Or, if Angus withdrew his financial backing and . . .

As the plane taxied round to the terminal she made herself stop worrying. She'd been paid a generous retainer, and had a watertight contract and comprehensive business plan in her handbag. She'd always wanted to be her own boss, to be in charge and this was her chance to prove what she was made of. The therapy centre might not belong to her but it was a million miles from *Pimlico Pamperers* and the humiliation of being dismissed without a reference.

She should enjoy the moment and leave all negative thoughts behind. She had a tendency to overthink things, so she stifled her misgivings; there was no place for second thoughts in her life.

Ten minutes later and laden down with luggage, she followed the squabbling sisters into the arrivals lounge where Cat spotted a familiar face in the crowd.

'Murdo! Murdo!' She waved her hand in the air and in her excitement dropped magazines, mobile phone and handbag at her feet. Smiling, Fliss picked them up and encountered Isla's furious expression as she scowled at Cat, and then at the crowd. Surely, Fliss thought acidly, the whole airport couldn't have earned her displeasure.

'For God's sake, it's only Murdo bloody Gordon not the sodding Dalai Lama,' Isla pulled Cat's arm down to her side with unnecessary force. Fliss searched for the man who warranted such a reaction, expecting an aged retainer along the lines of Private Frazer in Dads' Army. Old, bent over, crusty and speaking in a broad Scots' brogue.

'Isla, Cat - good to see you both,' they were greeted in an accent that was pure English public school. 'And you must be Miss Bagshawe?' Fliss did a double take as an attractive six foot two Highland god in kilt, T-shirt and belted leather Belstaff shook her hand. 'Welcome to Scotland.'

His hand was warm, firm and slightly calloused, presumably from working the land.

'Fl -Fliss, please,' she smiled, taking in his blue eyes, close cropped strawberry blond hair and healthy tan. Wow, she thought, her stomach giving a little flip of excitement; if all the men in Wester Ross looked like Murdo Gordon - then bring it on! Murdo gave her a quizzical look and Fliss realised that she was still holding his hand. Flushing, she released it and he was immediately set upon by Cat who embraced him in a fierce hug. He kissed her cheeks and then ruffled her hair in a brotherly fashion.

'Murdo. It's *ages* since I last saw you . . .'

'I thought you would have forgotten me with all the fun you've been having in London.' He raised a sandy eyebrow and pulled a comical face, leading Fliss to assume that news of their 'arrest' had travelled north ahead of them. 'It's good to have you back home. Both of you.'

'P-ul-ease,' Isla dragged out the word and gave him a withering look. 'Spare me the faithful retainer routine. You're only here because Ruairi has sent you as *prison detail*. So, save the Welcome to the Highlands crap, and get my bags!' She swept out of the airport like a princess, leaving them with her suitcases and hand luggage round their feet.

'Same old Isla. Sweetness and light,' Murdo observed as he picked up her belongings. Clearly, he was employed by the estate but his bearing and demeanour suggested he was more than simply a member of staff - and most definitely no one's servant. And that included Miss Isla Urquhart.

Outwardly, he appeared calm and unruffled by her rudeness but it was apparent from the set of his jaw and the anger in his eyes that he was far from amused by her attitude.

'Isla can be such a diva,' Cat apologised as they schlepped the heavy pieces of luggage towards the car park where a mud-splattered Land Rover was waiting. Shadow painted on the side doors was a lion with a sword in its paw and beneath it there was the motto: *Wha' Dares Challenge Me.*

Fliss's stomach performed a cartwheel in excitement - she was here, after all the preparation. She looked at Isla who, apparently less than charmed by the stunning backdrop, was leaning against the back wheel arch, arms folded, lips pursed. She gave them one last fierce look and then concentrated on watching the planes coming into land. Fliss thought she caught the shimmer of tears in her eyes and saw her bottom lip quiver. Plainly, she wasn't happy and was determined to make everyone else's life a misery, too.

Fliss felt annoyed that her first impression of Scotland was being spoiled by Isla's tantrum. Murdo was clearly of the same opinion because he frowned as he helped Fliss and Cat to climb into the Land Rover. Then he winked at Fliss as if to reassure her that Isla's behaviour was par for the course.

'Get in the car Isla,' Fliss snapped as she fastened her seatbelt and Isla made no effort to join them. 'I want to see Kinloch Mara even if you don't.' These past few weeks had been a trial and she wasn't in any mood for playing games with Isla Urquhart. Typically, Isla stayed where she was until Murdo switched on the engine and edged the vehicle forward. Left with no option but to climb in or get left behind, she snatched the door open with a muttered: 'Jeeeeze- ussss!' and flung herself into the front seat. But not before giving them all one last murderous look.

This behaviour seemed extreme, even for Isla, and Fliss suspected it had as much to do with her relationship with the gorgeous Murdo as it had with her being brought home to be grounded. She remembered the acronym **PINTA** which Becky had printed at the top of Isla's therapy notes in red felt tip. It stood for: *Pain In The Arse* and summed her up perfectly.

The Land Rover lurched forward as it left the car park and a beautiful Rough Haired Collie jumped over the back seat and sat between Cat and Fliss.

'Lassie . . . beautiful girl, how I've missed you,' Cat exclaimed. 'Murdo - I can't wait to see the new calves and to help you get the estate ready for the grouse shooting.'

'Yes. There's a lot to be done before Ruairi flies home. We've got some new retrievers - perhaps you can help with those, too.' He cast Cat a fond look, causing Fliss to wonder what alchemy was at work here that could change the wild child of Notting Hill into a country girl.

'My God now I've got to endure *Lassie Come Home* on a loop all the way back to Kinloch Mara. Don't make me puke. And do you *have* to kiss that smelly mutt, Cat? Mind you, Murdo's driving'll probably make me sick, anyway.' She gave Murdo a quick sideways glance look to see if he rose to the bait.

'I see that your temper hasn't improved for your stay amongst the Sassenachs, Isla,' Murdo responded as he slipped the Land Rover into gear and checked the traffic coming from the right. Fliss sensed a quiet steadiness in Murdo Gordon that any woman would be a fool to test. She could see a muscle tensing on his jaw line, the only visible sign that Isla's stinging darts were hitting home.

'Probably suffering from PMT,' Cat muttered below her breath, clearly not daring to antagonise Isla further in her present humour. 'Moody cow,' she added for good measure as she sank lower in her seat and gazed out of the window hugging Lassie.

Welcome to Bonnie Scotland, indeed! What had she let herself in for?

Fliss contented herself with the thought that when Ruairi came home Isla's behaviour would probably improve. Despite her posturing, Fliss gained the impression that Isla, more so than Cat, was dreading the arrival of their stepbrother in Kinloch Mara - and having to account for her behaviour. Fliss vowed to have the therapy centre up and running before he came home and give him no excuse to take her to task along with his stepsisters.

It was at least a two hour journey to Kinloch Mara where, according to Cat, the Gulf Stream warmed the Loch and palm trees and old French roses grew in the shadow of the hills. Leaving Inverness they made their way across the narrow neck of Scotland - but as the journey lengthened, the atmosphere in the Land Rover became highly charged. Cat and Isla traded insults and sniped at each other - obviously, a well-established ritual of childhood car journeys. Isla kept winding her side window up and down, fiddling with the radio and putting her feet up on the dashboard.

After half an hour Murdo pulled into a layby. 'Okay - Out. Both of you,' he addressed the squabbling sisters.

'Why?' demanded Isla, as Murdo leaned across her and pushed opened her door. 'I'm going nowhere. Wh - what are you doing?' Murdo marched round to her side of the Land Rover, the heavy pleats of his kilt swinging as he moved, giving a glimpse of tanned, muscular legs. He lifted her out of the Land Rover and deposited her unceremoniously on the ground. 'How dare you, Murdo Gordon?'

'Oh, I dare, Isla Urquhart. Now,' he grabbed her by the wrists and held her fast. 'Shut up - or you'll find yourself in the back of the Land Rover and Lassie can come and sit in the front with me. She's better behaved and has infinitely better manners. What is it to be?'

He let go of her wrists and held her firmly by the shoulders. The look that passed between them hinted at old history, unrequited passion and unfinished business. It was such an intense look that Fliss shivered and wondered, with a pang of yearning, what it must feel like to be held by a man capable of quieting his woman with just a look.

Giving her usual insouciant: 'Whatever,' Isla shrugged off his hands and got into the front seat without further protest. Murdo stood for a few moments looking towards the mountains, composing himself. Then he rubbed his scalp as though it was prickling in the summer heat, and climbed into the Land Rover. He drove on without another word and the rest of the journey passed in a tense silence. Fliss hoped that once she got to Kinloch Mara and became immersed in the therapy centre, she'd see little of Isla - which would suit her just fine!

Two hours later, Murdo pulled off the main road and started a long slow descent, leaving the mountains behind and following a minor road flanked by a mixed plantation of pine and deciduous trees. Eventually he stopped and pulled off the road, turning round to Fliss he gestured at the stunning view in front of them.

'There she is: *Tigh na Locha*, Fliss. The House by the Loch'

'Oh God.' Isla laid her head on her arms on the dashboard. 'Dead man walking,' she intoned, as if thoroughly dejected by the thought of the life she'd left behind in London.

'Don't be such a drama queen, Isla,' Cat slipped in one last dig as she and Fliss clambered out of the Land Rover with Lassie hard on their heels.

From their vantage point, the mountains behind them were hidden by trees and Fliss could see soft, rounded hills that swept all the way down to a large loch. The colours were dazzling; the green of the hills and trees, the blue sky reflected in the deeper blue of the loch and the ochre of the sandy beach which gave way to paler sand near a pebble path. The shore line dipped in and out of the expanse of water and in the distance, at vanishing point, the opposing shores appeared to link hands, cutting the loch off from the sea.

And, way below them, nestled in the trees with a wide lawn leading down to the waters' edge where it became a beach, was *Tigh na Locha*. Solid, ancient, a slice of Scottish history complete with white painted turrets and stepped gables, and with a look of permanency that said: 'I've been here for a thousand years. *Wha' dares challenge me?*'

After the car journey, the view of the loch was balm to her soul and Fliss let out a long, shuddering sigh. Unasked for tears prickled her nose and blurred her view. 'It's beautiful,' she said, a catch in her voice. Then she whispered softly so that no one could hear: 'I've come home.'

Chapter Nine

I've come home? Where had that fanciful thought come from? She looked at the beautiful view and a kind of peace settled on her. She knew it was whimsical, but she felt as if she'd visited Kinloch Mara many times in her dreams. She glanced quickly at the others hoping that they hadn't witnessed her fey moment. Luckily, they were wrapped up in their own thoughts . . .

. . . Isla - head bowed on the dashboard, the picture of misery. Murdo - striking an unconsciously heroic pose in his Kilt, thick white socks and biker boots as he gazed into the middle distance. And Cat - happily throwing sticks for the dog, her face flushed and healthy. Quite a change from the night of the party when she'd looked like an extra from Twilight.

'Did you say something, Fliss?' asked Cat.

'I said it's beautiful.' She made her way slowly back to the car. Encouraged by the romantic setting of the loch, hills, turreted castle and misty islands in the distance, Fliss could almost believe this overwhelming feeling of remembrance and homecoming was some long buried memory. That if she took a DNA test she would discover that she had Scottish genes running through her blood.

It wasn't like her to be so fanciful. Events over the last few years had left her little time for daydreams; it was level-headedness that had got her through college and hard work that paid the bills - not wild imaginings. Yet she couldn't rid herself of the notion that the novels she'd read, the movies she'd seen . . . The Flight of the Heron, Local Hero, Braveheart, the Thirty Nine Steps . . . had somehow coalesced in her subconscious to create an image so familiar that arriving in Kinloch Mara did indeed feel like coming home.

The Glen was working its magic on all of them, even Isla. But it didn't take long before she was back in character, tutting loudly as she held her mobile in the air and checked for a signal.

'About time Ruairi got a mobile mast erected on the estate. How am I supposed to keep in touch with all my friends if I can't get a signal? Oh - wait a minute, I forgot. They're all having a wonderful time in Ibiza and I'm stuck up here in highland hell, with you three.'

'Thanks for that,' Murdo said, grim-faced.

Fliss listened to the absolute silence. In place of the familiar soundtrack to her life: traffic, planes in holding pattern over London and people generating a hubbub of noise - there was the soft soughing of the wind in the trees and the call of birds deep in the woods. And something else . . .

'Listen Fliss. Can you hear the waterfall? I'll take you there. We can go exploring together,' Cat began enthusiastically, grabbing Fliss's sleeve. 'I'll show you the Jacobite cave where Bonnie Prince Charlie hid after the Battle of Culloden and -'

'Fliss's come here to work - she's not a guest,' Isla cut her short.

'Thanks for reminding me of that, *Miss Urquhart*.' Fliss's tone was sharp enough to penetrate even Isla's self-pity. 'Perhaps at the weekend?' she suggested to Cat and turned back to the Land Rover where Murdo was still admiring the view.

'I never tire of it,' he said. Then he gave Fliss a quick, worried look. 'Has anyone run your appointment past Ruairi? He has decided opinions about Mitzi's business schemes.'

'Unlike you, Murdo Gordon, we don't need Himself's permission for everything we do.' Murdo flushed at Isla's inference that he was little more than a hired hand.

'I'll take that as a no, then?' he asked Cat who had stopped throwing sticks for the dog.

'Chill, Murdo. Auld Aberdeen Angus is bankrolling Mitzi this time. Ruairi's got no say in the matter.' Murdo's expression made it clear that he thought differently. 'Dinnae fash yerself, Murdo, laddie. Come on, let's get home, I want to see Mumma.'

Fliss climbed into the Land Rover, glad she'd insisted on a contract of employment being drawn before she'd left London. It gave her security of tenure for six months - just to see how the therapy centre panned out. But one month had already passed as she waited for the go ahead to travel north with the sisters. That left her a scant five months to turn the therapy centre round and make it a viable concern.

Had she been a fool to get involved in Cat and Isla's hare-brained schemes? Time spent in their company was like real life Snakes and Ladders. Roll the dice, move forward, and up the ladder . . . get a job running a therapy centre. Yay! Roll the dice again; woops, no one's consulted Ruairi Urquhart about the centre - down a snake. Tough luck. Back to square one. Back to Pimlico and unemployment.

The therapy centre had Angus Gordon's financial backing, but it now appeared that everything hinged on the final word of the Laird of Kinloch Mara. The man with the charmless telephone manner apparently had power of veto over everything on the Kinloch Mara estate.

The Land Rover swept under a stone gatehouse at the end of a long avenue of trees. It rumbled over a wooden bridge, crossed a fast flowing torrent of a river, tinged brown by peat from the hills, and made its way along a tarmacadam drive before pulling up at the back of the house.

'We always enter the house by the back door,' Cat explained as Fliss glanced up at the ancient, turreted peel towers linked together by a central wing. 'We never use the front drive or open the big gates except when . . .' She leapt out of the Land Rover without finishing her sentence as the large, nail studded door swung open and several small dogs shot out, tangling themselves round her feet.

Murdo helped Fliss out of the Land Rover and they walked towards the house together, leaving Isla to sulk. He guided her along stone corridors with walls so thick that window embrasures had been cut into them and looked as if they'd once held shelves which stored household goods. The walls were painted the colour of buttermilk in order to shed light on the gloom, where - even in high summer - electric lights were burning and it was bone-chillingly cold. The passageway gave onto a large kitchen with an Aga, huge refectory table with bench seats, floor to ceiling painted cupboards and a batterie de cuisine hanging over a Belfast sink. The dogs were creating such a nuisance that Murdo chased them out and into the hall before beckoning Fliss to follow.

This part of the house was early seventeenth century and had pine panelled rooms leading off it. It was dominated by a large stone fireplace and a splendid cantilevered oak staircase which climbed up to a large landing. The front door gave onto lawns and gardens where, through magnificent ornamental gates whose gilded finials caught the sunlight, the loch could be seen.

'Mumma!' Cat shrieked as a petite blond in her early fifties came out of one of the rooms. Cat ran forward to kiss her but was held off at arm's length.

'You can't kiss Mumma, darling, she's had a little *work* . . .' Mitzi Urquhart held her face in profile and lifted her highlighted hair so the bruising on her jaw line became visible. 'And just the teeniest drop of Botox. But you can hug me; careful now.' As they embraced, Mitzi turned to Murdo and put her hand on his arm. 'Darling Murdo, thank you so very much for bringing my Puss Cat home. Fliss! Darling girl. Your coming was foretold by old Mrs MacLeish. She's a *taibhsear*,' she pronounced it *tav-sayer*, 'and has the sight; and is never wrong. My therapy centre will be a huge success. And where's Isla - sulking in the Land Rover? *So* like me at her age. Well, she'll come in when she's ready. Let's have a drink to welcome Fliss to Kinloch Mara.'

She didn't stop for breath, sweeping them along in her *Allure* scented wake towards a large drawing room where stone mullioned bay windows gave out across the water of the loch. She handed round glasses of neat whisky and toasted their arrival with: 'Slainte', which she pronounced slawnn-cha. 'Good health and welcome to our home, Fliss.'

'Slainte,' the others repeated, tossing their whisky down their throat with a deft flick of the wrist. Fliss followed suit and was left with streaming eyes as the fiery liquid caught her breath and scorched her throat.

'I'd have thought a girl used to drinking in nightclubs in London could

61

handle a wee dram,' Murdo laughed. He poured Fliss a glass of water and she drank it gratefully before replying.

'I normally drink white wine or cocktails,' she gasped - and they all laughed at her expression. 'To me, whisky tastes like cough medicine, only worse.' She regretted the words as soon as she said them; it was hardly diplomatic to make disparaging remarks about Scotland's greatest export upon arrival in the highlands.

But, clearly Mitzi found Fliss's declaration enormously diverting because she laughed, curled up in one of the four huge padded window seats and then indicated that the girls should join her.

'It's Midsummer's Eve and I've come over all other worldly, as though I've had breakfast with the fairies in the Great Glen.' She laughed, pushed up the sleeves of her cashmere sweater and waved her hands in the air. 'You do believe in fairies, don't you, Fliss.'

'I think I probably do,' Fliss laughed. 'In Kinloch Mara, *everything* seems possible, it's so unbelievably romantic.' It was clearly the answer Mitzi hoped for because she gave Fliss's hand a squeeze.

'I've organised a welcome home party for my gur-uls' (she pronounced it in a cod Lowland Scots accent). Like Murdo she spoke with a cut glass accent which would have been more at home in Chelsea or Mayfair. 'And you, too, of course Fliss.' Her gold bracelets jangled as she held Fliss's hands and then released them. Touched by the warmth of her welcome, the power of the whisky and the magical setting, Fliss began to relax.

Mitzi needed her. Everything was going to be all right!

'On the beach?' Cat asked excitedly. She and Fliss twisted round and looked towards the loch where tables, chairs and cooking equipment were being unloaded from trailers by uniformed staff. 'Mumma, you are a *darling*. And I'm going to kiss you,' she leaned forward carefully and kissed her mother's forehead. Then her face darkened. 'But, didn't Ruairi say that we were to live on neeps and tatties and be confined to barracks until he got home, Mumma? He'll go ape shit when he finds out we've had a party.'

'Don't worry, he won't find out,' Mitzi brushed her cares aside and turned confidingly to Fliss. 'I love Ruairi dearly, but he can be *such* a wet blanket. Now don't pull that face Murdo, you know it's true. Anyway, who could let June the twenty-first pass unmarked? Midsummer's Eve,' she gave a little shiver. 'Ill met by moonlight proud Titania, and all that.'

Fliss was charmed by Mitzi Urquhart, but she could well believe that Ruairi had his work cut out keeping a check on her *and* her errant daughters.

'My Cognitive Behaviour Therapist says I must keep upbeat through positive thinking, Fliss. Soon the nights will start drawing in - it'll be harvest and then in no time, Christmas. Even my SAD lamp can't counteract the effects of a gloomy Highland winter, deprived of love,' she said, seemingly referring to her widowhood of ten years. 'The most positive thing in my life right now is the resurgence of the therapy centre. If Ruairi starts raising objections, why - I - I'll spend winter in the Bahamas with Angus in his villa and *he* can organise Christmas at Tigh na Locha on his own.'

'No, don't do that Mumma. Look what happened last time . . . Fiona broke off their engagement and bolted just before the wedding, Ruairi left for the Far East and everyone was positively *miserable*.' Cat was openly alarmed at the thought of spending another Christmas away from home, familiar things, family traditions - and without her friends.

'Exactly. So you see, this party is like therapy, don't you agree Fliss?' Fliss nodded, somewhat bemused by Mitzi's flawed logic. 'So, don't you fret my darlings, I'll brave Ruairi.' She gestured for Cat and Fliss to get up, linked arms and walked with them into the hall. 'Besides, I have it on good authority that he's not expected home for another couple of weeks - and this is just a quiet little celebration. Only a hundred close friends. Oh, and did I say, you are to dress as a character from a Midsummer Night's Dream. Even you, Murdo. Oh, don't groan, darling, it'll be fun.'

'If you say so, Mitzi,' he had paled slightly at the mention of the number of guests she'd invited and the thought of dressing up as a six feet two fairy!

'I do say so. Would you rather that I had chosen The Wicker Man as our theme. The cult sixties version, with Christopher Lee and Edward Woodward, naturally. In my youth I looked a little like Britt Ekland, you know.' She fluffed up her hair and carried on talking about the merits of one film version against the other while Cat took Fliss upstairs to rest before the party.

Chapter Ten

S ome hours later Fliss woke with a start. Disorientated, she pushed herself up onto her elbows and tried to figure out why she was lying on a huge brass bed in a room with a turret window. Focusing on the nymphs and shepherdesses frolicking in the toile de jouy wallpaper she rubbed her eyes and stretched out on the bed, languorous as a cat.

She glanced at the clock on the bedside table and then sat bolt upright, all traces of sleep gone. Ten fifteen - it couldn't be! The clock was wrong; it *had* to be much earlier - the sky was as bright as day. Realising that she'd probably slept the clock round and missed Mitzi's party, she flopped back on the pillows, dismayed.

Some first impression she was going to make!

She reached out for her silk kimono someone had thoughtfully draped across the foot of the bed and shrugged it on. Feeling like a hung-over princess in the tower, she made her way to the window which looked over the rose gardens and the loch. Below her the party was in full swing. People were dancing on the sands in the luminous twilight and she couldn't wait to join them. As the last vestiges of sleep drifted away, she remembered Cat mentioning something about how, during the summer in Wester Ross, it never really got dark.

Then, just as she was turning away from the window her eye was drawn towards something black and malevolent squatting on the edge of the sands. A helicopter! Of course, it must have been the beat of its rotors as it landed which had woken her from her dreams. She moved away from the window, no longer feeling like the princess in the fairy story. Somehow, the black helicopter - so out of place on the gingerbread coloured sands - generated a sense of unease.

It was difficult to say *exactly* why she felt on edge. Her welcome to Tigh na Locha had been genuinely warm and friendly. She was here at Mitzi and Angus Gordon's invitation to sort out the therapy centre, had been treated like an honoured guest and given one of the best rooms in the house. So what was worrying her?

Not what - **who** - a voice whispered in her ear.

Until now she'd shut her mind to the possibility that Ruairi Urquhart could put a stop on the therapy centre. But here, where his word was law and even Mitzi seemed in awe of him, it now seemed a distinct possibility. Taking a deep breath, she counselled herself to think positively - when he jetted in from Hong Kong in a couple of weeks the centre would be up and running and there would be nothing he could do about it.

She knew she was a born worrier but - *this time* - she told herself sternly, there was simply nothing to worry about. 'I'll have oodles of time tomorrow to raise the topic of the therapy centre with Mitzi and Angus, ask a shed load of questions and get everything shipshape,' she told her reflection in the mirror.

Tonight was all about having fun.

But as she made her way over to the en suite bathroom and caught another glimpse of the black helicopter sitting on the sands, her blood ran cold. Something about it made it seem like an omen, a harbinger of bad luck.

Fun? What was she thinking?

She was here to do a job, not to be sucked into the Urquhart's charmed world of romantic castle in the highlands, staff to do their bidding and (from her financial viewpoint) money to burn. She had to keep her identity intact and her wits about her, if she was going to hold her own with Ruairi Urquhart. She was starting to think and act like Cat and Isla - the joint queens of procrastination. And that wouldn't do - it wouldn't do at all.

Putting everything from her mind, she concentrated on getting ready for the party. Her cases had been placed on top of the wardrobe, and someone had set out her toiletries on the glass topped dressing table. Walking over to a mahogany tallboy she opened the drawers and found her greying underwear and shrunken t- shirts neatly folded among scented drawer liners. A member of staff must have unpacked her case, hung her belongings in the wardrobe and put mineral water and a tin of biscuits by her bed while she'd slept. She cringed at the thought of some unknown hand unpacking her battered suitcase and making unfavourable comparisons between her Primark knickers and the silk and lace undies they more usually unpacked for house guests.

Drawn back to the window by the insistent thump-thump of the disco, she pushed it open. The delicious aroma of barbecued food wafted up, making her stomach rumble, reminding her she'd eaten nothing since breakfast.

Snatching a piece of shortbread out of the tin she munched it as she made her way to the bathroom to take a shower. The shower water was peaty brown from the hills and left her hair feeling soft and her skin glowing. She was just drying herself when Cat - channelling the *punk fairy on crack cocaine* look for the party - entered the room. She'd overdone the Goth pallor, heavily ringed eyes and face piercings; but, on closer inspection Fliss saw that her spectral paleness was entirely natural.

Her heart skipped a beat and her earlier disquiet returned.

'The shit's hitting the fan down there and heading in our direction.' Cat rubbed her hands together agitatedly and then tucked them under her armpits like a nervous teenager.

'*Our?*' Fliss questioned, wondering how she could possibly be in trouble when all she'd done was arrive at Tigh na Locha and slept. But Cat appeared beyond listening, let alone responding to her question.

In an obvious attempt to chivvy her, Cat picked up a paisley patterned bikini and folded length of sari cloth laid out across a button backed nursing chair. Ornate bracelets, earrings, anklet and a pair of flat sandals fell out of the folds and landed at Cat's feet. Scooping everything up, she tossed the improvised fairy costume onto the bed.

'Get dressed. Quickly!'

'Why?' Fliss was becoming immune to Cat and Isla's little dramas and refused to be rushed. 'My hair's soaking wet.'

'Never mind *that!* Ruairi's here. He's arrived in Angus's helicopter. That's it down there on the beach.' She muttered something in Gaelic, dragged Fliss back to the window and pointed at the helicopter. 'Now do you get it?' Like an understudy for Lady Macbeth, Cat's hand-wringing recommenced. Evidently, the day of reckoning had arrived sooner than any of them had bargained for.

Fliss sat down at the dressing table and tried to remain calm, but Cat's anxiety was contagious. 'Your stepbrother, Ruairi? Here?' she echoed, trying to gain herself some thinking time. Her mouth was dry and her tongue had glued itself to the roof of her mouth - whether as a result of nervousness or the two whiskies she'd drunk earlier on top of an empty stomach, she wasn't sure.

'Yes. Tonight of *all* nights. He's come straight from Hong Kong, jet lagged and in a foul mood . . . gone ape because he didn't know about the party . . . and we're supposed to be grounded . . . Mitzi's been spending money she hasn't got, or more importantly the estate hasn't got. And, worst of all - he knows all about the plans to revive the therapy centre. I left them having a *blazing* row - and with poor auld Angus playing Piggy in the Middle.'

At the mention of the therapy centre, Fliss's brain switched into a higher gear. She'd never seen Cat look so scared, so chastened - not even when she'd been arrested and taken to the police station. And that worried her.

'Get dressed. Mitzi wants you to come down to the beach and meet Ruairi ASAP. She's convinced that once you talk to him and go over your plans for the centre he won't think that it's just another of her *hare-brained schemes* - to use his words.' She rolled her eyes, leaving Fliss with the unflattering impression that she didn't believe her capable of dissuading Ruairi Urquhart from a course of action once his mind was made up.

'Why didn't you wake me earlier?' Fliss scowled and busied herself with moisturiser and toner.

But, Cat wasn't listening. She evidently had her own problems to think about; expelled from boarding school, poorly predicted A level grades, being taken to Ladbroke Grove Police station. It would all take some explaining - and with Ruairi patently in no mood to listen. Growing noticeably more distracted by the minute, Cat was drawn back to the window, the helicopter and the circle of people surrounding it. She kept muttering: *'Ohshit, ohshit, ohshit,'* under her breath, and biting the skin round the top of her thumb.

She glanced at her watch. 'Dealing with Isla will probably give him a coronary within minutes, so - hopefully - when we get down there he'll have run out of steam.'

'Really?'

'No – oh.' Her scathing look suggested that Fliss just didn't *get it*. 'He'll warm up on Mitzi, but he'll reserve the worst of his fury for Isla - and then *me*.' Her voice went up an octave and ended in a mouse-like squeak. Suddenly, Fliss felt sorry for her. She might be young and foolish, prone to aping her wilder, older sister - but she shouldn't be this terrified of her stepbrother.

'Give me five minutes,' she said with more composure than she felt. If she was going to meet the big bad wolf on his home turf she'd make damned sure that she was looking her best. The best she could, given the dressing-up-box collection of rags and tatters she'd have to pass off as a costume. Maybe she ought to wear something more . . .

'Five minutes! We don't have *five minutes*. When Ruairi says *now*, he actually means, like - yesterday?'

'Five minutes.' She had no intention of being harried by Ruairi Urquhart. She began towelling her hair dry and Cat left the room.

Minutes later Fliss stood in front of the mirror. Everyone might regard Ruairi Urquhart with shock and awe, but she'd show him that girls from Pimlico were made of sterner stuff. Besides, if she took a little longer to get ready he might have calmed down, got used to the idea of Mitzi's business and be more concerned with whipping his two stepsisters into shape than quizzing her.

Despite her brave assertions, her hands were shaking so badly she had difficulty ringing her eyes with kohl and making a bindi mark on her forehead with lipstick. She pinned up her long auburn hair, teased out some loose tendrils to frame her face and fastened on heavy silver drop earrings hung with little bells. Tucking yards of sari material into the top of her ridiculously small bikini, she knotted the rest over her hip.

Ever practical, she sprayed herself with insect repellent instead of perfume. She'd been warned about the vicious Highland midges and had no intention of being bitten alive and having to spend the rest of the week covered in tea tree oil. Looking more like a fairy from Bollywood than a highland glen, she descended the stairs with bracelets and anklets jangling and yards of embroidered cloth looped over her arm.

Leaving the house by the front door she made her way down to the beach, her heart beating like a crazy metronome at the thought of meeting the Laird of Kinloch Mara. She wondered if his entry in Burke's Peerage included "bully" and "thorough bastard" alongside his ancient lineage. There was only one way to deal with bullies and that was to stand up to them. She used that thought to shore up her confidence and prepare her for going head-to-head with this latter-day monarch of the glen.

Chapter Eleven

F ive minutes later, Fliss hurried along the path, psyching herself for the meeting with her nemesis. Ready to do battle on behalf of Mitzi and the therapy centre. She simply *had* to convince Ruairi Urquhart she was the kind of woman he'd be a fool to let slip through his fingers. Running the therapy centre represented a once in a lifetime opportunity and she wasn't about to give it up without a fight.

She couldn't face returning to London and unravelling everything she'd spent the last weeks putting in place . . . subletting her flat, the therapy equipment she'd put into storage. Not to mention the offer of a white van she'd turned down when she'd put her plans for a mobile therapy business on the back burner. She envisaged herself sleeping on the fold down bed in Becky's room, lying awake in the darkness, mulling over everything she'd lost - while Becky snored and ground her teeth for England. And Sir Ruairi Urquhart, Bart, congratulated himself on repelling another English invader.

That thought alone was enough to spur her on! Fixing on a confident smile, she ran towards the beach, past scantily dressed fairies, vampish Titanias and camp Oberons. A rocket shot into the sky and exploded above her in a technicolour shower. Startled, she stumbled on the uneven path and cannoned into one of the rose-covered iron arbours lining the path. The pain was excruciating and made her lose her grip on the sari cloth tethered to her bikini bottoms. It slithered free and snaked around her ankles, impeding her progress. Anxious not to keep *Himself* waiting, she gathered up the slack and hurried on. There was a horrendous tearing sound as the silk snagged on an ancient thorn and yanked her backwards.

She let out a groan of impatience and an expletive; this really was the last straw.

'Perhaps I can be of assistance?'

Her head span round towards a Victorian gazebo where she could just make out the dark shadow of a man. Annoyed at how unprofessional she must appear - she was, after all, the new manageress of Lady Urquhart's therapy centre - Fliss was keen to make an exit, stage left. But as she hoiked up her costume and gave the cloth one last desperate tug, she only succeeded in entangling herself further. The sudden movement sent rose petals falling around her like eco-friendly confetti at an upmarket wedding and her bikini bottom slipped past the point of no return.

'Oh, flippin' Ada,' she exclaimed, snatching up the free end of the sari and wrapping it around her like a sarong. Then she glanced towards the gazebo and saw that the stranger had got to his feet. Cat had warned her about Mitzi's louche male friends and their propensity for groping nubile young women in Tigh na Locha's dark passageways. She really had no time for fending off the unwelcome attentions of a Rod Stewart/Iggy Pop look alike. If he made one false move towards her in her present mood, he'd live to regret it.

'I'm fine. Really.' Her tone made it clear that his attentions were unwelcome.

'You don't look . . . fine. Not from where I'm standing at any rate.' There was a pause as she realised she was bent over the sari cloth with her bottom stuck up in the air like - like a duck diving for pond weed.

'Well, take it from me - I am.' She quickly unfastened the end of the sari that was threaded through her bikini bottom. But the other end had coiled itself round her calf and snagged on a silver anklet.

'I beg to differ.' In contrast to her dampening words, he showed a chivalrous regard for her dilemma. But she wasn't taken in by the whole knight in shining armour routine, not even when he asked for a second time, 'Are you *quite* sure you won't let me help?'

'I'm on my way to meet someone, actually. They'll be wondering where I am,' she added, just in case he was some kind of voyeur who got his kicks from spying on scantily dressed women. She looked over her shoulder to see if Cat or Murdo were within shouting distance.

'Who are you meeting? Perhaps I can reach them on my -'

'Don't bother trying to use your mobile. The Laird,' she couldn't help but spit the word out, 'has decreed - no phone masts on his land, so it'd be pointless.' Turning away from him, Fliss realised that she'd have to unfasten the anklet and sandal and abandon them on the path with the sari cloth. Then she'd be forced to run semi-naked down to the beach to find Ruairi Urquhart. 'Buggerbuggerbugger,' she repeated under her breath.

'I was going to say: *on my two-way radio.* Look - I *insist* on helping.'

She detected amusement in his voice and raised her head to glower at him. But she stopped in mid glare as a strikingly good looking man in his early thirties stepped out of the summer house carrying a two way radio. She was too preoccupied to wonder why a guest would need such a device or why he was wearing a business suit, white shirt and thin tie when everyone else was dressed for the revels.

Then she began to notice other telling details. The suit was obviously tailored and emphasised his broad shoulders, slim hips and long legs. His shirt looked like the finest Sea Island cotton and his tie was this season's Paul Smith. His hair - just two shades short of jet-black was well cut but dishevelled - as though he'd been running his fingers through it whilst mulling over some intractable problem in the gazebo. Though what would make a man with his air of self-possession leave the party when it was at its height, she couldn't imagine.

'May I?' He slipped the walkie-talkie into his pocket, crouched at her feet and curled his fingers round her ankle. 'Don't struggle - you'll only make things worse.'

Fliss tried to think of some stinging rejoinder that would let him know - should he be in any doubt - that she didn't need to be rescued. At least, not by him. She hoped that her body language - hands on hips, chin titled at a belligerent angle, other foot tapping on the gravel path, made it clear that his attentions were unwelcome.

'If you could just get a move on?' she commanded as he fiddled with the cloth. Then curiosity prompted her to ask, 'So, who - what are you - the event organiser?' She gestured towards the radio in his pocket and his lack of costume. Her words appeared to amuse him because he gave a short bark of laughter.

'I'm certainly not on the guest list, so, I guess that probably makes me *staff*,' his mouth quirked in a smile. Fliss suspected that at some level he was enjoying playing the rescuer, kneeling at her feet like a knight-errant while she was pinned to the rose tree like a gaudy butterfly. He shifted position, transferring his weight from one knee to the other and an explosive combination of his aftershave and musky pheromones wafted towards her.

'I - I . . .'

She took in a sharp breath, ready to deliver another crushing remark. But his intoxicating, manly scent overwhelmed her and she felt beset by the urge to draw his dark head into her naked body and cradle it there. She took a self-preserving half step away from him as her hormones kicked in and reminded her how long it had been since she'd slept with a man.

'A ram caught in a thicket,' he laughed, seemingly unaware of the effect of his touch on her bare skin. Pulling the sari free of the rose bush, he raised his head and sent her an appraising look from amazingly sexy blue eyes. Caught off guard, she let out a small "oh," as her womb tightened and then relaxed and a feather of desire unfurled deep within her.

'Would you please just . . . let me go?'

'Rambling Rector if I'm not mistaken,' he said, as though she hadn't spoken. For a wild moment, it felt like she was in an X-rated episode of Gardener's World - although this dangerously attractive man was light years away from Alan Titchmarsh. 'There all done.'

'Who *are* you?' She knew she was a fool to linger here, but there was something about the way he held himself, his Celtic colouring: dark hair, wide-spaced blue eyes and high cheek bones, which was familiar to her. One more question and then she'd keep her rendezvous with Ruairi Urquhart. 'Why aren't you in costume?'

'Let's just say I didn't know about the party until it was too late.' Apparently sensing her change of mood, he opened his hands and released her from bondage. Then he stood up, folded the sari into a neat rectangle and handed it over with a courteous dip of his head.

'Ditto,' she said indicating her own outfit. Another assessing look passed between them and she knew that - although he appeared to have himself under control, it probably wasn't a good idea to draw attention to her lack of clothing. 'I do know Cat and Isla, quite well, however,' she babbled, using the moment to cover the fact that her whole body throbbed for his touch. 'They're very . . .'

'They're certainly very *something*.' Now there was a different note in his voice, one she couldn't quite get a handle on. She guessed that in the past the sisters had done something to annoy him. So far, so predictable.

'Quite.' She gave him an oblique look - he didn't strike her as the kind of man they could behave towards with impunity. Neither could she imagine Mitzi leaving him off the guest list. Her 'hundred close friends' on the beach seemed to be drawn from *Who's Who* of the Western Isles.

'How *do* you know them?' he asked at last, his cobalt blue eyes suddenly suspicious, wary.

'From when I lived and worked in London.' Something was out of kilter, something she couldn't quite nail. She had the unsettling feeling that what she said next would be filed and later used against her. Time she left. 'Excuse me - I have to . . .'

Her words were drowned out by a salvo of loud bangs from the beach and she dropped the sari cloth onto the path. Simultaneously, they bent down to pick it up - and as she straightened, the top of her head came into contact with his chin. She absorbed the full force of the impact and bright stars of concussion flashed across her field of vision, merging with the fireworks going off all around them.

Temporarily stunned, she was dimly aware that her name was being called further along the path. Then her brain gave a warning pulse, the ringing in her ears amplified and darkness closed in on her. She felt herself falling - down, down - and reached out towards the stranger, as though some part of her knew that she could trust him. With one swift movement, he drew her towards him and gathered her into his arms - as though she weighed no more than a handful of the petals settling around them. She felt the soft touch of wool against her cheek, strong arms around her and she felt safe; the safest she had in years - even though she was in the arms of a perfect stranger.

Perfect . . .

Neither of them saw the fireworks shooting up into the pearlescent sky or heard the cheers that followed each extravagant effect. It was as if the clocks had stopped running and the rhythmic rise and fall of their breathing marked time instead. She moulded her body into his, prolonging the contact and enjoying the warmth radiating from him. Wrapping her arms around his neck, she turned towards him and then, as though it was the most natural thing in the world, they kissed.

The kiss at first was soft and exploratory. But as the dizzy beat of her faint receded, Fliss tightened her grip around his neck and pulled his head towards her. Boldly, she took the kiss a step further, probing the inside of his mouth with her tongue. In response, he shifted her weight in his arms, held her more tightly against his body and took command of their love-making.

He murmured something faint and indistinct against her hair and the cadence in his voice - if not the exact words spoken, sounded strangely familiar. Drawing back from the kiss, Fliss dredged up the memory of the night of her arrest - the plaque on the bench, the scent of tobacco plants and the phone call - as if it was vitally important that she remembered every detail.

'*Klingon*,' she said after a huge effort. She felt a shudder course through him as if he'd been in a waking dream and that single word had brought him to his senses.

'Fl -i -ss . . . Where are you?' Mitzi called out from lower down the gardens.

'Klingon - Fliss?' His face became hard, his expression calculating as if everything suddenly made perfect sense. 'Oh, ri-ight. I get it.' He looked at her with distaste as Mitzi, Murdo and Angus approached from the house and Cat and Isla advanced in a pincer movement up from the beach. 'This is a stitch-up, a sting; and I've fallen for it - hook, line and sinker.'

'Here she is,' Isla said crossly, clearly none too happy at being dragged away from the firework display to form a search party. But when she saw Fliss in the stranger's arms, she started to laugh.

When Mitzi and the others reached them, they stopped dead in their tracks, staring at Fliss with their mouths open. Why *were* they looking at her - at them *both* like that? Okay - maybe cavorting in the arms of the party planner when she should have been looking for Ruairi Urquhart reflected badly on her professionalism. But she couldn't quite understand why their reaction should be quite so extreme.

Unless . . .

'Oh, my god - *Klingon*,' she gasped. And the final piece of the jigsaw slotted into place.

'Greater love hath no woman, than she lay down herself for her career,' Isla intoned, regarding Fliss with ironic admiration. 'Way to go Fliss. I might have known you'd be prepared to go to any lengths to save Mumma's therapy centre. And, of course, your job.' Turning a jubilant face towards the man still holding Fliss in his arms she added, 'Hey, you guys - don't look at Fliss like that. You've gotta respect a girl for her determination to let nothing stand between her and her ambitions.'

'Enough, Isla,' said the man who was no longer a stranger.

'Enough? Oh, I don't think so.' Isla evidently had no intention of being denied her moment of triumph. 'It's probably a *bit* late for formal introductions, but the social niceties must be observed. Fliss, I'd like you to meet the Laird of Kinloch Mara. Our stepbrother. . . Ruairi Urquhart.'

Chapter Twelve

'You -your brother?' Fliss stammered as Ruairi Urquhart placed her on her feet and then took several distancing steps away from her. Aware that it must look as if she'd deliberately set out to seduce him in order to safeguard her position at the therapy centre, Fliss knew she had to set the record straight.

And quickly, too.

'Pleased to meet you,' she held out her hand. 'I'm . . .'

He blanked her and focused his attention on the search party grouped on the path before him. Humiliated and burning with mortification, Fliss linked her hands under the sari length to hide their shaking.

'Library, now please - all of you,' he commanded. It was clear from the deep frown that drew his straight dark eyebrows together that he was holding his anger in check.

'Yowzer. Whatever you say, Bro,' Isla saluted, ignoring his basilisk stare.

'Shall we?' Ruairi prompted, gesturing for Fliss to join the others. Plainly, it didn't occur to him for a second that she would do anything as reckless as defying him. Fliss hesitated, but decided that this was neither the time nor the place to make her stand.

So much for the highland hospitality she'd read about in the guidebooks. *Céad míle fáilte* - kaed meela fault-yih - a hundred thousand welcomes she'd been promised. Instead, she'd got the Urquharts - quite possibly the most *dysfunctional* family in the highlands and islands.

She held herself proudly as they progressed along the path, very much aware that her nemesis was right behind her - no doubt watching her bottom trying to free itself from the miniscule triangle of bikini. She stumbled once or twice and felt Mitzi's guiding hand at her back and threw a grateful look over her shoulder. At least she had *one* friend in Kinloch Mara.

As they entered the house and crossed the hall, Mitzi and the rest of the prison detail fell into step with the flip-flop of Fliss's sandals on the stone floor. As if she was performing some strange Bollywood version of a highland reel with tinkling ankle bells in place of the bagpipes. Shaking her head at the fanciful notion, she collided with Urquhart as she stopped at the foot of the stairs, unsure of where the library was situated. His expression wasn't encouraging as he moved to one side, peeled off from the main party and issued a command to a member of staff.

'Yes, Sir Ruairi, right away.' The young girl disappeared towards the kitchens. Fliss followed the family into the library where they took up various positions near a large partners' desk. Mitzi and Angus on a scuffed leather sofa, Cat by the marble fireplace and Isla on the very edge of the desk.

Fliss held back, wondering where to stand. Surely, what he had to say to his family should be said in private? Did she really need to hear him haranguing them? She pretty much guessed the outcome of this pow-wow and was mentally preparing herself for the long trip home to Pimlico.

But not before she'd said her piece to Urquhart - in private.

Moving towards the fireplace, she sat on the padded fender and stretched her hands towards the peat turves burning in the grate. She was disconcerted to find that she was chilled to the bone. It might be midsummer's eve but cool evening air blew through the open window and insinuated itself round the dark corners of the room, and her ankles.

The door opened and they all jumped, demonstrating just how jittery they were. But it was only the same member of staff bearing a tray of sandwiches, shortbread and a pot of coffee. She placed it on the fender and Cat reached out towards it.

'Supper. I'm starving,' she broke the depressing silence that had fallen on them.

'The supper was ordered for the English lady. By the Laird,' the girl announced, handing Fliss her silk kimono which she carried, draped over her arm. 'Will I be after fetching you some supper too, Miss Catriona?'

'You've been stuffing your face all night, Cat. Don't be such a pig. The staff has enough to do without running around after you - or Fliss, come to that.' Ignoring Isla's jibe, Fliss slipped on the kimono, grateful that she could at last hide her nakedness. Ruairi entered the room and held the door open for the young girl who scuttled back to the kitchen - no doubt eager to regale the staff with the behaviour of *themselves* upstairs. As she brushed past Ruairi in the doorway, she almost bobbed a curtsey.

No wonder he had such an inflated sense of his own importance Fliss thought, giving him an icy stare. But the effect was rather spoiled when her stomach gave a hungry growl.

'Do sit down and eat, Fliss darling. Before you faint clean away again,' Mitzi gestured towards the tray of food.

Fliss considered leaving the food untouched, just to make the point that she didn't want *anything* from Ruairi Urquhart. Neither would she be jumping every time he clicked his fingers. But common sense and good manners won the day. How would she be able to hold her own with the Laird of Kinloch Mara if she was weak from hunger? In a flash, she gained the measure of the man she had to convince the therapy centre was a good business proposition - and persuade to allow her to stay on at Tigh na Locha. Judging by the stubborn line of his mouth and the flinty look in his eyes, she doubted very much that anyone had made Ruairi Urquhart change his mind in a long, long time.

Evidently believing that he'd discharged his obligations towards her, Ruairi took his place behind the desk and Isla launched a pre-emptive strike:

'I have gathered you all together . . .' she said, mimicking Miss Marple perfectly.

Fliss had to admit that the scene *did* look like it'd been lifted straight out of an Agatha Christy novel. The family gathered in the panelled library, the tense atmosphere, the impending dénouement; and Murdo, the faithful retainer - with a long handled axe slotted through his belt - guarding the door in case anyone did a runner. Tense with anticipation, knowing full well that her turn would come, Fliss wondered who would be denounced as the murderer. Or, in this case, the mastermind behind the idea of resurrecting the therapy centre.

'All the usual suspects, I see,' Ruairi parried, looking at his sisters. 'Only this time a new character has joined the cast. So, what have we? Two punk fairies, one Titania, and - Julius Caesar; for the love of God, why Julius Caesar, Angus?' he asked despairingly of the large Texan.

'Mitzi said we were to dress as characters from Shakespeare. I kinda got my plays all mixed up. We don't read a whole lot of Shakespeare on the oil rigs, Ruairi.' Red faced and perspiring in the folds of a roman toga and with a crown of laurel leaves perched rakishly over one ear, Angus grinned lamely at them. Cat snorted and then coughed to cover it up when Ruairi flashed a warning look.

'I don't suppose you do.' Ruairi's lips were set in a forbidding line as he moved on to Fliss. 'I know Wester Ross has its monsoon season but I don't quite see where a Bollywood fairy fits into your vision of a Midsummer Night's Dream, Mitzi. Or why Murdo is dressed as a woodcutter.'

'Why to slay the big bad wolf when he crashes the party, of course. Duh.' Isla was shushed into silence by Mitzi who turned her big blue eyes on Ruairi.

'Ruairi. Sweetie . . . this little party has been all very last minute. Fliss and the girls only arrived today; hence the makeshift costumes . . . we've had to improvise, cobble our costumes together as best we could.' She picked at the layers of silk and gold organza that fell from her hand-embroidered bustier studded with seed pearls. It screamed *couture* at Fliss. 'I know you said to keep a lid on our spending, but we've been very frugal. The girls are wearing old ballet tutus, Doc Martens and . . . and, Angus has paid for his own costume, the caterers and, well - *everything*. It hasn't cost the estate - you - a bean.' Ruairi appeared to take her words at face value and she relaxed.

'Well that does rather present me with a problem, Mitzi.' He brought a sheaf of papers out of the desk drawer. 'Because someone called Vivienne Westwood is demanding payment for an exclusive costume designed for Lady Urquhart. The invoice runs into five figures - and is dated several months ago. Impromptu party, Mitzi? I don't think so.'

'I - I can explain,' Mitzi began.

'That's exactly what I'm hoping.' Ruairi folded his arms and gave her a deceptively charming smile, before turning to Angus. 'I thought we'd agreed, Angus - no more parties.'

'Hell, I know, Ruairi. But it was the only way to persuade Mitzi to leave that goddam spa - forward slash - ashram she'd booked herself into, and come home. Ah was nearly melting in the heat. Another week and ah'd've been a dead man. For sure. And Mitzi's face would have been frozen forever.' Taking one look at his huge frame and high colour, and Mitzi's smooth forehead Fliss sensed he wasn't exaggerating.

'Oh, Angus, how you do go on.' Mitzi slapped his hand. 'It was just a little top up,' she explained to Fliss who was by now the only one looking at her. The others were avoiding eye contact with each other and Ruairi in case they brought his wrath down on *their* head.

The tension in the room was palpable; there was an undercurrent of unfinished business and unspoken words between Ruairi, Mitzi and the girls. The whole family dynamic was out of kilter, but somehow Fliss couldn't envisage them signing up for Family Therapy, pouring their hearts out in an attempt to sort out their unresolved issues. People like them didn't; they bottled up their feelings and left them to fester for years. She wanted to understand the root of their unhappiness and dysfunction, spend time unravelling their collective past. Time she didn't have.

She was about as welcome as a plague bacillus at Tigh na Locha and the sooner she was back in London and quarantined the better. She turned away from the family scene and stared into the slow burning peat turves, letting her eyes swim out of focus.

She felt like she'd fallen asleep half way through a complicated movie and had woken up just as the final credits rolled - leaving her with a raft of unanswered questions. Just how strapped for cash *were* the Urquharts? They hardly looked like they were entitled to Family Credit. She knew that wealth was relative. But, if you owned a castle in the highlands complete with loch and acres of land, a house in uber-trendy Notting Hill and other assets - surely you could hardly consider yourself on the bread line?

'We'll talk about the party later, Mitzi,' Ruairi promised, as though suddenly remembering the reason he'd flown home earlier than expected. He turned the full laser beam of his blue eyes on Isla and Cat. 'I'm more interested in why you two think you can stay in the London house, without permission.'

'I didn't realise that we needed permission to stay in our *family* house.' Emphasising the word, Isla slid off the edge of the desk and sashayed over to Mitzi. She perched on the arm of the sofa and swung her black stockinged legs backwards and forwards.

'Well, for the record, you do. I only hope,' he added coldly, 'that nothing has been broken. And that you stayed well away from my mother's things in the attic.'

'Yeah, yeah, we know we're not allowed to touch them. You said.' Isla patted her mother consolingly on the shoulder. The reference to the late Lady Urquhart had clearly upset Mitzi and she was pulling a corner of her designer costume through her fingers. 'I'm nearly twenty. I *think* I can take care of myself and a knocked about old house.'

Ruairi chose to ignore her last derogatory comment.

'One would have thought so; but as it stands - I wouldn't leave either of you in charge of an empty shoe box, let alone a house full of antiques.' Fliss thought of the hammering some of those family heirlooms had taken on the night of the party and hoped that he wasn't planning on flying down to Notting Hill to take an inventory any time soon.

'We managed pretty okay. If you don't believe me, ask Fliss.' By now, Fliss was familiar with Isla's ploy of deflecting flak away from herself by sending it in someone else's direction. She'd used it to good effect when the neighbours had been baying for blood on the steps of the house in Elgin Crescent - and again in Ladbroke Grove Police Station. But she wasn't about to fall for it a third time.

Unhurriedly, she drained her cup and made a great play of rearranging the folds of her kimono. She didn't want him to think she was intimidated by him. Or that the epithets he'd levelled at his sisters: feckless, irresponsible, untrustworthy, could also be applied to her.

'I think you'll find the house exactly as you'd expect,' was her ambiguous reply.

'Which is?' Ruairi asked, clearly suspicious of her answer.

Then he yawned. For a split second he looked bone-tired, and if he hadn't behaved so appallingly towards her since they'd been discovered in the garden, Fliss might have had some degree of sympathy for him . . . Flying in on the red eye, helicoptering up from Heathrow to find a fancy dress party in full swing, and the contentious therapy centre resurrected. Instead, she hardened her heart and reserved her sympathy for herself - brought here on a fool's errand, and dispatched home less than twenty four hours later like an unwanted parcel.

'Nothing to add, Isla? Cat?' His interrogation continued despite his obvious exhaustion.

'D - don't think so,' Cat mumbled and moved closer to Fliss on the fender, evidently believing there was strength in numbers. In the ensuing silence the grandfather clock in the hall chimed the hour.

Midnight.

Ruairi glanced at his watch and Fliss calculated that his jet lagged brain was running seven hours ahead of theirs - the time difference between Hong Kong and Wester Ross. No wonder he looked shattered. He rubbed a hand over his eyes, got to his feet and then pushed his chair back from the desk.

'We'll resume this discussion in the morning. I want to know all about your arrest and the episode in the police station,' he addressed his sisters, now fully alert. 'Why Cat's seen fit to absent herself from boarding school before the end of term. And why Isla hasn't secured a university place for next term, and regards gainful employment beneath her.' Both sisters looked suitably crushed. 'Mitzi, we have your overdraft to discuss. I see you've maxed out on your credit cards, again. And, Miss Bagshawe -'

'Yes?' she started when he said her name.

'We'll discuss this foolishness about the therapy centre tomorrow, straight after breakfast.'

'Foolishness?' Fliss rose to her feet, ready to defend herself, but once more he acted as if she hadn't spoken. She was left with the unflattering impression that once she was back in London she'd be forgotten, and normal service would be resumed.

'I'll say goodnight, then. Pleasant dreams, everyone' His grim half-smile made it plain he knew they'd spend the night tossing and turning and honing their alibis. 'Breakfast will be at eight o'clock - sharp. Don't make me have to send a member of staff to fetch you out of bed.'

His parting remark was aimed at Cat and Isla, but Fliss felt that the little barb was for her benefit, too. She watched as he left the library and climbed the stairs towards the upper floors where, presumably, he had his lair.

Chapter Thirteen

The next morning, Fliss breathed in the scent of green, growing things through her open bedroom window, instead of the usual Chicken Hong Kong style that wafted over from the take away adjoining her flat in Pimlico. The beach and loch below her were shrouded in low-lying mist - like a scene from Brigadoon and she watched spellbound as the purple-blue hills were touched by cartwheeling shafts of sunlight.

Then, dragging herself away from the view, she focused on more pressing matters. She'd spent the last hour pouring over the contract drawn up between Angus, Mitzi and herself a few weeks earlier. It proclaimed her manageress of the Kinloch Mara Therapy Centre for an initial six month period stretching from May to October. But she knew if Ruairi Urquhart had any say in the matter she would never take up her post. Despite last night's resolution to square up to him and convince him of the viability of the centre, she knew in reality that the debacle in the rose garden had sealed her fate. Irrevocably.

But, she wasn't going down without a fight - she'd march into breakfast this morning and . . . A sound - somewhere between a cat being strangled and a dog baying at the moon drew her back to the window. Kneeling on the window seat, she beheld a spectral vision: a highland bonnet complete with eagle's feather, floating just above the shifting ribbons of mist. An errant wind blew off the loch and dispersed the fog to reveal Ruairi Urquhart, preceded by an ancient piper, making his way along the path from the beach.

It was a Kodak Moment.

The summer sun caught the clan badge which fastened the eagle feather to his Balmoral and turned it to burnished gold. The pleats of his kilt waggled aesthetically and his broad shoulders and slim waist were accentuated by a dark blue Scotland rugger shirt cinched in by a leather belt. He looked every inch the Laird of Kinloch Mara and the very embodiment of rugged, highland manhood as he stopped on the terrace where Murdo was standing by a small brass canon. With a nod from Ruairi, he pointed a remote control at the canon; it gave out a large boom and then shot back several feet on its wheels.

An unseen hand hoisted the Urquhart pennant on a flagpole jutting out from the ramparts, Ruairi and Murdo let out a bloodcurdling battle cry in Gaelic and raised a clenched fist in salute.

The rallying call reverberated against Fliss's breast bone and left her feeling unsettled by the sheer unapologetic *maleness* of it. Fancifully, she felt she'd witnessed something ancient and forbidden and sank back on her heels to ensure she was out of sight. Then she closed her eyes and let out a wail of frustration. *This* was the man she was up against: Monarch of the Glen - with knobs on. She might as well rip up her contract and start packing now. No way would she be able to persuade Ruairi Urquhart to change his mind about anything that concerned his house, his land or his heritage.

Then, breaking the sombre mood, the piper played a lively reel and led Ruairi and Murdo round to the front of the house.

There was a knock on the door and in contrast to the skirl of pipes and the canon's roar, Mitzi whispered hoarsely: 'Fliss darling, can I come in?' She entered without waiting for an answer, looking pale and wan in an eau de nil negligee and matching peignoir trimmed with marabou feathers. Fliss let out a pent-up breath relieved that it was Mitzi - and not a member of staff announcing that breakfast was served, and would she be after joining Himself in the dining room? Or the kitchen, or wherever last night's unpleasantness would begin all over again.

'Good morning, Mitzi.'

'How did you sleep, sweetie?'

She'd hardly slept a wink all night, twisting and turning in the 400 thread count Egyptian cotton sheets, corkscrewing into a silky cocoon, burning with humiliation over what had happened between her and

Ruairi. Reliving over and over the moment when he'd dropped her on the path like she had Ebola Virus.

'Not well,' she said succinctly.

'I've got a bit of a virus myself, actually. Must be something I ate.' Mitzi sat on the edge of Fliss's bed nursing a glass of alka-seltzer and a massive hangover.

Must be something you drank, Fliss mentally corrected before replying, 'I kept waiting for it to get dark but it didn't. All the guide books say that June's the best month to be in Wester Ross - long hours of daylight, the Gulf Stream warming the waters of the loch. Now I've seen it for myself . . .' she knew she was babbling but couldn't stop.

'No, I meant - how did you manage to sleep after Ruairi's little chat in the library?'

Little chat! It was like calling a tsunami a little local flooding. 'Well, he certainly left us aware of our shortcomings, didn't he?' She wasn't quite sure what Mitzi wanted from her. Did she want her to side with herself, Cat and Isla against Ruairi? Or, did she want *her* to throw in the towel and head back to England on the next available flight, making it easier for them to renege on her contract and avoid paying compensation?

She didn't know Mitzi very well, but somehow she couldn't believe her capable of that. For the moment it was best to withhold her counsel, take a deep breath and consider all the options before saying *anything*.

'Good. Good.' Mitzi pushed her blond hair off her face, without her makeup she looked all of her fifty plus years. 'I just wanted to remind you that Ruairi expects us down for breakfast at eight. On the dot.' She opened one bloodshot eye a little wider and gave Fliss a baleful look. 'He dragged Cat and Isla out of bed, ordered tea to be served in our rooms and then went for a yomp on the hills to check the shooting butts. His body clock's probably telling him that it's the middle of the day, or something.' She took a large swig of the alka-seltzer and pulled a face as it hit her stomach on the way to her liver.

'I saw him walk up from the loch,' Fliss nodded. She rather suspected that she had more to fear from the kilted warrior who'd dramatically staked his claim to his land beneath her window just now, than from the man in the sharply tailored suit who'd freed her from the rose bush last night.

'Yes, I heard Jaimsie playing *The Laird's Lament* and the canon going off.' Mitzi looked out to where the blue and silver Urquhart pennant fluttered above the house. 'Aye, Himself's in residence and the traditions must be observed.' There was a wistful note in her voice as if she was thinking about her late husband and the times the tradition had been observed in *his* honour.

'I suppose,' Fliss responded distractedly, having momentarily lost her train of thought.

'Anyway, darling, I wanted to check you were awake and to thank you,' Mitzi said, brightening up.

'Well - thank *you* for offering me the post.'

'No. Not *that*. The other thing. You know - what Isla said.' Beneath her death like morning-after-the-night-before pallor, Mitzi blushed.

'Other thing?'

'Yes.' She looked over her shoulder before spelling it out. '*S -E -X*. With Ruairi - to save my business. Darling girl, it was kind of you, but . . .'

'Mitzi! I was tired and hungry; I bent down to pick up the sari cloth, we banged heads, that's it!'

'Oh, yes, sweet pea. Quite; quite,' Mitzi patted her hand like they were co-conspirators getting their story straight. 'Then we turned up and spoiled *everything* . . .'

'Mitzi, really I -'

'No, darling. Don't say another word. You tried your best and I thank you for it. How did Isla phrase it? Greater love hath no woman etc.' She waved her hand in Fliss's direction and then drained her pick-me-up in one.

'Mitzi, you don't understand . . .'

'Although,' she frowned. 'It does appear to have gone spectacularly wrong.' She rubbed the cold glass against her forehead and closed her eyes. 'I've never seen Ruairi in such a mood; so angry, so - put out with us all. Not since Fiona did a runner - but, that's a story for another time.' She dropped her voice to a whisper. 'Actually, sweetie, he seems mostly put out with *you*.'

'Me? Oh, God,' Fliss's stomach flipped over and she tried to penetrate Mitzi's hangover. 'You've got to . . . to intercede with Ruairi; explain that my faint was genuine. Mitzi, please; you really must . . .'

'Of course. I understand. That's the tack we'll take.' Like all the Urquharts, Mitzi had perfected the art of switching off from what she didn't want to hear. She patted Fliss's arm, patently misunderstanding her meaning. 'You need time to prepare.'

'Prepare? Prepare for what?' But Mitzi rushed on without pausing for breath.

'Put on your prettiest dress and apply your war paint. You'll need to look your best when . . .' Her telling pause did nothing for Fliss's confidence, especially when she added: 'But I'm sure Ruairi will be perfectly charming to you this morning. Last night will be ancient history - forgiven; forgotten.'

'Wanna bet?' Fliss was thoroughly alarmed at the thought of meeting Ruairi Urquhart and the rest of the family after Mitzi's Sunday tabloid revelations. No doubt the tom-toms had been busy spreading the message throughout the glen that Ruairi Urquhart had been seduced by a wanton, half-naked, Sassenach fairy.

'I'm sure you'll be able to win Ruairi round. Just explain to him that you weren't going to have sex with him to save the therapy centre. That he got it all wrong.' Mitzi winked theatrically at Fliss to let her know that she considered the opposite to be true. 'Bless you for trying though, darling girl.' She gave Fliss's arm a squeeze of gratitude and then got to her feet. 'Ruairi's a tough nut to crack.'

'Mitzi, that *wasn't* what I was doing,' Fliss got to her feet, appalled.

'Well, you'll be able to explain it all to Ruairi,' Mitzi said as she left the guest bedroom. 'I believe he wants to have a little tete-a-tete with you after breakfast.'

'I bet he does,' Fliss muttered as Mitzi left, closing the door behind her. She threw herself on the large brass bed, looked up at the ornate plasterwork on the ceiling and prayed for divine inspiration to get her out of this fix.

Then it came to her in a flash: *she'd phone a friend!*

Chapter Fourteen

'You wot?' Becky spluttered down the crackling line from Walthamstow to Kinloch Mara. 'It sounded like: you *almost* had sex with Ruairi Urquhart. How can you *almost* have sex with someone?'

'That's what I'm trying to tell you. Put down your straighteners and listen.' Monday was Becky's day off and Fliss pictured her sitting at her dressing table about to begin the daily ritual of applying her makeup and rearranging her hair extensions before she hit the Bluewater centre.

'My God, you're a fast worker,' Becky said admiringly. 'You only got there yesterday, and you've already *almost* had sex with someone?'

'Well, it wasn't sex - exactly. A case of mistaken identity might be more accurate.' Fliss ran last night's events over in her mind as she explained. 'You see, I was wearing a bikini, dressed as a fairy and –'

'Time out . . . You were dressed as a *fairy*?'

Maybe ringing Becky hadn't been such a good idea. She should have known Becky wouldn't be able to get past the *sex part* - and focus on the seriousness of the situation. Optimistically, she'd hoped that Becky would have some words of wisdom regarding how she could face the family over breakfast this morning.

'It was a fancy dress party and beach barbecue, right? But that's not the point; the point is . . .'

'The point is, Fliss, sweetie, you *nearly* had sex with the big bad wolf. Ohmigod. That must be against the law. A fairy and a wolf; it's like a bleeding nursery rhyme gone wrong. Or, an episode of Being Human, only with a werewolf instead of a -'

'Becky! Concentrate. This isn't funny. I didn't know he *was* Ruairi Urquhart at that point. Okay? I thought he was a party guest who was kind enough to free me from a rose bush.'

'Rose bush? Where exactly did this hot date take place?'

'Beneath a rose arbour - and it wasn't a hot date. It was a completely embarrassing situation if you really must know. Now the Urquharts think that . . .' Fliss tailed off, sensing that Becky had zoned out after hearing the buzzwords: sex, bikini, hot date.

'You can tell me what a rose arbour is another time. Tell me what he looked like.'

The phone line was now so clear that, if Fliss closed her eyes, she could imagine she was sitting on Becky's rumpled bed swapping details of what they'd got up to the night before. She could almost smell the hair straighteners scorching another mark onto Becky's dressing table. In spite of the situation, she smiled.

'You're missing the point, Bex. I'm in trouble, here.'

'Tell me what he's like,' Becky insisted. 'I have to get a picture of the two of you together - well, perhaps not *that* picture! But you get my drift.' Fliss sighed; Becky could only think and move at her own pace, and was not to be rushed.

'Tall. Slim. Dark hair. Blue eyes. Smelled of some divine aftershave - Chanel or Jo Malone at a guess, Oh, and did I mention he is bloody rude, self-opinionated and doesn't look as if anyone's said *no* to him in a long time?' She glanced towards the door, paranoid that someone was on the other side listening and would report her scathing description back to Himself.

'What was he wearing - a hairy suit?' Becky broke into her thoughts.

'A hairy suit?'

'You know. Was he dressed like a wolf?'

'No, you idiot, he was wearing a business suit. He'd just landed in his helicopter, and . . .' She gave a short-tempered tut, willing Becky to get on message.

'Helicopter. He has a *helicopter*?'

'Well, I don't know if it's his, exactly; it might belong to that other guy I told you about - Mitzi's boyfriend - Angus Gordon.'

'Jeesuz - Fliss. *How could you resist him*?' Becky sang, like this was a scene from Mamma Mia and Fliss was Meryl Streep. 'Gorgeous. Own helicopter and castle in Scotland. What's not to like? So, just how far *did* you go? First base?' she asked matter of factly and then laughed.

'What's so amusing?' Fliss demanded, not quite seeing the funny side of her predicament.

'This is like one of those 0875 Chat lines. You know. Hello. This is Sheena in the Highlands; I'm wearing a kilt and no knickers.' The line went silent Fliss's end and eventually Becky picked up the vibe. 'Ok. I'll shut up and listen.'

Fliss continued. 'He freed me from the rose bush. I bent down to pick up my sari cloth; we banged heads and I saw stars. I was about to keel over - *not* so romantic - fireworks went off around us. He caught me in his arms.' She didn't mention their passionate kiss; she didn't want even her best friend to know how idiotically she'd behaved. Becky, however, quickly dismissed the subtle nuances in the tale and concentrated instead on the bigger picture.

'Fireworks. Buff bloke. Not romantic? Bloody hell, Fliss, you're hard to please. Well, it works for me. Tell me there's more - pleeease,' she begged.

Now it was Fliss's turn not to be rushed.

'At that point, Mitzi, Murdo, Cat and Isla came up from the beach and . . .' she tailed off. *The moment was over and the damage was done.*

'Murdo, Angus? Oh, never mind.' Becky quickly dismissed the secondary characters and waited for the resolution. 'So - you weren't actually . . . you know, getting down and dirty when they found you.'

'Well, hardly. I'd just fainted, remember.' She was glad that Becky couldn't see her blush or the long strand of auburn hair she was twining round her finger. 'They called out my name. *He*,' she still couldn't quite bring herself to call him Ruairi, 'put two and two together. We stood looking at each other. It was then that the penny finally dropped - for me, at least. He got there a nano second ahead of me. Naturally, Isla took great pleasure in introducing us.'

'Naturally?' Becky let out a shriek of outrage. 'The skinny cow. I bet she did. You get all upset; but *she* gets the chance to put one over on her brother.'

'He thought I'd faked the whole episode in order to compromise him. Thought I was offering myself on a plate so that he'd give the therapy centre the green light.'

'Were you?'

'Becky!'

'Well! I know how much this job means to you.'

'Not *that* much, I can assure you.' Fliss suspected that she sounded like an outraged dowager next to the ever-pragmatic Becky. 'Then Isla implied that I *was* willing to lay myself down for the sake of the centre. Planned it even. And, judging by the conversation I've just had with Mitzi, it's clear that she thinks so too. And if she thinks it, then Ruairi Urquhart - and no doubt half the estate - believes it. Trust me; the clan network works faster than Twitter during an inner city riot round here.' She paused to give Becky the chance to come up with some words of comfort.

'Now. Don't go all huffy on me, Flissy . . . but.' Her tut of exasperation could be clearly heard 500 miles away in London. 'Bloody hell - how come you din't know who he was? You're supposed to be the one with brains. Din't you wonder why he was wearing a suit when everyone else was in fancy dress?'

'I know, I know. I was so anxious to keep my appointment that I wasn't thinking straight. I assumed that he was a guest who'd received an invitation too late to organise a costume, or one of the event planners.' There was a pause as Fliss acknowledged that Becky was right - she'd been an absolute idiot.

'Okay. So . . . you stood your ground and explained that it was all a misunderstanding?' Becky painted in the final scene.

Silence.

'Not quite.'

'Wot?'

'We were escorted to the library where he laid into each member of his family in turn. I think my bollocking has been reserved for this morning after breakfast when, no doubt, I'll be given my marching orders.'

'Blimey, Fliss, you've only been up there one day and look what you've got yourself into.' Becky sighed extravagantly. 'Look; I'll throw a sickie - come up and . . .'

'And do what, exactly?' Fliss knew Becky would spend her holiday money on an air ticket without a moment's hesitation. 'No. This was my big chance and I've screwed up. I've got to tough it out; at least put the record straight before I leave.' It went quiet, and she could almost hear the cogs in Becky's brain shifting up a gear.

'Okay. Here's what I think. You're being paid silly money for a job you can do blindfold. He sounds like a right bastard. But . . . and here's the thing . . . from what you told me, the business is being bankrolled by whatshisname?'

'Angus.'

'Well -'

'Well?'

'How can Ruairi - Smart - Arse - Urquhart sack you when he don't employ you? Plus - if he makes *them* sack *you*, you're owed, babe. Big time.'

'That's true . . .' Fliss wondered why she couldn't have figured all this out for herself. Perhaps she was too close to the problem. 'But, even if he does agree to my staying on, how could I face him - day in, day out - with him thinking me some kind of second-rate Mata Hari who'd used her body to get what she wanted?'

'Mata Hari? Who the bleedin' hell is Mata Hari? Some kind of Indian Head Massage therapist?' Fliss laughed in spite of the seriousness of the situation and started to explain, but Becky didn't give her the chance. 'Listen Fliss, the question you should be asking is - how can he face *you*? He's made himself look a right plonker in front of his family - that's what's really buggin' him, if you want my opinion. Accusing you of dropping your drawers to keep your job? I mean, as if! In fact, babe, I'd say that he owes *you* an apology.'

Fliss's spirits lifted. She knew Becky was only saying what she'd have worked out for herself, if she'd had the time to think clearly. But, the clock was ticking and she had the breakfast meeting to get through before she flew home. After that, she'd steel herself to march up to Angus and Mitzi and demand compensation for her disappointment, time and trouble. Even if it meant that in doing so, she'd confirm Ruairi Urquhart's impression of her: *Good Time Girl on the Make.*

'Maybe you're right,' she said and sighed, knowing that her reputation was well and truly tarnished.

'There is another way,' Becky suggested.

'Come home and admit I'm a failure?'

'Who says you're a failure? My cousin'll soon find you another white van and you can set up your mobile therapy business, like you'd planned. You can doss down on my floor until your flat is available again. I'd be like old times.'

The words *doss* and *old times* made Fliss shudder.

Cradling the phone between her chin and her shoulder, she walked over to the turret window and looked out over the loch. Truth was, she didn't want to go back to her other life. At least - not yet. The thought of leaving the glen gave her a sharp pang of homesickness although she'd been there less than twenty-four hours. It wasn't the obvious grandeur of the place, or the Urquharts' lifestyle that made her reluctant to leave. It was something deeper - a feeling of belonging.

The feeling was all the more unexpected because Ruairi Urquhart and probably the rest of his family probably couldn't wait to see the back of her. But how could she feel so deeply about a place she hadn't seen before yesterday? Was there some kind of highland magic at work, a magic that had begun to weave its spell the moment she'd set foot in Kinloch Mara.

'You know what you ought 'a do - get one in first. Kick some Scottish ass. Show them that they can't mess with the Flisster.' Becky's words blew away her fanciful thoughts. 'Ring and let me know what's going on. Anyway, why doesn't he install a mast on his property? It's a pain not being able to get you on your mobile.'

'You and Isla have something in common at any rate, she's been complaining about having no mobile phone signal.' Becky gave an indignant snort at the thought of having anything in common with Isla Urquhart. 'I'll ring you as soon as things have been settled here. One way or another,' Fliss added, full of gritty determination.

'OK. Love you Thelma.'

'Love you Louise.'

Fliss held onto the phone long after the line went dead and thought over what Becky had said. *Stand your ground. You've got nothing to lose. Fight for what you want.* She pictured their twin tattoos and gained strength from the sentiment if not the image.

Carpe Diem - Seize the moment.

That's exactly what she was going to do: go down to breakfast and kick some Scottish Ass.

Chapter Fifteen

When Fliss finally made her way downstairs, all fired up to say her piece to Ruairi Urquhart and clear up any false impressions he might harbour about her, she did a double take.

Isla was standing at the foot of the staircase, looking more like an extra from Balamory than the Notting Hill wild child she considered herself. She'd scrubbed her face free of heavy Goth makeup, removed all piercings and was wearing kilt, white blouse and sensible shoes. It was a transformation worthy of Extreme Makeover and clearly in honour of her interview with Ruairi pencilled in for after breakfast.

She looked younger, less confident and the family resemblance between her, Cat and Ruairi was more marked this morning - black hair, pale skin and piercing blue eyes. Catching Fliss's amused look, she fired an opening salvo: 'If you ever mention to *anyone* that you've seen me dressed like this, I'll -'

'You'll do what? Embarrass me in front of your friends and family? Get me arrested and then sacked? Or have you thought up some new humiliation this morning? No? Then do me a favour, Isla - back off and *shutthefuckup*.'

Her outburst left Isla gasping for air like a newly landed fish. She couldn't have looked more stunned if the stag head on the wall had burst into *Flower of Scotland*. Fliss had barely raised her voice, but her body language coupled with her use of the *f word* made it plain she wasn't taking prisoners this morning. She drew some grim satisfaction from Isla's look of shocked disbelief. Previously, she'd found the Urquhart sisters' *nothing can touch me* confidence slightly intimidating. But no longer. Mitzi's revealing tete-a-tete this morning and Isla's mischief making last night had changed everything.

This was the day when worms turned and squadrons of Gloucestershire Old Spots flew over Tigh na Locha. *Show them that they can't mess with the Flisster*, Becky had advised - and that's exactly what she intended! Turning smartly on her heel and leaving a gobsmacked Isla in the hall she joined Mitzi and Cat in the dining room. Four places had been laid for breakfast. Did that mean that Ruairi Urquhart wouldn't be joining them and she'd been given a reprieve? Not that she sought one. She was on a roll and wanted to say her piece to Himself before her anger and her nerve, ran out.

Mitzi raised her head, smiled absentmindedly and then shuddered at the sight of Cat wolfing down great slabs of home-cured bacon and white pudding.

'Coffee, Morag,' she instructed a young girl standing by. 'Black. Gallons of it. Fliss darling, help yourself.' She gestured towards silver chafing dishes, battered by age and daily use, ranged on a long sideboard.

Now that the first confrontation of the morning was over and her adrenaline levels had returned to normal, Fliss was ravenously hungry. Mindful of the long journey home she'd be undertaking after breakfast, she piled her plate high with the Full Scottish and took her place at the table.

Eventually, Isla joined them - noisily scraping back her chair, banging crockery and announcing her presence with as much fuss as she could. Fliss fully expected to receive one of her death stares but Isla was too occupied glaring at the piper on the terrace playing a medley of reels and laments.

'Mumma. Make him stop. Please . . .' she whined, putting her hands over her ears. 'He's killing me.'

I wish! Fliss thought as she shook out her linen napkin with a snap and applied herself to breakfast. Mitzi opened the French doors, shaded her eyes against the bright sunlight and addressed the piper. 'Jaimsie. I think you've played long enough this morning . . .'

'But Himself's home. The clan pennant's been hoisted on the battlements. Have ye no seen?' Visibly scandalised at the traditional welcome being curtailed, he nevertheless let the air wheeze out of the bag and the pipes fall against his shoulder. 'I'll away then - but Himself willnae like it.' He sniffed and left in a great huff to scare the wildlife down by the loch instead.

'Coffee, Miss?' Morag broke the blissful silence that followed his departure and poured strong black coffee into Fliss's cup. Fliss glanced at Cat and saw that she, too, had opted for a brother-appeasing outfit of kilt, plain blouse and no makeup.

'I'd kill for a tall skinny latte,' Isla muttered, pushing her empty plate aside and giving Fliss and Cat's breakfasts a disgusted look. 'At Joseph's or Daylesford.'

'Or a macchiato,' Cat agreed with a mouth full of sausage. Then she waved her fork in the direction of the French doors and spluttered out a warning: 'Ruairi.' Heart hammering against her ribs Fliss watched him advance through the gardens with Jaimsie in attendance.

'The Monarch of the Glen. In all his glory,' Isla announced with sour humour as Ruairi pushed open the French doors and the piper struck up the same bloodcurdling tune as before. Isla cast her stepbrother a provocative look and muttered: 'The condemned woman did *not* eat a hearty breakfast, despite knowing that she was about to be hung, drawn and quartered.'

Ignoring her sarcastic greeting, Ruairi paused on the threshold and took a deep, calming breath before entering. His ominous expression suggested that before the morning was over he would have asserted his authority over his family, sacked an extraneous therapist and restored order to Kinloch Mara.

However, he didn't look on top of his game - he was unshaven and his clear blue eyes were red-rimmed. Although the fresh morning air had brought colour to his cheeks, his skin had a pallor that suggested he'd spent most of the night pacing about in his lair. That pleased Fliss - it would do him no harm to suffer; she doubted that anyone had managed a good night's sleep after last night's family conference in the library.

But it was obvious his wrath was directed solely at them, because he laid a gentle hand on the old piper's shoulder and spoke to him quietly in Gaelic. Jaimsie touched his hand to his Glengarry, gathered his bagpipes under his arm like a much loved pet and walked away.

'Ladies,' he addressed them. The temperature - which had dropped by several degrees when he opened the French doors, plummeted even lower as he waited for their response. 'Ladies?'

Isla and Cat eventually managed a mutinous 'Morning, Ruairi,' while Mitzi croaked a feeble, *Ruairi, darling* without raising her head. In one sweeping glance, he registered Fliss's lack of greeting, Mitzi's hangover and his sisters' apathetic welcome. Was it Fliss'smagination, or did he save his most withering look for her? She'd already guessed that she was at the top of his hit list this morning and that look confirmed it.

'Coffee, sweetie?' Mitzi asked in an obvious attempt to placate him and stop the morning from deteriorating further. She gestured for Morag to come forward with the coffee pot. 'Breakfast?'

'No thanks, Mitzi. I had breakfast. Hours ago.' He swept off the Balmoral, complete with eagle feather - and tossed it onto the table. His glance at his battered Fossil wrist watch intimated that they should have been up at dawn and done half a day's work by now. During the uncomfortable silence, Fliss wondered if she'd imagined the physical connection which had fizzed like a high voltage current between them last night. This morning it had been replaced by something altogether more measured and calculating.

Well, that made it easier to leave Kinloch Mara and her dream of managing Mitzi's therapy centre. She wouldn't stay where she wasn't wanted or give him the satisfaction of knowing he had sent her spinning off into space with just one kiss. Unexpectedly, she was overwhelmed by feelings of disconnection, a loneliness that chilled her to the marrow. She gave a convulsive quiver and Ruairi turned in her direction, as if he'd felt the frisson, too. And - just for a moment, it seemed like they were the only people in the room and she thought she detected something beneath his scornful regard; something close to regret.

But then his scowl was back in place and it was business as usual. His gaze narrowed, became more speculative, cynical even - and it was plain that he'd interpreted her plaintive look as another form of entrapment. A sting to elicit his sympathy and to get what she wanted.

I won't fall for the same trick, twice, his searing look told her.

Evidently missing the look that had just passed between them and no doubt hoping to distract him, Isla fired the first shot. 'Couldn't sleep, Ruairi? Too much on your mind? Overexcited by the fireworks?' She tipped her chair onto its back legs and swivelled it skilfully on one leg. 'I hope you two weren't playing musical bedrooms in the wee small hours of the night. Such a bad example to set the children,' she nodded towards Cat who corpsed and nearly choked on her sausage.

Ruairi's expression showed he was in no mood for Cat's silliness or Isla's posturing. 'We'll discuss the party and your latest escapade in Elgin Crescent, later. For now I'll settle for knowing who banished Jaimsie down to the loch?' he raised an eyebrow at Mitzi.

'Ruairi sweetie, I only asked him play a little further off from the house because Isla had a headache.' Judging by Ruairi's expression that was the wrong answer.

'To be honest, Ruairi, it did sound like he'd been playing the same tune for over an hour,' Cat leapt to her mother's defence while she slathered marmalade on thick buttered toast. 'All bagpipe music sounds the same to me, anyhoo.' She dismissed her heritage with a casual wave of the butter knife.

'Jaimsie plays the pipes every morning when the Laird's in residence,' Ruairi continued with studied patience, but his fingers beat an irritated tattoo on the back of the chair. 'The Laird's Lament was Papa's favourite, as I am sure we all remember.'

'Of course we do.' Mitzi looked positively crushed and drew her peignoir more tightly round her slender frame and sighed. Tangible feelings of sorrow, loss and happier times remembered, hovered in the air between them.

'Although, I suppose it is perfectly reasonable to dispense with hundreds of years of tradition because Isla has a hangover. Cat can't distinguish a Strathspey from a reel - despite my having spent a fortune on her dancing lessons, and you have other things on your mind, Mitzi.'

At the mention of *dancing lessons*, the sisters exchanged one of their spooky, telepathic looks. Cat bowed her head over her plate, hiding a smirk which Fliss suspected had nothing to do with Jaimsie being banished to his own quarters. But she had no time to give it further thought because Isla leapt to her mother's defence.

'That's a bit harsh, Ruairi.'

'Perhaps we could continue this discussion in the library, Isla.' He waited for her to get to her feet, his measured breathing the only indication that he was deeply, furiously, angry. 'I'll see you other ladies in . . .' he glanced at his watch. 'Five minutes. Suitably dressed,' he gave Mitzi's nightdress and negligee combo a despairing look as he and Isla left the room.

'Yes, of course. The library; in five minutes,' Mitzi answered, sending Fliss an apologetic smile. 'I'm afraid that means you, too, sweet pea. Until this business with the therapy centre is sorted out, we can't make any plans. But do finish your breakfast first.' She got up and left the room.

Therapy centre! What therapy centre?

A quick tour of the house with Cat yesterday had revealed nothing as obvious as a therapy room. Fliss had hoped to have a surreptitious look round after breakfast to locate it so she could torture herself on her flight home with the thought of what she'd be leaving behind. Her appetite suddenly deserted her and she pushed away her half-eaten breakfast and left the table. At least she could get a few breaths of fresh air and take a last look over the loch before she was fired for a second time in less than a month.

Entering the hall, she spotted her luggage, handbag and brand new jacket neatly stacked at the foot of the cantilevered staircase and an electrical charge exploded in her brain. Seemingly, she and her luggage were about to be thrown off the estate and put on the first available flight home as soon as Ruairi Urquhart had finished with her. Her meeting with him would be a show trial, with him as judge and jury and with the verdict already decided.

She pictured him dusting off his hands as Murdo's Land Rover disappeared down the long drive with her in the passenger seat. One problem dealt with; good riddance to bad rubbish. Tension prickled her scalp and her blood pressure raised a couple of clicks as the phrase jarred in her brain. *Good riddance to bad rubbish?* Well, she'd see about that . . .

What are my belongings doing here?' she demanded of Murdo who was tending to the fire.

'Good morning, Fliss.' Murdo turned and smiled at her, but she could tell from the tell-tale flush that spread over his fair skin that the madness in the garden and its aftermath were still fresh in his mind. Did he belong to the camp who believed that she was a scheming hussy who'd set her cap at the Laird of Kinloch Mara?

'Did you bring my cases downstairs?' she repeated, hoping that the answer was *no* - she liked Murdo and didn't want to pick a fight with him.

'Cases?' he queried, 'I'm afraid you've lost me there, Fliss.'

'Excuse me, Miss. I did.' Turning, Fliss saw a member of female staff carrying a plastic holdall full of cleaning materials looking at her anxiously. 'I was sent by the Laird to pack your things, bring them down here and put them by the front door. They'll be moved shortly.'

'The Laird told you to pack my things, did he?'

It was one thing for her to leave Kinloch Mara in high dudgeon, but quite another to be dismissed like an unworthy servant. Small wonder he could hardly bring himself to look at her this morning!

There was an eruption from the library and all heads turned as Ruairi raised his voice. 'Gap year? You've been on a gap year since you left school two years ago. If you don't take up your university place this autumn I'll find you a job on the estate. Mucking out the stables, driving the guns over to the butts, painting fences if needs be. And before you ask, there's no way you and Cat will be flying down for the Notting Hill Carnival this year. I think the Royal Borough of Kensington and Chelsea has had quite enough of you.'

He came out of the library followed by a chastened Isla. She rushed past them, dashing tears from her cheeks and openly furious that they'd overheard Ruairi get the better of her. Murdo made as if to go after her but Ruairi laid a hand on his arm and shook his head. Fliss wondered as Isla ran up the stairs and slammed her bedroom door, what bound Murdo and Isla together.

'Leave her, Murdo. She needs time to cool off and think over what I've said.'

He rubbed his hands over his stubble, stretched his arms above his head and yawned. A gap appeared between the waistband of his kilt and the bottom of his rugger shirt. Fliss traced the line from his taut abdomen to where a sprinkling of dark hair disappeared below his belt. She sucked in an extra breath at the thought of where that tapering line led to, feeling suddenly very hot. Catching her look, he pulled down his shirt and straightened the leather sporran over the front of his kilt.

'Is there a problem?' he asked Murdo, looking directly at Fliss as if her name and *problem* were synonymous.

'Well, now that you mention it. There is,' she cut in before Murdo had a chance to answer.

High colour stung her cheeks and stole along her décolletage because she knew he'd seen her checking him out. He was standing so close that the rough wool of his kilt grazed along the sensitive skin on the side of her hand and she dragged it away, as if scalded by the contact. Furious with her reaction to his nearness, she decided that anger was the best defence against raging hormones and wild imagining about what lay under his kilt.

'How dare you send someone to pack my belongings and - and *dump* them by the front door without so much as a by your leave?'

'I was simply helping you on your way,' he replied, using the same calm, *there, there, dear* tone that had infuriated Isla earlier.

'*Helping me on my way*?' She spoke in italics and her voice rose in a shriek. 'It's been decided, then - I'm leaving Tigh na Locha?'

'It seemed the most sensible arrangement, given the circumstances,' he said, cool and in command.

'*Circumstances*? I take it you're referring to last night.'

'What about last night?'

The sharpness in his tone showed that he wasn't as cool about the whole episode as appearances might suggest. But she couldn't decide whether he was mad with her for - as he believed, lying over her identity; or, with himself for having fallen for a honey trap. Either way, it was clear he didn't want to be reminded of his moment of weakness, or how easily he'd been duped into holding her in his arms.

'Well?' He waited for her answer. Fliss took a deep breath, from what she'd observed of Ruairi Urquhart, she needed to be composed and in control if she was going head-to-head with him.

'What I have to say to you is best said in private. Not in front of . . .' she nodded in the direction of Murdo and the girl. There had been too many witnesses to her cringe-worthy moment in the garden and she had no intention of repeating the experience.

'Your scruples do you justice,' he said, his eyes darkening to sapphire as he gave her a shrewd once-over. And Fliss knew in his eyes she was nothing more than an amoral chancer who'd used her charms to compromise him and so safeguard her job. It was a reputation unfairly won and she had no intention of leaving without setting the record straight.

'I dare say I'm as principled as you.' Her unequivocal look was designed to remind him how he'd flirted with her on the path, held onto her ankle longer than was necessary and had gathered her into his arms - when he could just as easily have guided her to a bench. She hadn't forced him to kiss her, had she? It took two to tango - or in this case, dance the Highland fling, and she wanted him to admit it.

'Remind me never to come to you for a character reference,' he said dryly.

'In case you doubt my integrity, why don't you search my bags for the family silver?' Impulsively, she upended the contents of her holdall onto the flagstones and tossed the empty bag at his feet.

The jumbo box of tampons which had been tucked in amongst her underwear burst open, scattering tampons everywhere. Ruairi looked at the white paper cylinders littering the hall floor as if they were radioactive. One of the tampons rolled as far as the log basket before ricocheting off it and heading back towards him like a heat seeking missile. It finally came to rest by the toe of his boot.

Plainly, that was a bridge too far.

'We'll continue this discussion in private,' he said, his lips set in a thin line. Holding her firmly by the elbow, he half-escorted, half-dragged her through the hall towards the library.

Furious at being manhandled and crimson with mortification at the sight of her sanitary protection scattered all over the floor, Fliss cast a helpless look at the young maid. The young girl scooped up the tampons and pushed everything back into the holdall before zipping it up. Fliss had a sinking feeling that the incident with the tampons would pass into legend and be recalled long after she was back in London, flipping burgers.

She resisted the childish impulse to snatch her elbow out of Ruairi's grasp. But once they were in the library and standing before the partners' desk, she looked down at her elbow and then slowly up at his face.

Getting the message, he released her.

Chapter Sixteen

'I'm sorry if my touch offends you,' Ruairi said, although his expression suggested the opposite.

'Not just your touch, if we're being totally honest,' Fliss replied. She'd show him he wasn't the only one with issues to resolve and matters to put right.

'I doubt you know the meaning of the word, Miss Bagshawe.'

'What do you mean by that?' she demanded, her face flaming.

He guided her towards a faded turkey rug in front of the desk and indicated that she should stand there. Furious at being manhandled for a second time, she sidestepped the rug and took up position on the neutral ground of the polished floorboards.

'Last night's performance,' he jerked his head towards the rose gardens, visible through the library window, 'was worthy of a BAFTA.'

'A BAFTA?' She had the uncomfortable - and frankly ludicrous feeling, that she'd been summoned to the headmaster's study to explain her behaviour. Time she seized the initiative, asked a few questions of her own and let him know that she was no pushover. As she considered what to say next, he walked over to the partners' desk and picked up a cheque book and pen. 'First of all,' she began, putting her points in order, 'you've got it all wrong. You've got *me* all wrong.'

'I don't think I have.' He leaned against the edge of the desk and riffled the pages of the cheque book. Then, with the pen poised over a blank cheque, gave her a contemptuous look. 'I think I've got you bang to rights.'

Now she got it!

The luggage in the hall, the blank cheque waiting to be written, were cues for her to exit stage left - with a month's salary in her handbag in lieu of notice. Well, if he thought she was leaving Kinloch Mara with her piece unsaid, he'd seriously underestimated her.

'Explain what you meant earlier by *not just my touch*.' He caught and held her gaze, making it plain that women didn't usually find his touch repellent.

'I meant that you've insulted me by implying that my collapse in the rose gardens was an act to secure my position as Mitzi's manager. Is that what *you* really think? What you *all* think?'

His eyes ranged over her - from her newly washed hair, past her bare legs in summer shorts to her feet in their delicate sandals. His scrutiny was offensive and almost certainly designed to provoke her into saying something unguarded. She looked down at her painted toenails and saw how, in his eyes, they summed up the difference between them. The hardworking laird, wearing what looked like his second-best kilt, frayed rugger jersey and scuffed boots - and the grifter on the make, with her fashionable summer clothes and hard-edged city girl gloss.

She was angry; not just with him, but with her traitorous body and the way it remembered the touch of his fingers across her ankle, his lips against her hair, his whispered words - and wanted more. She dismissed the memory and the feelings it evoked, knowing his version of events went something like . . . She'd arrived in Wester Ross to scam Mitzi and Angus, but upon meeting the Laird, had decided that he was the bigger prize and blackmail was a more profitable venture.

'And didn't you fake it?' He drew her back to the here and now and it sounded as if the answer actually mattered to him. Then the calculating look was back in place. 'Why else would a girl like you leave London unless it was to further her career as a gold-digger? You have the floor Miss Bagshawe.'

A girl like you. He invested such contempt and scorn into the phrase that Fliss winced. Seeing the distrust in his eyes she knew it wasn't going to be easy to make him revise his opinion of her. But she would give it her best shot. When she left here it would be with her head held high and with him admitting he was all wrong about her.

'I came here to do your family a favour. Yes, a favour,' she repeated as his mouth quirked sardonically. 'Then I find out that there's no job.

There doesn't even appear to be a therapy centre. I fainted in the garden because we banged heads and I was tired and emotional. That's it.'

'Okay, Miss Bagshawe, let's assume for a moment that you had no idea who I was.' His wolfish smile - which she would probably have found sexy under different circumstances - showed his scepticism.

'Yes. Let's . . .'

He registered her sarcasm and looked towards the door as though he itched to wrench it open and throw her off his land. A vein throbbed at his temple, indicating that he found her continued presence in his house aggravating and annoying in the extreme.

'I think that we were both carried away last night, but for different reasons.'

'Oh, really?' Fliss resented the implication that while *he'd* acted the gentleman and rescued a fainting guest, *she'd* seized the opportunity to compromise him - accuse him of assault, even - and use it as leverage to extort money from him.

'The time difference, fireworks, whisky on an empty stomach. I wouldn't normally,' he paused, searching for the right word, 'act like that. Especially not with . . .'

'. . . staff?' she prompted.

'A guest,' he corrected.

'For the record - neither would I.'

'No?' His disbelief was insulting.

'I fainted. You caught me. End of.' She gave a 'whatever' shrug, affecting an air of nonchalance. But this time she hung back, waiting for him to give some hint of what was going on in his head before she spoke.

'I think,' he said carefully, 'we both acted rashly. I've had all night to think about it. Jet lag,' he explained, as if to make plain he hadn't lain awake thinking of *her*. 'I've reached the conclusion that the best solution for everyone is . . .'

'. . . that you sack me.' Fliss launched a pre-emptive strike. 'The last

111

twenty four hours have been a nightmare. And that's the *honest* truth. Take it or leave it.

'Sack you?' Fliss was so beleaguered that she didn't register the query in his voice.

'But *you* can't sack me,' she ploughed on, 'because I don't work for you. I'm employed by Mitzi and Angus.' She rifled through her leather tote and brought out her contract which was cracking along the folds from the number of times she'd read it. Smoothing it out, she used two paperweights to flatten it on the desk by his left hip. 'And Mitzi won't be able to sack me, because . . .'

She was about to say *because I resign*, when he cut across her.

'Because you'll sue for wrongful dismissal and make a tidy profit out of her? Out of all of us,' he concluded, implying that they'd finally reached the crux of the matter.

'Got it all figured out, haven't you?' She took an angry step towards him and then checked herself. He might look every inch a highland landowner but he thought and acted like a barracuda. Standing this close to him, she could see where his thick dark eyelashes were paler at the tip, the sunburn beneath his stubble, the strong brown arms that had caught and held her safe. Then, as he leaned forward his body's sweet scent undercut by his aftershave pulsed towards her, taking her back to last night. And, in spite of everything, she couldn't deny her reaction to him. Or that she wanted to be back in his arms, kissing him until they were both dizzy.

Then the voice of reason cut in and reminded her that he was about to have her run off his land and thought her little more than a scheming opportunist. It was the douche of cold water her overheated senses needed and made her realise that her untrammelled response to him was more dangerous than anything he could say, or do.

'I'll tell you what I've figured out - your Lairdship - *I'm* the injured party here. I've travelled to this godforsaken corner of the UK; almost bankrupted myself and sublet my flat. Do you have any idea how difficult it is to find and hold onto a decent two bedroom flat in Pimlico? Of course you don't – you've got your mini-mansion in Elgin Crescent to fall back on every time you fancy a trip up to London.'

'You seem keen to make assumptions about me,' he cut in.

But she wasn't listening; she was on a roll and couldn't stop. 'Now I'm going back to London to start job hunting - in the height of the summer, in the middle of a recession - fighting students for every vacancy that comes up.' He looked almost sympathetic for a moment but then his expression became shuttered, closed up. 'I wouldn't have lost my job in the first place if . . .'

Whoa. Too much information.

'Don't stop, things were just getting interesting,' he prompted. But she clamped her mouth shut; she didn't want him to learn the exact circumstances of her hasty departure from Pimlico, or to make things worse for Cat and Isla.

'I demand compensation,' she said, steering the conversation away from Elgin Crescent. She'd hoped to leave Kinloch Mara with her reputation restored, some compensation for her wasted time and with him put firmly in his place. Instead, she'd just confirmed what he'd suspected all along - she'd taken a punt in coming up here, and they'd be well shot of her.

'At last . . . How much is it going to take to get rid of you?' Ruairi opened his cheque book and reached behind him for a pen. Unaccountably, his words cut her to the quick and made tears prick her eyes.

'How much do you usually pay?' She wanted to hurt him, make him feel as wretched as she did at that moment. So she pushed him a little harder: 'What's the going rate, in your experience? Something tells me I'm not the first woman you've had to pay off.' She knew no such thing of course, but it pleased her to deflect his poisonous dart back at him.

She hardly recognised the creature that she'd become this morning - defiant, rebellious and provocative. But she couldn't back down now. She had to get her hands on the cheque, tear it into a thousand pieces, throw it back in his face and walk out of Tigh na Locha with her head held high.

But he wasn't finished with her – yet.

113

'Difficult to say,' he drawled. 'Sleeping with the Laird isn't a procedure we usually employ when interviewing staff.' Unfazed, he started to fill in the cheque. Fliss didn't know whether to feel triumphant because her ruse was working or dejected because he thought her capable of extortion. 'But don't worry, you'll get every last penny owed to you. I'm sure you're not the type to give anything away for free.'

He wrote the cheque, signed it and tore it out of the book; even from her topsy-turvy viewpoint Fliss could see that the amount was substantial. It was plain he wanted her off the estate and out of his life - lock, stock and therapy table, and with no chance of her ever returning.

'Just ring for a taxi so I can leave you and this place behind,' she said in what she imagined was a fair imitation of a gold-digger's harsh voice.

The cheque was within reach of her fingers now; all she had to do was snatch it from him, rip it up and wipe the cynical *I know all about women like you* look off his face.

'My pleasure. You'll be pleased to know that this godforsaken corner will be as glad to see the back of you, as you are to leave!' He opened the flap of his leather sporran and brought out some loose change. 'Here. I'll even throw in the tip for the taxi.' She ignored his outstretched palm and the crumpled notes nestling there. All that mattered was the cheque . . .

'*Ruairi. Come in,*' a voice crackled into the silence. Putting the cheque book down, he reached for the walkie-talkie on his desk.

'Ruairi. Over'

'I think we've caught those poachers. Can you drive over to the sea loch? Over.'

'On my way. Over and out.' He clipped the walkie-talkie to his belt and pushed himself off the desk. 'I'm sorry to delay your departure, Miss Bagshawe. We'll complete this - transaction - when I return.' It was pretty clear he thought she'd take the cheque and run, because he folded it up and put it in his sporran. Obviously, the Laird of Kinloch Mara regarded catching poachers a top priority, whereas sacking unprincipled therapists came just above cleaning out the septic tank and drenching his sheep for worms.

Hoist by her own petard, Fliss was forced to stay in role until the final curtain call. But was she capable of bringing this BAFTA winning performance to a successful conclusion?

'What about my cheque. And the taxi?' she persisted.

'Are you *so* desperate to leave Tigh na Locha?'

'As desperate as you are to see me go.'

'You, Miss Bagshawe, are the most provoking . . .'

He closed the gap between them in one easy stride, laid a scorching hand on her bare arm and pulled her close. So close that her breasts touched the hard musculature of his chest and her nipples sprang to life at the contact. She sensed he was torn between throwing her over his desk and finishing what they'd started last night - and getting her off his land as quickly as possible.

She read the warring emotions in his face; felt the anger that made his heart race and thud against her breastbone. Her breath snagged and for an instant she experienced fear and exhilaration in equal measure. She didn't know what he was capable of and didn't want to find out. With remarkable self-possession she stared him down and snatched her arm out of his grasp.

'That's the third time you've manhandled me. It'd better be the last.'

'My apologies.'

He pushed her away as though her skin leached acid and shook his head in apparent disbelief at what had just passed between them in this room, closeted away from the rest of the house. Fliss sensed that she'd caused him to forget his duties as laird and his obligations as host. Evidently that ran contrary to his code of civilised behaviour and disturbed him. He gave her one last measuring look, as if to confirm that his instincts had been right about her, and then put as much distance between them as was physically possible.

For her part, now that her temper had abated, Fliss wanted to apologise for her outré behaviour and the stinging things she'd said. She wanted him to know that *this* wasn't who she was. That far from regarding Kinloch Mara a godforsaken corner of the universe, she'd fallen in love with it and didn't want to leave . . . for reasons she could not as yet articulate.

It was suddenly important that he understood that she'd been play-acting and she didn't want him, or his damned money. She'd pay Angus back every penny of his retainer even if it emptied her bank account. She was poor, but she'd been in worse straights. All that mattered was to leave here with her reputation restored.

But she wasn't given the chance. With a terse nod, he took the paperweights off the contract and locked it in the desk drawer along with the cheque book. Giving her the widest berth possible he walked past her and into the hall, uttering the portentous words:

'Wait here. I haven't finished with you by a long chalk.'

Chapter Seventeen

F liss stood rooted to the spot as Ruairi flung open the library
door and strode into the hall, past Mitzi and the girls who were
gathered in a huddle.

They'd obviously heard his parting shot: *I haven't finished with you
by a long chalk*, because they cast anxious glances at Fliss as Ruairi left
via the front door. Evidently intent on channelling his anger and sexual
frustration into catching the poacher.

Fliss groaned, knowing she'd just made a complete fool of herself.
Her precious contract was locked away in the desk drawer and she'd
blown her chance of severance pay. What had she been thinking? If Cat
and Isla - who'd known Ruairi all their lives, couldn't steal a march over
him, what chance did she have?

The Laird of Kinloch Mara was wilier than the poacher he'd set out to
catch.

Hands shaking, she took lipstick and mirror out of her bag and set
about repairing the ravages to her hair and makeup. Her spirits sank
even lower when her reflection looked back at her in the compact's
mirror. Her face was red and blotchy, an unbecoming nettle rash had
spread over her décolletage and her eyes were wild. Some blackmailing
femme fatale she'd turned out to be. She affected a quick repair job,
put the lipstick and mirror back in her tote bag and pulled the leather
drawstring together. She made her way into the hall to retrieve her
luggage, ring for a taxi and put Ruairi Urquhart and Kinloch Mara as far
behind her as possible.

If things hadn't looked so bleak, she might have been tempted to
laugh at the sight that greeted her. Mitzi was ostensibly polishing the

hall table with a handkerchief that looked as if it was made entirely from cobwebs. Cat was showing sudden interest in a small dog curled up near the fire and Isla was regarding her with something akin to empathy. It was clear from their sheepish expressions and the guilty way they'd sprung apart when Ruairi had flung open the library door they'd been blatantly eavesdropping.

'You've been Cluedo'd, Fliss.' Isla held out her hand, their earlier argument apparently forgotten. 'Welcome to the club.'

'Cluedo'd?' Fliss shook her hand.

'Yes. You know . . . like the board game? By the Laird. In the library. With a length of lead piping concealed in his sporran.'

'Make that a tongue lashing and you're not far off the mark,' Fliss responded with a weak grin. They nodded sympathetically and she realised she'd been admitted into the exclusive 'Cluedo' club - whether she wanted to be a member or not. She hitched her bag more securely onto her shoulder and looked around for her suitcases.

'Lost something, darling?' Mitzi asked.

'Yes. My suitcases. They were right there.' She pointed at the foot of the stairs.

'Suitcases, darling? Why they've been moved -'

'By Ruairi?' Fliss asked with such vehemence that they took a step back from her. Judging from their expressions they didn't seem to regard her outburst as anything out of the ordinary, clearly assuming that the interview with Ruairi had pushed her over the edge.

'Well . . . yes,' Mitzi picked her words carefully.

Fliss formed a letter 'T' with her hands. 'Okay, time out. Would one of you please tell me where my luggage is? No - wait, let me guess. In Murdo's Land Rover ready to be taken to the airport? But I won't be going anywhere with Murdo, or anyone else. I have unfinished business with *Himself*,' she spat out. 'After that I'll need my suitcases, a taxi . . .'

'The Dower House,' Mitzi managed to slip in when Fliss took a shaky breath.

'The Dour House?' Fliss muttered, completely misunderstanding. 'Everything's dour round here, from what I can make out - thanks to your stepson. Why should a house be any different?'

Mitzi took a tentative step forward and stroked Fliss's arm as though she was one of the Gordon Terriers who'd been up against a larger, fiercer dog in a fight and lost. When Fliss didn't push her away, she took Fliss's hands in her own.

'The Dower House, darling,' she repeated. 'Or to give it its other name: *The Wee Hoose*. Come on, I'll take you there,' she offered with the air of one who didn't understand why the suitcases were so important, but was willing to go along with it for the sake of peace and quiet. 'And, on the way you can explain why you want a taxi.'

'Du-uh!' Isla put in as she and Catriona waited in the hall for Ruairi's return - no doubt frantically thinking up excuses to explain what had gone down in Ladbroke Grove Police Station. 'She wants a taxi, Mumma, because she's been in this madhouse for less than twenty four hours and wants out. That goes for me, too,' she called after them as they left the house.

Linking her arm through Fliss's, Mitzi led her down through the gardens, past the gazebo and towards the loch. After the confrontation with Ruairi, Mitzi's inconsequential chatter, gentle hand stroking and the rhythmic crunch of the gravel under their feet was soothing. It had been a long time since anyone had made her feel like a much-loved daughter who needed to be indulged and made to feel better. Memories of her mother, who had died of cancer and of her father who had died soon after, crowded in on her. The gravel path to the Dower House shimmered through a haze of tears as she recalled the all-encompassing love she'd taken for granted and which had been snatched from her so cruelly . . .

Would she ever feel safe or cherished again?

Then - as she always did - she banished the memory of those dark days until she felt strong enough to deal with it. She dashed away the tears from her eyes with the back of her hand and took a gulp to steady herself. Mitzi obviously sensed her distress and gave her arm a little squeeze and then passed over the handkerchief she'd used to dust the hall table.

119

'I'll be alright. You'll see. Ruairi's bark is worse than his bite. Go on. Blow.' Fliss blew her nose and gave a watery smile as, arms linked, they crossed a springy lawn starred with daisies, rounded a large clump of rhododendrons and came upon the Dower House.

'Oh; but it's lovely,' Fliss exclaimed throatily, as she caught her first sight of the gabled Victorian house with its fretwork eaves, porticoed veranda and panelled front door. The paintwork was dusky blue, there were hanging baskets on either side of the wooden columns that supported the veranda and a climbing rose flanked the front door. Lloyd loom sofas and a large glass-topped table sat in the shade of the veranda, overlooking a lawn which levelled out to a shingle beach. This in turn gave way to sand the colour of gingerbread as it ran down to the loch.

The stonework was grey and the lighter stone of the mullioned windows gave the Dower House a look that said: *Come and stay a while*. Overwhelmed by the magical, healing quality of the place, Fliss let out a sigh and wished she *could* stay forever.

'It is lovely,' Mitzi agreed with a mournful little smile. 'And much better than *suttee*, I'll agree. But sad, all the same.' They stopped at the front door and she rooted in her quilted Chanel shoulder bag before pulling out a large key worthy of the Tower of London.

'*Suttee*?' Fliss tried to follow Mitzi's train of thought. 'You mean when Hindu widows committed suicide by throwing themselves on their husband's funeral pyre?'

'Oh, don't mind me, I'm just being melodramatic, darling,' Mitzi said, opening the well-oiled door and leading Fliss into a square hall flagged with Minton tiles. 'You see, traditionally, when the Laird dies, his widow moves out of Tigh na Locha - which is known as the *Big Hoose,* and comes to live here in the *Wee Hoose* until her own death. That means she isn't in the way of the new Laird's wife and the running of *his* household.'

They walked into the shuttered sitting room with its bright kelim rugs and comfortable, if slightly faded, soft furnishings. Mitzi opened the shutters and the light poured in from the loch, showing well-cared-for rosewood furniture and family photographs in silver frames.

'Why don't you live here?' Fliss couldn't resist prompting Mitzi to tell more of the story. 'It's beautiful.'

'You see - the children were very small when Hamish died.' She picked up a photograph of a handsome man in full Highland dress with a young boy on his knee. Recognising the fierce expression, Fliss guessed this was Ruairi and his father. 'Ruairi was only twenty four years old and studying for a Masters in Land Management and Conservation at St Andrew's when his father died. As the twenty-ninth Laird, he was needed to run the estate and sort out affairs - including a *massive* inheritance tax bill. He came home from university and never went back to complete his degree. He gave it all up for us, for Kinloch Mara and the people who depend upon him. And we've been a thorn in his side ever since.'

'I'm sure that's not true, Mitzi,' Fliss demurred, feeling it was beholden upon her to say something uplifting. Mind you, she'd only known Ruairi Urquhart for twenty four hours - if she didn't count the phone call weeks ago - and already he'd made her feel like an endangered species. About to be hunted to the point of extinction or driven off his land.

Anyway,' Mitzi continued, kissing then polishing the frame with the edge of her cashmere cardigan before replacing it on the side table. 'Ruairi wouldn't hear of us leaving Tigh na Locha because the girls were so young, so we've continued living there. However, I think the time has come for us to move out,' she added sadly, no doubt thinking of the uncomfortable atmosphere in the house this morning. 'Put a bit of space between ourselves and Ruairi. And the wife he will, one day, bring home.'

'Do you think so?'

'Yes - we should have moved out years ago and left the way clear for Ruairi to find a bride and bring her home. I think the idea of moving into the Big Hoose with us still in residence was one of the things that put Fiona off. Drove her away.'

Fiona - that name again.

Fliss experienced a pang, which she was quick to identify as a twinge of sympathy for the unknown woman who was to have been his bride. Urquhart might be a catch, the sex would probably be great, but she'd bet the last of her savings that he'd be the very devil to live with.

She restrained herself from asking if there were any future Lady Urquharts waiting in the wings. That was way too personal. Instead, she imagined girls of impeccable Scottish lineage circling above Ruairi's head in holding pattern . . . like planes at Heathrow, waiting for Mitzi and the girls to vacate the premises and be given permission to land. The thought made her smile as Mitzi led the way back into the hall, off which she saw a dining room, very modern kitchen and a study. Mitzi gestured for her to enter a second sitting room, opening plantation shutters to reveal comfortable chairs and sofas and - looking slightly out of place - a flat screen TV that was probably visible from space.

'Ta Da!' Mitzi announced, walking through a set of French doors and into a large conservatory. 'The therapy room.' She picked up a remote control and pressed it. There was an electrical whirring as a brass and rattan fan stirred the air and the blinds rolled back to reveal a view of the loch on one side and the steeply tiered gardens on the other side. A second set of double doors gave onto a patio with steamer chairs, low rattan tables and a furled, calico umbrella.

'My equipment!' Fliss rushed towards the boxes stacked along one wall next to white rattan cupboards waiting to be filled. In pride of place in the middle of the conservatory was the brand new therapy couch she'd ordered. 'How - I mean, where . . .'

Mitzi laughed. 'Has everything come from? Let's just say Angus pulled a few strings once you'd sent us your rough business plan and list of 'basics' to get the centre up and running. Mention his name in commercial circles and people tend to spring to attention.' She couldn't resist a proud waggle of her head. 'Also, to my shame, when I first came up with the idea of the Therapy Centre last year I got no further than having the conservatory converted and ordering lots of lovely things from catalogues. Sadly, ordering a beauty therapist proved to be rather more difficult. So everything's been here since last November. Waiting for you to arrive,' she added blithely, 'just as Mrs MacLeish foretold.'

'Foretold?'

'She is a taibhsear - and has second sight. I told you when you first arrived. She also said that you and . . .' Mitzi's cut glass accent slipped, took on a softer cadence and she gave Fliss a straight, searching look that made the fine hairs on the back of her neck rise of their own volition. But she didn't finish the sentence. 'You've been so excited you've probably forgotten. Well, it won't have to wait any more.' Mitzi was back in the here and now and spoke in more business-like tones as Fliss went over to examine the creams and products

She was dismayed to find that many of them were out of date and would have to be reordered. But that was do-able. Overcome with delight at finding that the therapy centre did exist and was in such a fantastic position, she forgot that she'd vowed to put as much distance between herself, Ruairi Urquhart and Kinloch Mara as possible - only fifteen minutes earlier.

'Angus has flown over to his own estate. He'll be back soon, but don't worry; he's written a cheque for everything you've spent so far - and a little extra to cover expenses.'

'Mitzi, I -' Fliss thought of all the things she'd said to Ruairi about the therapy centre. How she'd thought it only existed in Mitzi's fevered imagination. Now she felt humbled and very, very stupid.

'When Ruairi, Angus and I discussed it last night, before you met for the first time,' there was an imperceptible pause, indicating that she hadn't forgotten the embarrassing episode in the gardens. 'Ruairi was impressed by your business plan, in spite of himself,' she added encouragingly. It was as if she sensed there was bad feeling between them and wanted to make it all right - in true Mitzi fashion. 'Angus might be a 'gazillion-aire' as the girls put it, but he's no fool. He told Ruairi that if it all went pear-shaped it was my dream and his money, *"doon the stank"* as they say - not the estate's.'

'But, Mitzi, you don't understand - I've been fired by Ruairi. And I think at one point,' Fliss cast her mind back to the heated interview in the library, 'I might even have resigned . . .'

123

'Darling girl,' Mitzi took her by the hands and laughed delightedly. 'Ruairi will have forgotten all that by now. He'll be happily playing cops and robbers on the hills with Murdo and the other gillies trying to find a poacher. It's probably only Jaimsie's cousin, Jaimsie MacMor; he's been helping himself to salmon from our rivers for as long as anyone can remember. Ruairi won't be a problem, you'll see.'

Fliss gave her a far from convinced look. 'But you don't understand. I think I may have *upset* Ruairi in the library. Said things I didn't mean . . .'

'Darling girl, Ruairi makes everyone feel like their head is about to explode and goads them into saying rash and ill-considered things. He can't have thought seriously about sacking you. It was his idea to move you to the Dower House . . .'

And further away from him Fliss thought darkly.

'. . . so you can get the therapy centre up and running ASAP,' Mitzi warbled. She gave Fliss another warm hug, openly delighted she was showing signs of wavering and clearly convinced that her therapy centre would soon be open for business. Fliss managed a weak smile as she walked round the conservatory touching cardboard boxes, looking at the fluffy towelling robes in their polythene wrappings. She drew in deep breaths and kept her back towards Mitzi but when she turned round, she had a foolish grin on her face.

'OK. I'm game if you are.'

'Thank you Fliss, this means so much to me. And Angus, too. He's dying to meet you under . . . slightly different circumstances.' Fliss thought back to her skimpy costume and Angus red and perspiring in his toga. 'And to discuss the business plan in more detail and make any amendments and changes you both think necessary. Oh, and look at this.' She pulled open a plastic bag on a pile of clothing to reveal a black tunic and matching three-quarter-length trousers. The legend: Fliss *Bagshawe, Manageress* was emblazoned on the left-hand side. She raised an eyebrow and waited for Fliss's reaction.

'Mitzi. I - don't know what to say.'

'The wonders of the internet, hmm? Got all this equipment without setting foot outside Kinloch Mara. Cat showed me how to order everything online. I had a great time. Bet you thought that I wasn't serious about my project. Ruairi made that mistake too. And to be honest, I have had one or two failed enterprises.' She glossed swiftly over those. 'But with your expertise, Angus's war chest and my address book we're going to be a huge success.' She put the uniform down gave Fliss another *Allure*-scented hug.

'Thank you, for giving me this chance, Mitzi. I won't let you down.' It was as much as Fliss could manage without her voice cracking, overwhelmed by all that had been accomplished in such a short a time. 'But I think I need to have another word with Ruairi.'

Demonstrating her selective deafness Mitzi ignored the last comment. 'The monogrammed jacket was couriered here from Inverness. I wanted it to be here when you arrived. Try it on, darling; I want to see how you look in it.'

Fliss looked around to make sure they weren't overlooked and slipped off her t-shirt and shorts. Feeling a little self-conscious standing in just her underwear, she pulled on the wide- legged trousers and struggled into the tunic. It fastened Chinese style along her collarbone and had a mandarin collar.

'How do I look?' She caught sight of herself in a long mirror and pulled a wry face. If she was sent packing, at least she'd had her fifteen minutes of fame as the manageress of Kinloch Mara therapy centre. Maybe they'd even let her keep the uniform.

'Fabulous, darling. Very Zen. Oh, I can't wait for the appointment book to fill!' She handed Fliss a leather bound appointments diary with *Kinloch Mara Holistic Therapy Centre* tooled in gold letters on the front. 'All my friends will be green with envy.' She clapped her hands and then looked out through the conservatory window. 'Look, it's Ruairi - let's ask him what he thinks of your new uniform.'

'Mitzi. I'd rather you didn't.' Fliss was horrified at the thought of seeing him so soon after their confrontation in the library. Now she'd be forced to eat her words about putting as much distance between herself and Kinloch Mara as possible. 'Please . . .'

'Don't be silly darling, you look gorgeous.' Completely

misunderstanding the reason for her reluctance to show off the uniform, Mitzi unlocked the side doors of the conservatory and beckoned Ruairi and Murdo inside. 'Any luck with the poacher, darlings?' Ruairi made his way round to the side of the house, the wind ruffling his hair and teasing the eagle feather in his highland bonnet.

'Jaimsie MacMor, as usual,' he replied and entered the conservatory with Murdo.

Murdo gave a dry laugh. 'His excuse this time? That the salmon had apparently committed suicide by leaping out of the water and he'd just happened upon it while out walking his dog. Being a kind soul he thought he'd put it out of its misery. We confiscated the salmon and let him go with a ticking off. He's a good beater and the Twelfth will be on us sooner than we realise, and we'll have need of him.'

They all laughed except Ruairi. Either he took the poaching of his fish seriously or was displeased to see Fliss in her uniform, commanding the therapy centre as though her position was now de facto.

'The Twelfth?' Fliss asked, anxious to steer the subject away from herself.

'The Glorious Twelfth of August, Miss Bagshawe,' Ruairi replied, formal and distant. 'The start of the grouse season. Not that I'd expect you to know that.' His tone implied that there were many things on his estate a city dwelling Sassenach wouldn't understand.

'The estate's biggest money earner,' Murdo put in more kindly.

'Soon to be followed by the profits from the therapy centre,' Mitzi added, clearly missing the *'as if'* look Ruairi exchanged with Murdo. Feeling patronised Fliss sent him an inimical look, but he was too busy casting a dismissive eye over the packing cases and the empty shelves to catch it. Clearly, shooting grouse and catching poachers was important Man's work and all this - frippery - held little interest for him.

Murdo, evidently picking up the vibe, tried to break the tension by drawing Fliss back into the conversation. 'Although, this year we'll start on the thirteenth because the twelfth falls on a Sunday. No shooting on the Sabbath, Fliss. The Sabbath is strictly observed on Kinloch Mara.'

'Quite right, too,' Ruairi put in swiftly and gave Fliss and Mitzi a meaningful look.

This prompted Fliss to interject: 'I have no intention of working at weekends, in case you're worried,' then she bit her lip. Damn. Now she'd admitted that she was having second thoughts about leaving.

'Oh. I'm worried Miss Bagshawe, by the whole idea of you.'

'Well, you needn't be. The centre's going to be a great success,' Mitzi soothed, clearly misinterpreting his meaning. 'My girlfriends - and *their* girlfriends' girlfriends - will be very supportive and then word will spread. There's nowhere between here and Inverness where you can get a good massage, let alone a Brazilian.'

Ruairi flinched at the graphic picture *that* conjured up. He coughed to clear his throat and shared a slightly desperate look with Murdo. Mitzi seemed to take his silence for approval and pushed Fliss forward to stand in front of him.

'Doesn't she look cute in her uniform? Ruairi? Murdo?' she prompted as neither man answered, obviously unsure of the response expected from them.

'Aye, bonnie,' Murdo replied in a broad Highland accent and winked. Fliss wanted to crawl under the therapy couch and hide from their scrutiny.

'Ruairi?'

'Cute, indeed,' Ruairi agreed poker-faced. But she knew that he was running the word through his mind and coming up with alternative definitions of *cute*;

clever . . . sharp . . . clued - in . . . *devious*.

Ignoring his cold look, Fliss walked round to the other side of the couch, and staked her claim. Ruairi looked as if he'd like to say more and was undoubtedly holding back for when they were alone to voice his disquiet. He glanced down at her clothes, which lay in a pile at his feet - the discarded clothing had an erotic, abandoned look, as though she'd shrugged them off for a lover. Fliss remembered her nakedness in the garden, the uncooperative sari cloth and blushed. Bringing his head up, Ruairi sent her a scorching look which showed he hadn't forgotten the moment in the garden - or the scene in the library, either. With mock gallantry he bent down, retrieved Fliss's clothes, and folded them - lingering unnecessarily over the operation, in her opinion - and handed them back to her.

'Thank you,' she responded expressionless.

'There. Friends,' Mitzi beamed, totally misreading their body language. Ruairi looked as if he wanted to wipe his hands clean after touching Fliss's clothes and she felt like burning them because they'd been contaminated by his touch. Murdo, witnessing the exchange and clearly understanding what was going on, took Mitzi by the arm.

'Come on, Mitzi - we've got the clearing up to supervise after last night's party.' He steered her firmly through the open doors. 'Ruairi?' he questioned as he made no attempt to follow them.

'I'll be with you in a minute,' he replied, not taking his eyes off Fliss.

'See you later, then,' Mitzi called over her shoulder, evidently believing the therapy centre was a done deal and she had no further worries on that score. Fliss and Ruairi watched them leave and when they were sure they were alone, whipped round to face each other, dropping all pretence of civility.

'I asked you to wait for me in the library.'

'You *told* me to wait for you in the library; there's a difference.'

'In semantics?'

'In good manners.'

Seemingly, the walk on the hills had done nothing to improve his mood and her snarky remark brought angry colour to his cheeks. She placed her clothes on the therapy bed, put her hands on either side of the pile and faced him across it, unwilling to give an inch.

'I'm guessing that Miss Bagshawe no longer requires a taxi?'

'You guess correctly,' she countered. 'I've spoken to Mitzi and decided to stay on.'

'I'm glad that's settled, then.' The disdain in his voice made it clear he'd suspected that'd been her intention from the outset. That her posturing in the library was nothing more than a piece of theatre, designed to wring more money out of Mitzi and Angus, himself.

A BAFTA winning performance indeed.

She started to explain but realised it was pointless. No matter what she said or did, he'd put his own spin on her reasons for staying. Frantically, she hunted through her brain for a telling phrase that would draw this conversation to a close, put him in his place and leave her with the last word.

Murdo ended things by re-appearing at the conservatory door. 'Sorry to interrupt, Ruairi, Fliss - but Angus has arrived back from inspecting his estate and wonders if he could have a word with you about the wolves.'

Wolves! Oh, why was she *not* surprised to learn that he was an expert on that particular species?

Ruairi gave her a hard look as if waiting for her to make some quip. 'Oh, don't stay on my account,' Fliss said, gathering up her clothes. 'I've got a hundred and one jobs to attend to in order to get the therapy centre ready. And we wouldn't want to keep the wolves waiting, now would be?'

'I'm leaving Miss Bagshawe, but rest assured, I'll be back.'

'I'll look forward to it,' she said with her sweetest smile. But when he and Murdo left, she let out a shaky breath.

Last night, she'd vowed that if he wanted a fight over the therapy centre she'd give him one - and, fundamentally, nothing had changed. There could only be one winner in this contest and she'd do her damnedest to make sure it wasn't Ruairi Urquhart!

Chapter Eighteen

Two days later, Fliss heard footsteps in the hall of the Wee Hoose and guessed it was Murdo doing the daily rounds and checking if she was okay. She reached over to switch the kettle on, glad of the company. She hadn't seen Cat and Isla since the 'cluedo' remark in the hall, and apart from scheduling a meeting with her for tomorrow, Mitzi and Angus had pretty much left her alone.

As for Himself, he'd stayed away, too - something she found more ominous than reassuring. She suspected that Mitzi and Angus had told him to back off and give her some space and it pleased her to think someone was fighting her corner. But, if his parting shot was anything to go by, she suspected it was only a matter of time before he paid another visit.

'I'm in the kitchen, Murdo,' she called. 'Kettle's on. Tea or coffee?'

'It's Ruairi - and I take my coffee dark and strong.'

Heart thumping, she left the sink and walked into the hall where she found him unfastening his muddy boots. In spite of the antagonism between them she checked out the way his t-shirt rode up and exposed his tanned waist and lower back, the long line of his legs in combat trousers and the firm buttocks which the camouflage material could not disguise. She realised that she was unconsciously weighing up his potential as a lover and the father of fine, strong children and pulled herself up sharply. That was a bridge too far! She'd obviously been deprived of human companionship for too long if these dangerous thoughts were percolating through her brain. Dry mouthed, she cleared her throat as he turned round to face her.

'I've been expecting you,' she stated, more fiercely than she'd intended.

'Is that your oblique way of telling me that I'm not welcome?'

'No, it's not.' She wondered how much of what she'd been thinking showed on her face. 'But I'd like my contract returned. You had no right to lock it in your drawer for -'

'Safekeeping? Insurance? I think I have every right. I get the feeling that there's more to you than first impressions would suggest. I wouldn't want you to leave Kinloch Mara just as we're getting to know each other and reaching a consensus on where we stand on the therapy centre.'

'Leaving? Who says I'm leaving?' She ignored the latter part of his sentence. She didn't want to get to know him any better. And as for him learning more about her, that information was strictly on a need to know basis.

'Two days ago, you were desperate to get your hands on my cheque and get the hell out of here. In fact - correct me if I'm wrong - I think you resigned at one point? Tell me,' he prompted, 'what had made you change your mind.'

'I -' Fliss bit her lip. She could hardly say I only wanted the cheque so I could rip it up, throw it back in your face and make you eat your words. He'd never believe her.

'Enlighten me,' he perched on the edge of the hall table, arms folded, and waiting for her answer. It was the same pose he'd struck in the library, and judging by the cynical twist to his lips, he was expecting more lies from her. 'I'm listening.'

'I hadn't seen the therapy centre until Mitzi brought me down here. To be honest, I was beginning to think it didn't exist and Cat and Isla had brought me up here on false pretences - as one of their little *jokes*.' The words *honest* and *false* hovered between them and Ruairi's expression left her in no doubt as to which adjective he thought best fitted her.

'Does Angus strike you as the kind of man who'd have a contract drawn up if he wasn't serious?'

'On the face of it - no.' The silence between them lengthened. Then he smiled - a charming smile that showed off his perfect white teeth, and made him appear younger and less formidable. And dangerously more attractive. But the smile didn't quite reach his eyes and he changed the subject - making her doubly suspicious of his motives in turning up unannounced.

'I'm anxious to get to know the newest employee on my estate, Miss Bagshawe, so tell me a little more about yourself. For example, you must have been pretty desperate to leave London and travel all the way up to Wester Ross for a job.' He made it sound as if the Vice Squad - not to mention the Serious Fraud Squad - were hot on her heels and she'd come to Wester Ross to lay low until the heat died down. He paused, evidently waiting for her to contradict him.

'I needed a job. Simple.'

'Something tells me that there is nothing simple about you - or your intentions, Miss Bagshawe. And there's the rub - Mitzi has no references for you, other than Cat and Isla's enthusiastic recommendation. I believe they hired you and other staff from the salon where you worked in order to raise money for Comic Relief in March?' He made the innocent fundraiser sound like a cross between Sodom and Gomorra with dancing boys and animal sacrifice thrown in, and intimated that *Pimlico Pamperers* doubled as a lap-dancing club after hours. 'What I want to know, before I agree to let you stay in my house is - who exactly *are* you, Miss Bagshawe?'

His blue eyes were openly hostile and suspicious and his smile had vanished.

'Rest assured the family silver's safe, if that's what's bothering you!' she snapped.

'I think that was established when you emptied your holdall.' Fliss cringed as she recalled how the tampons had scattered in all directions before rolling towards him, tapping against his boots.

'I've already told you - I'm a fully trained therapist. I was working at a salon in Pimlico, when I decided to go freelance.' She gave the heavily edited version of her reasons for travelling north. Not exactly a lie - but not the whole truth, either. The fact she'd been sacked and had grabbed this opportunity to escape the dole queue was strictly on a need-to-know basis. And, as far as she was concerned, he didn't need to know. 'I learned through Cat and Isla that Mitzi was looking for a therapist, and I thought - why not?'

'Why not, indeed?'

'I'm good at my job. As you will find out if you give me half a chance.'

'I'll do better than that. I'll give you a long rope to play with and watch you tie yourself in knots.' Fliss let out an indignant breath, but he continued. 'I have a feeling about you . . .'

'And I have one about you! You like everything your own way, don't you? You aren't used to being . . .' she searched for the right word, 'countermanded. The bottom line - *Sir* Ruairi - is that I have a contract that runs until the end of October. In that time I'll turn this centre round, make it a success.'

'Really?'

'. . . and make you eat your words,' she ignored his interruption. 'And while we're having this frank and open discussion I'd like to make a few things clear to *you*. One, I hope you accept that the *episode* in the garden was completely unrehearsed and genuine. I never want it referred to again. Understand?'

'Go on.' She ignored the quelling look that said she was in no position to dictate terms.

'Two. I am *passionate* about the therapy centre and committed to making it a success.'

'That's a given. Three?' His earlier appraisal was replaced by a cooler, more speculative look, as if he was trying to work out the reason behind her volte face.

'My *only* interest is the therapy centre . . . and I want to be left to get on with the job of running it.' She hoped that her cutting look made it clear that she had no designs, romantic or otherwise, on *him* - or any other man on the estate. He nodded, and although he listened politely, she sensed that he was waiting for his chance to state his rules of engagement.

'I'm sensing an addendum here. Please, continue.' Fliss could feel the metaphorical rope he'd mentioned coiling round her like the serpent in the garden. Much as his hand had curled round her ankle under the rose arbour. She shook her head and dismissed the beguiling image.

'I want everything to be on a business footing from day one. Just so's there's no confusion between us.' She sent him another forthright look. He might be used to women falling in a dead faint every time he flashed those sexy blue eyes, but *she* was immune to his charms. She'd made a fool of herself twice - but she'd make damned sure it wouldn't happen a third time.

'Message received. Loud and clear,' he tipped her an ironic salute. 'And, finally . . .'

'More?' he feigned surprise.

'I want to be answerable to Mitzi and Angus, exclusively. I don't want you muscling in every five minutes and questioning my every move.' There. She'd laid out her manifesto and now she steeled herself for his reaction.

'Only four demands? I'm lucky to have escaped so lightly.' She winced as his expression morphed from speculation to barely suppressed hostility. She needed to get away from him, so she picked up a box of supplies to carry into the conservatory - but he barred her way.

'Excuse me,' she breathed heavily, keeping her cool in the face of such provocation.

'One,' he moved aside and then followed her into the therapy centre. 'Rest assured that last night will not be referred to again. Not by me at any rate - although, I can't vouch for others. You must realise that everything that happens in Kinloch Mara is of interest to the people who live and work here. Especially if it involves the Laird, his family and those in his employ.'

She was just about to point out that she wasn't one of his employees but changed her mind as her heart sank. Used to the anonymity of living in London, she'd failed to appreciate that she was now part of a living, breathing Scottish soap opera.

'Quite,' Ruairi replied with discernible satisfaction as he caught her woebegone expression. 'But cheer up. Think of all the free publicity this gossip will generate. They'll be queuing round the loch just to check you out. Shall I go on?'

'Why not?' She shrugged unconcernedly, but used the excuse of putting the box on the floor to conceal her expression. Damn the man - was he a mind reader or something?

'Two. I fully appreciate that you are passionate about the therapy centre. But, like my sisters, you probably have bursts of enthusiasm about most things and don't see any of them through.'

'For starters,' she interrupted, cut to the quick by his presumption and regaining her spirit. 'I'm *nothing* like Isla - or Cat. I've had to make my own way in the world since I left school. Something you might not understand.' She shot him a fierce look, implying that he was a grown up version of the posh boys who hung round the bars in Notting Hill and Holland Park. 'I'm a fully qualified holistic therapist; my specialism is Alexander Technique and Reike. I was London area finalist and Salon Based Beauty Therapist of the Year. I've got certificates, press cuttings and a rose bowl to prove it.'

'I don't doubt your capabilities for a second.' *Your capability to wheedle your way into our confidence and relieve us of the family jewels,* his look inferred. 'And, you do look the part, I'll give you that.' It almost sounded like a compliment, but clearly wasn't meant as one. 'Which brings me neatly to point two (b).'

'To be or not to be?' Fliss gave a brittle laugh. What kind of man, she seethed, thought in subparagraphs? She suspected that, at some level, he was actually enjoying this cross-examination. Seething, she watched as he walked round the conservatory prodding boxes with his foot, picking things off the shelves and replacing them. Then he hoisted himself onto the therapy couch, stretched out his long legs and crossed his feet at the ankles – like the effigy of a crusader in a country church.

'If you don't mind, I have lots to do this morning.' She walked over to the conservatory doors and pushed them open, but he linked his hands behind his head and ignored her invitation to leave.

'Why is there a hole in one end of the couch?' His question came from left of field and caught her by surprise.

'Is that point Three? Or are you asking a supplementary?' She glared

135

at him, stretched out on *her* brand new therapy couch so full of himself. Her blood quickly reached simmering point and she was beset by the urge to push him off the couch and onto the floor. He might consider himself laird of all he surveyed, but he'd *never* be master of her. 'Don't you have a poacher to catch, grouse to count - or whatever it is that lairds do? If you want to continue this conversation, book a consultation with me.'

She dropped the heavy appointment book on his lap and allowed herself a satisfied smile as he gave out a little 'oof' in protest. 'That's the first time I've seen an appointment book used as a lethal weapon,' he commented dryly as he flicked through the empty pages. Then he looked up at her and for an unsettling moment she thought she saw amusement in his eyes and him struggle to hide a smile.

Oh no - that wouldn't do - that wouldn't do at all.

She didn't want to think there might be a nice side to him. It suited her to believe him one hundred and ten per cent bastard - arrogant and overbearing. Only by reminding herself how impossible he was and his low opinion of her, would she be able to maintain her defences against him. Banish for all time the unguarded moment when he'd kissed her like he'd meant it and her response. And how one glance at his fit arse in the hall had sent her body clock on an alarming countdown.

'For the record, I don't answer supplementary questions,' she said snarkily to cover her wild thoughts.

'Oh, I'm sure you only divulge what you want people to know about you, Miss Bagshawe.' His dart struck home and she was back to hating him - *that* she could deal with. 'But please - enlighten me, anyway.' He drew the conversation back to the therapy couch but she knew he was capable of double-speak and knew more about her than he was willing to admit.

'It's where you'd put your face - if I was giving you a back massage. Otherwise you'd *suffocate*. The vehemence with which she expressed the word suggested that suffocation was too good for him.

He gave a sudden, unexpected bark of laughter.

'You must school your features, Miss Bagshawe. Your face betrays you.' Again, she caught a flash of humour in his eyes as he pushed

himself off the couch. 'I hope you're more circumspect with your clients
... Point three.'

'You really are pushing it, your Lairdship.' She knew of course, there
was no such title in Debrette's Peerage but it pleased her to have
something to goad *him* with; a counterpoint to his mocking *Miss
Bagshawe.*

'I won't come calling unless invited. However, you're on my land, in
my house. If I don't like what I see, I'll throw you into the back of the
Land Rover and take you back to Inverness, myself. Handcuffed and
protesting all the way, if necessary.'

Handcuffs? Ropes? She was about to make a reference to kidnap and
bondage when she stalled, overwhelmed by the thought of being tied
up by him, held hostage - and at his mercy. She stole a quick look at him
to see if he'd caught the moment and the tell-tale heat flaming her
cheeks. His eyes had darkened to deep blue and his pupils were dilated.
On any other man she might have considered it a look of sexual arousal
- but she knew he considered her as alluring as a rattlesnake, and
dismissed the thought. He was probably just thinking up another
sarcastic phrase to lob over the net at her.

'Thanks for the warning. Same goes for me. Only, I won't give notice
- I'll just up and go. My first task *when* you leave,' she nodded towards
the conservatory door, 'will be to memorise the number of the local cab
firm. The second will be to find out exactly where I am: post code, GPS,
ley lines, drovers' track, ordinance survey coordinates - whatever it
takes to find my way back to civilisation. Should the need arise.'

'I see.'

She could tell he didn't like her insinuating that his highland kingdom
lay somewhere beyond the pale and close to the end of the earth. She
remembered what Cat had told her about Fiona - the runaway bride.
How she'd bolted when his back was turned, and how it was Kinloch
Mara and its remoteness that had driven her away. And possibly the
remoteness of its laird, she speculated?

'And another thing - would you please stop calling me Miss

Bagshawe. My name is Felicity. Felicity Amelia if you want to be precise. But I answer to *Fliss*.'

'Felicity Amelia - how very Austenesque. You can call me Ruairi - or the Laird. You may also refer to me as *Himself* - but never to my face.'

'Is that like a respect thing?' she gave him a *get-over-yourself* look.

'It is.'

'And what about Big Bad Wolf?'

'Big Bad Wolf?'

'Cat and Isla's nickname for you. As in, who's afraid of . . . ?'

'. . . the Big Bad Wolf. Oh, yes - I get it.' He started to laugh, apparently amused rather than angered by the reference. 'It's a game we used to play when they were children. Like - what's the time Mr Wolf? I used to chase them round the garden and into the tree house and they'd scream for . . .' Then he clammed up, making it clear that he considered revealing more about his family than was strictly necessary a bad move.

'I see.' Unaccountably, it stung that he didn't trust her.

'Knowing that; how do you feel about me, now?' he asked, with one of his sudden mood changes as he levered himself off the therapy couch.

'In what way?' She frowned, had he seen the flush of colour that had washed over her earlier?

'Are *you* afraid of the Big Bad Wolf, Ms Bag - Fliss?' He stood inches away from her, waiting for her answer.

She could smell the outdoors on his clothes and in his hair, count every freckle on his skin; feel his breath on her cheek. His use of her Christian name sent a frisson sliding along her nerve endings, leaving her skittish and unsettled. It was time to re-draw the battle lines.

'Should I be?' she asked, adopting the pose of a hard-edged *nothing can faze me,* city girl.

'Oh, I think so. Don't you?'

He handed her the appointment book, sauntered back into the hall, collected his boots and was out of the house before she had time to frame her answer.

Chapter Nineteen

E arly the next morning Fliss was standing by the front door of the Wee Hoose waiting for Murdo. Much as she loved living in the Dower House and getting the therapy centre ready, she was beginning to feel a little stir crazy. Since arriving in Kinloch Mara, she hadn't been off the estate other than to walk along the loch shore or up to Tigh na Locha to collect deliveries for the therapy centre. She'd begun to treasure her nightly phone conversation with Becky that kept her abreast with what was happening at *Pimlico Pamperers* and with their friends.

She'd read somewhere that the houses in Port Urquhart were painted different pastel colours like those in Tobermory and Portree. She was looking forward to seeing them and indulging in some much needed retail therapy. Although Isla had declared that Port Urquhart was the world's repository for American tan tights and crocheted crinoline-lady toilet roll covers.

She knew she'd better make the most of the trip because she had a business meeting scheduled with Angus, Mitzi and Ruairi later that afternoon. However, as the Land Rover drew up and parked on the beach, she was surprised to see Angus Gordon climb out of the vehicle instead of Murdo. He walked up the short incline from the shore to meet her and waved his hand.

'Don't bother coming up, Angus. I'll come down.' She locked the door behind her and put the key in her tote bag.

Angus looked like he'd been kitted out by the costume department of a Sunday night period drama. Notes: *Angus Gordon, Billionaire Texan oilman, searching for his Scottish roots; desperate to be accepted by laird and family.* Puce-faced and sweating in shooting breeks, belted tweed jacket with suede inserts on the gun shoulder, checked shirt and brogues, he looked miles away from the air-conditioned comfort of his Texan homestead.

'Good morning, Angus, you look very -' she struggled for the right word.

'Hot?' He climbed into the driver's seat, switched on the engine and fired up the air conditioning. 'I am. But I feel I've gotta take my responsibilities seriously and dress the part.' His accent was a strange fusion of Texan drawl and 'Scoddish' brogue.

'I was expecting, Murdo,' she replied, wondering which *responsibilities* he was referring to.

'Ruairi had somethin' real important for Murdo to do, so I said I'd drive you into Port Urquhart.'

'Thank you, Angus. Although I do have a current driving licence and am *quite* capable of driving myself.' Reading between the lines, she guessed that Ruairi didn't think his right-hand man should act as her chauffeur.

'I'm sure you are, honey, and probably Ruairi'll be happy for you to do just that,' Angus soothed, obviously detecting the irritation in her voice. 'Once I've driven you there and pointed out the hazards.'

Fliss couldn't imagine what hazards he was referring to unless fire-breathing dragons still roamed Wester Ross. It was typical of Ruairi to make arbitrary decisions about how and when she could leave his land without consulting her. It took several calming breaths before she regained her equilibrium.

'Angus . . .' None of this was his fault and it was unfair to inflict her frustration on him. So she smiled at the large Texan fondly.

'Yes, honey?'

'I just wanted to say . . . thank you for giving me this chance. I won't let you - or Mitzi - down.'

'I know you won't, sugar.' He patted her hand as they passed over the wooden bridge and under the gatehouse that marked the eastern boundary of the Kinloch Mara estate. 'I can tell you're a hard workin' girl and my investment is in safe hands.'

'Thanks. Would you mind telling Ruairi that?'

'Sure will. Mind you,' he added as they reached the main road and the Land Rover began to pick up speed, 'this whole therapy centre thang ain't just about making money.'

'It isn't?' Fliss wondered if that was the difference between millionaires and other mortals. Money only became an issue when you didn't have enough of the stuff. 'What's the point of my being here and turning the centre around, then?'

'It's about Mitzi - making her happy. You're a bright kid; kinda thought you'd've had it figured out by now.'

'Happy?' Fliss tore her gaze away from the distractingly beautiful scenery of mountains and loch and concentrated on what Angus was saying.

'She's never quite come to terms with being a widow. Don't suit her. She's the kind of woman who needs a man to take care of her.' A man like him, Fliss guessed as he squared his shoulders. She sensed he was keen to apply for the vacancy and to kick Mitzi's other boyfriends into touch. 'She's been running away from the Highlands ever since I've known her; ashrams, shrinks, Prozac, every quack therapy you can name.' He drew breath as he slowed down to avoid a ewe and her lambs on the road. 'Reckless business ideas; spending time abroad because she can't live without sun in the winter.'

'I know that feeling,' Fliss put in, feeling that she ought to add something to the conversation.

'She's damned near driven Ruairi crazy - leaving him to deal with those girls when it's her responsibility as their mother. Taking their side against him often as not. Like they can't be whupped into shape because their daddy died when they were young.'

Fliss stared ahead at the road winding downhill and caught a glimpse of the sea shimmering in the distance. She heard the frustration in Angus's voice and guessed that it stemmed from trying to make Mitzi own up to her responsibilities and help her daughters to face up to theirs. Did Angus relish the task of taking *them* on, as well as their mother? She rather suspected they came as a package.

141

'So how does a Texan oil man end up in Wester Ross and Kinloch Mara in particular?' She moved the conversation along and tried to lighten the atmosphere in the Land Rover.

'I was acting as a consultant to the oil industry in Aberdeen.' He caught her look and grinned: 'Yeah. That's why the girls call me *Aberdeen Angus*. My ancestors came from hereabouts, but during the nineteenth century were evicted from their land during the *Fuadaich nan Gàidheal* - the Highland Clearances - to make way for the laird's sheep. Like many other Scots they emigrated to Canada, and then moved to the West when it began to open up, utilising their skills as cattle wranglers. Then, when oil was discovered in Texas they moved there.'

'And here you are...'

'Two hundred years later...'

'Back where it all started?'

'Kinda. I met Murdo when I was givin' a talk to students at Aberdeen University where he was studyin'. Stayed with him for a while - turns out he's some kinda cousin o' mine; a hundred of times removed. Through him I met Ruairi and the family and, well I kinda grew to like it here; the scenery, the hardworkin' people. So, I bought myself an estate no one thought profitable and turned it round with some help from Ruairi and Murdo. Hell, it even came with a lairdship - now, ain't that funny?'

'And?'

'Well,' he glanced at her as they drove along a deserted stretch of road. 'I plan to marry Mitzi, if she'll have me; take care of her and the girls - so they don't need to draw money from the estate. Help Ruairi, too, as an investment.'

'Investment?' Perhaps Angus could help her understand who Ruairi Urquhart *was*; and where he was coming from.

'Guess you know the estate's running on empty? Hamish's will settled such a generous trust fund on Mitzi and the girls that - after death duties were settled - Ruairi was left with little more than the title, the houses here and in Nottin' Hill, and some property in Port Urquhart. And of course the land, which makes up most of his inheritance.'

'So what's with the wolves?'

Angus laughed. 'That's Ruairi's scheme to turn part of the estate back to how it was hundreds of years ago and combine tourism with land conservation. It's called *Wilding*. He leaves Murdo to run the estate while he goes abroad to encourage ex-pat members of Clan Urquhart - which is scattered all over the globe - to support his scheme financially. Sometimes I go with him.'

So *that's* why he was in Hong Kong on the night of the party. And why, when Mitzi and the girls squander money which should by rights be ploughed back into the estate, he goes ballistic. Angus slipped down a gear as the Land Rover crawled along a steep downhill section of road that led to the sea. The stunning scenery became of secondary importance as Fliss concentrated on learning more about Ruairi. She sensed that Angus wanted her to understand what drove the Laird of Kinloch Mara and to prepare her for the business meeting scheduled for after lunch.

'You mentioned investing in the estate?' she prompted.

'Sure. I wanna give Ruairi an interest free loan so that he can make the improvements the estate's crying out for. Help him get his conservation scheme off the ground. Maybe try some of his radical ideas on my estate, too. But he's too damn stubborn and proud to accept my offer'

'Angus. You are a good man.' She turned sideways to smile at him and he blushed to the roots of his russet hair.

'Ah figured that once Mitzi and the girls come live with me, Ruairi'll be free to marry and bring his bride home. He sure as hell needs the love of a good woman to sort him out. Although, he don't seem too keen - after what . . . happened with Fiona, to take the plunge again. Though Mitzi's been trying to help out with her matchmaking skills.'

'Why do I find that thought alarming?' Fliss joked and they regarded each other with identical, comic faces.

Bring his bride home.

Fliss experienced a pang similar to the one when Mitzi had

mentioned the well-bred girls queuing up to be Lady Urquhart. Then she'd dismissed it as no more than a feeling of pity for the unfortunate woman who would live in the Big Hoose and lie beside Ruairi in the Laird's Bed. And that's how she preferred to go on thinking of it. No way was she interested in the Laird of Kinloch Mara, other than in a purely academic sense where she conceded that he was a handsome man. But *so* not what she needed in her life right now.

She listened with half an ear as Angus rattled on. 'No woman wants to start married life with three other women in the house, cloggin' up the pipeline.' She smiled at his oil industry metaphor.

'I suppose not.'

She was reminded of her current run of bad luck where men were concerned. She rarely got a second date because men preferred women who didn't bail on them at the last minute because they couldn't afford to turn down a lucrative after-hours appointment. And until now it hadn't bothered her that work and ambition had taken precedence over romance. The way things had turned out, it was probably just as well that she didn't have a boyfriend ringing her every night and begging her to come home.

She couldn't afford to get side-tracked by any man right now - Ruairi Urquhart least of all.

'We're here.' Angus swung the Land Rover into a parking space and walked round to help Fliss climb down. 'Port Urquhart.'

'Thanks, Angus.' Small wonder Ruairi had such an inflated idea of his own importance. How many men could actually say they had a town named after them?

'An hour be long enough for y'all? This ain't exactly Inverness.'

Fliss glanced round at the painted houses in pink, yellow, blue and creamy white arranged around the L-shaped harbour. They brought to mind the sugar almond houses in Elgin Crescent where this crazy adventure had begun. With one sweeping glance she took in the fishing boats, café and a couple of gift shops, an open-all-hours supermarket and a chemist. She'd make her purchases, buy a take-away coffee from the café and drink it sitting on the harbour wall looking out to sea and try to assimilate everything Angus had told her.

'I take it we're all done here?' Angus asked Fliss, Ruairi and Mitzi in a business-like manner a few hours later.

'I haven't quite finished with Ms- Fliss . . .' Ruairi began, gathering his papers together and getting to his feet.

'Now, Ruairi, darling, don't be so tiresome. Of course you've finished with Fliss,' Mitzi interjected, moving away from the Pembroke table where the meeting had been conducted. 'You don't need to concern yourself with her or the therapy centre any longer. We've explained all that.' She waited for Fliss to corroborate her statement.

'Absolutely. No, need to worry . . . R - Ruairi.' Fliss stumbled over his name - it felt too strange and intimate to use it, given their contentious relationship. She felt more comfortable using *Sir Ruairi* or *Himself*, it kept a degree of separation between them. But she supposed they had to move forward. She gathered her note book, pens and invoices together, hoping that no one had noticed that her face and the tips of her ears were scarlet after the warts and all meeting.

Angus and Mitzi had been perfectly calm and reasonable throughout but had made it plain to Ruairi that the centre was going ahead, with or without his approval. And if it turned out to be the flop he predicted, then Angus would have all the equipment disposed of and everything put back to rights - at his own expense.

'Fait accompli,' Ruairi conceded, far from happy. 'But there *is* one last thing. I asked Fliss a question a couple of days ago and I'd like an answer to it. I wonder if you would give us a few moments alone.'

'A *few* moments,' Mitzi agreed, giving him a stern look, 'no more. Fliss has been grilled enough for one day. We'll wait for you in the therapy centre.' She held her hand out to Angus, and Fliss realised that there was more to Mitzi than blonde highlights, expensive clothes and a reckless spending habit. She knew how to land herself a Texan Oil Baron and could handle the proud Laird of Kinloch Mara. Mitzi caught her look as she closed the door and winked, as if to say - softlee softlee catchee monkey.

'I'm not answering any more of your questions until you've returned my contract and ripped up your insulting cheque,' Fliss opened with when she was sure they were alone.

'They're staying in my drawer for safe keeping. Who knows when I might need them?'

'I could sue you for - oh, I don't know - wrongful something or other,' Fliss spat out.

'If you dared.'

'Oh I dare! And as to your question . . . Prepare yourself for a shock, your Lairdship - unlike everyone else within a hundred mile radius of Kinloch Mara - I'm not afraid of the Big Bad . . . of you.' Even as the thought took shape she knew that in *one* respect she was afraid of him. Or, at least of the sexual chemistry that crackled and fizzed between them, almost as strong as the antipathy that drove them to argue every time they met.

'You aren't?' He took a challenging step closer as if his physical presence could make her back down, change her mind.

She took two steps away from him. Their relationship was complicated enough without adding a sexual element. She returned his provocative look, measure for measure and wondered if he felt as conflicted as she did. Then she dismissed the idea as preposterous; judging from his demeanour, it would give him greater pleasure to throw her off his land than over his four-poster bed.

'In that case -'

However, Fliss never heard the end of his sentence because the door leading from the conservatory was flung open and Cat and Isla burst in. They were followed at a more sedate pace by Angus and Mitzi, who tapped her Philippe Patek watch with a manicured fingernail to remind Ruairi his time was up.

'Hey, lovin' the look, Fliss.' Cat pointed at the uniform Fliss had left hanging in the therapy centre. 'Oh - can I have one, too, Mumma? Angus?'

'Why, darling?' Mitzi gave her a puzzled look.

'Well, I was thinking - maybe I could help Fliss. You know - with unpacking and everything.'

Fliss schooled her features into a semblance of joy but her heart plummeted. The last thing she wanted was Cat opening boxes; unpacking products before she'd ticked them off against invoices and making a complete mess of her system. Then becoming bored and leaving her to tidy up. But everyone was looking at her expectantly, practically willing her to give a positive response.

'Wonderful,' she choked out, ignoring the imperceptible rise of Ruairi's eyebrow which said: *let's see you wriggle out of this one.*

'Well, we think you're wonderful, too. Don't we Ruairi? So clever and talented.' Mitzi extended her hands, drew Fliss and Cat into a warm embrace and sent Ruairi an admonishing look.

'Talented doesn't even *begin* to describe Fliss,' Ruairi said. But only she caught his barbed look which inferred this was a mere skirmish and the battle royal lay ahead. Then he smiled a white, disarming smile, the one Fliss was learning to be especially distrustful of. 'In fact, I hope to avail myself of her skills as a linguist, sometime soon.'

'You're good at languages, Fliss?' Mitzi asked. 'That's bound to come in handy when the therapy centre expands and we start having foreign visitors stopping in en route to their holiday destination in the highlands. Which languages are you fluent in?'

'Well, I'm not . . .'

'Klingon,' Ruairi said without missing a beat.

'Klingon?' Mitzi repeated.

'He means, Korean,' Fliss improvised, wishing he'd go away. But she guessed that by telling him that she wasn't easily intimidated, she'd unwittingly issued a challenge to the alpha male in him. And he couldn't just walk away from *that*.

Oh, why did she have to act so provocatively?

'I'm sure we'll get lots of K- Korean visitors,' Mitzi put in uncertainly.

'I'm looking forward to hearing Fliss speak the language of the Klingon people again, very soon.' It was with a sinking feeling that Fliss realised that he not only remembered the phone conversation in the

Elgin Crescent gardens but knew that she'd lied on that occasion, too. Or - at the very least, been economical with the truth.

But that was a discussion for another time his look told her.

'I might have known that Fliss'd be a cunning linguist. Probably knows all about Tantric sex, too.' Isla said snarkily. Cat was the first to get Isla's pun and let out a shocked laugh, glancing round at the adults to gauge their reaction.

Predictably, Ruairi wasn't amused by Isla's bad manners or her double entendre. 'Apologise to Fliss. Immediately, Isla.'

It was a couple of seconds before Fliss realised that he'd sprung to her defence - and her heart gave a glad little skip. Even though she knew his reaction stemmed more from his innate good manners and sense of what was appropriate, than from any desire to act as her champion.

'Sorr - eee, Fliss-sss,' Isla responded unconvincingly. From her gleeful expression, it was plain that she was exacting revenge for having been sworn at in the hall a couple of days previously. Then it was Ruairi's turn to receive some of her vitriol. 'How much longer are you going to be down here? If I am to be busted, I need to know the length of my sentence so I can start organising my diary for the next few weeks.'

'I'll be as long as it takes, Isla.'

'But, I need an answer,' Isla persisted, but Ruairi was not for moving.

'Answers, answers. What *is* it with questions and answers today? I've had enough of them. Now all of you - scoot.' Mitzi shooed them into the hall and the direction of the front door.

'But Mumma,' Isla protested. 'Aren't you coming back up to the Big Hoose with us?' It was clear that she wanted her mother to act as buffer between Ruairi and herself.

'Not at this very moment, darling. I've got the organisation for the Open Day to discuss with Fliss and Angus. We couldn't have picked a better time of year for it, what with the grouse season almost upon us and everyone returning for the Clan Gatherings and Highland Balls.'

Clan Gatherings? Highland Balls? Open Days?

Ruairi threw his hands up in a gesture of defeat as he followed his stepsisters out of the house.

'Oh, don't fret about Ruairi.' Mitzi read Fliss's mind like she was gifted with second sight. 'The Highland Balls are part of the Scottish Season and our obligation as landowners; noblesse oblige - and all that. We raise thousands of pounds for charity, darling. Thousands. Then of course there's the Urquhart Gathering in mid-September followed by our own Ball - which draws the season to a close. You're going to be really busy. We might need to get you some help. What do you think, Angus?'

'Whatever you and Fliss decide is fine by me,' he ducked under the low doorway and followed them through to the kitchen where Mitzi busied herself at the coffee machine.

'An Open Day is *such* a good idea. You know - demonstration facials, let people look round the centre, champagne, little nibbles and goody bags,' she was really getting into her stride. 'You leave that side of things to me - and Angus,' she extended her hand towards her tame Texan. He took it and kissed it reverentially and then crashed down on one of the bar stools. Next to his height and girth it looked like it had been designed for a Hobbit.

'But Mitzi, don't you think it's all a little . . . excessive? Not to mention expensive?'

Angus entered the discussion, 'Fliss, honey, don't you know it pays to advertise? Anyhoo, most of this can be written off as expenses. Don't you worry 'bout a thing. It's my money and how I spend it is my business. It's one way of payin' back Ruairi for his kindness and hospitality.'

Mitzi patted his arm absentmindedly, her absorbed expression showing that her mind was on higher things . . . the design of the goody bags, the colour of the balloons and what to serve with the drinks.

'I wonder,' she began, almost to herself. 'Would it be too OTT if I had a uniform, like Fliss's, only with "Mitzi Urquhart, Proprietress" embroidered on the tunic. What do you think, Angus?'

'Mitzi, I think you need a new dress; several new dresses. Then you can pick one for the Open Day. What say we fly down to London for a few days and let Fliss get on with unpackin' and sortin' out the centre? In the meantime you can ring round all your girlfriends and ask them to save the date.'

'Excellent!' She came up behind Angus, draped her arms over his shoulder and kissed the top of his russet head. 'Isn't he just a darling; he always comes up with a practical solution to our problems.'

He winked at Fliss who responded fervently: 'He certainly is.'

'Now, you and Fliss go inspect the therapy centre and I'll finish off the coffee. Ya'll think I can be trusted with that?'

'If you can put out wild fires in Texan oil fields, cope with my naughty daughters and put up with Ruairi's dark moods, darling, I think we can trust you to make the coffee. Come on Fliss; I want to show you some old photos of the house I've found and which I think would be just *perfect* for the flyers.'

Chapter Twenty

Fliss awoke with a start as the canon in front of the Big Hoose heralded in the new day. Getting out of bed, she opened the casement windows and stepped onto the Juliet balcony but was too late to catch Ruairi and Murdo beating the bounds. She could hear the strains of a Strathspey reel played by Jaimsie on the terrace, its tune so haunting that it was several seconds before she realised she was holding her breath.

Exhaling, she gave a wry smile.

Since arriving at Kinloch Mara a month ago she'd spent most of the time bracing herself for the next disaster, or counting to ten before responding to one of Ruairi Urquhart's more cutting remarks.

But on a morning like this - when the sun danced on the sea loch, she felt alive and full of optimism. Her upbeat mood was due, in part, to living and working in the Wee Hoose. Compared to her flat in Pimlico it was like living in a palace, but there was more to it than that. Its ancient stone walls radiated a sense of tranquillity and healing, and she wondered if it had its own *genius locus*. A gentle spirit of the place, which was responsible for restoring her sense of balance after each bruising encounter with Ruairi.

Just thinking about him was enough to prick her bubble of contentment and make her question if her mood was less to do with a benevolent highland spirit - or more with the fact that he'd stayed away from the Wee Hoose since their business meeting three weeks ago.

Which suited her just fine!

She had plenty to occupy her. Mitzi had chosen the first Saturday in August for the open day. By then, everyone would have returned to their estates in preparation for the grouse shooting. There would also

151

be Americans, Canadians and Australians staying in the grand houses nearby as paying guests; immersing themselves in the whole highland experience, complete with midges, antiquated plumbing and peaty brown bath water. They would be here until the end of September and if the therapy centre wanted to attract their business, it had to be ready - like, yesterday.

The rest of her clients would be drawn from Mitzi's friends, who were legion - if the crowd on the beach on Midsummer's Eve was anything to go by. Fliss wasn't in the least daunted by the task because she had faith in her own ability. The only fly in the ointment was over six foot tall, dark of hair and unpredictable of temper.

She sighed as the last strains of the reel drifted away and hurriedly got dressed. She had boxes to unpack this morning and would leave her shower until this evening when Murdo was due to call in.

Half an hour later, seated at the breakfast bar nursing a second cup of coffee and tapping a biro against her teeth, she contemplated the appointments diary. As she ran a finger down the impressive list of names, she experienced a jolt of excitement. The success of the therapy centre would mean a fistful of feathers in her cap and the satisfaction of having Ruairi retract every derogatory remark he'd levelled at her since her arrival on his estate.

The thought made her smile as she cleared away the breakfast things and put the milk back in the fridge. Mitzi had given her the choice of dining en famille each evening or fending for herself - and she'd opted for the latter. She didn't want to relive the controversial breakfast of her first morning over dinner every night, like a damaged DVD sticking on the same scene.

Being an only child, she hadn't appreciated that families got on better when they weren't playing to the gallery. Maybe when the therapy centre was up and running, she'd join the Urquharts for the occasional evening meal. But until then they were an acquired taste and best enjoyed sparingly she decided, snapping the appointment book shut and tucking the pen behind her ear.

She heard her name called out, and froze. Had simply thinking about Ruairi conjured up his presence? She'd been dreading meeting him again as they'd hardly parted on good terms. There was unfinished business between them and she suspected he was biding his time. Waiting for her to drop the pretence of hard working therapist determined to reverse the fortunes of Mitzi's centre, and revert to type. Then, as he saw it, he'd have his suspicions about her finally confirmed.

But it was only Cat, calling 'Fl - i -ss,' as she made her way through from the conservatory. She'd taken to calling in most mornings to help, and despite her initial reservations, Fliss'd found her engaging company and a cheerful worker. With Mitzi and Angus away, the only other people she saw on a regular basis were Murdo and the wee girl who came to clean the house.

'Hi,' she called back, 'any deliveries for me this morning?'

'Yes. Lots. Murdo's bringing them down as soon as Ruairi can spare him.'

'Good.'

'I can't wait to see what we're unwrapping today. It's, like, so cool?' her inflection rose at the end of her sentence. 'Just like Christmas.'

'I'm expecting the machine for removing hard skin from feet and elbows to arrive today,' Fliss informed her.

'Ugh. Gross. I don't know how you do that. Touching people's feet. Let alone give them Brazilians . . .'

'I'd be a pretty poor sort of beauty therapist if I didn't want to touch my clients. Although,' she continued, full of mischief, 'once, when I clipped a client's toenail it went sailing through the air landed in my cleavage.'

'Double gross,' was Cat's shuddering response. 'So, what's first?'

'I'm waiting for the posters, flyers, and tariffs to come back from the printers. Hopefully, Murdo's nephew - Lachlan, is it? - can start hand-delivering them. Mitzi's already given her girlfriends the heads-up and the appointment diary is filling. These flyers are for the locals who'll be our bread and butter trade once the initial excitement of the Open Day dies down and the summer visitors leave.'

She didn't have time to ponder over what would happen to her when her contract expired at the end of October. Would Mitzi keep her on? Or would she be heading south with the geese at the end of autumn?

Cat took on a haughty expression. 'They'll come all right. They'll be queuing round the loch to book an appointment. For the price of a beauty treatment they get the chance to come onto the Kinloch Mara estate and gawp at us up at the Big Hoose.'

'At Ruairi's insistence we've roped off a designated area at the side of the Wee Hoose where clients can park and make their way to the centre without disturbing anyone. Clients will arrive in ones and twos for their appointments. It's hardly likely we'll be attracting coach parties,' she added sharply, being rather bored with this particular argument.

Didn't they want Mitzi's business to succeed? Were the Urquharts too grand to sully their hands with anything as vulgar as *trade*? Cat looked suitably chastened for a few seconds then bounced right back.

'The flyers will be fabby, you'll see,' she said in a clear attempt to placate. Fliss didn't comment, it was a sore point that Mitzi had asked Isla to design the artwork for the flyers, posters, letter headings etc. And had dispatched them to the printers without seeking her approval. That task would have been a delight for her, given the career in fashion and design she would have chosen if her life had panned out differently.

'I hope so,' she said, tight-lipped. Since the *cunning linguist* jibe, she'd avoided Isla and it galled her to think that she'd probably executed the commission with ill grace - and made a complete hash of it.

Cat was quick to pick up the vibe and to reassure her.

'Honestly Fliss - don't worry. Isla has a real talent for that sort of thing. She has Mumma's flair for design, too. If only Ruairi didn't insist on us going to Uni, life would be peachy. I mean, I'm not in the least bit academic . . . I've been sent to so many crammers to prepare me for the International Baccalaureate that I've lost count. I keep trying to tell him it's a waste of money, but he won't listen,' she prattled on as they crossed the hall and went through the small sitting room to the conservatory.

The therapy centre was beginning to resemble the treatment room Fliss had first envisaged. Beauty and holistic products were arranged on white rattan units with towels, robes and disposable slippers stacked neatly beside them. The treatment couch had a large roll of disposable paper positioned at one end - a length of which was stretched over the bed and covered by a cream cashmere blanket. At its foot, Fliss had laid out a towel, disposable slippers and a waffle bathrobe ready for her first client.

Waxing and exfoliating equipment was set out on a glass and chrome workstation that wouldn't have looked out of place in an operating theatre. Cosmetics, pots of nail varnish and beauty products for clients to purchase were enticingly displayed on freestanding shelves which backed on to the house. The air was redolent with essential oils from an electric incense burner/humidifier that Mitzi had seen in a spa in London and ordered at great expense.

'The trouble is,' Cat continued, the calming properties of Rosa Damascene essential oils seemingly unable to take the edge off her anxiety, 'Ruairi had to leave university when Papa died. He feels he missed out and wants to make sure that the same thing doesn't happen to us. He's a real brainbox, and as far as he's concerned it's university for Isla and me - or gutting herring at the smoke houses in Port Urquhart.'

Now *that* was something Fliss'd pay good money to see!

'What do you want to do?' Fliss kept her thoughts private, feeling a little sorry for Cat. The contrast between the drunken teenager she'd put into the recovery position on the night of the party and the fresh-faced girl in front of her couldn't be more marked. Sure - some of the heavy eye makeup and ear piercings were back in place. But she wasn't a bad kid - simply almost ruined by a toxic combination of maternal deprivation and over indulgence.

'Don't laugh - but I'd like to be a veterinary nurse. I'd give *anything* to get hands-on experience at a practice in Port Urquhart.' Cat's sigh signified that her ambition was out of the question.

Fliss had seen her groom and work the dogs, help with the herds of pedigree highland cattle and sheep, drive out with Murdo to check the grouse nests and get the shooting butts ready for the Glorious Twelfth. She'd cheerfully mucked out the stables and cleaned the horses' livery, so Fliss guessed she must be serious about wanting to be a veterinary nurse.

'Why don't you simply tell Ruairi that you don't want to go back to boarding school and take A Levels? If you came up with a serious alternative - such as looking for work experience in Port Urquhart, maybe he'd listen to you . . . help you, even. He must be on first name terms with the local vets?'

'I guess . . . do you think he'd be able to find me a placement?'

'Something tells me that the name Urquhart might wedge open a few doors,' Fliss observed dryly. 'But, he's your brother. You know him better than I do!'

'That's the problem - I do.' They rolled their eyes in an unplanned synchronised movement and then collapsed in a fit of giggles.

'Okay, complete change of subject - do you know where I can find the key for the large cupboard under the stairs?

'Oh, *that* cupboard . . . I do, but it won't be much use to you. Cat fished a heavy key out of an Arts and Crafts vase on the window ledge in the sitting room and Fliss followed her back into the hall. Cat then opened the cupboard door and switched on the light.

A hoarse 'wow' was all Fliss could manage as she entered the cupboard, which - Tardis like, was much bigger on the inside. It was stacked to the roof with a miscellany of expensive goods. Cashmere twinsets, jars of organic honey, bottles of malt whisky, hand thrown pottery, boxes of homemade fudge and self-published poetry anthologies in Gaelic.

'What *is* this?' she asked. 'Is Mitzi storing up funeral goods to accompany her into the afterlife?'

'This is just *some* of the junk left over from Mumma's failed attempts at running a business. Not to mention the stuff she's bought off her girlfriends when *their* businesses went tits up.'

'There must be thousands of pounds of stuff here. Why doesn't Mitzi just get rid of it? Put it on eBay?' In a moment of epiphany, Fliss suddenly understood why Ruairi was reluctant to let Mitzi re-open the therapy centre. More money down the drain, money that could be better spent on the estate. 'How could Mitzi - where has the money come from to buy all this - ah, Angus?'

'Give the girl a lollipop.'

'Does Ruairi know about this cupboard?' Cat arched a *what do you think* eyebrow as she switched off the light, locked the door and handed the key over to Fliss. Leaving Fliss with the impression that she'd passed on the responsibility for the cupboard along with the key.

'Now you know why Mumma's so anxious for the therapy centre to work out. When she's impressed Ruairi - and made him eat his words, she'll tell him about her secret stash, the money she's lost and offload it - somehow.'

'No pressure then.' Fliss's heart bungeed all the way down to her Birkenstocks. 'Ruairi . . .'

'Yes?'

'**Ruairi!**' they exclaimed in unison as he came through the sitting room and joined them in the hall.

'We - I - didn't hear you come in.' Fliss reddened, knowing they must look the picture of guilt standing with their backs against the locked door, arms folded defensively across their chests. Surreptitiously, she slid the large key into the pocket of her shorts. Cat, seemingly drawing upon years of being caught out by her brother, threw a *sorry, I'm out of here* look over her shoulder. Then she left, slamming the front door behind her.

'I wasn't expecting you,' Fliss began, wishing she had an escape route, too. She'd wanted her next encounter with Himself to be on her terms, when she was feeling confident and assured - not caught out like a naughty schoolgirl with a secret.

'Evidently.' There was no mistaking his inference that she was up to no good and he'd caught her in the act.

Doing *what* exactly she wanted to ask?

157

Dipping her hand in the till; ordering duplicate equipment and sending half to a lock-up in Pimlico for her use after her contract expired? Seducing half the men under seventy on the Kinloch Mara estate starting with Jaimsie the piper and finishing up with Murdo Gordon?

She sucked in a lungful of air and held onto it, like a pearl fisher preparing for a dive. At this rate, she'd have to carry a supply of paper bags around with her in case she hyperventilated every time their paths crossed.

'Was there something you wanted? Something *specific?*' she asked, releasing the breath.

'I've stayed away - as per your instructions - but I'm curious to see how you're getting on.'

'Very well, thank you.'

'That was . . . short and sweet.'

'Well, I'm rather busy.'

'Show me.'

'That was . . . curt and succinct,' she volleyed back. She started to walk towards the therapy centre, paused and then turned to face him, hands on her hips. 'You know, this is all getting rather tiresome. Does it have to be different day, same argument every time we meet?'

'Of course not. *Please* show me,' he amended with a smile that would have been heart-meltingly attractive - *if* she'd been taken in by his Mr Nice Guy act.

'Follow me,' she said, moving away from the cupboard. He had an uncanny knack of knowing exactly what she was thinking and this secret was on a strictly need to know basis - for Mitzi *and* the therapy centre's sake.

Crossing the hall, she felt his eyes on her. Typical of him to come calling unannounced and catch her off guard she thought, glimpsing at her dirty shorts, shrunken t-shirt and skanky hair in the mirror above the pier table. The last thing she wanted was to give him an unrivalled view of her cellulite and less than Persil-white underwear so she gestured for him to precede her into the second sitting room. Then she paused at the door to the conservatory and gave him a sharp look which warned he was on *her* patch, at *her* invitation. And he'd better remember it.

She gestured for him to enter the therapy centre and he made his way from the display unit to therapy bed, touching things and nodding without commenting. She knew she'd done a good job but suspected that hell would freeze over and the camels perform Torville and Dean's Bolero before he'd admit it.

He examined the humidifier with some interest and she used the breathing space to study him unobserved. He wasn't wearing his usual kilt but a pair of faded black Levi 501's which clung to his thighs and fitted snugly over his sexy rump. He looked tanned and relaxed, the result she suspected of being at home and doing what he loved - looking after his estate.

His customary rugger jersey had been exchanged for a long-sleeved t-shirt that bore the legend: HARD ROCK CAFE - HO CHI MINH CITY. It was close fitting and outlined the planes of his chest; and for a moment she was back to the library when, frustrated by her obduracy, he'd pulled her up close. Fleetingly, her breasts ached as she remembered how it'd felt to be held captive against the hardness of his upper body. Then she dismissed the frisson as nothing more than a surge of pre-menstrual hormones and reminded herself that he was a shark. An attractive one, admittedly - but a shark none the less.

'Well. Go on,' she said, giving his buff body one last sweeping look before adopting her default position; brain engaged, hormones disengaged. 'I'm bracing myself.' For dramatic effect, she held on to the therapy bed like she was on the rolling deck of a ship - preparing herself for his next sarcastic comment.

'It certainly looks the part,' he said with slow deliberation, followed by one of his trademark pauses which implied that all of it - the therapy centre, the equipment and her cutesy uniform were nothing more than smoke and mirrors.

'It - looks - the - part,' she repeated slowly. 'I'll take that as a compliment, shall I?'

'It was meant as one,' he added smoothly and then changed the subject. 'Will it be ready in time for the Open Day?'

'It's ready now. Mitzi had converted the conservatory and ordered most of the equipment last summer when . . .' she paused - realised that she was on dodgy ground, and then rushed on. '. . . When she first came up with the idea of opening a therapy centre. All I had to do was make logistical sense of everything, re-order out of date stock and complete the process. We're good to go; all we need are paying customers. The appointment book is already three quarters full for the first month.'

'I won't ask to see the appointment book. Last time you nearly bludgeoned me to death with it.' He delivered the line straight-faced but his lips quirked in a half-smile. 'You've set it up much quicker than I expected.' This time she took it as a compliment.

'That's because I'm good at my job.'

'I'm sure you are.'

'Meaning?'

'Just that. You're good at what you do.'

'I'm good at what I do,' she parroted, sensing the sting in the tail. 'How can I convince you that I'm here for one reason and one reason only? This therapy centre represents a once in a lifetime chance for me - a chance to have my dream come true.'

'And what might that be?'

'To run my own business. To open my own salon.' For a second his suspicion wavered, then the scepticism was back in place and she was stung into replying more forcefully. 'But of course all that's secondary to my primary purpose in coming to Kinloch Mara.'

'Which is?'

'To seduce its Laird, scam Mitzi and Angus out of a shedload of money before making my way south leaving you with a mountain of unpaid bills, a ruined business and egg on your face.' He took a step forward but she turned her face away from him and held him back with a *speak to the hand* gesture. 'Don't bother to deny it; your expression says it all. And if you really must know - I'm getting rather fed up with this particular argument.'

'Look, I didn't mean . . .' he began, openly taken aback by the vehemence of her outburst.

'Oh, I think you did. And to be quite honest, I think your bating of me has gone far enough.'

She walked over to a rattan unit and made a great play of arranging products. Damn the man. In less than five minutes he'd made her hormones zing, her blood pressure surge to a dangerous level, destroyed her peace and most probably exorcised the friendly spirit she'd been sharing the house with these past few weeks.

She was dismayed to find tears of anger and frustration stinging her eyes. Don't you cry, don't you dare cry. Don't give him the satisfaction of knowing that you care about his opinion of you.

'Was there something else?' she asked in a husky voice.

'Actually, yes.' Now it was his turn to appear unsure of himself. 'I've come to ask you to dinner.'

'Dinner?' She swung round to face him, not caring if he saw the sheen of tears in her eyes. She hadn't seen that one coming. 'With you? You mean - like a *date*?

A date? How had that slipped out? A lengthy, embarrassed silence stretched out between them.

'God. No,' he responded at last, with just a little too much vehemence than was necessary, or flattering. 'Not a *date*. I meant - dinner up at the Big Hoose. Mitzi and Angus are arriving back tomorrow afternoon and the fatted calf - well, fore rib of beef to be more accurate - has been brought out of the freezer to mark the occasion.'

Now it was his turn to shift uneasily on the spot, tear *his* eyes away from *her* and focus on the view of the loch through the windows. A flush of colour swept across his cheeks but she couldn't decide whether it was an outward sign of his displeasure at being practically propositioned by her; or his discomfiture at everything the word *date* implied.

She cringed, willing Kinloch Mara in that instant to be transported to the edge of some tectonic plate where a fault line could open up and swallow her whole.

161

'I misheard. I thought you said . . . *great,*' she began, back-pedalling in an attempt to preserve her dignity.

'Yes . . . Crossed wires. I imagine that a date would be the last thing either of us wanted.' He waited for her to contradict him, his expression bland.

'My feelings exactly,' she was quick to assure him, desperate to move the conversation along and to escape his all-too-perceptive blue eyes.

'Good. Good.' He rubbed his finger along the side of his nose and pushed his fingers through his hair, betraying his uncertainty. He let out a deep breath, pushed his hands into the back pockets of his black jeans and focused his attention on the loch once more. Now that they had decided - by tacit agreement - not to be at each other's throat every time they met, it appeared that they lacked the necessary vocabulary to communicate with each other.

Unsure what to say, and not wanting to be the one who took the first step toward total rapprochement, Fliss muttered a noncommittal: 'Fine . . .'

'So, I'll send Murdo down then. About eight o'clock, tomorrow evening.'

'Murdo?'

'To escort you in to dinner.'

Ah, now she got it. He didn't want to walk through the garden with her in case there was a repeat of the rose bush and sari incident. 'I'm hardly going to get lost, am I?' she asked with her usual asperity and they were back to square one.

'It's traditional. The Laird escorts whichever lady is staying at the Dower House in to dinner. But I thought - in the circumstances - you'd find Murdo a more acceptable choice?' He looked genuinely puzzled, as if he couldn't understand why there was ice in her grey-green eyes.

'Dress code?' she snapped, moving the conversation along. She didn't want him thinking she was some chav who'd turn up for dinner wearing jeans and a sequined boob tube.

'Formal. Mitzi's got a new dress, apparently, and wants to show off.' His crooked, uncertain smile hit her somewhere in the region of the solar plexus and her heart snagged for a beat or two. 'You know Mitzi.'

Boy did she know Mitzi!

She tried to respond to his light-hearted banter but her facial muscles felt like they'd been botoxed. All she could think of was Mitzi's *cupboard of shame*, how she had the key to it - and his reaction when he found out about it. She wasn't sure how, but somehow it would all end up being her fault, just like everything else.

She didn't think he'd be smiling then.

More secrets and lies. More trouble stored up for the future. She walked over to the rear entrance to the conservatory and - getting the message loud and clear, he followed her. She felt like she should say something innocuous, so everything would be on a neutral footing when they next met.

'Eight o'clock then,' she said, expecting him to nod his head and leave. To her surprise, he stopped halfway through the door, gave her one of his burning looks, followed by a quirky smile.

'That's a date.'

Then he strode through the gardens like he was yomping across the moors on some extreme survival challenge. And she was left wondering if she'd imagined it, or if they'd just shared their first joke.

Chapter Twenty One

That evening Fliss watched as Murdo fired up a propane gas cylinder contained inside what looked like a World War Two bomb.

'Does that device work?' she called over from the veranda.

'It will certainly attract the midges,' he said as he checked that the burner was lit. 'This bad boy gives off a scent they can't resist.'

'Chanel No 5? Essence of haggis?'

'It works by releasing carbon dioxide and water vapour from combusted propane mixed with small amounts of octenol.' Then, realising he was being teased, he added: 'Now you mention it, a smidgen of haggis wouldn't go amiss. The main thing is to make the midges go towards the machine and away from the ladies in your therapy centre. There.' He stood back to admire his handiwork and cleaned his hands on a cloth.

'I've no idea what you just said - the science bit. But if it works then I'm all for it. Would you like that drink now?' Murdo joined her on the veranda, sitting on an ancient Lloyd Loom chair. Fliss pushed a glass of Merlot across the glass topped table to him. 'So, how come the midges don't bite you?'

'Well, hairy legs help for a start.' He stuck his legs out for inspection, raising his kilt above his knees and drawing his feet to one side like a shy Victorian maiden. Fliss giggled. 'That's better. I was beginning to wonder if Ruairi had robbed you of your sense of humour - not to mention your spirit.'

'I'm okay. I'm a brilliant therapist - if I say so myself, and want to be left to get on with what I do best and make the centre a success.'

'Isn't that what we all want?'

'I'd have thought so. But with Ruairi, I'm never sure.'

'Och, don't mind Ruairi . . .'

'But that's the thing, Murdo. I *do*. I want to prove him wrong about me.'

'Well, now you can. My machine will deter the midges and your expertise will attract the ladies.' He grinned, took another sip of Merlot and clinked glasses with her. 'To the Kinloch Mara Therapy Centre and the best therapist in the Western Isles.'

'If not the entire world. Slainte.'

'See. You've been here less than three weeks and already you're speaking Gaelic like a native. And, do you mind my asking, what did Ruairi mean about your being able to speak Klingon?'

'Just his idea of a joke. A very bad joke designed to remind me exactly who is boss around here. As if I could forget.' She smiled to take the sting out of her words, Murdo was trying to put her at her ease and make her feel at home. There was no need to snap his head off. There was only one head she wanted to see roll.

Murdo's profile was cast into relief by the citronella candle, lit to keep the midges at bay until the machine was fully functioning. With his fine features, strawberry blonde hair and sympathetic blue eyes he was a catch for any woman. She felt drawn to him, not only because of his physical attributes but also because of the many kindnesses he'd shown since he'd picked her up at Inverness airport.

It would be so very easy to . . .

But no, she wouldn't go down that road. She was in enough trouble as it was and knew - however much she might deny it - that Isla had prior claim to this proud Highlander. However, she sensed something between them tonight - a potential for friendship if nothing more, and didn't want to ruin it with flirtatious behaviour or a throwaway remark. They sat in companionable silence for several minutes watching the setting sun sending bolts of red and orange fire across the waters of the loch towards them.

'Kinloch Mara is the most beautiful place I've ever seen. If I was Ruairi I wouldn't be able to leave it, not even for a second.' She let the tension of the last few weeks slip from her shoulders as she sipped her wine.

'You could almost imagine yourself sailing towards *Tir na nOg*,' Murdo mused and then gave a self-deprecating laugh as though he was being too fanciful.

'Tir na *what*?'

'A mythical land in the west. A story for tomorrow night, perhaps?'

'There *is* one story I'd like to hear,' she began, sensing that the opportunity might not present itself again.

'Which story is that?'

'The one about Ruairi. The family. Mitzi. Angus,' she began, feeling her way forward. 'Where *you* fit in. You're all Scottish - no matter how the girls pretend they belong in Albert Square and not Elgin Crescent. Yet you all sound more English than I do.' They exchanged a humorous look and then Fliss sobered. 'I've been invited to dine with the family tomorrow night. I've been putting it off ever since I arrived here and I feel I can't hold out any long. Trouble is, I don't want to say anything out of turn.'

Murdo nodded in understanding. 'Where do you want me to start?'

'The bench in the Elgin Crescent Gardens?'

'Okay, the bench. Ruairi's father dedicated it in Mairi's memory the summer after she died. She'd travelled down to the Royal Marsden for chemo sessions and, sadly, the end came rather sooner than anticipated. She died in the house in Elgin Crescent but was brought home for burial in the family church overlooking the loch.'

Now, Ruairi's possessiveness over the house in Notting Hill made perfect sense. It had hardly been touched in over twenty years because it was his last link with his mother. Small wonder he didn't want Cat and Isla holding a party there, trashing the furniture and breaking things.

Fliss was drawn back to her own history and the council house she had to vacate when her parents died because it was needed for a family with children. She'd been offered a one bedroom flat on the other side of London, miles away from everything and everyone that she knew, and had turned it down. If it hadn't have been for Becky's parents taking her in, she didn't know what she would have done.

'Go on,' she urged.

'Ruairi was eight and had just started his first term at boarding school in Berkshire, and it was thought best for him to remain there. Hamish couldn't cope with his own bereavement, let alone Ruairi's. Ruairi was dreadfully homesick and so it was decided that I should attend the same prep school - with Hamish paying the fees, to provide companionship for Ruairi. Hence my 'English' accent,' he gave a self-deprecating laugh. 'During the long holidays Ruairi and I returned to Kinloch Mara and he stayed at our house.'

'*Your* house? Why?'

'My father was Hamish's factor and Hamish thought that my dad could prepare Ruairi for the day when he became Laird. When I, in turn, would become *his* factor. It helped of course that our house was full with children: my brothers, sisters and cousins, so Ruairi had a ready-made family and was never lonely.'

Fliss wondered where Mitzi fitted into the story. She liked her and didn't want to imagine her jumping straight into a dead woman's shoes, let alone her bed and marrying Hamish while he was still raw with grief. As if anticipating her question, Murdo carried on.

'Mitzi was an old friend of the family - in fact, I believe that all three of them were related through some distant cousin - as many highland families are. Just as Angus and me are cousins several times removed. Anyway, Mitzi and Mairi had been at school in Edinburgh together, but lost touch after their Highers - A levels,' he explained, seeing her puzzled expression.

'So they knew each other pretty well then?'

'Yes - including Ruairi, when he wasn't at boarding school or staying over at our house. You know how it is, children playing in the background while their parents' friends drift in and out of their lives during the summer. Tennis parties, highland gatherings, balls, shoots - that sort of thing.'

'I see.' Fliss thought of her own summer holidays which had consisted of two weeks in Hastings with her mum and dad and the

Castertons, their next-door neighbours and best friends.

She looked towards the beach and pictured the boys following Murdo's dad around and learning about land management from him. She remembered the photograph of Ruairi in the sitting room, eight years old and at his father's side; doubtless trying to make sense of his mother's death and his father's swift remarriage. Now she understood that his fierce expression hid grief and bewilderment. Her heart contracted unexpectedly and she cursed herself for a fool. Better she should save her sympathy for herself and not waste it on a man who'd shown her no quarter since she'd set foot on his land.

Small wonder then, that Murdo was more like a brother to Ruairi. But she wanted to know more, much more, so she continued her gentle probing. 'What had become of Mitzi in the intervening years?'

'She'd been in Val d'Isere running a training school for Chalet Girls. Until she . . .'

'Got bored with it? Let me guess, there was an entanglement with a minor German aristocrat, some Eurotrash royals and compromising photos in the Sunday red tops?' Fliss giggled again, relaxing in Murdo's easy company.

'You guess correctly.' He laughed and turned towards her. Their gazes locked over the citronella flame, and as the seconds stretched out, Fliss knew she had to break the intimate mood.

'So far, so predictable. Then what?' She pushed a bowl of olives across to Murdo.

'Brought home in disgrace. Confined to her father's estate to help with the picnics for the guns . . . enrolled in another 'safe' Sloaney Cookery/Secretarial course to keep her out of scandal's way. Until they found some man crazy enough to marry her.'

'Are we quite sure it's Mitzi we're talking about here?'

'I agree. For Mitzi . . . read Isla.'

He took on a sombre look, as if wondering if the same fate would befall her. Sensing that Murdo felt he was being disloyal to the Urquharts by revealing the skeletons lurking at the back of the family armoire - and suspecting that this opportunity might not present itself again, Fliss pressed him further.

'And did they?'

'Did they what?'

'Find some Deb's delight to marry Mitzi?'

'No. Just as she was going to start her course in Edinburgh - London was thought too distracting for her, Mairi had a late miscarriage. She got back in touch with Mitzi who came home to look after her. Soon after that, Mairi was diagnosed with cancer.' The facts were stated without embellishment. Perhaps he felt a little embarrassed at discussing such intimate matters with someone who was, after all, a comparative stranger.

'And Ruairi?'

It always came back to Ruairi - didn't it?

'Boarding school, summers here with my family, winters abroad with cousins in Canada. Or in Texas with Angus and me. When Hamish remarried, things changed. Not just for Ruairi, but for everyone who lived on the estate. Don't get me wrong, Mitzi's great and I love her. But she wanted things done differently.'

'What kind of things?'

Murdo's brow puckered as he remembered. 'The usual female things. Curtains changed, rooms painted, furniture removed. Oh and parties. Lots of parties . . . you know Mitzi. But no one minded all that, she made Hamish laugh again and was more like a big sister than a step-mother to Ruairi.'

'Then along comes two baby stepsisters; spoiled, adored?' Fliss could picture it now, the scowling adolescent, the new wife and the pretty little sisters, no doubt the apple of their father's eye. She had a sudden understanding of what Ruairi had faced, virtually alone.

'He felt pushed out, I guess - excluded,' Murdo became quieter as he relived those days.

Difficult days . . .

Fliss drew a parallel between what Ruairi had endured and what she had gone through when her own parents had died. It had been a defining moment in her life and made her the person she was today.

169

She'd been eighteen when these cataclysmic events had overtaken her. Ruairi had been eight. Now she better understood him. She had come to terms with her loss but a slick of ice remained around her heart, the last vestiges of bereavement. Perhaps Ruairi felt the same? Now, six years on, she wondered if she'd ever be able to remember happier times without being swamped by feelings of desolation. Feelings that she kept at bay by working hard and being positive in her outlook.

'Go on,' she prompted Murdo, but it became clear from his expression that she'd learn no more tonight. She'd save her questions about his difficult relationship with Isla - and Fiona the Bolting Bride for another time.

On cue, two Border Terriers rounded the corner of the house. They barked delightedly when they saw Murdo, their scratchy little paws scrabbling at his bare knees as they tried to jump up at him.

'Down dogs,' he commanded and they did as they were told, sitting obediently at his feet, tongues lolling out of their mouths as they caught their breaths. Their otter-like heads and dark eyes gave them a comical, dour expression at variance with their wagging tails and ecstatic whimpers as they waited for permission to roam free in the undergrowth.

'Meet Buffy and Angel,' Murdo introduced the dogs.

'Buffy and Angel?' Fliss shook paws with the two most unlikely vampire slayers in Wester Ross.

'Cat's choice I believe.' Murdo pulled a face and joined in with her amused laughter. Suddenly, the dogs lost interest, pricked up their ears and looked past them. 'Their pedigree names are . . .'

'*Coquetdale Cullen* and *Reedwater Rover of the Glen*, if you want the shortened version.' Isla joined them on the veranda. 'I bred them myself,' she added with just enough emphasis to let Fliss know that behind her bad girl façade there lurked a true countrywoman and the Laird's sister. 'You're wanted up at the Big Hoose,' she snapped at Murdo, clearly put out to find them enjoying themselves on what she evidently considered the firm's time.

'I've got things to finish here,' Murdo replied, nodding towards the anti-midge machine. 'Ruairi knows where I am. If he wants me, he can get me on the walkie-talkie. You needn't have come all the way down here just to tell me this, Isla.' His tone implied that he was impressed by her altruism, but his frowning look suggested the opposite.

Isla's all seeing, all knowing gaze swept over the veranda - taking in the candle, wine glasses and dish of olives on the table.

'*Quite* comfortable in the Dower House are we?' She gave Fliss the impression that she was still in a massive sulk with her, Murdo, Ruairi, - the whole world in fact.

'*Quite*; thank you.' Fliss folded her arms to make the point that Isla was trespassing on *her* patch. She was answerable to Angus and Mitzi - not to the Laird of Kinloch Mara and certainly not his uppity sister. Isla might be the daughter of the house but as far as Fliss was concerned, she could butt out. Clearly, Murdo was of the same mind because he made no effort to leave. Getting the message, Isla gave them one of her death stares, clicked her fingers and brought the dogs to heel.

Fliss got the impression she'd like to do the same to them! Murdo waited until Isla was out of sight before draining his glass and gathering his tools together. Although he kept his own council, Fliss felt downhearted for him because it was plain from the stoop of his shoulders that the bruising encounter with Isla had demoralised him. 'If there's anything else . . .'

'No. I'm fine. Thanks.'

'My pleasure. Now don't stay out too long in the dusk - the midge machine won't be fully effective for two days.' Swinging his tool kit over his shoulder he made for the path which led to the Factor's cottage further along the shore. He half-turned, 'Just one more thing.'

'Yes?'

'It was Ruairi's idea to have the midge machine installed down here. He paid for it; not Angus - I thought you should know that. You've got off on the wrong foot with each other; Ruairi's a great guy and a loyal friend. You'll see.'

If I'm here long enough, she thought.

Going into the Wee Hoose, she closed the door behind her. As she slid the bolts home, she wished that Murdo's magic machine had the power to keep the Urquharts at bay as well as the midges.

Then her life would be just peachy.

Chapter Twenty Two

A gust of wind stirred the voile curtains and sent the casement windows in Fliss's bedroom crashing back on their hinges. Getting up from the dressing table, she looked through the slanting rain at the bruise coloured clouds scudding across the loch. She closed the windows and shivered, it was like a scene from Independence Day. She'd been warned that the summer weather they'd enjoyed recently wouldn't last and it looked like the weather mongers were right.

Downstairs, the grandfather clock struck the quarter hour and reminded her that she was running late. She caught her frown in the dressing table mirror as she put the finishing touches to her make-up and gave a sigh of exasperation. She'd spent two sleepless nights denying how much it rankled that Ruairi had asked Murdo to escort her up to Tigh na Locha tonight for dinner instead of escorting her himself.

She'd gone over what he'd said countless times, trying to make sense of it: *I thought - in the circumstances - Murdo would be a better choice.* What circumstances was he referring to? Was asking Murdo to deputise for him his subtle way of underlining the differences in their situations without spelling it out? His way of sparing her feelings? He was the laird and she was the therapist; she got it, she really did - and fully understood that it wasn't appropriate for her to be escorted into dinner on *his* arm when she was on Angus's payroll.

But his actions - and this was her sticking point - not only highlighted their respective places in the Kinloch Mara hierarchy, but defined the boundaries of their relationship. It appeared that he still regarded her with suspicion and was hedging his bets until she dropped her guard and revealed her true colours.

173

She'd decided soon after meeting Ruairi Urquhart that she wouldn't let his opinion of her - good or bad - influence her in any way. So what had changed?

The grandfather clock struck the hour.

Pushing herself away from the dressing table, Fliss gave a huff of annoyance at the conflicting thoughts running through her mind. Spraying a fine mist of Clinique *Happy* into the air, she walked through it and let the droplets settle over her hair and underwear. Then she slipped into her only posh frock - a vintage wrap dress she'd found in Oxfam on Westbourne Grove Road, collected her clutch bag and went downstairs.

As arranged, Murdo was waiting for her in the hall and dressed for the worsening weather in a full-length waxed coat and an Akubra. He looked like a cross between a dandy highwayman and a hunky cowboy. She fixed a smile on her face - better not shoot the messenger.

'I'll just get a coat and umbrella and I'm good to go, Murdo.' She nodded towards the jumble of waterproof coats, wellingtons and umbrellas in the canopied porch. She negotiated the turn in the stairs where the tread narrowed, holding the hem of her maxi dress in one hand and her strappy sandals in the other.

'Not Murdo. Ruairi.' She stopped dead in her tracks and her heart stuttered at the sound of his voice.

'What is it? What's happened?' she asked, suddenly fearful. There must be an emergency or bad news, what other reason would he have for coming down here?

He removed his Akubra, shook the raindrops off it and then glanced up at her, rubbing the back of his hand over his eyes. And in that moment she saw beyond the man who troubled her waking hours and kept her from sleep - and realised what his life entailed, his obligations towards family and his estate. He looked so careworn, so bowed down by responsibility that, in spite of everything, her heart contracted and she sent a silent wave of sympathy towards him. And all the negative thoughts she'd harboured about him only minutes earlier, vanished.

'We've had to cancel dinner I'm afraid. The phone connection between here and Tigh na Locha is down at the moment - it often happens when it blows a gale. I wanted to warn you to batten down the hatches and stay indoors until the storm blows itself out. I'm on my way to join Murdo, apparently there's an emergency up on the main road.'

'Thanks for thinking of me,' she said and immediately wanted to kick herself. *Thanks for thinking of me?* What was she - twelve years old?

He was simply concerned over her welfare, as he would be for any tenant on his estate. She shouldn't read any more into his words or his actions. Embarrassed, she concentrated on watching the rain water run off his wellingtons and soak into the turkey rug, anything other than looking at him and giving away too much of her innermost feelings. When she'd regained her composure and raised her head, she became aware of how the rain had dampened his hair and clung to the edges of his lashes, making them darker, thicker. He looked like an organic part of the wild domain over which he was laird and in her heightened state, she imagined she could detect the scent of the storm on his clothing and the wind in his hair.

'My pleasure,' he replied politely, breaking the mood.

'What about Mitzi and Angus?' she asked to gain a breathing space.

'Fine. They flew in ahead of the storm and are safe and sound up at the Big Hoose. I'm sorry that all your effort has gone to waste.' He nodded towards the wrap dress that picked out the green flecks in her eyes and accentuated the copper threads in her hair. 'We'll reschedule for next week.' His eyes darkened and his pupils dilated - all the better to see her with, she thought wildly, as he took in her hair, make-up and bare feet with a second, more comprehensive sweep.

'Oh well.' She licked her lips, her mouth feeling suddenly dry. 'Beans on toast for supper instead of Aberdeen Angus beef.' She laughed at her pun but Ruairi didn't join in. '*Now* what have I said?' She clicked her tongue in exasperation; sometimes it was hard going with him. Was it really worth the effort she asked herself, and glared at him?

'Sorry, I'm just a bit preoccupied. And I should be going . . .' Yet he made no effort to leave. 'I've had to initiate the Kinloch Mara Emergency Plan. Two mini buses full of wedding guests are stranded on *our* side of a collapsed bridge. The river's in spate and the emergency services can't get through by the usual route and will have to go the long way round. And, as you can see, it's too windy to send up a helicopter.'

Realising what an airhead she must appear, talking about beans on toast when his mind was on rescuing people stranded in the worsening storm, Fliss felt she had to make amends. On impulse, she abandoned her high heels on the stairs and walked towards the weatherproof coat and wellingtons in the porch.

'What are you doing?' Ruairi asked as she lifted the hem of her dress and pushed her feet into a pair of wellingtons. 'Didn't you hear me? Dinner's been cancelled.'

'I heard you,' she replied patiently, 'and I'm coming to help.'

'Help? You?' Ruairi raised a sceptical eyebrow. She knew she looked all *wrong* - from her pinned up hair fastened with diamante clasps, full war paint and posh frock, down to the wellingtons which were several sizes too big for her.

'I'm tougher than I look,' she said, squaring her shoulders.

'I don't doubt that for a second,' he said with some of his usual asperity. But it was accompanied by a smile. 'But I really don't see how your skills as a beauty therapist will be of much help to us tonight.'

Fliss ignored the subtle put-down.

'There's more to me than aromatherapy and tea tree oil. Which you'd find out if you gave me a chance,' she said employing a brisk tone. 'For your information, I was a St John's Ambulance cadet . . .'

He didn't need to know that her dad had encouraged her and Becky to join to keep them off the streets and out of trouble. Or that she and Becky had agreed, hoping that as first aiders they'd get free access to gigs and football matches. Not to mention wall-to-wall boys. But, during their five year stint, she'd gained triage skills, become a competent first aider and learned how to deal with people who were anxious or in pain.

'You never cease to amaze me, Miss Bagshawe. But I haven't got time to debate the issue, Murdo's gathering the team together and I must join them.' He picked his walkie-talkie up off the pier table, jammed the weather-beaten Akubra back on his head and turned his back on her.

Fliss felt dismissed, but swallowed her hurt pride. She put her hand on his arm and forced him to turn round. 'Seriously, I really *could* help. I have triage skills and could act as first responder when you bring the injured back here. Hold the fort until the medics arrive. That sort of thing,' she trailed off. Then she looked up into his face, pleading to be given the chance to be taken seriously; to show what she was made of.

The *real* Fliss Bagshawe.

He gave her a measuring look and it was as if the scales had fallen from his eyes and he as seeing her for the first time. *Really* seeing her. And although he frowned down on her hand on his arm, he didn't shrug it off. In fact, it seemed that - just for a second, he actually welcomed the physical contact and her reassuring, comforting touch. As though intimacy and tenderness had been missing from his life for a long time. The air around them felt charged, electrified, but whether that was because of the storm and the falling barometer or the way his arm muscles flexed under her hand, Fliss couldn't say. Whatever the reason, they both took a deep breath and of one accord took a step away from each other.

And it was down to business.

'I guess we'll need all the help we can muster tonight.'

He took a heavy riding mac off a coat peg and held it out for her to slip her arms into. She knew he was only acting the gentleman and she shouldn't read anything more into the gesture than that, but she was touched by his show of good manners. She shivered. *Not* because his fingers had grazed the back of her neck when he'd untucked the collar, *or* because his breath touched her cheek. But, because the coat was cold and damp from hanging unused in the porch - or at least, that's what she told herself.

Then, not caring for her carefully styled updo, she removed the clasps holding it in place, shook her curls loose and crammed on an unflattering but practical sou'wester.

'Ready?' His voice was gruff, as if watching her shaking her curls free had affected him in some fundamental way.

'Ready,' she replied, buttoning up the last fastening on the riding mac and shoving her shoes in her coat pockets.

When Ruairi opened the door, the force of the wind blew her backwards into his arms and he caught her and steadied her against his chest. She thought she could feel the heat from his body pulsing through two thicknesses of coat - and wondered if that was possible, or if it was just her imagination. They stayed in that position longer than was strictly necessary, neither of them seemingly keen to break free.

Then Fliss muttered her thanks and they drew apart. And she was glad, as they made their way up the windswept path towards the Tigh na Locha that conversation was impossible and her burning cheeks couldn't be seen in the darkness.

They entered the house via the kitchens where volunteers were heating soup and spreading sandwiches. Ruairi said a few encouraging words to them en passant and Fliss saw the respectful way they responded to him. She didn't know what constituted the Kinloch Mara Emergency Plan but she guessed that if Ruairi and Murdo had drawn it up, it would be near enough bombproof.

Murdo, Cat, Angus and Mitzi were waiting for Ruairi in the hall.

'Fliss has volunteered to organise triage for the stranded passengers until the emergency services arrive. I want everyone to help her, once they've finished their allotted tasks,' Ruairi ordered, without preamble.

'Good for you, Fliss,' Murdo said, patting her shoulder encouragingly. 'Our designated first aider is stranded on the other side of the bridge. As is our local GP, Jack Dunbar.'

Isla chose that moment to saunter out of the dining room a little worse for wear. She gave them a scalding look, clearly none too pleased that Murdo's hand was resting lightly on Fliss's shoulder. Since the episode on the veranda, she'd been very cool towards Fliss - freezing her out, giving her a killing look and behaving like a dog in the manger where Murdo was concerned. Fliss moved away from Murdo; she liked him and enjoyed his company, but had no intention of being party to whatever game the two of them were playing.

The thought was quickly dismissed as Ruairi and Murdo pulled on neon safety jackets and hurried back towards the kitchens looking suitably manly and heroic. Isla turned towards the stairs, making plain that none of this had anything to do with her. She made her way unsteadily upstairs and Cat was about to follow suit when Fliss grabbed her by the arm.

'Are you mad! Don't you see that this is your big chance to prove to Ruairi how capable you can be in a crisis? Your helping tonight could be the very thing that makes him think twice about sending you to a crammer this summer. Perhaps even persuade him to find you the placement at the vet's in Port Urquhart you're so keen on.'

Cat threw her arms round Fliss's neck.

'Fliss - you are a bloody genius.'

When Fliss disentangled herself from Cat's enthusiastic hug, Mitzi and Angus were standing by the fireside waiting for her instructions.

Letting her take the lead as if it were the most natural thing in the world.

Chapter Twenty Three

'Several years ago, a landslide blocked the road to Kinloch Mara and we only *just* managed to hold the fort until help arrived,' Cat explained as Fliss set up her triage station in the hall. 'Ruairi vowed that he wouldn't allow that to happen again and drew up a contingency plan - after consulting the emergency services and WRVS, of course. But essentially the Kinloch Mara Emergency Plan is his baby.'

The pride in her voice was unmistakable and Fliss hid a smile. Cat had certainly changed since the night of the party when she'd called Ruairi everything from a pig to a dog. Ever since their heart-to-heart in the Wee Hoose two days ago she appeared to have gained a new respect for him - and a developing understanding that he had her best interests at heart.

'We certainly appear to have everything necessary to cope with an emergency,' Fliss replied as she laid out the first aid equipment on a carved chest draped in white cloth. 'Antiseptic, butterfly closures and cold compresses; bandages and sterile dressings; tweezers, barrier gloves and some generic analgesics. That should keep us going until the emergency services arrive.'

'Urgh. What about *this*?' Cat held up a box containing a defibrillator. Fliss took it from her and pushed it out of sight under the hooded porter's chair.

'I'm not trained to use one of those. It's best that we don't let people see it. In my experience, even the most unflappable person can freak out at the sight of medical equipment.'

She half expected some flippant remark from Cat, but she was carrying out tasks without a fuss, obviously seizing the opportunity to show herself in a positive light to Ruairi and increase her chances of becoming a veterinary nurse.

By the same token, Fliss knew this was her big moment, a chance to show how capable she was in a crisis. She was mulling over the idea and composing herself for what lay ahead when the first of the Land Rovers pulled up in front of the house. Jaimsie, who'd been vigorously stoking the large fire in the grate, raised his head and announced self-importantly: 'It's Himself.'

'Oh,' Cat responded, nervously.

'Just do everything I say and you'll be fine.' Hiding her own nerves, Fliss put a reassuring hand on Cat's arm. Despite her brave words, her fingers were transformed into thumbs and the rolled up bandage slipped out of them as Ruairi swept into the hall - waxed coat billowing out behind him, leaves and debris swirling in his wake.

Full of authority, he paused in the doorway and took in Fliss's triage station, the staff and volunteers going about their allotted tasks and Cat folding blankets with one encompassing glance. For a few seconds everyone stopped and turned towards him, seeking reassurance and leadership. Although they were in the middle of a full blown emergency, Fliss sensed that he welcomed the opportunity to be put to the test. He was the Laird of Kinloch Mara - it was what he'd been born to.

Removing his Akubra, he skimmed it Frisbee-like towards a stag's head mounted on the wall. It caught on one of the stag's antlers and perched there at a rakish angle. This was clearly a well-practiced trick and made everyone laugh, releasing the pent-up tension in the hall.

'Spot on, double - oh - seven,' giggled Cat, playing Miss Moneypenny to his Bond. He flashed a smile as he slipped off his neon safety waistcoat and tossed it onto a chair.

'You've all been busy. Well done. Everyone's skills will be called upon this evening.' He addressed them collectively but Fliss felt his remarks were addressed to her alone. She sensed his scorching regard and stress on the word *skills* was his way of warning that her Florence Nightingale Act had better be genuine. Not some new game she'd thought up to take advantage of the situation.

She knew she was here under sufferance. She didn't need him ramming it home every five minutes. Especially not tonight when she needed to be on top of her game and remember her first aid training from years ago. She glared back at him, look for look, and hoped he got the message!

As if suddenly recalling why Fliss was wearing a large apron over her wrap dress and had set up a triage station in the hall, Ruairi shook off his mood.

'Mitzi and Angus?' he asked.

'In the kitchen, supervising food and drink for our - your - unexpected guests,' she answered crisply, hoping he hadn't noticed her trip over the pronoun.

'Isla?' he asked, holding his hands out towards the fire.

'Upstairs.'

'Par for the course.' He curled his lip and Fliss suspected there would be fresh confrontations over breakfast tomorrow and was glad she had her bolthole to scurry back to when tonight was over. Isla was a fool, a show of penitence now and Ruairi's attitude towards her could alter significantly. But it was a compromise she was seemingly unwilling to make.

No need for Cat to go down the same road, however.

'Cat's been a godsend. She's got a real talent for helping me - and helping others.' She brought Cat forward, willing him to say something positive to her.

'Well done, Squirt,' he said, obviously picking up the vibe. He peeled off his coat, handed it to Jaimsie, came over to ruffle Cat's hair and laid a brotherly hand on her shoulder. Fliss felt the love between them, and guessed that despite the heavy brother act she'd witnessed on several occasions, there was great affection and trust there, too.

'Thanks, Ruairi,' Cat beamed.

'Right; you seem to have everything under control here, Fliss. I'll leave you to it. Jaimsie - the fire can look after itself - away and get a wee dram for everyone, if you please.' The grin that split Jaimsie's craggy face showed that it pleased him very much indeed.

'Oh, but - it's not a good idea to give alcohol to people who might be in shock or suffering from hypothermia. It goes against the fundamental principles of emergency first aid.' Fliss bit her lip, knowing she sounded like some starchy ward sister and steeled herself for his reaction. The General Medical Council might view Ruairi's cure-all askance but in these parts, giving guests a shot of whisky was in keeping with highland hospitality.

'Come, Nurse Bagshawe, surely you won't deny your patients a dram of *uisge beatha*.' He pronounced it *ish-ga ba-ha*.

'I'm afraid I must until they've had something to eat and a warm drink inside them,' she replied firmly. Her heart hammered against her breastbone as she waited for his wrath to descend.

'Highly commendable,' was his surprising reaction. 'I bow to your superior knowledge in these matters. We'll hold it in reserve until you give us permission to administer it. It has healing and antiseptic properties you know,' he said poker-faced. But she could tell from the light dancing in his eyes that he was teasing her.

'If you say so,' she stammered, thoroughly wrong-footed by his backing her up. She gave him a far from convinced look and stood with one hand on her hip and with the other holding a disposable thermometer. Like she was indeed Nurse Bagshawe.

Then they caught the inimical glance that Jaimsie the piper was sending towards them, openly furious at being denied a dram of the Laird's finest malt. His expression was so comical that Fliss burst out laughing. Ruairi, hiding his own amusement, said something soothing to Jaimsie, in Gaelic.

'I hope you're not undermining my authority,' Fliss said giving him a mock-stern look as Jaimsie brightened up and walked off towards the kitchens.

'I wouldn't dare. I thought it best to let Jaimsie have his *uisge beatha* or he'd be playing the Urquhart Funeral March on his bagpipes every morning for the next week as we beat the bounds past the Wee Hoose.'

'I know. I've seen you . . .'

She clammed up - she didn't want him thinking she hid behind the curtains in the hope of catching a glimpse of him marking out the limits of his ancestral acres. Even though that was exactly what she did. Ruairi's brow puckered, as if he was trying to figure her out and get a handle on the sea change taking place between them. Then, as the first travellers were brought before Fliss's triage station, he issued orders to the staff and volunteers - and it was all hands to the pumps.

Time passed quickly as a steady stream of travellers of all ages passed through Fliss' hands. She showed Cat how to clean and dress a wound, assess each traveller for injury and decide on treatment. Fortunately, most of the travellers were well enough to be dispatched almost straightaway to the kitchen for sandwiches and a mug of good strong tea.

'We were on our way back from Oban and a family wedding when the weather got worse,' an elderly gentleman explained, as Fliss cleaned his grazed knuckles with an antiseptic wipe. 'I never thought we'd end up anywhere as grand as this.' He looked round the hall with its imposing staircase, family portraits and air of gracious antiquity. 'Never mind having the Laird himself carry me out of the mini bus.'

'Aye, we'll no forget tonight in a hurry,' his wife added and looked over at Ruairi. 'The likes of us . . . in a place like this,' she echoed her husband's words.

Fliss looked at the scene through their eyes. Ruairi and Murdo looked the part in their plaid trousers - or trubhas - in contrasting tartans, short dinner jackets with silver buttons on the turned back cuffs and dress shirts. The ladies in their evening dresses and Angus in his tux with Gordon tartan cummerbund all added to the overall effect. In the short time she'd lived here, she'd grown accustomed to this element in the Urquharts' lives: the grandeur, formality and respect for the past. But to the wedding party from Glasgow it must look very fine indeed.

'Aye, and if ye dinnae mind me saying so, Lady Urquhart - you're a lucky lassie,' another female wedding guest whispered to her 'To be married to such a fine man.'

'Oh, but I'm not . . . and he's not,' Fliss reddened as she realised that Ruairi had overheard their conversation. Turning away, she concentrated on tending to the old lady's sprained wrist and said no more. But as she bound up the injury, she allowed herself to imagine how it would feel to be the mistress of this fine house and wife to its laird. Raising her head, she caught Ruairi's unfathomable look as if he was pondering on the old lady's words, too. She had a light, fluttering sensation in her stomach as she returned his enigmatic look and then a darker thought struck her.

What if he was wondering how Fiona would have coped tonight? Imagining *her* graciously binding up the old lady's injuries and whispering soothingly to her; a lady born and bred? Perhaps his look showed that he wasn't over her, that he was hoping one day she'd come back into his life and that she was a usurper.

Enough. Fliss pulled herself together and stripped off her disposable gloves. Tonight was her chance to show what she was made of, not wonder if Ruairi Urquhart was nursing a broken heart. With the air of someone used to coping with emergencies she asked Cat to escort the old lady and her husband down to the kitchen and then walked over to Ruairi who was speaking to one of the gillies. She coughed to gain his attention, not daring to lay her hand on his arm twice in one night.

'I think most of the wedding party will need to spend the night here and see what the morning brings. No one is seriously injured, so perhaps you ought to tell the emergency services to stand down? Tomorrow, it might simply be a case of ferrying our visitors to Port Urquhart or the nearest large town and having the mini buses pulled out of the ditch by a tractor.'

'You're right,' he conceded, his straight black eyebrows drawing together as he gave weight to her words. 'Other places might have greater need of the Fire and Rescue Services than we do.'

'Sorry - have I overstepped the mark?' she asked, trying to read his expression. 'Naturally, it's for you to decide what's best in these circumstances. I have an organising gene that has a tendency to take over if I don't keep a rein on it. My friend Becky reckons I was born with a clipboard in my hand and a pencil behind my ear.'

'Don't apologise. I'm like that myself, like things done and dusted.'
This time his smile was designed to smooth any ruffled feathers. The
delicious fluttering of a few minutes ago returned; it started in the pit of
her stomach and travelled upwards to her heart. Just as Ruairi looked as
if he might qualify his statement, the hall door slammed back on its
hinges and Murdo entered with a woman in her early thirties.

It didn't take long for Fliss and Ruairi to realise that she was heavily
pregnant.

Chapter Twenty Four

'I found this lady near the entrance to the estate. Her car has a flat tyre.' Murdo handed her over to Fliss, went back outside and returned moments later carrying a large holdall.

'I'm Fliss; welcome. You've chosen the wrong night to get a flat tyre.'

'I certainly chose the wrong night to drive to Inverness, that's for sure,' was her spirited reply.

'You went out shopping in *this?*' Ruairi asked incredulously, taking in the storm with a sweeping gesture.

'I know. After four children, you'd *think* I'd have enough equipment to open my own branch of Mothercare, wouldn't you. But, oh no, I had to make one last trip to Inverness before I'm too huge to fit behind the wheel of the Discovery.' Despite making light of the situation, she looked slightly shame-faced. She pushed her blonde hair out of her eyes and gave a small moan, and appeared grateful when Fliss guided her towards the porter's chair by the fire. 'I'm Shona McAlester, by the way.'

'Ruairi Urquhart, Laird of Kinloch Mara,' Ruairi came forward and shook the hand of his new guest. He gave her an anxious look. 'When's the baby due?'

'Not for another three weeks. I carry a bag of things round with me, just in case.' She indicated the holdall that Murdo had left by the front door. 'We live on the far side of Kinloch Mara, and have taken over a small hotel there. My husband wanted to do the shopping for me, but I *insisted* that he stayed at home and looked after the other wee ones. I said to him: *Archie, stop fussing; after four children I think I'd know if number five was about to put in an early appearance.*'

Fliss got the impression that Shona was probably insistent about

187

many things!

'Five children? Wow.' Cat moved closer to the fire, inspecting her like she was one of their brood mares about to foal.

'Are you sure you're OK?' Fliss asked as Shona rubbed her lower back. For a moment she felt absurdly like Prissy in Gone with the Wind who famously knew nothing about delivering babies. She fervently hoped Shona would spend an uneventful night at Tigh na Locha and be on her way in the morning. Dealing with an expectant mother in her third trimester was a different ball game to cleaning a graze and sticking a plaster over it!

'I'm fine. Just got a bit cramped in the car. A cup of tea and I'll be right as rain. If someone could just ring my husband and let him know what's happened.' She rooted in her large tote bag, found a business card and handed it over to Ruairi. 'Something tells me I'm going to be hearing lots of I told you so's when I get home.' She gave Fliss a cheeky grin but winced as she sat down, stretched out her legs and examined her swollen ankles.

'You rest while Ruairi makes the phone call and I'll check you over for injury. Cat, would you fetch Shona something to eat and drink from the kitchen?' Fliss laid a cool hand on Shona's wrist and discovered that her pulse was racing.

'I've got twitchy legs and backache from trying to sleep in the car,' Shona elaborated. 'I tried to call the emergency services but there was no signal. Lucky Murdo found me.'

'Yes, it's a dead zone round here,' Fliss informed her and couldn't resist casting a look at Ruairi. Maybe this emergency would make him change his mind about allowing a mast on his land.

'Sorry I just need to . . .' Shona walked round the hall to restore the circulation to her calf muscles and massaged her back just above her hip bones with both hands. 'Oh no . . .' She moaned as a steady trickle of fluid dripped down her legs and pooled at her feet. Ruairi stood rooted to the spot but Fliss rushed forward to help. 'My waters have broken,' she informed unnecessarily. 'I'd better . . .'

'There's a cloakroom just through the hall where we can clean you up.' Fliss picked up the holdall Murdo had left by the door before turning to Ruairi. 'Do you think someone could . . .' she nodded at the slick of amniotic fluid on the hall floor.

'I'll get that attended to,' he said briskly. 'You do whatever is necessary to make our guest comfortable.' Although she was dealing with an emergency Fliss's heart leapt at his use of 'our'. It made her feel like she was part of the team; his team - and it was a good feeling.

At the mother-to-be's insistence, Fliss left her alone in the cloakroom; but she was equally insistent that the door was left unlocked and slightly ajar. When she returned to the hall, Ruairi was waiting for an update.

'Well?'

'That is one stubborn lady!' Ruairi shot her a look that suggested women as a species were as stubborn as a troupe of seaside donkeys. 'I think in the circumstances you should send for your GP, or is there a midwife in the vicinity?'

Ruairi thought long and hard before answering. 'Our GP's the other side of the washed away bridge, but there's Mrs MacLeish. She was a practice nurse in the surgery at Port Urquhart before she retired. I suppose we could call on her.' He looked through the window to see if the storm had run its course. 'I'll ring Jack Dunbar and ask Murdo to fetch Mrs McLeish. Can you step into the breach until they arrive? I'll also try to raise Callum McDonald, our local police officer - he's bound to have dealt with this kind of emergency before.'

Murdo put his wet coat back on without complaint and went out into the storm, while Ruairi walked into the dining room to make the call. Fliss re-tied her apron in a business-like manner before returning to the cloakroom to help Shona. Thirty minutes later, there was no sign of Murdo with Mrs McLeish and Ruairi hadn't been able to raise Callum McDonald. Shona had already snapped Fliss's head off several times for asking her to sit down when plainly she wanted to pace the hall between contractions.

When it became obvious that Shona wouldn't be able to climb the stairs to the guest bedroom, Fliss - with Cat and Ruairi's help - followed

Dr Dunbar's instructions and prepped the library to act as a makeshift delivery room. They covered the leather chesterfield with a shower curtain, which they had rubbed down with antiseptic spray. A lace trimmed, monogrammed linen sheet was spread over that in an attempt to make everything appear less clinical and Shona more comfortable. There was a fire burning in the grate and Cat brought armfuls of scented candles from the dining room. Under instruction from Fliss, she was busy arranging cushions at one end of the couch and covering a pillow with an old towel. 'I've seen cows and horses give birth but this'll be quite different, won't it?' she asked Fliss concernedly.

Fliss didn't answer; her experience of childbirth was limited to what she'd seen on Holby City or Doc Martin, but she kept that to herself. When Mrs McLeish arrived, hopefully all she'd have to do was follow the retired nurse's instructions.

As the wind rattled the front door in its frame, Shona was wracked by another contraction. Stubborn to the last, she refused to lie down on the makeshift bed, preferring to walk around the hall supported at the elbow by Mitzi whose hand she was gripping tightly. But at least she'd seen the sense of changing into a nightdress from her holdall and the dressing gown Cat had brought down from upstairs.

'How far apart are the contractions now?' Cat asked Fliss anxiously, her blue eyes large and frightened in her pale face.

'Every five minutes,' Fliss said, checking the grandfather clock.

'Shouldn't she be lying down or something?' Ruairi asked, looking to Fliss for guidance and reassurance - like she was an expert in childbirth.

'You try telling her that! When I spoke to Dr Dunbar earlier, he said we should take the lead from Shona.' Fliss tried hard to keep the quaver out of her voice. 'Seeing as this will be her fifth child, the doctor said she - and her body - will know better than any of us what's required.'

'Christ - I hope he's right,' was Ruairi's fervent prayer. Then he turned to Cat who was hovering anxiously by the library door biting her nails. 'You've done brilliantly this evening Puss Cat. Why don't you take the little ones who've had their supper up to play with your old toys in the nursery? That's the best help you can give us for now. And tell Isla to stir herself and help you.'

'If you're sure you don't want me to help with the birth?' she asked, openly relieved.

'That's fine. There are plenty of us to help Fliss until Mrs MacLeish gets here.' He exchanged a worried glance with Fliss; clearly thinking the same as her - what was taking Murdo so long? Providentially, at that moment the walkie-talkie on the hall table crackled into life.

'*Ruairi, it's Murdo - over.*' Ruairi headed for the library to take the call and Fliss followed close behind.

'Ruairi. Go ahead.'

'I can't get through to Mrs McLeish. The Port Urquhart road's closed to traffic. I'll have to go round via Kinloch Head to fetch her. But that'll take the best part of an hour. Over.'

Ruairi and Fliss looked at each other. With the contractions just minutes apart, the baby could arrive before Mrs MacLeish got there. Ruairi took a deep breath and looked long and hard at Fliss. Fully aware that she was their best hope if they wanted the baby delivered safely, Fliss nodded.

'Just get here as soon as you can. But don't take any risks. Over and out.' The walkie-talking went silent. 'You heard?'

'I heard.'

'Now what?'

'I know Shona might not want to - but I'd feel happier if she came into the library. She can walk around in here just as well as in the hall. I think we've done our best to get it ready under the circumstances. When the contractions come closer together we'll be ready.'

'You sound very sure.'

'I'm not.' She gave a brave little smile as she discarded her soiled apron and put on a clean one. 'Once Shona's settled, I think you should ring Dr Dunbar or Nurse McLeish and ask them to talk us through the birth - step by step. Or if all else fails, ring 999 and they'll put us through to someone who can help.'

'Good idea. You stay here; I'll send Shona in and you do the rest.' He put the walkie-talkie down on the desk and pulled the house phone out of the waistband of his tight trews. He made as if to leave but then turned round. 'You're doing a great job. I can't thank you enough.' He laid his hand on Fliss's upper arm and her heart swelled with emotion.

'I'll do my best for Shona,' she croaked. 'Now, go.'

She was relieved when he didn't argue. After all, this was his house, his emergency plan - maybe she should let him take the lead and stop being so hands-on. But she was the so-called expert tonight and Ruairi obviously knew when to step back. It felt good to be working shoulder to shoulder with him and at last to show him what she was capable of.

Taking a deep breath, she positioned the bib of her apron so that it sat squarely over her breasts and covered the gap in her wrap dress. Next, she made sure that everything was just as the doctor had ordered. *Everything* included: two electric kettles full of hot water, a large jug of cold water, two medium bowls for washing hands, two empty bowls, a saucepan in which Cat had boiled scissors and a pair of laces donated from her new trainers. They'd also laid out disposable gloves, towels, blankets, cotton wool, sanitary towels, large bin liners and some antiseptic hand sanitiser. It was the best they could manage in the circumstances and she knew that if her dad was watching he'd be proud of his cadet daughter. That made her throat constrict, but she pushed the thought away as the door opened and Ruairi ushered Shona and Mitzi into the library.

'Now darling, do everything Fliss says and you'll be fine,' Mitzi said, giving Fliss a much-needed confidence boost.

'Are you sure you're up for this?' Ruairi came over and asked her quietly, their heads almost touching as he bent forward to hear her reply. Maybe he thought that she'd been sucked into helping before she'd had time to think about what 'helping' might entail. Fliss nodded, forgoing this last chance to back out.

'I want - I'd like to see this through,' was her determined reply.

'As long as you're certain,' he gave her a crooked smile. 'Rather you than me. Although I suppose one day I'll be in a similar situation,' he said, evidently thinking ahead to the birth of his first child. They exchanged a significant look then Fliss turned away and it was down to business.

'I want everyone to wash their hands, sanitise them and put on a pair of disposable gloves and a disposable apron. Ruairi if you man the phone and stand at Shona's shoulder - that should give her a little privacy. Mitzi - between us, you and I should be able to follow the doctor's instructions. At least until the midwife gets here. Mitzi, you're the cheerleader for the team; keep the flannels ready.' She gave Shona and Mitzi a confident smile. 'Ruairi, ring the doctor, please.'

The contractions were coming thick and fast as they waited for the doctor to answer. Jack Dunbar picked up almost straight away and they heard him tell Ruairi - via speakerphone - that unless something went badly wrong the baby would be born very soon. Following his instructions, Fliss and Mitzi checked Shona discreetly before announcing that she was almost fully dilated.

Fliss looked up at Ruairi for reassurance, doing her best to appear calm and collected although her heart was racing and her hands were shaking. Mitzi was holding Shona's hand and mopping her décolletage and the back of her neck with a wrung out flannel, recounting the birth of her two daughters to distract her between contractions. Fliss was relying heavily on the fact that between them Mitzi and Shona had given birth six times - and should have a good idea of how this went.

She started slightly as Dr Dunbar's voice came across loud and clear.

'I don't need to tell you that you're in the final stages of labour Shona. Now you'll want to push, but don't do that just yet. I want you to get into position: lying on your side, squatting or whatever feels most comfortable for you so that the baby can slip out easily onto the pillow which I believe Lady Urquhart is holding.'

Fliss handed Mitzi a pillow draped in an old, clean towel and they stationed themselves by Shona, kneeling in front of the fire. Shona's expression swung between pain and anxiety and Fliss sensed that she wanted no fuss; simply to get the birth over with and ensure the baby arrived safe and well. Stubborn to the last, Shona was insistent that they didn't ring her husband and tell him the fix she was in. Time enough for that, she said, when the baby was safely delivered and in her arms.

God willing thought Fliss as she and Ruairi exchanged a look over Shona's head.

'*Now Lady Urquhart, hold the pillow close to where the baby will emerge, ready to catch and support it.*'

Mitzi did as she was told and Shona let out a guttural yell and blasphemed. 'That's it, darling. Let it out. Swear if you want to; no one to hear you but us. I remember when Isla was born I used language that would have made the Moderator of the Church of Scotland faint.'

Shona managed a feeble smile.

'Ruairi, you could stand the phone over there on the table, ring out the flannel and give it to Shona - or take over from Mitzi and mop Shona's brow for her.'

'*Can you see the baby's head?*' Doctor Dunbar asked.

'Yes!' Fliss declared loudly so that the he could hear her.

'*Now, Shona - push gently with the next contraction, you don't want tearing and stitches if you can help it.*'

This time Shona only managed a nod as she gritted her teeth, held onto Ruairi's hand and gave one last push with the contraction. Fliss's eyes were drawn to where the miracle was taking place, trying to listen to the doctor and not obscure Mitzi's view of the birth. By now the baby's head had emerged and they could see thick dark hair wet with blood and mucus.

'*Now Fliss, feel round baby's neck for the umbilical cord.*'

Gingerly Fliss did so, giving thanks that massage and aromatherapy had made her hands and fingers slender and supple. Mitzi watched anxiously, pillow at the ready while Ruairi mopped Shona's brow.

'Found it.'

'*Lift the cord over the baby's head and loosen it. Gently now. You're nearly there.*'

'Can you do it, Fliss?' Ruairi asked, straining to see whilst trying to give Shona some privacy. Fliss nodded and then realised that mime wouldn't be much use to the doctor on the other end of the line.

'Yes. I've . . . done it.'

The fire was burning at her back and sweat trickled down her spine and heat suffused her face. Her hair flopped forward, but she knew better than to touch it and risk cross infection. As if reading her mind, Ruairi leaned over and tucked the loose strands behind her ears and they shared an eloquent look. Although she was burning hot, Fliss shivered at his touch; then she puckered her brow in concentration and was back in business.

'*This next part is crucial, Fliss. Make space for the baby to slip through the umbilical cord on the next push . . .*'

Fliss didn't have time to think or reply as Shona let out one last painful scream and delivered the child. It slid out of her and onto the pillow Mitzi was holding, followed by a gush of blood-coloured water that soaked them. Fliss looked down at the little scrap that had been delivered almost into her lap and sank back on her heels.

'*Can someone please tell me what's going on?*'

'The baby's been born, safely I think,' Fliss shouted at the phone. She looked towards Mitzi for confirmation but she was too choked up to reply and simply nodded.

'*Good. Now rub baby gently up and down its back until . . .*' The baby took several deep breaths and let out a mewing cry. '*Good. Good. Now, if the cord's long enough - put the baby on mother's breast. Skin to skin. Replace the soiled towel with a clean one and cover mother and baby with a blanket to keep them warm. If the cord isn't long enough . . .*' Fliss did as instructed, and then took the soiled pillow away from Mitzi who shuffled forward on her hands and knees and took over flannel duty from Ruairi. '*Hello Ruairi. Tell me what's happening.*'

Ruairi picked up the phone and held it closer so that Fliss could speak to Dr Dunbar. 'The baby's trying to suckle. Mother and baby appear to be fine. What about the cord?' she asked anxiously, not sure if she could deal with that aspect of the birth.

'*There's no rush to cut the cord as long as it isn't pulled tight.*'

Fliss checked that it wasn't.

'*If you pick the cord up between your fingers you can feel the baby's pulse. Within 10 minutes the pulse should stop. Then I'll tell you how to cut the cord.*'

Fliss, Ruairi and Mitzi glanced at the saucepan containing the scissors and the sterilised laces. Fliss tentatively felt the cord for the pulse and nodded at Ruairi.

'Fliss's has found the pulse, Jack.'

'That's good. Now clean up the room but leave mother and baby as they are. I'll ring back in ten minutes with more instructions. But for now - have a wee dram to wet the baby's head and stand down.' And with that, he hung up.

Fliss stripped off her disposable gloves and put them in one of the two large bin bags she'd kept to one side, along with the soiled pillow and towels. She pushed her hair off her face with the back of her hands, tried to lever herself into an upright position but her legs refused to cooperate. Ruairi put the phone down and was at her side in two swift strides.

'You okay?' he asked. He helped her to her feet, oblivious that her blood-streaked apron was soiling his dress shirt and trubhas. She leaned against him, grateful for his strength and support. The look that passed between them recalled the moment in the rose gardens when she'd reached out to him and he'd caught her. The moment before the world had come crashing round their ears and everything changed. Fliss couldn't find the words to express how she felt; she wanted to lay her head on his shoulder, close her eyes and sleep for a hundred years, knowing she was safe in his arms. Instead, she moved away from him and ostentatiously rubbed her thighs. .

'Pins and needles. I'll be OK once the circulation returns. The baby - is it a boy or a girl?'

Due to the heat of the moment and their relief afterwards, no one had thought to check. Laughing, Mitzi raised one corner of the blanket and looked under the clean towel.

'A wee girl. A beautiful wee lassie . . .' Her voice broke and she reached out tentatively to touch the baby's dark head.

'A girl,' Fliss breathed. The besotted look on Shona's face made her imagine how her own mother must have felt when she'd held her in her arms for the first time. Tears filled her eyes as she was beset by a fresh pang of loss - but there was no time for sentiment. Sanitising her hands,

196

she slipped on another pair of disposable gloves and a fresh apron.

Her job wasn't over. Yet. There was the cord to cut, placenta to deal with and . . . Unexpectedly, a wave of nausea washed over her as she thought of everything that could have gone wrong with the birth. The adrenalin that had seen her through the last hour ebbed away and she had to grab hold of the curled end of the chesterfield to steady herself.

Ruairi left the room and returned with three tots of whisky and a cup of tea for Shona and they did as the doctor had ordered and stood down. Their ten minutes of grace were barely up when the library door opened and Murdo brought in a little bird of a woman with cornflower blue eyes and thick white hair. Ruairi and Mitzi looked relieved to see her and greeted her in Gaelic. She went over to Shona and examined the baby who was already suckling.

'The cord is still intact?' she asked Fliss.

'Yes, Doctor Dunbar said to wait until I couldn't feel a pulse.' Realising that this was telling her granny how to suck eggs she trailed off. Nurse McLeish washed her hands and put on a spare pair of surgical gloves and looked at Fliss with a twinkle in her eyes.

'You've come this far, lassie. You'll no be in the way; let's finish the job together. How's Mother?' she asked Shona in that way medical people have of talking to their patients in the third person.

'Tired but fine. Once you've dealt with the cord and the afterbirth I'd like to ring my husband, Archie.'

'Of course. Now, Lady Urquhart, could we have a pack of frozen peas and fresh towels please?' She laughed at Fliss's expression as Mitzi left the library to do as asked. 'Dinnae worry, lassie, I'm no making an omelette. The peas are to use as an ice pack to put on mother's bottom to take away the sting . . .'

Ruairi and Murdo - clearly deciding it was time for a swift exit - headed for the hall. Fliss mouthed: *chicken* at them, Ruairi laughed and Fliss knew things were good between them. Fliss and Nurse McLeish rolled up their sleeves and got down to the task of dealing with the cord, expelling the placenta, putting a tiny nappy on the new-born and cleaning Shona as best they could.

Later, the family gathered round Shona in the library and watched her nursing her new daughter.

'We'd already chosen the name for the baby,' she explained as she sipped a cup of tea and ate a cracker spread with peanut butter while everyone else drank champagne. 'Iona for a girl and Hamish for a boy.'

'Hamish?' Mitzi repeated. 'That was my late husband's name. How sw - sweet,' she said, though her voice faltered. Everyone appeared to be on the verge of tears - some hormonal, some emotional and Fliss was glad that there were enough staff and volunteers to take care of the stranded travellers as her reserves of energy were spent.

Conscious that she, Mitzi and Ruairi were wearing blood stained clothing, Fliss put her champagne glass down carefully on the table and rose to take her leave. Mrs McLeish was going to spend the night with Shona and Iona. Tomorrow morning, Murdo and Ruairi would take mother, baby and midwife home safely, weather permitting.

Her job here was done. 'I'm going back to the Wee Hoose to get cleaned up, if no one minds?'

'Mind? Who could refuse you anything tonight, Fliss darling?' Mitzi looked round the family circle - the drama of the birth even having roused Isla and brought her downstairs. 'The Urquharts are in your debt. You've been a brick.' She sent Ruairi a sharp look through her tears as though expecting him to disagree. 'An absolute brick.'

Even Isla regarded Fliss with new respect.

Ruairi shook his head as if to assure her that she had no worries on that score and raised his glass: 'To Fliss. Kinloch Mara's new midwife.'

That was the final straw. Fliss took in a shuddering breath, and when she released it, promptly burst into racking sobs, which she struggled to get under control. Mitzi and Cat began to fuss over her, but there was only one pair of arms she wanted to hold and comfort her.

'I - I'm fine; really. I'm just dog-tired and my dress is beyond the help of Bold 3 in 1.' She made light of her emotional outburst not wanting to reveal that the unexpected kindness Ruairi had shown her this evening was the real reason for her tears. She dashed them away with the back of her hand and smiled at Shona. 'Little Iona has arrived safely and that's all that matters, isn't it?'

'We'll get you another dress, if that's what you want,' Ruairi promised, putting his glass down on the table and moving over to her. The room went suddenly quiet and the atmosphere seemed to thicken and grow heavier. Fliss realised that Nurse McLeish was staring at her and Ruairi unblinkingly, with her far-sighted blue eyes.

'There will be another wee one.' She touched Iona's dark head and then added something low and lilting in Gaelic. 'Within the year.' Everyone else was staring at the taibhsear as though what she said should be taken seriously. Then she gave a little shudder as though a ghost had stepped over her grave. 'Ach, babies; it's the best o' times when the wee ones are born.' And - just like that, the heavy atmosphere lifted, like the sun coming out after a thunderstorm.

'I'll get my coat and take Fliss home,' Murdo said.

But Ruairi forestalled him. 'Thanks, Murdo - I'll see Fliss back to the Wee Hoose.'

He walked into the hall and the family exchanged a telling look. He returned moments later with the ancient Burberry and unflattering sou'wester Fliss had worn earlier. Removing his Akubra from the deer's antlers, he shrugged on his waxed coat and helped Fliss into hers. Her arms were so heavy she could barely raise them high enough to slip into the sleeves of the riding mac.

Then they were out in the storm. Fliss was so tired that her vision blurred and the strong wind funnelling down the loch rocked her on her feet. Ruairi put his arm round her shoulders and drew her protectively into his side, shielding her from the wind that threatened to bowl her over. It took every ounce of Fliss's willpower not to turn her head, bury her face in his neck and pretend that it was the wind which had pushed her there.

She wanted the journey to the Wee Hoose to last forever but soon they were standing in the canopied porch under the security light, looking and feeling suddenly self-conscious in its unforgiving glare.

Ruairi bent his head to say something - but the wind carried his words away and Fliss shook her head to signify that she couldn't hear him. Removing his hat, he bent his dark head towards her and whispered in her ear.

'I've been wrong about you, Fliss. And I'm sorry.'

As he withdrew from her, his lips grazed her cheek. The wind gathered strength, pressing him forward and forcing him to hold onto the porch's wooden buttresses to prevent him from knocking her over. There was a confusion of limbs and flapping coats as long strands of Fliss's auburn hair whipped across their faces and the storm battered on around them. In spite of their best efforts, they found themselves standing so close together that it was an effort to focus on each other's flushed faces without their vision blurring.

Sensing it was what they both wanted, Fliss closed her eyes, raised her face and mutely, brazenly demanded to be kissed. She felt Ruairi take a step away from her and her heart sank at his rejection. But when she opened her eyes, she saw the flame burning within him - the uneven rise and fall of his chest and his hands balled into fists at his sides - and she realised how conflicted he was. She felt a sense of victory - she hadn't misread him; he wanted to kiss her as much as she wanted to be kissed. But like her, he was afraid of where the kiss might lead.

She watched warring emotions flicker across his face, saw the struggle as desire overruled good sense. Then he let out a slow breath, as though the fight was too much for him and he was glad it was over. Then he kissed her. The kiss was brief and exploratory. Almost as if he was trying it out for size, and didn't want to deepen and prolong it because he knew that way lay danger. Once they took that step there would be no turning back – for either of them.

Fliss felt behind her blindly for the door handle and pushed the heavy old door open with her bottom – knowing that an open invitation for him to enter the Dower House was written on her face. But evidently, he was stronger than she was. Taking a further step away from her, he raised his hand to her cheek and held it there for several long seconds. Then, with a regretful smile he bowed courteously, dropped his hand and then turned on his heel and disappeared into the inky, windswept darkness.

Lizzie Lamb

Chapter Twenty Five

After the storm subsided, Shona and her baby were driven back to her hotel on the far side of Kinloch Mara to be checked over by her family doctor. But not before she'd pressed a business card into Fliss's hand with a whispered promise.

'I owe you, Fliss. If there's ever anything I - or my family - can do for you, you have only to ask. If things don't work out here -' she gave Fliss a knowing look and nodded towards Ruairi who was carrying her bags to the Land Rover. 'Remember that you have friends on the other side of the loch . . . the bit where His Gorgeousness doesn't call all the shots. Seriously, I mean it.'

'I won't forget,' Fliss promised. Was she so transparent that everyone in Kinloch Mara knew her business, knew about her growing attraction for Ruairi? 'I want full visiting rights to Madam; you know that, don't you?'

She bent her head and kissed Iona, inhaling the intoxicating scent of vanilla, baby powder and milk that clung to her. It was also a convenient way of hiding her expression. She didn't want Shona - or anyone else - to have even an inkling of what had passed between her and Ruairi last night. Now, standing in the bright, rain-washed morning she wondered if the kiss they'd shared in the darkness wasn't some remnant of a fevered dream, conjured up by the storm and the stress of delivering Baby Iona.

'Tell me to mind my own business and - oh, hell, I've never been able to mind my own business so why should I start now? I sense something between you and Ruairi; something . . .' Shona was forestalled as Murdo opened the back passenger door and beckoned her to climb in. Handing Iona to Fliss she got in, wincing as she shuffled along the bench seat. Fliss kissed Iona's dark head one last time before handing her back to

Shona. 'Come and visit. Both of you.' She extended the invitation to Ruairi who had come round to check that mother and daughter were safely fastened in.

'We'll keep in touch,' he promised, not giving the slightest indication there was anything untoward in Shona's assumption that he and Fliss were an item. He closed Shona's door, climbed into the front passenger seat and rolled down the window. The warm look he sent Fliss made her breath catch in her throat. A surge of adrenaline sent hormones scudding through her veins and hot pins and needles travelling the length of her arms, down to her fingertips. 'Will you be in the Wee Hoose later, there's something I need to discuss with you?'

'Certainly. I'll be waiting for you.' She answered lightly, but trepidation knotted her stomach and her euphoria plummeted like mercury in a cooling thermometer. She was a fool, she castigated herself; it was only to be expected - he wanted to tell her that last night had been a mistake. He shouldn't have kissed her. She shouldn't get any ideas about what the kiss signified - it had happened in the heat of the moment; and now - in the cool light of day, he was furiously back-peddling.

'Later, then,' he gave her a brief smile before he wound up the window.

'Laters.'

Wearing a fixed smile, she stood until the Land Rover was out of sight and then let her shoulders slump. Crestfallen, she made her way into Tigh na Locha to fetch her mail. As she entered the hall, Isla sauntered downstairs in her dressing gown and tartan pyjamas although it was almost noon. Fliss wasn't in the mood for another close encounter of the barbed kind and was about to leave when Isla called her back.

'Fliss; wait - I have a favour to ask.'

'A favour. Really?' Fliss regarded her suspiciously; Isla was at her most dangerous when she was being charming. If Isla noticed her less than enthusiastic response, she gave no indication.

'I've got a stinker of a hangover and I'd love an Indian Head Massage - but I can't be arsed to get dressed and schlep all the way down to the Wee Hoose. Would you mind carrying out the treatment in my bedroom?' It was on the tip of Fliss's tongue to refuse but she changed her mind. There was bad blood between them. This might be a chance to consign the incident in the rose garden, telling her to *shutthefuckup* - and Isla's unfounded suspicions about herself and Murdo to the recycle bin.

'Sure. No problem - I'll go and fetch my equipment. I'll even throw in an eyebrow shape and upper lip wax - if you like.'

'I like,' Isla grinned and then shut her eyes as though the effort was too much. She stumbled her way towards the dining room while Fliss, trying to put Ruairi from her mind, left for the Wee Hoose.

Fifteen minutes later, Fliss was heating up a pot of wax and sorting through bottles of essential oils in Isla's bedroom. What had once been a large bedroom had been converted into a studio-cum-sitting room, with a futon in the corner doubling as a bed. The futon was almost buried under its own weight of discarded clothes, shoes, magazines, paperbacks and make-up. The only space Fliss could find to set out her stall was on a table which held a laptop, several notepads and a pile of sketchbooks.

Over by the window, a large easel had been placed to catch the morning light. Next to it was an X-shaped frame which held prints and sketches. In another corner, there was a kitchen unit complete with sink and draining board; and above it were shelves stacked with paints, inks and brushes. A wash line was strung diagonally across the room and drying prints and lithographs hung from it in lieu of laundry. The room smelled of paint, linseed oil and a heady, musky perfume - and something slightly earthy and mouldy smelling. Most likely traces of Isla's secret cannabis smoking sessions that went on up here.

Although distracted by Ruairi's parting shot, Fliss nevertheless found a free corner of her mind to decode the scene before her.

Here was an Isla she didn't know - one who was artistic and talented, too, by the look of things. She moved over to the cluttered dressing table where Isla had blue-tacked rough sketches for the therapy centre flyers around the mirror: a pen and ink drawing of Tigh na Locha overlaid with the centre's opening hours, contact details and an introductory offer of ten per cent off a range of therapies. Just as she was grudgingly conceding that Isla had done a good job, the artist -in-residence wandered in from the en suite bathroom and sat on the futon blow-drying her hair.

'I wouldn't go to a lot of trouble,' Fliss advised above the noise. 'You'll have to wash your hair after the Indian Head massage - because of the oils.'

'No problemo, my hair felt so skanky I couldn't let you touch it.'

'I've had to deal with a lot worse.' Fliss gestured for her to sit on a straight-backed wooden chair, feeling very much that they were circling round each other like dualists wondering who was going to score the first hit. Draping a towel over Isla's shoulders, she poured oil into the palm of her left hand, rubbed her hands together and applied a firm but light pressure on Isla's cranium.

'You did brilliantly last night.' Isla closed her eyes and let Fliss's fingers work their magic. 'The family is massively impressed. I must say - I didn't think you had it in you . . .'

'Thanks for the testimonial,' Fliss remarked sardonically, uncertain where Isla was going with the whole you're *my new best friend* act.

'That came out wrong. It was meant as a compliment.' Now Fliss was doubly suspicious. Isla only schmoozed you when she wanted something. Like when she'd invited her to the party in Elgin Crescent because Mitzi needed someone to run the therapy centre. And look where that had got her! 'By the end of today the story will be right round the loch. That - coupled with the flyers I've designed, will bring in the punters. The advance publicity will ensure that the Open Day is a great success, too. I think Mumma and Angus are hoping to invite the local press to cover it.'

'Good.' Fliss's fingers worked through Isla's hair and the scent from the oils intensified as her hands warmed to their task.

'Mumma said that Ruairi - *ouch*!'

'Sorry. Was the pressure too hard?'

'A bit.' Isla settled herself more comfortably in the chair, relaxed and closed her eyes. 'Mumma said that Ruairi,' she tensed at the mention of his name, clearly expecting Fliss's fingers to dig into her scalp for a second time. 'Mumma said that he was singing your praises to old Nurse McLeish shortly before Angus drove her home. Looks like you're flavour of the month . . .' Fliss stopped the massage and let the words hang in the air for a few seconds before continuing with her rhythmic kneading.

'Your point being?'

'My point is *this*,' Isla swung round to face her - straddling the chair cowboy fashion, with her arms across the back. 'Cat told me you're going to persuade Ruairi not to send her back to the crammer at the end of the summer. That you're going to help her get a work placement at the vet's in Port Urquhart.'

'I think Cat's being a little bit too optimistic. I merely suggested that she should -'

But Isla wasn't listening.

'So, what I wondered . . . what I *hoped* was - maybe you could do the same for me? Persuade Ruairi to let me concentrate on my art instead of going to university.'

'I really don't think . . .'

'Ask him to give me a year to gather together enough samples of my work to hold an exhibition in Port Urquhart next summer when the tourists return. Maybe even make it an annual event - THE PORT URQUHART ARTS FESTIVAL.' She sketched the letters in the air like it was already a done deal. 'After that, maybe a foundation course at a Scottish University with a view to transferring somewhere more - urban, to specialise for the last three years before graduating with honours.'

Clearly, Isla had great belief in her own abilities - but no surprises there.

'More urban?' Fliss knew exactly where this was leading.

'Yeah, like Chelsea Art School.' Isla gave a casual shrug, making it seem like she hadn't given the idea much thought. But Fliss knew that Isla did nothing without thorough planning and ensuring that all the odds were stacked in *her* favour.

'Chelsea?'

'That'd be my first choice. But I'd be quite happy to attend the Slade. I could live in the Elgin Crescent house in term time - thus saving Ruairi oodles of money on accommodation and just come home in the hols. I wouldn't need him to fund my degree course; my trust fund will take care of that. I'd even attend Edinburgh School of Art, if I had to - as a last resort, naturally. Much too close to Ruairi for comfort,' she laughed. 'You have his ear, Fliss; so - whatd'ya think?'

'Think?' Fliss gave her a severe look. 'I think you've overestimated my powers of persuasion and my standing with Ruairi. I merely *suggested* to Cat that she should work harder to improve her relationship with Ruairi and - maybe - after a month or two, have a frank discussion with him and tell him what she really wants to do with her life. Why don't you do the same?'

'What? Are you mad? You don't talk things over with Ruairi. You present him with fait accompli and leave him no room for manoeuvre.'

'Hasn't worked up until now - has it?' Fliss pointed out candidly, and then gestured for Isla to turn round so she could continue with the massage. 'Besides, up until last night Ruairi and I couldn't spend more than five minutes in each other's company without going for the jugular. Flavour of the month? I don't think so.'

'No, you're wrong. It may have been like that in the beginning, but Ruairi's mellowing. He's seen how hard you've worked; the way the therapy centre is taking shape and how - by some miracle - you've drawn Mumma away from London and back to Kinloch Mara, like she can't get enough of the place. That's *never* happened before.'

'He's said nothing to me.' Fliss gave a casual shrug although her heart sang as Isla's words sank in. Had she really - finally - won Ruairi over?

'No he wouldn't. Ruairi doesn't work like that. You have to work hard to earn his respect; his approval. But he gave me another lecture this morning about how little I contribute to the estate - compared to Cat and you. Especially *you.*'

Fliss thought of his whispered words last night. *I've been wrong about you, Fliss. And I'm sorry.*

'Really?'

'Really.'

'So why does he constantly scowl at me and look like he'd like to send me packing?'

'Unresolved Sexual Tension, sweetie. Plus - he's never been any good at admitting when he's wrong.' But Fliss only heard the first three words.

'What do you mean by - by . . . '

'Unresolved Sexual Tension? Oh, come on, Fliss; don't deny it. You two should get a room. Ouch - that hurt -' Isla said as Fliss's nails inadvertently grazed along her scalp, 'and proves I'm right. I've seen the way you look at him when you think no one's looking. Like you can't get enough of him. Like you'd like to eat him up in one greedy gulp.' Hot colour swept over Fliss and she was glad that Isla was facing away from her.

'I do *not,*' she protested weakly. But Isla was having none of it.

'Of course you do. And as for my sainted brother . . . brooding Mr Rochester is his default mode. But the way he looks at you? As if he can't quite figure you out? Why, he could give Darcy, Heathcliff and Rochester a run for their money,' she laughed. 'It's as if he can't make up his mind whether to shag you witless or have you thrown off the estate and out of temptation's way.'

'No. No, you've got it all wrong.'

Or maybe, just maybe, Isla had it all right!

'Can't remember the last time he had a girlfriend,' Isla carried on blithely. 'Let alone got laid. Unless, of course he's been visiting the massage parlours and lap dancing clubs in Hong Kong.'

'Isla! That's a vile thing to say. Besides, I thought . . . well, Mitzi told me that he's one of the most eligible bachelors in the western isles. That there are aristocratic girls desperate to be the next Lady Urquhart.'

'And they are! However, he hasn't shown interest in any of them, not since Princess Fiona did a runner and left him nursing a broken heart and a bruised ego. And, I will admit that in the past Cat and I *may* have gone out of our way to scare a few off. Not that it took much doing - they're such lightweights. But you're different, made of sterner stuff. You've stayed the course, weathered Ruairi's bad moods and made him eat his words. Not quite what Cat and I had in mind.'

'*Had in mind*? Is there something I'm missing here?' Fliss took hold of Isla's skinny shoulders and spun her round.

'I thought - well, Cat and I thought - that with Mumma's plans for the therapy centre resurrected, Ruairi would be too occupied trying to stop it happening. Too busy getting rid of *you*, that he'd have no time left to devote to *us*. Bringing us to heel; grounding us; stopping our allowances - that sort of thing . . .'

'I don't get it. Don't you want Mitzi's business to flourish?'

'Well it doesn't really matter one way or the other, does it? She's going to marry Angus and have so much money that she'll be able to bathe in champagne. The therapy centre will come a very poor second to *that*.'

'Don't you think that Mitzi *needs* the therapy centre? To prove to Angus that there's more to her than half-brained business ideas, a secret stash of unsalable goods under the stairs and a predisposition to run away from her responsibilities to you and Cat. She should be the one disciplining you, not Ruairi,' Fliss pointed out, not quite believing that she was fighting Ruairi's corner.

'Urquharts don't have to prove *anything* to anybody,' Isla rounded on her, plainly not considering it Fliss's place to tell it like it is. 'Not that I'd expect *you* to understand that.'

'Don't come over all daughter-of-the-house with me, Isla Urquhart. It might have worked once when I was actually in awe of you; but not any more. As for running away from responsibility - like mother, like daughter? You have a God given talent - why do you have to go all the way to London to attend art school? What are *you* running away from?'

Tellingly, Isla's gaze slid towards a silver-framed photograph on her dressing table - a family group of Ruairi, Murdo, Mitzi, Cat and herself enjoying a barbeque on the beach. She looked about fourteen or fifteen, so it must have been taken a good five or six years earlier. Murdo had his arm round her shoulder and she was leaning into him as though he was her hero and it was the most natural thing in the world. He looked like he'd won the lottery and was the happiest man alive.

Fliss remembered the atmosphere in the Land Rover when Murdo had picked them up from the airport. The way he'd taken Isla by the shoulders as though he wanted to shake all the silliness and posturing out of her. The burning look they'd exchanged in the layby and how he'd quieted her with a glance. Now she got it:

Mitzi was running away from her widowhood.

Isla was running away from her feelings for Murdo.

'Unresolved sexual tension? Well, you'd know all about that - wouldn't you?' Fliss looked at the photograph and then slowly back at Isla. 'Do you have some inflated idea of your own importance and think that Murdo's not your equal? If you can't see Murdo's worth then you're a fool.'

Isla got up, pushed the chair back, removed the towel from her shoulders and threw it down on the chair seat like a gauntlet. 'Not such a fool that I haven't noticed you and Murdo huddled together. Laughing. Sharing drinks on the veranda of the Wee Hoose. Him visiting you every day.'

'On Ruairi's instructions,' Fliss put in, keeping her temper. 'To check that everything's ready for the Open Day? Make your mind up, Isla. Either its Ruairi I'm after, or Murdo.'

'Or both,' Isla spat out jealously.

'Oh - kay,' Fliss let out a long breath. 'And are Angus and Jaimsie the piper on my *To Do List*, too? You really are a dog in-the-manger, aren't you?'

'Meaning?'

'Meaning you don't want Murdo but you don't want anyone else to have him, either.'

'Think you've got it all figured out, don't you?' Isla's blue eyes blazed with suppressed anger.

Fliss shrugged. 'Forget it - this conversation is getting us nowhere. I'll finish your head massage and -'

'Tell me one thing,' Isla demanded, grabbing Fliss urgently by the wrist. 'Will you speak to Ruairi on my behalf?'

'As I've tried to explain, I haven't offered to act as go-between for Cat and Ruairi I don't think I should for you, either. Talk to your brother, instead of pushing him into a corner and you might be surprised at his reaction.' She pulled her wrist free of Isla's death grip and rubbed the reddened skin with her free hand. 'Your family needs to sit down and talk to each other.'

'Spare me the psychobabble. I don't need your insightful comments and neither does my family.'

'Suit yourself.'

Fliss gave another shrug and Becky's acronym sprung into mind. P.I.N.T.A - pain in the arse. Although monumental pain in the arse would be nearer the mark this morning.

'Oh don't worry,' Isla assured Fliss, her eyes hard as flint. 'I intend to do just that.'

'Nothing new there, then,' Fliss commented unconcernedly.

If she was burning her bridges with Miss Isla - up - her - own - bottom Urquhart, so be it. She gave Isla a *bring it on* challenging look, the one that had seen her through many dodgy situations on the mean streets of Pimlico, and gathered her equipment together.

The therapy centre Open Day was next week, she was half way to earning Ruairi Urquhart's approval and was hero of the hour for delivering little Iona safely.

What was the worst Isla could do?

Chapter Twenty Six

Fliss was standing by the kitchen sink deep in thought, staring across the beach towards the loch when Ruairi called out to her.

'Fliss?'

'In the kitchen.' She pulled herself out of her daydream, turned round and acted as though she was totally cool about everything that had happened last night. But her heart was thumping and her mouth was dry as sand when Ruairi walked into the kitchen.

'Fliss - about last night . . .' he cut to the chase.

Knees buckling and blood pressure rocketing, Fliss was glad she had the sink unit to lean against for support. She shut her mind to how sexy he looked in combat trousers, faded Superdry t-shirt and ancient gilet. She ignored the way the light from the window gave his hair a dull bloom, like a chough's wing; and how his eyes - usually so flinty and full of mistrust - were now regarding her with a mixture of amusement and something deeper.

Something more dangerous.

'Tea. You'd like a cup of tea wouldn't you?' To maintain her tenuous grip on reality she fetched mugs, teabags and sugar out of the cupboard and made a great play of arranging them on the island unit; using the action to delay the moment when he said: *last night was a mistake. Can we put it behind us and pretend it never happened?*

'No, I wouldn't like a cup of tea. Can you please stop behaving like a demented Stepford Wife and listen to me for a few minutes.' He leaned against the larder unit, folded his arms across his chest and gave her an impatient look.

Minutes? What did he have to say that would take *minutes* to deliver? Clearly, things were a lot more serious than she thought.

Distracted, she started spooning sugar into Ruairi's mug - six heaped spoons of the stuff.

'Are you trying to give me diabetes?' He laughed, covered the floor in three long strides, took the spoon out of her hand and placed the sugar out of harm's way. Then, quite unexpectedly, he took her hands in his and stilled them. Aware that she had to maintain an appearance of dignity if she was to cope with his rejection, Fliss freed herself from his grasp. 'Relax.' He gave her a lopsided smile. 'I just wanted to thank you for everything you did last night. And to say . . .'

'It was nothing - n- othing,' she stammered. But when he captured her hands for the second time, she didn't snatch them away.

'Hardly nothing. You started the night off as first responder and by the end of it had safely delivered a baby. And throughout you remained cool, calm and collected.' His eyes never left her face, and his thumb slowly massaged the blue veins on the underside of her wrist. He looked as if he was a different person this morning and was seeing the world - and her - through new eyes. And it was a revelation to him.

'Well,' she gulped as his touch did crazy things to her pulse, 'probably two out of the three.'

He laughed at her quip and then was suddenly sober. 'I've been hard on you since you set foot in Kinloch Mara, Fliss - and I'm sorry.' The last three words made goose bumps break out all over her; and when he bent his dark head and kissed her upturned wrists, she found it hard to breath. But she knew she had to concentrate, ignore the siren call of her body and say her piece.

'You did what you felt was right. But you were wrong; *very* wrong. You've made my life difficult - almost impossible - because of a preconceived idea you had about me and my intentions. Which have *always* been to make the therapy centre a success, to hope that I might be regarded as a friend of the family - and be treated as such - for as long as I remain in Kinloch Mara.'

'Believe me - I've been a lot harder on myself.'

'Oh really? In what way?'

213

She snatched her hands away. It would take more than honeyed words and the rhythmic stroking of her erogenous zones to win her over. His apology was long overdue and she wanted it in its entirety: chapter, verse and available for download.

'You know - yomping over the hills, hardly getting any sleep, taking no pleasure in food and drink.' He ignored her less than enthusiastic response. 'Snapping at the staff - including poor old Murdo. Everything tasted like ashes in my mouth; and when I did managed to swallow something it stuck in my craw, because I knew - deep down - how unfair I was being towards you. But I couldn't stop myself suspecting the worst of you; it became a compulsion. A daily fix I couldn't do without.'

'And -'she prompted.

'I want to make amends.'

'How do you propose doing that?'

'Well - for starters . . .' He ran his fingers through his thick hair, making it stand on end like a cockscomb. 'I thought I'd ask you out on a date.'

'A date?'

'Yes. What do you say? I've got to sail over to the island in the middle of the loch - An t-Eileen Molach - to check the equipment.'

'What sort of equipment?'

'We monitor the island for evidence of global warming and pass on the data to Scottish Natural Heritage - Dualchas Nadair na h-Alba, if you want the full Gaelic version. What's so funny?' he frowned.

'Is *come over to the island and help me check my equipment,*" the Gaelic equivalent of "come up and see my etchings"?'

'It is, if you want it to be,' he informed her with a wicked grin. His cobalt eyes darkened and he gave her a searching look, clearly trying to gauge her mood. It was as if he was wondering how to proceed, how to win her over; little knowing that he had her at: *I've been wrong about you and I'm sorry.*

'I - I'd like to sail over to the island with you. For scientific purposes, you understand.' She tried to hold out against him, to prolong her cool regard but a bubble of happiness threatened her outward show of sang-froid. It welled in her throat and came out as a hiccup of laughter.

Everything was going to be all right between them. Inside she was doing a happy dance, while to all outward appearances she remained as he'd said earlier: cool, calm and collected.

'Purely academic,' he agreed, nodding solemnly. 'Now?'

'What - *now*?'

'It's the global warning, you see, it waits for no man.'

'I thought that was time and tide,' she corrected.

'Time, tide *and* global warming wait for no man. I'm shocked to find that amusing Miss Bagshawe.' He tutted and shook his head like an old professor of climatology as she laughed.

'There.' She covered her face with her right hand and when she lowered it, her expression was grave. 'Better?'

'Much better.' There was a definite glint in his eye as he took a step towards her, pressing her back against the sink. 'Still, it all might be an act. You might come over to the island, help me check the equipment and collect stats and then not take it seriously.'

'Oh, I'm taking this seriously; believe me.' Boldly, she bought her face closer to his and concentrated on his lips, the stubble round his chin, the laughter lines fanning out from his gorgeous blue eyes. Then his features swam out of focus and she was forced to close her eyes or go cross-eyed. So she didn't see his head bending towards her, or the corresponding flush of colour spread along his cheeks as he drew closer. But she felt the kiss when it came, so soft and light that it was over in a second - leaving her wanting more. She let out a little moue of regret that was matched by Ruairi's throaty groan, as though he'd tired of their playacting

'Enough, Fliss. For the love of . . .'

Putting his hands on either side of her hips, he drew her into his body. His arousal was unmissable and her nipples hardened in response as warm heat, like melted dark chocolate being freed from the centre of an exotic desert, spread through her. They kissed properly for the first time. It was an untidy kiss - a clash of lips, teeth and questing tongues as they sought out the essence of each other. Then Ruairi placed one hand behind her neck and pulled her more tightly into the clinch as though he couldn't get enough of her.

His stubble grazed her soft skin. She felt his heart hammering against her breasts and revelled in the knowledge that she had won this proud man over. He released her from the kiss and she became aware of the hard edge of the sink against the small of her back, their rapid breathing and the bruised feel to her lips. She raised her fingers to his mouth, wonderingly, and he drew them into his mouth and sucked each one in turn – his eyes never leaving her face. Lost in the moment, she tipped her head back and closed her eyes as he took the weight of it in his hand. Then, after long seconds, he released her fingers with a playful nip.

'I take it that means,' he coughed, to clear his voice, husky with desire, 'that you would like to come to the island?'

She slipped sideways out of his grasp and made a great play of straightening her clothes. 'For purely scientific reasons you understand,' she said firmly. Although she guessed that the sparking light in her grey-green eyes made her intentions pretty clear.

'Very well, you'll need to change,' he said pragmatically, although his roving gaze seemingly revelled in the sight of her tight fitting t-shirt and shorts. 'Otherwise you'll be a feast for the midges. Trousers, socks and a long sleeved top. We'll both spray ourselves with insect repellent - the midges will be dancing after last night's storm. But there's a beach on the island - the island's name: An t-Eileen Molach means shingly beach - where the midges will leave us alone. We can have a picnic there.'

'Oh, should I make sandwiches and a flask of coffee,' she reached out for the cupboards but he caught her hand and drew her into his arms again.

'In true Blue Peter fashion, there's one on the boat I made earlier.'

'*You* made earlier?' she raised an eyebrow.

'Okay, the kitchen staff made earlier. What's the point in being laird if you have to make your own sandwiches?' he asked and gave her another stonking great kiss before freeing her. 'Five minutes. Then I'm gone.' He glanced at his watch and then gave her a get-on-with-it look that turned her insides to molten chocolate once more.

'I'll be down in four.'

'Three and a half,' he admonished and rooted in the fridge in search of something to drink while she scooted upstairs, with wings on her feet.

Chapter Twenty Seven

Ruairi led the way through the rhododendron bushes and along a well-trodden path before fetching up at boathouse. A jetty reached out into the loch like a pointing finger and moored at the end was a boat which took Fliss's breath away. She'd been expecting a dinghy with an outboard motor and a couple of life jackets tossed casually in the back to take them to the island. Instead, here was a beautiful launch all burnished teak and glass - with a cabin taking up half the deck, and a scallop edged canopy on brass stanchions covering the remainder.

'Wh- what is it?'

'It's a 1920's saloon launch commissioned by my great- great-grandparents shortly before their wedding. See the name?'

'*The Heart of the Highlands*. Oh, that's so romantic.' Embarrassed by her outburst Fliss ran along the jetty to touch the gleaming prow with its brass fittings, coiled ropes and inlaid teak gratings.

'My great-great-grandfather was gassed in the closing stages of the First World War,' Ruairi explained when he caught up with her. 'A hurried marriage was arranged because he wasn't expected to live - and, less romantically, because the Urquharts could see my great-great grandmother's considerable dowry slipping out of their hands. At one point, it was uncertain whether the priest would be administering the last rites or conducting a wedding service. My great-great-grandmother nursed him back to health and the boat was their wedding present to each other.'

'How romantic is *that*?' Fliss asked as she clambered on board and then grimaced as she realised she'd used the word *romantic* twice in under five minutes. He must think her an idealistic airhead! 'So was it a love match in the end?' she asked, to move the conversation along.

'Oh yes, they weren't denied their happy ending,' Ruairi smiled. Then his face clouded over briefly, as if he was thinking about his and Fiona's story, which didn't have such a happy conclusion. The more Fliss learned about their disastrous engagement, the more she longed to find out. But today - she told herself firmly - was neither the time nor the place for twenty questions.

They climbed on board *The Heart of the Highlands* and the deck rocked beneath their feet. Fliss let out a little yelp and grabbed at his sleeve. That appeared to bring him out of his dream because he caught her by the elbow, then after a moment's hesitation, pulled her into his arms. He tilted her chin and regarded her with apparent wonderment; and then he spread his hands along the small of her back and bent his head to kiss her. Their mouths touched - and the gentle swaying of the boat at its moorings was forgotten as his hand found the hollow between her shoulder blades and he deepened the kiss. Fliss's heart lurched at the intensity of emotion channelled into the kiss and twined her fingers into his thick dark hair. When they finally pulled apart, they were both breathless and she was surprised that she could stand unsupported.

'Woops.' She tried to make light of her reaction to being kissed so thoroughly, but the current pushed the launch against the side of the jetty and she was pushed into his arms. 'I'm such a landlubber,' she laughed, moving from him on the pretext of examining the beautiful launch.

She let out a long, shaky breath. Time to slow things down or she'd burst into flames and the vintage boat would be reduced to a pile of charred timbers beneath her feet. As if reading her mind, Ruairi gave a rueful smile and then guided her to a companion seat near the helm, located in the middle of the deck. He slipped a life jacket over his head and then passed one to her and left her to tie the fastenings. Patently thinking it was best to keep physical contact between them to a minimum.

'We're sailing over to An t-Eileen Molach,' he said. His voice was gruff and betrayed his pent-up emotion.

'*Shingly beach*. See, I remembered.'

'So you did. I'll reward you later.' He gave her a look of such promise that she shivered with anticipation at what might unfold on the island, far away from prying eyes.

She smiled to herself, secretly wondering at the change in him - from bad tempered wolf to sexy, beguiling laird. Surely, this change in him - in her - was too sudden to be more than pure physical reaction. Too unexpected to be real? She held on to the thought and used it to armour herself against the full onslaught of his charm which was slowly chipping away at her resolve. All she wanted to do was lay down with him on the padded couch under the glass-sided saloon and make love until the sun sank below the western hills.

But she knew that wasn't a good idea and wrapped her arms around herself as her skin prickled all over with goose bumps. In contrast, Ruairi appeared in command of his emotions as he turned the key in the ignition and steered *The Heart of the Highlands* out into the open water. A picnic basket had been placed on a table in the middle of the glassed-in saloon next to an apple box containing scientific equipment. So it was a bona fide expedition after all! That would give them something to think and talk about other than themselves and keep the atmosphere light and teasing.

Not to mention help them to keep their hands off each other.

'I can't believe the change in the weather from last night. Little Iona was certainly born on the back of a storm.'

'It often happens that a summer storm blows itself out as quickly as it arrives.' Clearly, he was following her lead and manoeuvring the conversation onto less controversial topics. 'Don't worry about sailing conditions - the weather's set fair for today. I checked the forecast and the barometer. Apart from which, the boat has a draft of two feet - which means it will float in very shallow water, making it ideal for mooring close to the island.'

They fell silent as *The Heart of the Highlands* made its way along the loch, the beautiful scenery providing the necessary distraction to the thoughts running through their heads.

The gently sloping hills on either side of the loch appeared to touch and Fliss was disappointed to think that their journey would soon be over because they'd reached the far end of the loch. But as they rounded each promontory, the loch stretched out before them all the way to the sea. The sky was a pure, clear blue and at vanishing point, where the faint outline of an island could be seen, puffy clouds hung over the distant hills.

It was all too perfect for words.

The wind ruffled Fliss's hair and she was filled with a sense of happiness and well-being. She felt so at home in this beautiful setting, drinking in the colours and scents of Kinloch Mara, that her senses - already under siege from Ruairi's passionate kisses - were momentarily overwhelmed. A sob rose in her throat. Feeling suddenly foolish - and anxious to escape Ruairi's knowing gaze, she leaned over the side of the launch and trailed her fingers in the water as the launch chugged along.

'Be careful. The *each-uisge* has been known to drag unsuspecting maidens down to his lair.'

'*Ech ooshskya,*' Fliss copied his pronunciation as she took her place back by his side. 'Sounds like the Gaelic for whisky: *ooshkie bah-ha*. So it must be something to do with water?'

'You learn quickly, young apprentice,' Ruairi laughed and put his free hand on her shoulder. 'Must be all that Klingon you picked up as a child.' Fliss had a suitable retort ready, but then she saw the laughter in his eyes and smiled back. 'Sorry, I couldn't resist.'

'Well, you should have tried harder - Klingon, indeed.' She pretended to be offended but her heart leapt in her ribcage and she revelled in his praise. 'I - I *would* love to learn Gaelic,' she began hesitantly, 'so I can speak it to my clients. But . . .' *I'm only passing through. Like the birds that fly away at the end of the season.*

The unspoken thought hung in the air and Fliss experienced a pang of sadness. She never wanted to leave this beautiful place and for the first time in years she felt that she actually *belonged somewhere*. Then she pulled herself up sharply, no point in spoiling the day worrying over what the future held, so she changed the subject.

'What is an *each-uisge*, exactly? A monster?'

'A water horse. The old legend tells how An t-Eileen Molach was guarded by a particularly fierce one. But a fearless Urquhart ancestress - for, it goes without saying that Urquhart women laugh in the face of danger - sailed over to confront the beast and demand that she and her descendants be allowed to land on the island.'

Urquhart women laugh in the face of danger.

Fliss was transported back to the night of the party when Isla had been totally unconcerned at the prospect of being arrested and charged with affray. Now she realised it was her way of scoring points off Ruairi, no matter what the cost to herself.

'And?' she prompted, dismissing Isla from her thoughts.

'The water horse agreed, on condition that he was allowed to father a child on her.' He took in Fliss's expression and laughed. 'Men, huh? I'm only telling you how it was in those days.'

'Not *so* different from now. Go on,' she sent him an arch, *I don't believe any of this,* look.

'A child was born. A boy - with sand in his hair and on his chest. A sure sign of union between a human and a water horse. This was the Urquhart who conquered Kinloch Mara all the way to the sea and claimed it for himself - with the help from his father the water horse.'

'That is a weird and wonderful story. But everything about Kinloch Mara is so magical that I'm half inclined to believe it.' She looked up at him, feeling a sense of freedom at being able to reveal - at last - how much she'd grown to love this place. He smiled, and his grip on her shoulder tightened as he swallowed hard and visibly struggled to hide his emotion.

'Is that what you really think about Kinloch Mara?' he asked, staring ahead with the wind ruffling his dark hair. It was plain that he didn't want to look at her and influence her in any way. Fliss, sensing that her answer mattered and that it was important to be completely honest, thought for several long seconds before she spoke.

'This *is* a special place. Supernatural, almost.'

'Ah; you feel it, too.' After that, there seemed nothing left to say and they remained silent - watching the dark mass of An t-Eileen Molach draw nearer.

The island was almost entirely covered in tall pine trees, different from any she'd seen before. Some were past their prime and leaned drunkenly against their neighbour, like they'd had a hard night carousing in Port Urquhart. Others grew tall and straight - a metaphor for all that was best in highland manhood.

Ruairi threw the engines into reverse and tossed a small anchor with a buoy attached to it over the side.

'Come on,' he pulled Fliss to her feet. They'd anchored a little way off from the shore and Fliss looked warily over the side of the launch.

'How do we . . .'

By way of an answer Ruairi took off his boat shoes, laced them together, slung them round his neck and then dropped over the side. He held up his hands and asked Fliss to pass him the picnic basket.

'I'll come back for the scientific stuff - and you.'

'I can wade ashore.'

'What. And risk losing you to the *each-uisge*? No way,' he laughed at her stubborn expression. 'You stay in the launch; then you can pass me the apple box on the next trip, otherwise I'll have to climb back on board for it.'

'Yes, Cap'n,' she saluted, ironically. He waded through the shallows with the picnic basket, returning minutes later for the apple box of test tubes and monitoring equipment. Then it was her turn. She didn't want him to think she was a wimpy southerner, so she slipped over the side into water which came up to her crotch.

'Uh - uh. M - My God, you didn't tell me the water was so *cold*.'

'You are *such* a Sassenach. The loch gets its waters from the hills - although it is warmed by the Gulf Stream.'

'It doesn't feel like it.'

'That's why I told you to wait until I fetched you. Now we're both wet. Come on, I'll get a fire going on the beach and soon warm us up.' He took her by the hand and led her through the shallows; the look he shot her enough to send the blood racing through her frozen extremities and bring the colour back to her cheeks. As they waded ashore, Fliss hoped that the cold waters would cool their ardour and help to keep her mind on higher things.

Half an hour later, Ruairi had a fire going on the beach well away from nearby vegetation, although after last night's downpour he'd judged it unlikely that anything would catch a stray spark.

'The trees are so tall and slender,' Fliss remarked, looking upwards as she drank hot chocolate laced with hazelnut syrup while her trousers dried on a makeshift clothes horse. 'I'm used to the trees in London parks being deciduous and wide enough to give shade from the sun. But these are magnificent.'

'These are the remnants of the Caledonian Forest that once spread over Scotland. When climate change brought a wetter, warmer environment their roots became waterlogged and they died. There are clusters of the original Caledonian Forest to be found throughout Scotland - our nearest is Beinn Eighe near Inverewe.'

'A bit like overwatering the plants on the kitchen windowsill?'

'Exactly. Now . . . *Dulchas Nadair na h - Alba* - Scottish Natural Heritage,' he paused and shot her a considering look. 'Are you sure you want to hear all this? Most women aren't interested.'

'I'm not *most* women.' He gave her an old fashioned look that suggested he'd worked that one out for himself. 'I want to learn more about this island and your heritage.' The steady look, she sent him demanded that he take her interest seriously.

'Okay; but I warn you, I can be quite evangelical on the subject.'

'I'd expect nothing less.' She was surprised when he leapt to his feet and held out his hand.

'Come on. If you dare.'

'Dare what?'

'See the island from the best vantage point. Be warned though, you'll need a head for heights and nerves of steel . . .'

'I braved the water horse, didn't I?'

'Aye, ye did that,' he said in his best highland brogue. 'Yer a brave lassie, and no mistake - braving the habitat of the *each-uisge*, but . . .'

'But nothing! Let me put my trousers back on.' She was very aware of the Brazilian cut lacy underwear beneath the tartan rug she'd wrapped round herself like a sarong. She got dressed - much as she had done as a child on Clacton sands when she'd changed into her swimming costume on the beach beneath a large bath towel. She saw his amused, engaged look as she tossed the rug aside and stood in her still damp clothing.

'Don't laugh at my modesty. You have the blood of an *each-uisge* running through your veins. I'm not sure you're entirely to be trusted - alone on this island with an unmarried female.'

'Very proper,' he drawled. The look he gave her suggested that the same thoughts had been running through his head on a loop ever since their arrival on the island. Taking her hand he led the way through the plantation of pine trees, their passage muffled by a thick carpet of pine needles and moss. Eventually, they stopped at the foot of one tree which looked three quarters dead and leaned against its neighbour at a forty five degree angle.

'If you're sure.' Ruairi gave her a chance to back out of whatever he had in mind.

'I'm sure. Bring it on.

'Very well. You go first.'

'First?' She hung back while he demonstrated how to climb the pine tree using a long knotted rope dangling from its canopy.

'I'm right behind you. I'll catch you if you slip. Don't worry; the Urquharts have been climbing this tree for as long as I can remember.'

She was about to say: *But I'm not an Urquhart*, but stopped herself in time. Instead, she substituted: 'If the tree's dead, why don't you chop it up for firewood?'

'I'll pretend I didn't hear that, Miss Bagshawe. It might look dead to you, but its home to crypto-fauna - small creatures you can't see but who thrive in this woodland habitat.'

'Okay. I'll try not to tread on any - crypto fauna? - as I make my way along it.' She shinned up the tree branch by branch, trying to ignore that Ruairi had a grandstand view of her bottom and still wet underwear pressing against the thin stuff of her trousers.

Luckily, she'd always been a bit of a tomboy so it didn't take long before she dismissed the thought and relished in the challenge instead. Soon she was at the top of the tree leaning into its canopy and shading her eyes as she looked out towards the horizon.

'I didn't realise that Kinloch Mara was so *big*,' she said as Ruairi came up behind her. Two thoughts immediately sprang to mind: one, it was no surprise that he was proud of his inheritance. And, secondly - no wonder mothers in the Highlands and Islands considered him a catch for their daughters, although relatively impoverished.

'You climb trees surprisingly well - for a girl,' he teased, standing with his arms on either side of her, his chin resting on top of her head. 'See there? Straight ahead at twelve o'clock?' She caught his signature aftershave as he pointed out over the pines and his sleeve grazed her cheek. She took in a deep breath and held it. 'The sea. The old Gael name for our settlement is Ceann Loch na Mara: the head of the loch by the sea. But over time it became Kinloch Mara - easier to say, I guess.'

Fliss sighed deeply and leaned back against his chest almost without thinking. 'I love the history and culture as well as the scenery of Kinloch Mara. Bit different to Walthamstow where I grew up - or Pimlico where I have my flat.'

'Everyone's location is exotic to someone else,' he breathed into her ear and turned her round to face him, taking care that she didn't lose her balance. 'You're exotic and intoxicating; know that?' She shook her head and looked down at the ground and then wished she hadn't. She suddenly had a sense of how high up they were and lost her nerve and her footing. She lurched forward and clung to him as though her life depended on it and the intense moment passed. 'Come on, let's climb down and I'll show you more of the island. Then we can take our samples and head back.'

Five minutes later they were carrying the apple box between them, the test tubes and phials clinking together like champagne glasses as Ruairi explained how global warming was raising the temperature of the water in the loch.

'We have to send water samples to be analysed to see if the water is becoming more - or less, acidic. Changes in the loch's temperature and alkali balance affects what can grow on the island. Some of the rare native species we've got here: tooth and wood hedgehog fungus could be swamped by foreign invaders such as New Zealand Pygmy Weed and Nuttall's Pondweed. The peat bogs on the island are host to an amazing collection of dragonflies and we don't want to lose that because the climate's becoming milder and damper.'

'Tooth fungus?' she questioned as she watched him fill the phials with water from a peat bog where weeds grew round the margins. It was the perfect habitat for dragonflies and she longed to return in August to see them shed their nymph skins and morph into beautiful creatures with iridescent wings.

'Yes. Tooth fungus - here's some. When Cat was little she called it the 'tooth fairy' and thought that the fairy lived on our very own island. I didn't like to disillusion her.' Fliss knelt down and examined some pinkish brown stripes on the fungus which did look like a row of teeth.

'You know, Cat's a great girl and has been very helpful, setting up the therapy centre.' Maybe this would be a good time to broach the subject of her training as a veterinary nurse. 'She's practical and hardworking and I - I've had several heart-to-hearts with her.' She took a deep breath before continuing. 'She says she doesn't want to go to university but would like to become a veterinary nurse.'

'She does?' he looked surprised.

'She's got a great way with animals and . . .' she didn't say any more because she could tell that he was mulling over the idea.

'A veterinary nurse? Hmm. I suppose I *could* call in a few favours and organise some experience for her at the vet's practice in Port Urquhart over the summer and see how she gets on. To be honest, I was beginning to think that Cat wasn't cut out for academic life, given her last few reports.'

'That'd be great,' Fliss added casually, not wanting to overplay her hand. 'It'd keep her occupied, on the estate and far away from London and temptation. I'm sure Murdo would be happy to keep an eye on her.'

'I'll give it some thought.' Then he changed the subject. 'While you were drying out your clothes I checked that the monitoring equipment hadn't been damaged in the gale, and took the latest readings of air pollution so I can email the results to Scottish Natural Heritage.' It was clear that he took the job seriously and Fliss felt sudden sympathy for him - being pulled away from his degree course when his father had died.

'*Dulchas Nadair na h - Alba.*' She read the name on the label Ruairi stuck over the phial, rolling the strange vowel sounds around her tongue.

'Work's over for today. I brought you out onto the island as a reward for everything you did last night, not to use you as an unpaid lab assistant. Come here.' He spread the rug over a small mound of moss and springy heather which, as she sank down onto it, Fliss discovered was almost like a mattress topper. 'Fancy a wee nip?' He brought a hip flask out of the pocket of his combat pants and passed it to her. Fliss wasn't sure that she'd ever learn to like whisky but she took a sip and handed the flask back to him. He leaned on his elbow and twined one long strand of her hair round his finger, using it to pull her closer.

'Freckles,' he grinned. 'You've got freckles. Lots of them. Must be your auburn hair and pale skin,' he reflected, apparently in no hurry to release her. He traced his fingers over her cheeks and lips and examined her face, minutely. 'Quite a combination; and your eyes, are they grey or green?'

'Bit of both, I guess.' All her life, Fliss had hated her freckles, but given the way he was examining her face, she thought she might learn to love them.

During the pleasurably drawn out seconds, Fliss reached out and curled her fingers round the exposed skin on the underside of his wrist where the ragged cuff of his shirt fell short. Reaction to the touch sparked between them like an electrical charge. For a moment, the world became peripheral, the entire universe contained in this sunlit glade where the light filtered through the pine trees and the whine of midges sounded in their ears.

Then Fliss took hold of his other wrist and, catching him off guard, rolled him onto his back and straddled him. Unhurriedly, without taking her eyes off his face, she undid the buttons of his shirt and traced her fingers over the fine dark hair on his chest. Putting his hands behind his head, he closed his eyes and allowed her to trace the line from the firm column of his neck to just above the waistband of his combat pants where the dark hair tapered downwards. Although he appeared unmoved by her far from clinical examination, she felt the rapid beat of his heart beneath her outstretched palm and his penis press against the inside of her thigh, strong and impatient to be released.

'Looking for something?' he asked huskily, keeping his eyes closed.

'To see if the legend of the *each-uisge* is true and you've got sand on your chest.'

'This much *is* true.' He flipped her over on to her back and putting his hands on either side of her face, pressed the length of his body against hers. Now it was Fliss's turn to close her eyes and part her lips as she revelled in the length of him and his weight on her. He let out a sexy growl, lowered his head and kissed her with such diligence that for long moments all that could be heard was their ragged breaths and the soughing of the wind in the pines. Fliss untucked his shirt and moved her hands inside so that her fingers fanned out across the strong planes of his lower back. Then, carried away by his kisses, she slid her fingers underneath his belt and raised her pelvis towards him instinctively, seductively.

That seemed to ignite a new fire within them and she parted her lips and touched his tongue with her own. She felt his stubble graze along her jawline as her hands cupped his buttocks and she pulled him against her. Giving a deep rumble of regret Ruairi pulled away from her, fastened his shirt and tucked it back in his trousers.

'God, Fliss - I.' He appeared unable to form words, let alone form them into a sentence that would express his feelings.

Aware that she'd acted uncharacteristically, Fliss came to her senses and touched her hot cheeks with the back of her hands. What must he think of her? Get her on the island and she loses all her inhibitions, practically rips his clothes off him and offers herself up on a plate. When he turned round, he had the dazed expression of a man who'd been struck by a *coup de foudre* and had found the experience unnerving, yet strangely pleasurable.

'I think I'd better warn the *each-uisge* just what he's up against. He won't stand a chance,' Ruairi gave a throaty laugh as he folded up the rug and gathered the picnic hamper together. 'We'd better head back for the Heart of the Highlands - otherwise, I can't guarantee my behaviour.'

'I'm sorry - of course,' Fliss bent over the apple box containing the samples to hide her embarrassment.

'Don't be sorry, Fliss.' Taking her by the arms, he raised her to her feet. 'I'm not. It's just that,' he took a deep breath and rushed on. 'Look I'm not sure where this is going; so let's not force the pace. Okay'

'Okay.'

'Up until last night we couldn't stand to be in the same room as each other and . . .'

'And?'

'Well, all *this* has been a bit . . . unexpected.' Evidently reading her expression, he hurried to qualify his statement. 'Not that I have a problem with that. It's simply that we both have a lot on our plate at the moment. You with the therapy centre - me with a fundraising trip planned to raise money for the regeneration of Kinloch Mara's natural environment. I'll be going back to the Far East in a just over a week and I'll be away for a couple of months. I don't want to start anything I can't finish. Or,' he continued sombrely, 'make promises neither of us, ultimately, will be able to keep. Understand?'

She didn't, not really; but she nodded anyway and her heart turned over. *Just over a week*? No sooner had they found each other than it would all be over. She was sensible enough to know that by the time he returned, things would have changed - their lives would have moved on.

She'd be returning to London and he'd be preoccupied with his conservation work and - as was his duty - finding the next mistress of Kinloch Mara.

All they had was here and now.

She must have looked thoroughly cast down because he tipped up her chin with his forefinger and kissed her gently on the lips. 'You have conquered the water horse, quite unmanned him. Let that be enough for now.'

He framed her face between his hands, gave her one last kiss and then started packing up the picnic things. Taking his lead, Fliss knelt down to help, taking care not to brush against him - even accidently. Carrying the picnic basket in both hands and with the apple box of scientific equipment hoisted on Ruairi's shoulders they made their way back to *The Heart of the Highlands* and the real world.

Chapter Twenty Eight

Half an hour later, with the taste of Ruairi still on her lips and the scent of him in her hair, Fliss skimmed through her emails on the laptop in the therapy centre with a dreamy smile on her face. The latest email was from Becky and had a hyperlink attached to it; so, unable to settle or to concentrate on her 'to do' list after the interlude on the island, she opened it. The link took her straight to a YouTube viral entitled: *A Farewell to Notting Hill* and showed Isla and Cat in an empty tube carriage, decked out in tartan and plainly up to no good.

Isla was first to speak, her eyes bright with mischief. 'I'm Kurr-ssty and this is -'

'Morag,' Cat cut in. They bowed solemnly to each other and then nodded to the camcorder operator.

To the strains of "Scotland the Brave", Isla performed a sword dance with two crossed pokers in lieu of claymores and Cat danced a highland fling. Although they executed a faultless sequence of steps, the overall effect was marred by Isla's hiking boots, oversized badger pelt sporran and a kilt long enough to trip up Murdo Gordon. By way of a contrast, Cat's kilt was so short her knickers were visible - unsurprisingly, they were in matching Urquhart tartan.

'So far, so predictable,' Fliss murmured, recognising the brass pokers as the ones which had fallen out of Isla's rucksack and onto the hall floor the morning after the party. Then the track ended, they bowed solemnly to each other, moved the pokers to one side and spoke directly to camera.

'This next dance is entitled *A Farewell to Notting Hill*. It's dedicated to our stepbrother who's infringed our human rights by denying us the right to party. To paraphrase Braveheart: You can take away our allowances; you can send us back to Scotland. But,' continued Isla passionately, 'you'll never take away our . . .'

'FREEDOM!' Cat interjected, punching the air.

Some amateurish editing followed, after which the sisters reappeared in killer heels. To the opening bars of The Pussycat Doll's: *"Don't You Wish Your Girlfriend Was Hot Like Me?"* they whipped off their kilts to reveal thongs, hold-up stockings and t-shirts emblazoned with the family crest. A lion holding a sword in its paw above the motto: *Wha' Dares?*

Clearly, the point of the viral was to prove to Ruairi – and the rest of the world - that they did.

Using one of London Transport's poles - better designed for clinging to in the rush hour, they bumped and ground their way through a routine that wouldn't have been out of place in some sleazy lap dancing club. Then, off camera, someone shouted: 'Oi! What you gels doin' in 'ere?' and the video ended.

'Oh - My - God,' Fliss enunciated slowly.

Her chilled out, loved up mood evaporated as she realised they'd kept her out of the loop and purposely hidden the existence of the viral from her. Becky had been right - they were the Spawn of Satan and not to be trusted. It was the night of the police station all over again. Plainly, despite everything she'd done for them - bigging Cat up to Ruairi, supporting her efforts to become a veterinary nurse; and the pains she'd taken to avoid doing Isla an injury every time she queened it over her, counted for nothing in their eyes.

They were the daughters of the house, the Laird's sisters and she was an employee - evidently not worthy of inclusion to their circle of trust. She'd been a gullible fool to consider them her friends, she seethed. Naively, she'd allowed the romantic setting of a castle in the highlands - with its attendant sexy laird, and her appointment as manageress of the therapy centre, to blind her to the reality of how things stood on Kinloch Mara.

Perhaps they thought - if they'd told her about the viral - she'd grass them up to Mitzi and spike their guns before they were ready to spring their surprise on Ruairi. Well, whatever their reason, this was her wakeup call, and she heard it loud and clear. Feeling thoroughly used and sick to the pit of her stomach, she slammed down the lid of the laptop and sat fuming in her seat for several minutes. However, as her anger subsided, she began to see things in a different light. Had Cat and Isla - albeit unintentionally, done her a favour by casting her relationship with Ruairi into relief, forcing her to ask the question: *was he out of her league, too?*

She'd lowered her defences and allowed him get closer than any man had in a long time. But was she punching above her weight? Could their relationship ever be more than midsummer madness; a highland fling? As she saw it, there were two Ruairis. On Shingle Beach, there was Ruairi the man - who could turn her boneless with one blistering kiss. But once on his estate, he morphed back into Sir Ruairi Urquhart, Laird of Kinloch Mara, bowed down by responsibilities, duties and obligation.

Which one was the real Ruairi? Ultimately, would he let her down, exactly as his stepsisters had done?

Once the flood gates opened, the doubts began to crowd in, thick and fast. He was right - so much had happened between them, possibly too quickly for it to be real. She let out a groan of frustration as a gamut of mixed emotions washed over her. Wrapping her arms around her to ward off the twin demons doubt and indecision, she walked into the hall and straight into Ruairi.

'Hey, you,' he greeted her, 'time to come clean.'

'C- come clean?' her voice wavered. Had he come to tell her that what had happened on the island was a big mistake?

'My desk is bowing under the weight of papers I should be sorting through. Murdo's waiting for me by the shooting butts, I have a host of calls to return, but . . .' He stopped and looked at her questioningly, as if sensing she'd taken a step away from him.

'But?' she prompted, preparing herself for the worst.

'All I can think about is you.' Showing none of her hesitancy, he pulled her into his arms and buried his face in her neck. Giving her no time to protest, he searched for her mouth and then kissed her long and hard, as if trying to recapture the magic they'd shared on the island.

When they finally drew apart, Fliss felt light-headed, as if she'd just stepped off a merry-go-round. She knew she had to put distance between them if she was to reassess her feelings in the light of what had just unfolded. With a supreme effort, she walked unsteadily towards the kitchen, calling over her shoulder: 'Coffee?'

'Coffee?' he repeated, as though the last earth-shattering kiss had robbed him of the ability to think straight.

'Yes. A drink made from grinding the roasted beans of a certain African bush before turning them into -' He strode purposefully into the kitchen and cornered her by the island unit, leaving her with nowhere to run, nowhere to hide.

'Aren't we a bit old for kiss chase?' he grinned, drawing her back into his arms. 'I don't know how you expect me to drink coffee when what I really want is . . .' He didn't finish the sentence but his passionate look said everything. 'May I?' For one heart-stopping moment, she thought he was asking permission to kiss her again. Instead, he moved her aside and reached in the cupboard for the biscuit tin.

'What do you want?'

She knew it was time to take up a defensive position and not fall for this disarmingly *open* Ruairi who seemingly delighted in simply being with her. She reminded herself that he'd come down to sort things out, and as it stood - they'd probably end up making love over the granite island unit with nothing resolved.

'May I have a Hobnob?' he asked, taking her by surprise and opening the biscuit tin. It was as if he sensed her hesitation and uncertainty and wanted to bring a little humour and normality to the situation.

'It falls to the lady of the house to *offer* biscuits to a guest. Not for the guest to help himself,' she said, willing to play along even though her brain was in turmoil.

'You see yourself as the lady of the house, do you?' he asked, suddenly, deadly serious.

'For now,' she replied quietly, just in case he thought she was getting ahead of the game and imagining herself as the next Lady Urquhart. She quickly filled two mugs with coffee and when she passed his mug to him, he curled his hand round her fingers before letting go. Then he settled down on the bar stool and reached out for one of the Hobnobs.

'You wanted to talk,' Fliss prompted.

'Yes. I wanted to apologise . . .'

'You've already done that.'

'I know; but I wanted to apologise properly for my attitude and behaviour towards you. If we're to go forward, we need to clear the air, be honest with each other. Agreed?'

'Agreed,' she said quietly, although her heart leapt when he said *If we're to go forward.*

'Okay - cards on the table. I thought you were a honeytrap. Someone Isla had brought up from London to distract and compromise me. Make me lose focus and not ask awkward questions about what'd happened in the police station, Cat being excluded from another boarding school, Isla maxing out on her credit cards - and the advisability of Mitzi re-opening the centre.'

That was quite a list. 'I see.'

'And why Isla thought - even for a moment - that it was fine to open up the Notting Hill house without my permission and use it like some student squat. My mother died in that house . . .'

'I know.' She laid a hand on his arm. 'I've seen the bench in the garden and the inscription on it; that must have been a terrible time - you were no more than a boy . . . I was sitting there when I answered Cat's phone and the Klingon conversation took place. You must have thought you were talking to a crackhead.'

'Ah, yes. Klingon. I was so stressed out that night! Shipstone, our next-door neighbour, had already rung me several times to complain about Isla's partying . . . I think I might have behaved quite objectionably towards you.' He looked so rueful that Fliss took a slug of scalding hot coffee to hide how affected she was by his mea culpa.

'That night seems a lifetime away. So much has happened since then, especially in the last twenty four hours.' She trailed her fingers along the back of his hand almost absentmindedly; innocent of the effect of her gentle touch until he removed his hand and sent her a long, steady look that almost melted the marble worktop that separated them.

'I've come to realise,' he began, 'that maybe the therapy centre isn't such a bad idea, after all. It's brought Mitzi back to Kinloch Mara when she usually spends as much time away as she possibly can. You've helped Cat find her work ethic and won everyone over with your dedication and commitment.'

'I'm glad,' she said consideringly, 'that you've realised the difference between what you thought I was - and who I am.'

'Murdo's been singing your praises since day one, telling me what a fool I've been,' he pulled a rueful face. 'Although you've got to admit, when you fainted in my arms it did seem like a sting.' For a few seconds they were lost in thought and Fliss remembered how safe she'd felt in his arms. Like she belonged there.

'Believe me, it wasn't.'

'I know that, now.' Ruairi reached across and captured her hands. 'Angus, Mitzi - and even Cat, have been your champions from the beginning. How you coped when you delivered Iona - no one could fake that. I saw your competence and steadfastness - and I was in awe of you. Perhaps I should take Murdo's advice, lighten up and let the family get on with their lives without me. Now, what's made you smile?'

'The night of the party my friend Becky advised me to lighten up and get -'. She didn't finish the sentence; she didn't need to because he got the gist of it.

'Maybe they've got a point,' he said. 'Forget about friends and family, it's *us* I've come down here to discuss.' Putting his mug aside, he got up and starting pacing the kitchen. 'I can't get you out of my head, Fliss. You've been there since the moment you stood under the rose arch, tugged at the sari cloth and petals cascaded around you - and you refused to let me help.

'Surely that should have told you I wasn't a honeytrap?'

'At the time, it seemed like you were playing hard to get. I've been such a fool.' He struck his forehead with the palm of his hand, turned

237

and gave a self-deprecatory grin. The fact that he was man enough to admit his mistakes only served to make him dangerously more attractive.

Now it was her turn to fess up . . .

'There have been times when I've felt like packing my bags, walking out and thumbing a lift all the way to Inverness. But I know that when I do leave Kinloch Mara I'll be leaving part of me behind.' She was taking an enormous risk in dropping her defences and laying herself bare. It was unlike her to exchange prudence for recklessness but her gut instinct told her to trust him. Let him know not only of her desire for him, but of her yearning never to leave this place.

In a moment of epiphany, she understood that the invitation to stay - as friend, lover, therapist, whatever - had to come from *him*. That would be his declaration of intent and she'd know then he was serious about her; and that what they felt for each other went beyond a quick fumble in the heather and stolen kisses in the kitchen.

'Fliss I won't lie to you. I've never felt like this about any woman,' he said, as if reading her mind. 'And, believe me, most of the girls in Wester Ross and beyond have been paraded past me in an attempt to get me to settle down and produce lots of little Urquharts.' He laughed, but something deep within Fliss contracted at the thought of a nameless, faceless, woman bearing his children.

She filed the thought away to mull over later and concentrated instead on what she said next. 'Isn't that your duty, your destiny? Doesn't it come as part and parcel of - all this?' She waved her hand to encompass the world outside the kitchen window. 'Can you have one without the other?'

'It's common knowledge that there's little or no money to run all - *this*.' He walked over to the window and looked out over his estate. 'That - coupled with the fact I'm out of the country for much of the year, deters prospective fiancées. Kinloch Mara is the most beautiful place on earth but it can be snowed in for weeks at a time. We're miles from shops, access to Edinburgh and London; all the usual comforts a woman expects.'

She slanted a look at him - was he really so unaware of his own attraction? Okay - so he came with baggage and a bunch of debt, but who didn't these days? And, in any case, his concept of poverty was in a different league to hers. The right woman, the one meant for him, wouldn't allow such things to drive her away - not if she really loved him. Her thoughts turned briefly to Fiona, the Bolting Bride.

'Sorry, that sounded a bit self-obsessed,' he apologised, giving a diffident shrug.

'Snap.' She laughed to lighten the atmosphere and then went on to explain. 'Although, with me it's more a case of: love you; hate your job. Few men are willing to put up with the long hours I work, or to play second fiddle to my determination to have my own business.'

'Then they are fools and you deserve better. The fact you have ambition is one of the things I most admire about you. My sisters could learn a lot from you.' He drew her to her feet and regarded her seriously. 'You're plucky and determined - any man who can't see that is an idiot.' She gave him an old-fashioned look, hadn't he behaved like an idiot towards her until last night? Catching her look, he had the grace to laugh. 'Guilty as charged M'lud,' then his smile faded. 'But it would be a lot to presume, though, wouldn't it?'

'What would?'

'To expect any woman to bury herself in Wester Ross?

'That,' she said slowly, 'would rather depend on the woman.'

For several moments, they were lost in thought and neither of them spoke, although it was clear each had more to say. His life was constrained by his obligations to clear his debts and hand the estate on to his eldest son. Her life was a constant struggle to make ends meet and she was driven by a longing to feel a sense of security - of simply *belonging*, that had been missing from her life since her parents' deaths.

Thanks to Cat and Isla, she was more aware than ever that she and Ruairi came from different worlds. Once she left Kinloch Mara their relationship would be over, how could it be otherwise? Perhaps these snatched moments were all she could hope for, and if that was the case, she had a simple choice: take it or leave it.

As though sensing her conflict, Ruairi gave her a swift kiss.

'Can I come back later? Finish this conversation? The estate calls - and you've got the Open Day in a few two days' time.'

'Of course.' She didn't say that she'd been ready for about a week. Clearly, she worked at a different speed to everyone round here.

'In the meantime -'

'Yes?'

He leaned across the table and put the lid back on the biscuit tin. 'Let's not share the Hobnobs with anyone else.' She saw the wisdom in his words. In a few days, he would be off to the Far East to continue his fundraising tour and when he returned, her six month contract would be up for review.

It would take Nurse McLeish with her gift of second sight to predict what would happen after that.

Chapter Twenty Nine

'And . . . smile. Fliss, hold the baby just a wee bit higher so that we can get a shot of the four of you together. Do you think you could manage a smile, Sir Ruairi? *Please*?'

'Is it really necessary for me to be photographed? People won't want to see my face above your article. It's Fliss, Shona and the baby who are the stars.'

'Och, that's where you're wrong, Sir Ruairi. Our readers will lap it up: *Laird Delivers Premature Baby During Storm of the Century*.' The reporter from the local newspaper sketched the strapline in the air. 'And free publicity for the therapy centre is not to be sniffed at,' he pointed out, earning one of Ruairi's dark looks.

'Hardly the storm of the century, though, was it? And it was Fliss who delivered the baby. Not me.' As if distracted by the image of Fliss rocking Iona, he appeared lost in his own thoughts. He squared his shoulders, settled the Glengarry more securely on his dark hair and collected himself. 'And - to be strictly accurate, it's Lady Urquhart's business venture.' He indicated Mitzi who, resplendent in a silk cocktail dress and feather fascinator, was standing outside the therapy centre talking to Angus and Murdo. 'But I bow to your superior knowledge in these matters.' The reporter, obviously missing his ironic inflection, concentrated on getting copy for his story.

'And Shona. Maybe you could give us a bell when the wee one's about a couple of months old and we'll come back and take some follow-up snaps.'

'Will do. And thanks for mentioning our hotel. It'll give us a real boost.' She'd recovered quickly after Iona's birth less than a week ago, and was an advert for blooming motherhood. Her husband, Archie, had stayed at home with their four children but had promised to come and visit as soon as things were a bit quieter at the hotel.

'No problemo.' The reporter gave Ruairi an oblique look as if to say: *at least someone round here appreciates us.*

'All done here?' Fliss asked, handing the baby to Ruairi and getting out of the chair. 'I've got rather a busy day ahead.'

'Yeah, that's great. Stand down ladies - and you, too, Sir Ruairi. Jimmy, get a photo of the laird and the therapist with the bairn before we go, will ye. That'll look great with the article. Great idea of yours, Lady Urquhart - to combine the story of the baby's delivery with the opening of your therapy centre,' he schmoozed as Mitzi joined them.

'Oh, it was all Mr Gordon's idea really,' Mitzi said.

Fliss bit her lip to stop herself laughing at the hapless reporter. Despite his earnest schmoozing, no one appeared to want to claim credit for anything that happened the night Iona was born, or subsequently.

Cat and Isla bustled into the conservatory.

'Mumma . . . Make Ruairi change his mind!' They turned woebegone faces towards Ruairi who was holding Iona like she was a ticking time bomb. Using their entrance as his cue, he handed the baby back to Shona who gave him a look that implied he was wimping out.

Mitzi, self-appointed counsel for the defence opened with: 'Darling Ruairi. Let them attend the Open Day. For me?'

'Not even for you,' Ruairi replied, his expression stony. He glanced towards Fliss as if half expecting her to plead the sisters' case.

To signify that she considered this a family matter, she made a great show of counting the RSVPs and checking them off against the guest list. Her hands were shaking as she laid the cards out on the therapy bed. If he was this obdurate over their missing the Open Day because of their behaviour in Elgin Crescent, she feared what his reaction would be when he found out about the viral.

'This all looks very impressive.' He changed subject smoothly, indicating the caterers, party planners and the treatment room with a nod of his head. He checked out her Zen-inspired uniform of jet black tunic, three quarter trousers and Birkenstocks. 'You look the part, Fliss;

very professional. Wouldn't you say so girls?' he prompted his stepsisters who muttered something indistinct.

'Thank you, Ruairi,' she replied uncertain of his mood. Judging by his deadpan expression, he appeared to have reverted to default mode. So different from the passionate man who'd carried her across the waters of the loch to *The Heart of the Highland*s, she thought - her heart heavy.

'It must make you very proud to see all your hopes for Mitzi's therapy centre come to fruition, especially after your tireless search to find a therapist, Isla. You are to be congratulated on finding such an excellent one. Fliss has turned out better than any of us could have hoped.' Recalling what he'd said about believing that Isla had set a honeytrap, Fliss wondered if Isla detected the inference behind his words.

'Yeah. ri -ight.' Isla dismissed Ruairi's barbed comments with a *whatever* shrug. However, Fliss thought that she'd seen a flash of apprehension cross her face.

'In fact,' Ruairi went on, 'I've been half expecting you to surprise us with a happy dance to celebrate.'

Isla's head whipped round. 'What do you mean *happy dance*?'

'Isn't that how youngsters celebrate success these days?'

'I have no idea what you're talking about,' Isla said. But it was clear, from the way her gaze swung between Ruairi, Mitzi and Murdo that she was thinking on her feet.

Ruairi was only too happy to elucidate. 'A highland fling, for example, wouldn't be out of place, would it Cat? And I'm sure - if only we had the time, Isla could perform a sword dance that would impress all of us.'

Cat went very pale under her thick foundation and took a step away closer to her mother. Mitzi and Angus looked at Ruairi uncomprehendingly. But Murdo looked as though his heart had been shish-kebabbed by a claymore, or perhaps more accurately, the sight of the woman he loved cavorting on YouTube in her underwear. It was obvious that Ruairi and Murdo knew all about the viral and Ruairi was playing cat and mouse with Isla.

'Well, maybe the girls can perform a set piece at the Highland Ball Ruairi, darling.' Mitzi as usual supported her wayward cubs. But it was clear from her puzzled expression, that she was unsure what misdemeanour they were being held to account for. 'So, they can stay and enjoy the Open Day - can't they?'

'No, they can't, Mitzi. Nothing has changed. These two *pussycats* are coming out on the hills with Murdo and me to check the shooting buts.'

'Pussycats?' Mitzi looked at him as if he'd gone mad.

'Pussycat *Dolls* to be precise. Isn't that right girls?' Ruairi grinned, openly enjoying their discomfiture.

Instead of raising Cain as they'd seemingly expected, he appeared to find the whole episode ironic and entertaining. Isla, plainly put out that her complicated plan to wind Ruairi up had come to nothing, glared at Fliss - as if suspecting she was responsible for this sea change in their brother and even of grassing them up. In a flash, Fliss realised that it was Isla's reaction to the viral she should have been worrying about - not Ruairi's.

'Ruairi, you are a complete pig!' Isla spat, as he mimicked her insouciant *whatever* shrug. 'Haven't we been punished enough?'

'Let's take stock . . . You've danced semi-nude on the London Underground in some ill- thought-out scheme to exact revenge for being grounded. As a result, you've made yourselves look ridiculous. I'm assuming that *wasn't* part of your original plan?'

'Semi-nude? London Underground? Will someone *please* explain?' Mitzi begged.

'I think - given the circumstances, your punishment is very lenient. So . . . to the hills!' He rubbed his hands together as though yomping over the heather and bracken was the most exciting thing in the world. Then he added with black humour, 'I hope you've slapped on as much midge cream as you have make-up; otherwise you're going to be eaten alive until we get away from the loch.'

He turned his back on his stepsisters and winked at Fliss. Then he and Murdo headed for the fleet of Land Rovers full of gillies and equipment waiting on the beach

'Buck up girls.' Mitzi dropped her voice to a conspiratorial whisper. 'I

don't know what you've been up to but it can't be *that* bad. Do as Ruairi
says and we'll have the cousins over while you're at Angus's. We can
have barbeques and tennis parties. All kinds of fun. But, hush - not a
word to Himself.'

'Mitzi, they are supposed to be grounded,' Angus protested and he
and Fliss exchanged a look of fellow feeling. 'Honey, you've gotta get a
handle on those girls, back Ruairi up - not undermine him. Who knows
what they've been up to in London?' He gave Fliss a searching look as if
he suspected she knew more than she was prepared to say. 'And Mitzi,
I'm not so sure I want those damned cousins in my house, drinking my
booze, smoking dope and getting out of hand.'

'But Angus, darling, I was so much worse at their age.' She smoothed
down her silk cocktail dress, obviously remembering past indiscretions.
'There was an Italian Count once, in his palazzo on Lake Como. I had to
escape out of a window wearing only a silk chemise when his wife
turned up.' Angus looked like he wanted to say more but was choosing
his battles.

Shona took Iona off for her mid-morning nap and Fliss gathered up
the RSVPs spread over the therapy bed. Leaving Angus and Mitzi arguing
over how to discipline her daughters, she went into the sitting room to
ponder over Ruairi's unexpected reaction to the viral.

A couple of hours later, the Open Day was in full swing. There had
been a steady flow of guests all afternoon but after a polite look round,
they'd shown more interest in drinking Mitzi's champagne than listening
to Fliss extolling the virtues of the range of therapies on offer. The
whole enterprise resembled an upmarket garden party with guests in
their summer finery and bunting festooning the path down from Tigh na
Locha.

True to form, within five minutes Mitzi had sloped off to gossip with
her girlfriends and left Fliss to get on with it. However, Angus had taken
it upon himself to coerce guests - in the nicest way possible - to book

several sessions with Fliss while they were rosy with champagne and full of his caviar.

'Phew,' Fliss remarked at the end of an eyebrow shaping demonstration. 'Time for a break, I think.' She glanced at Angus, flushed and perspiring in his khaki chinos and blue Ralph Lauren shirt.

'Wait there,' he ordered, pointing to an empty table and two chairs outside the conservatory doors. Obeying, Fliss sat down, kicked off her Birkenstocks and rested her feet on a stool. In a flash, catering staff appeared with champagne, a silver tray full of nibbles, two plates and linen napkins. Shaking out a napkin, Angus laid it across her knee.

'Tuck in kid,' he pushed a plate towards her. 'You deserve it.'

'So do you, Angus. I've learned a lot from watching you today. Talk about the hard sell,' she gestured towards the appointment book. 'I'm booked up for the next two months - and that's before we've even started taking bookings from the general public. I may have to take on an assistant at this rate.' She regarded him with new respect and guessed that persistence and drive had made him his first million. She raised her glass to him: 'Slainte.'

'Slainte. Well, I enjoyed it. Hell, I ain't much for small talk and besides, it's Mitzi's day, not mine. I want to thank you for everything you've done, Fliss. You've anchored my wandering star, made her realise that she can make a life here in Wester Ross with me. She's happier than I've ever known her.'

'I think you should claim the credit for making Mitzi happy, Angus,' Fliss said, and squeezed his hand.

'Talking about me, sweetie?' Mitzi asked, joining them. 'Now Fliss, enough with the boring demos. Come and meet my friends, your clients. You too, Angus, no more hiding.'

'Sure, honey.' He put down his glass and got to his feet, reluctantly.

'They're all anxious to meet the girl who's got my business venture off the ground.' Like Angus, Fliss felt worn out and in no hurry to meet Mitzi's friends but good manners and business sense dictated otherwise.

'Okay. Just give me a moment will you?' Fliss asked.

'Yes. But do hurry up, sweetie, Ruairi will be back off the hills soon.

The girls are packed and ready to be helicoptered over to Angus's estate.' She carried on as though nothing had happened between Ruairi and his stepsisters that morning and it was obvious that she'd dismissed the whole incident from her mind.

'*If* they're coming over to stay,' Angus scowled, clearly not thrilled at the prospect of providing open house for Mitzi's young relatives.

Mitzi took his arm and guided him through the conservatory. 'Now, don't be a cross old Texan bear, Angus. Ruairi won't want them under his feet when he's getting ready to return to Hong Kong, will he?' They carried on debating the subject and rejoined their guests outside.

Fliss's joy evaporated at the thought of Ruairi leaving the day after tomorrow. She hugged the appointments diary to her chest as familiar feelings of emotional displacement washed over her. If - as now seemed increasingly likely, Mitzi and Angus were to marry, the girls would live on Angus's estate. With a wedding to plan, Mitzi's enthusiasm for the centre could vanish overnight. Fliss had a sudden vision of her carefully sourced therapy equipment being stashed under the stairs with the detritus of Mitzi's other (failed) business ventures.

Would Angus extend her contract at the end of its six month period? Or, would the therapy centre close down for winter and re-open in the spring? Did they expect her to take temporary work in London (if she could find it) and return when the snows had melted? She'd made no attempt to find a permanent replacement for herself, hoping that at the end of the contract she'd be invited to stay on

'Ur - rrrr.' She gave a cry of frustration as she took the appointments diary through into the kitchen. She knew she had a tendency to spoil the moment by worrying over something that might never happen. And was capable of grinding to an emotional halt over events that were beyond her control.

It wasn't as if she could prevent Mitzi and Angus marrying and setting up home. She couldn't stop Ruairi from continuing with his Far East fundraising tour just because their relationship was changing. She touched the tattoo on her hip through the thin material of her uniform:

Carpe Diem. In truth, it had been more to please Becky than for any other reason that she'd had the tattoo in the first place. But it was a timely reminder that she should enjoy herself and seize any happiness that came her way - however temporary. She had no control over the future. All she had was one more day with Ruairi and she'd better make the most of it.

Chapter Thirty

Later that evening, showered and changed, Fliss walked into the kitchen and found Ruairi peeling back the cling film on the left over canapés and pouring himself a glass of champagne.

'I wasn't expecting you.' She felt as if she'd descended in a very fast lift and her body was no longer governed by the laws of physics. For a few seconds she felt weightless and then the world righted itself.

And breathe . . .

'Is that your oblique way of telling me that I'm not welcome?' Ruairi knocked back the vintage Krug in one thirsty gulp as though his mouth was dry, or he was in need of a champagne buzz.

'No - never that,' she replied, sending him an honest, open look. 'Are you hungry? There's plenty of leftovers, can I get you something?'

Something of her inner turmoil must have shown on her face because he put the champagne glass down and gave her one of his considering looks. Then he shrugged off his gilet and threw it and his Glengarry onto the counter top.

'Come here, you mad woman.' Unable to resist his cajoling tone, Fliss walked into his arms and laid her head on his chest. For a moment they simply stood drawing comfort from the physical contact, and - one by one, her worries melted away.

'Less of the mad woman, if you don't mind,' she answered back with her usual asperity, her voice muffled by his rugger shirt. 'I can see that changing your diet from Hobnobs to caviar and Krug has had an adverse effect on you.'

'That's better. I thought you'd lost your sense of humour,' he murmured against her hair. Then he held her at arm's length and grinned, his cobalt eyes dancing with mischief. 'Well, come on. Put me out of my misery.'

For one crazy moment, Fliss thought he was asking her to rip his shirt off, throw him over the island unit and make love to him. Although she schooled her features, her expression must have given her away because he threw his head back and laughed uproariously.

'Engaging as that thought is, I actually meant - tell me all about your day of triumph. Isn't this the moment when you say: I told you so - the therapy centre is going to be a great success.'

'*I told you so; the therapy is centre is going to be a great success,*' she parroted, applying the brake to her runaway senses. 'I'm booked up for the next two and a half months. Right up to the time you return from the Far East.'

'Show me. Then, if you still want to ravish me on the granite worktop I'm all yours, but I think it would be bloody cold and uncomfortable when there are sofas and beds going begging in the house.' As intended, that made her laugh and the awkward moment passed. He looked into her face, clearly sensing something else was bothering her. 'What is it?'

'Murdo. He looked positively stricken over the viral. Look, I know it's none of my business, but what's the deal with him and your sister?'

'Simple. When Isla was growing up she hero-worshipped Murdo. Then, when she was about fifteen, the Urquhart cousins - bloody fools - started teasing her, calling her Mrs Murdo, the Factor's wife. Telling her that she'd marry him and give birth to a ginger haired brat every year until she was too old and raddled for any other man to want her.'

'Nice one.' The Urquhart cousins sounded a load of trouble and Fliss hoped never to make their acquaintance. 'And I suppose she was at an age to take that sort of thing to heart?'

'Absolutely. So for the last five years she's been giving him the run-around, wanting him; not wanting him. Murdo's waiting for her to grow up but he won't wait forever. In fact, I think she's just used up the last of her nine lives with him.'

'The YouTube viral, you mean? I'm surprised that you took it so calmly,' she began, anxious to know what his take on it was.

'When I first found out I was furious and then I realised that was exactly the reaction Isla wanted. I figured that, by *not* acting according to plan, I'd spike her guns. Obviously, the viral and bringing you up here as a honeytrap - not to mention resurrecting the therapy centre against my wishes, were her way of paying me back for grounding her and Cat.'

'It all seems a bit Machiavellian and over the top, even for her. Why does she do these things?'

'Because she can?' Ruairi shrugged. 'Papa spoiled her and Cat rotten. Luckily, I've been able to reverse the damage with Cat, but Isla - well, she's a completely different matter - out of control and out of hand.'

'I found out about the viral just after we'd been on the island and have been stressing over it ever since,' Fliss confessed.

'Because you knew about it, but didn't say anything to me?'

'Yes.' Now it was out in the open she felt better.

'Let me put your mind at rest. I've known about it for some time - it's not exactly something that Isla could hope - or even want to keep secret. I was waiting for the right moment to play my ace. I think my timing was bang on, don't you?'

'Yes,' she agreed, anxious to explain herself fully so there were no further misunderstandings. 'You see, I decided - no matter what had happened between you and me, I couldn't grass them up.'

'Rest assured, Fliss, I wouldn't expect you to betray a friend - even two as undeserving of your loyalty as Cat and Isla.' Her relief was palpable and he must have felt it, because he changed the subject and held out his hand. 'Come on, show me your appointment diary, Angus says it's almost full.'

Leading him into the drawing room, she made him sit on the yellow brocade Knowle sofa and placed the diary across his knees. With her kneeling at his feet, Ruairi turned over the handmade pages and ran his finger down the list of names. As she waited for his judgment, she spent a pleasurable few moments studying the way a shaft of amber light streamed through the west facing windows and touched his dark hair, how his eyelashes curled down over his sunburnt cheeks and a tuft of dark hair poked out of the neck of his t-shirt.

'Very impressive Miss Bagshawe. I'm detecting the hand of Angus in this roll call of the best families in the highlands?'

'You should have seen him. He was a complete star. Twisted arms gently up backs and applied velvet thumb screws. He worked his little cotton socks off today.'

'Big cotton socks, surely, in Angus's case?' Ruairi closed the diary and handed it back to her. It was tooled in the finest leather and slightly cumbersome; it slipped out of her hands and landed at their feet. 'Butter fingers. Let's hope you do better with your clients.'

'Usually the best hands in the business,' she said and held them out for inspection.

'I'll be the judge of that.' Ruairi pulled her towards him so that she was kneeling between his knees. 'As you know, many Highlanders believe in *Taibhsearachd* or Second Sight.' Regarding her seriously, he turned her hands over and searched her palms as though the future lay there. Then he traced slow circles on the sensitive skin at the base of her wrists with his thumbs, his eyes on her as he waited for her reaction to the rhythmic stroking of her erogenous zone.

'L - like Nurse McLeish?' Fliss stammered.

'She certainly knows how to do spooky,' Ruairi was suddenly serious, 'and her predictions usually come true.'

'A baby within a year,' Fliss mused. 'I wonder whose'

'Well, as long as it's not Cat or Isla's I don't really mind.'

'She certainly came over all fey when Iona was born, made my blood run cold and shivers run down my spine.' The slow circling of her wrists now moved down to her palms and was having much the same effect. She marvelled at his composure when every nerve in her body was zinging. 'You were saying - about second sight?'

'Well, if I had the sight, I would know what your reaction would be when I did *this*.' Swiftly he changed places so that she was sitting on the sofa and he was kneeling at her feet. 'Then *this*,' he pushed a strand of hair behind her ear. 'And finally, *this*.' He pushed her gently down onto the sofa and then bent his head towards her.

His kiss was soft and tentative. Closing her eyes Fliss surrendered to it, breathing in the warm scent of his skin. She heard a sensuous moan, but it took several seconds before she realised she was the one who'd made it. A more physical reaction followed close on the heels of her moue of surrender as Ruairi pulled her close, deepened and prolonged the kiss. A current of electricity crackled between them and triggered a sort of madness in her. Weaving her fingers into his thick dark hair, her tongue found his lips and boldly pressed them apart. Then the tenor of their kisses became more urgent and this time it was Ruairi who gave a deep cry of such longing that a delicious charge surged through Fliss on hearing it.

'Fliss. My God - stop.' Briefly, he put her from him and sat back on his heels, evidently feeling that it fell to him to call a halt before things got out of hand. He ran shaky fingers through his hair and struggled to bring his breathing under control. Fliss looked back at him, knowing her eyes were shining, her hair tousled, and her lips bruised from their furious kisses.

'I don't want to stop,' she replied with a confident brazenness that surprised her. 'Do you?'

'What do you think?'

He swung her knees up onto the sofa, laid her on her back and placed a cushion under her head. Hooking his hands under her knees, he pulled her forward and then joined her on the sofa, his pelvis thrust against the soft curves of her body. His breath snagged as he whispered against her ear: 'Is this what you want, Fliss? If you're unsure, now would be the time to call a halt.'

He paused in their lovemaking long enough to tip her chin up. She opened her eyes, sighed and laid two fingers against his lips.

'I want you more than I have ever wanted any man in my whole life. Can't you tell?' She knew it was time to be honest with each other. Even if nothing - apart from the success of the therapy centre, had been resolved. Life couldn't always be orderly and organised, she realised that now. Sometimes a leap of faith was required. She felt ready to take that step with Ruairi - and without looking down to check that a safety net was in place to catch her when she fell.

'Then - it's what we both want,' he responded huskily.

His hand, which had been holding her chin, slid down the column of her throat and came to rest on the row of pearly buttons that fastened her low-cut camisole. Bending his head, he kissed the line his hand had just traced; and then, slipping his hands underneath the hollow of her back, tilted her pelvis upwards and closer to him. Fliss caught his hair in her fists and pressed his face into her breasts, throwing her head back and exalting in her ability to make this proud man want her. She was so lost in the power of his lovemaking that when he raised his head and sent one last, questioning look before unfastening the remainder of the buttons, she felt bereft. But the feeling was fleeting as Ruairi's lips soon found the warm hollow of her clavicle and then continued downwards.

In command, he raised his head and looked into her face, as though he needed to be doubly sure before their lovemaking passed this point. Wordlessly, Fliss took his hand and laid it on her breast, her look establishing there was no going back. Ruairi pushed the fine material of her camisole aside and his lips found her nipple, which was pushing up against her cotton bra. He grazed it with his teeth through the material and then pushed her bra cup aside, revealing her breast in all its glory.

'Christ, oh Fliss . . .' His warm mouth covered her nipple and he murmured something indistinct against her skin. She held his head and urged him closer to her breast, encouraging him, willing him not to stop as his hand slid along her thigh.

Then - a sound. A different sound

For long seconds, neither of them registered what it was, or where it was coming from. Then Murdo repeated his call.

'*Ruairi. Ruairi? Do you read me? Over.*'

Dazed, they glanced towards the kitchen where Ruairi had left his gilet. With a regretful sigh, he rolled off Fliss, scrambled onto his feet and fetched the two way radio, muttering about wanting to throw it in the deepest part of the loch.

'This'd better be an emergency,' he said, assuming the mantle of Laird of Kinloch Mara and answering Murdo's call. 'Hi, Murdo. What's the problem?' His eyes stayed on Fliss's face as he knelt down by her side, reached out and cradled her breast. Fliss turned her face into the back of the Knowle sofa, closed her eyes and revelled in his touch.

'One of Mitzi's guests has had too much to drink and hit the gate post on the north drive with his Merc. The police are here but he's refusing to be breathalysed. In fact, he's already pushed Callum McDonald into the wee moat that runs under the bridge. Over.'

'Damn. Can't you deal with it, Murdo?' Then, evidently remembering he was responsible for everything that happened on his land, he pulled himself up sharp. 'Okay. I'll be there in five minutes.' With that, he hung up and clipped the walkie-talkie onto his belt.

'Trouble?' Fliss asked unnecessarily, propping herself up on her elbows - very much aware of her nakedness.

'No more than to be expected with Mitzi's crowd.' Drawing a dark mustard cashmere comforter off the sofa, he covered her with it. 'Nothing for you to bother yourself with, Fliss. Wait there, I'll be back. Fifteen minutes - tops.'

'Is that a promise?'

'It's a promise.'

He bent lower and kissed her hard on the lips before drawing apart with extreme reluctance. She caught his yearning look and desire squirmed like a beguiling serpent in the pit of her stomach.

Ruairi sprinted through the hall and out of the house like an ardent lover.

And for the first time in her adult life, Felicity Amelia Bagshawe did as she was bidden.

Chapter Thirty One

A tap on her bedroom door woke Fliss the next morning. She stretched out languorously - then remembered the humiliation of trying to maintain her seductive pose on the sofa until it dawned on her that Ruairi wasn't coming back. After that, a sleepless night wondering what she'd done wrong and why he'd got cold feet. And finally, the realisation that she'd been a fool to drop her guard and show how much she wanted him.

There it was again. Knock, knock, knock.

'Fliss. Can I come in?'

'Go away.' She pulled the covers over her head and wished Ruairi Urquhart half way to Hell - or Heathrow.

'*Please* may I come in . . . I've got breakfast and an apology.'

'Didn't you hear me? Just. Go. Away.' The door opened a crack and Ruairi entered bearing coffee and toast on a tray. Fliss gave him and the breakfast a scathing look. Sitting up in bed, she pulled the duvet higher so that only her eyes were visible. She hoped they were sparking with anger and sending out the message that things had changed since last night.

'It's the best I could rustle up in the circumstances. I've spent all night with that fuckwit - sorry - Hugh Auchinloch in A&E having the gash on his head treated, and insisting that he give a blood sample to the police.' Lowering her fourteen-tog yashmak Fliss registered that he was wearing yesterday's clothes and in need of a good shave.

'You smell of - whisky,' She wrinkled her nose. So, while she'd been languishing on the Knowle sofa getting colder by the minute he'd been knocking back the uisge beatha with his irresponsible friends.

'That's because Auchinloch threw the contents of his hip flask over Murdo, Callum and me in a drunken fit - like we were ghosts and he was exorcising with holy water. Although in a way it *was* holy water; a twenty five year old single malt from his family's distillery near Spey Bridge,' he made a feeble joke. 'The eejit.'

His use of the archaic word made her smile.

Plainly emboldened, Ruairi edged further into the room, put the tray down on the bedside table and sat on the edge of the bed. He handed Fliss a cup of very strong coffee and toast on a plate. She drew her knees up to her chin, making sure the spaghetti thin straps of her nightie didn't slip off her shoulders and give him the wrong idea. She wouldn't be going down *that* particular road this morning - thank you very much. No matter how sexily crumpled he looked or how much her body yearned for his touch.

'Apology?' She sensed a distance between them that hadn't been there last night. As if he was already thousands of miles away in Hong Kong and back on the money-raising slog amongst ex-pats.

'Yes, another one. I hope you didn't . . . wait too long for me.' His pause showed he felt awkward about last night. 'By the time I was able to get to a pay phone - the mobiles don't work round here, as you know - it was late. Very late. I couldn't get the picture of you . . .'

'Lying on the sofa waiting for you?' *Like an eejit*, she felt like adding. 'Oh, don't worry. I gave it fifteen minutes - realised you weren't coming back - and then got on with tidying up the therapy centre.' Pride made her hide the truth that she'd languished on the sofa for more than an hour.

'Fifteen minutes?' It was plain he thought she should have waited a bit longer before giving up on him.

'Give or take. I could hardly just lie there - now, could I?' She blushed at the picture she must have presented, hips tilted at an inviting angle and her breast exposed - albeit underneath the cashmere comforter.

'No. I'm sorry.'

'So you've said.'

During the ensuing silence, Fliss drank her bitter coffee and hid her expression behind the mug. Bleak-faced, Ruairi looked out of the window obviously regretting his impulse to visit her, and searching for a suitable exit line.

'This was a bad idea.' He rubbed his hands over his stubble and then raked his fingers through his hair - a tell-tale gesture which, she was beginning to realise, meant he was on the back foot and unsure of himself. Getting up, he put his mug on the tray and then turned to face her. 'We never seem to get a clear run at this. At *us* - do we?'

'There's always something or someone in the way,' she agreed, her froideur beginning to melt in the face of his discernible regret.

'Story of my life.' He gave a mocking smile and pulled the cuffs of his rugger shirt down over his knuckles as if he was suddenly chilled. And in a blinding flash, Fliss understood. As Laird of Kinloch Mara, his life was as curtailed by duty as hers was by lack of opportunity and poor prospects. It was hard for either of them to break free.

The Laird and the Therapist.

It sounded like a salacious headline in a Sunday red top, but there was more to their relationship than that. Last night, they'd made a connection beyond the physical and they both knew it. Hugh Auchinloch's drunken accident had probably saved them from making complete fools of themselves and starting down a road that could only lead to heartbreak.

The Therapist and the Laird.

Fliss sensed what it must have cost this proud man to come to her bedroom. Not as many men would have done - to pick up where he'd left off last night - but to explain and apologise. And she'd thrown his apology back at him. He'd taken the first step, now it was down to her to swallow her pride and reach out to him this time.

'I think,' she began and slowly lowered the duvet, 'that I fancy the Full Scottish up at the Big Hoose with Jaimsie playing a reel on the terrace outside the dining room. Not, The Laird's Lament, mind; something livelier - that Strathspey reel he often plays in the mornings when I watch you beating the bounds with Murdo.'

There. It was out; she'd given *him* something back - a confession that she hid behind the curtains every morning in the hope of catching a glimpse of him.

'I think I know the one,' he said, gentleman enough not to acknowledge her confession. But when he turned towards her, his eyes were shining and he couldn't conceal his joy at her volte-face. 'Shall we say half an hour? Afterwards, I'd like you to come up on the hills with me there's something I'd like to show you.'

'More etchings?' she raised her eyebrow.

'A Brocken Spectre - if we're lucky.'

'A *what* spectre? Like *Most Haunted*?' Now her curiosity was piqued.

'You'll see.'

'What should I wear?'

'Plenty of protection against the -'

'Spectres?'

'The midges.'

He bent down and took the mug from her slack fingers, his face just inches from hers. Fliss sensed that he badly wanted to kiss her and his ardent look showed how much he wanted to climb into bed with her and conclude last night's lovemaking. But, clearly he thought better of it, because he turned on his heel and left her to finish her coffee and cold toast alone.

An hour later, they made their way along a ridge towards a triangulation point high above Kinloch Mara. They walked in silence, aware only of the uneven ground, the damp atmosphere and drop below them hidden by enshrouding mist and cloud. The grass was wet and Fliss was glad of her waterproof walking gaiters, otherwise, her jeans would have been sodden. Out of breath from having walked up a punishing incline, she stopped and pressed her hand into her right side where a painful stitch was making itself felt.

'I am *so* out of condition,' she said and flopped onto a large boulder.

'Here,' Ruairi rooted around inside his rucksack, found a bottle of water and passed it to her. She took a large swig from it and handed it back. Without taking his eyes off her, he drank from the same bottle and wiped the back of his hand across his mouth. The gesture was highly erotic and Fliss felt as if she'd been kissed by proxy when she took her turn with the water bottle. His searing look made it plain that last night's interrupted lovemaking hadn't been consigned to the past; it had simply been put on hold.

'I'm surprised you don't bottle your own water off the hills. Remember the episode of Only Fools and Horses where Del and Rodney sell tap water as Peckham Spring Water? Maybe you and Murdo could set up a profitable sideline doing that. Aren't landowners supposed to diversify or die?' Fliss made the joke to cover her churning emotions - this man rocked her to her core, even when he was just drinking from a water bottle!

'Diversify, yes; break the law? No.' He held out his hand and pulled her to her feet. 'Come on. Not far now until you see the spectre.'

'Is this one of those rituals where the heir is shown some hideously deformed monster mummified behind a brick wall on coming of age and is sworn to secrecy? Like the monster of Glamis?' She gabbled on as goose bumps travelled the length of her arms - was he *really* going to show her a ghost?

'I'm impressed that you know your Scottish history. But no; it's nothing like that. Wait and see.'

They climbed higher and were soon above the clouds with the sun on their backs. Ruairi's grip on her hand tightened as they climbed the last few feet to the summit. Then, taking her by the shoulders he looked down into her eyes.

'Do you trust me?' Her teeth were chattering with a mix of fear and anticipation but she nodded. He positioned her so that the low sun warmed her back and the mist-shrouded valley was in front of her. 'Close your eyes and put your hands out like you're flying. Now don't move. I'm going to take a few steps away and then I'll ask you to open your eyes.'

She heard the long grass brush against his waterproof gaiters, smelled the crushed blades beneath his boots and heard the wind singing in her ears. Behind her closed eyelids it was semi-dark, but she wasn't afraid; she knew he wouldn't place her in any danger. Holding her arms out like Kate Winslet on the prow of the Titanic, she gave a nervous giggle.

'Aren't you supposed to say: "I'm King of the World"?' She rocked on the balls of her feet in borrowed boots that were too large for her. 'Oops.'

'Okay. Open your eyes.'

It took a few seconds for her to become accustomed to the light, and then she saw it. Not a ghost or a spectre, but her own form cast as a huge shadow onto the cloud bank below her. She wiggled her arms up and down like she was indeed flying and her shadow followed suit. When she saw the nimbus around her 'shadow's' head - all red, gold and green, like a pre-Raphaelite saint's, she drew in a breath and instinctively reached out for him.

He'd taken precious hours out of his busy schedule to bring her here and share something special with her. Her eyes pricked with tears and she knew in that instant that she was falling, deeply and irrevocably in love with this proud, complex man.

'Oh My God. What is it?'

She clung to him as if she couldn't believe her eyes or trust her brain to make sense of the tumultuous feelings rocking her. Their shadows merged onto the clouds and the nimbus of light encompassed them, making it seem like they were literally standing beneath the arc of a rainbow.

'It's called a Brocken Spectre and it's a natural phenomenon.'

'But how - how does it happen?' she asked in a whisper.

'Okay - here's the science bit. First, the weather conditions need to be perfect - like today. The *spectre* - in this case, you - must climb to a high point while the morning sun is low in the sky. That's why I got you out of bed so early.'

'I get that bit, but . . .' Ruairi pulled her into his side and silenced her with a kiss.

'The spectre must stand with her back to the sun so the shadow is formed. The spectre's halo - or glory - occurs when droplets of water

261

are suspended in the air and sunlight reflects off them, shines back toward the sun and . . . us.'

'Wow.' The word was inadequate and hardly described the spectre or what she was feeling.

'*Wow* - indeed. You make me feel King of the World - know that?' Unexpectedly serious, Ruairi turned her round and looked as if he was committing her face to memory. Then he drew her into his arms and kissed her. If they hadn't been lost in the kiss they would have seen themselves surrounded by glory as the light shimmered and diffracted around them. Ruairi was first to break off. 'Forgiven?'

'Nothing to forgive.' To hide the catch in her voice she moved away from him and their shadows broke apart. 'But, Ruairi how can this work - you and me?' He turned his back on the Brocken Spectre as if it was too distracting, and looked instead across the wide acres of Kinloch Mara just visible through the shifting mist.

'Fliss, it's no secret I was in a relationship which I thought would go the distance. But it didn't - and the fault's entirely mine. My fiancée - Fiona, was used to the diversions of Edinburgh, London and Paris, foolishly I brought her to Kinloch Mara where none of those things exists.'

He drew breath as though it was important that she understood. She knew how much it cost him to admit that he'd failed at something as fundamental as getting his bride to the altar and making a life with her, so she gave his hand an encouraging squeeze.

'Go on . . .'

'It can be really bleak here in the winter when the tourists leave and everything shuts down. That particular winter, Mitzi and the girls decamped for Angus's villa in Barbados in early December as soon as their term ended at boarding school. As a result, Fiona spent a lonely Christmas at Tigh na Locha, waiting for me to return home from Australia. When I came back for the New Year I was so immersed in estate business that I didn't see how isolated and neglected she was feeling. Now, looking back - I realise that I didn't court her enough or pay her enough attention. That was the kiss of death on our relationship.'

Fliss knew that in Fiona's place she would have stayed at his side, reading by the big fire in the library while he and Murdo went over the accounts. Driving out with him to rescue animals caught in the snowdrifts. Organising parties and making Tigh na Locha so welcoming that he would never want to leave. She would have cemented their relationship with nights of passion in the Laird's old-fashioned bed, making love until the weak sun pushed through the curtains and drove everything else from their minds.

Not because she felt it was her duty as his fiancée, but because it was what she wanted to do, as his woman.

'But then, I imagine that any woman - cut off by the winter snows, miles from Edinburgh and its allure would find it hard to settle to life as the laird's wife.' He excused Fiona's desertion by putting the blame squarely on himself.

'Not every woman,' she demurred. But he was too lost in his own thoughts to register her moue of protest.

'Eventually, the reality of being the laird's wife, the social demands of the role and her position in the community hit home. That, coupled with the realisation of the years of hard work necessary to make the estate profitable, proved a bridge too far. The gilt wore off the gingerbread - in this case, me - and she left. One month before we were due to walk down the aisle together.'

'When - how?' Now she was hearing the whole story she wanted all the gaps filled in.

'She packed her cases one morning while I was out on the hills with Murdo, called a taxi and left a note with her engagement ring - a family heirloom - explaining why she couldn't marry me.' Pain was etched on his face and Fliss wanted to find the faithless Fiona and shake her, make her realise what she'd thrown away. But she also felt a grudging sympathy for the runaway bride - Kinloch Mara was undoubtedly beautiful, but Ruairi's love came at a price. That price was sharing the burden of lairdship and helping to preserve his inheritance for the next generation. It was his life's work and any prospective wife who didn't understand the importance of his birthright was the wrong candidate for the position.

'Maybe it was for the best . . .' she began, taking his hands in her own. But Ruairi was lost in the past and seemed almost oblivious to her presence. Moving away, he stepped over to the edge of the ridge, rested his hand on the triangulation point obelisk and stared into the middle distance. Momentarily, Fliss was transported back to the night of the party when she'd imagined him - tall, dark, and kilted - striding romantically along a highland mountain ridge.

That fantasy had become a reality.

'When she left, it became clear that that it was asking too much of Fiona - of *any* woman to give up *everything* for me. Or, to expect anyone to understand what Kinloch Mara means to me.'

'Wouldn't that rather depend on the woman?' Silently, Fliss willed him to see the difference between the fiancée who'd broken off the engagement and . . . well, herself.

'You think?' His brow furrowed in concentration, as though that hadn't occurred to him.

'I *know*,' she said simply, too proud to tell him how much she loved Kinloch Mara. Or to beg for the chance to prove him wrong.

She longed to explain how - in her humble opinion, the estate could become profitable and he could stop travelling the world and spend his every waking moment on his beloved estate. She'd driven round Kinloch Mara on many occasions with Murdo in the Land Rover and seen its untapped potential. Words, phrases and ideas were buzzing around inside her head like angry wasps, demanding release. She knew she had to say her piece, her future - their future - depended on it.

Taking a deep breath, she opened with: 'Don't you think it's time you thought outside the box? Stopped thinking what you can't do and concentrated instead on what *could* be achieved in Kinloch Mara with a little imagination and some forethought?'

'Such as . . .'

'Accept Angus's offer of an interest free loan, use it to establish your conservation scheme and build up ecotourism on the estate. It's what you were studying at university, wasn't it? Angus reckons you could probably make twice as much if you ran ecotourism alongside the more traditional aspects of estate management: farming, shooting and deer stalking.'

'And you and Angus would know all about that, would you?' She was so focused on delivering her speech that she didn't detect the ice in his voice.

'Yes! We - Angus, Murdo and me, have discussed how the estate could easily accommodate eco-friendly lodges . . . built well away from Tigh na Locha.' Her eyes were bright with missionary zeal as she outlined the plans neither Angus nor Murdo dared broach with him because he was so protective of his inheritance.

Only she, it appeared, was prepared to go head to head with him.

'Go on.'

'Stressed out businessmen and women would jump at the chance to experience Kinloch Mara's peace and tranquillity. You could build a profitable health spa to run alongside the eco-tourism, licence it for weddings etc. - make it a complete package. And that's something I could help with.'

'You've been giving this some thought, haven't you?' This time there was definite frost in his voice.

'I've had plenty of time to talk it over with Angus while I've been setting up the therapy centre.' She turned and smiled, convinced that he'd see how diversification coupled with Angus's financial help could make his estate thrive. One glance at his darkening countenance was enough to wipe the smile off her face and douse her enthusiasm. 'What? Have I said something wrong?'

'Ah, yes; the therapy centre. Do you really think that Mitzi will sustain her interest when she has Angus's oil millions to spend? If the therapy centre closes then you're out of a job . . . And what would happen to the health spa and eco-friendly lodges then? It can't work; and to think otherwise is no more than a pipe dream.'

'Well I think you're wrong.'

'It's my land, my responsibility and I think I know what's best for

Kinloch Mara.'

'Do you now?'

'You've done a wonderful job of setting up the therapy centre and everyone's grateful. But you're returning to London in a few months and no one - least of all me - would blame you for trading Kinloch Mara for the big city. No one expects you to stay forever, or would think any the worse of you for leaving.'

There it was again; that damning little word: *expect*. Why did everyone assume what she wanted, instead of asking her? If he asked her, she would say she wanted to stay forever. Then it occurred to her that maybe history was repeating itself and he was pushing her away, sacrificing his own happiness for the sake of the estate. Just as he had done with Fiona.

'That's the difference between you and me, isn't it?' she asked, aware she was ramming her point home with a little too much vehemence. But she was fighting for something significant, even if he didn't realise it yet.

'What is?'

Having gone this far she knew there was no turning back. She took a deep breath and ploughed on, ignoring his warning frown.

'You - running away from the estate, the place you love. Using the fundraising scheme as a convenient cover for the fact you haven't yet come to terms with your father's death, or your fiancée getting cold feet.' She steeled herself as their argument played out in mime, silhouetted on the clouds below.

'You know nothing about it,' he said quietly, but with a wealth of emotion in his voice.

'I think I do. I've lost my parents and -'

'It's not the same thing at all,' he said, his jaw tight.

'How? Do you think because you live in a grand house the pain and loss is any different? Only the scale is different. And - and at least you still *have* your family.'

He gave a snort of derision.

'Mitzi and the girls? Let me tell you about them, shall I? Isla made my ex-fiancée's life a misery; calling her Princess Fiona and saying she turned into a troll at sundown - like the character in Shrek. Mitzi, despite her promises, made no effort to leave the Tigh na Locha or give a firm date when Fiona and I could take it over and get married. She preferred having the girls in boarding school so she could go gallivanting round the globe, spending Angus's money. Or any man foolish enough to subsidise her extravagances. Dressing it all up as a desire to escape the Scottish winter; getting sympathy because she was a widow with two wayward daughters. Then refusing to back me up when I tried to rein them in.'

'But that's all changed - hasn't it? Mitzi's ready to move onto Angus's estate, Cat's keen to train as a veterinary nurse and Isla . . .'

'I think the YouTube viral sums Isla up rather neatly.'

'She has a God-given talent for art. Which you would see if you stopped being so *bloody* towards her and opened your eyes,' she declared passionately, even if she was no friend of Isla's. 'I know she's acted like a fool, but why not encourage her to take a foundation course at a Scottish University and then see if she's got what it takes to make a career out of her paintings. You might be surprised.'

He glanced at his battered Fossil wristwatch and turned back to her, grey-faced, as though the argument was all too familiar - and he didn't have the time or energy to go over it all again.

'And what do you get out of this?' he asked cuttingly.

'Me? I - I don't understand?'

'Well, according to your plan everybody wins. So I'm asking . . . what's in it for you?' She didn't like the way he looked at her; it was as if he'd reverted to default mode: shuttered and suspicious.

'Nothing - except I'd be willing to stay on and help to set up the eco-lodges and health spa - if asked.'

'No surprise there, then,' he said coldly.

'Meaning what exactly?'

He shrugged, gave her a telling look and turned away from her. Then she got it.

Evidently, he believed that she'd somehow convinced Angus and

Murdo what a good idea the proposed Kinloch Mara Health Spa and eco-lodges were and had offered to run the spa side of the venture. Providing her with a job for life - or, at least for however long it took before she got bored with the idea. The last hurdle - as he apparently saw it - would be getting him onside, and she was evidently prepared to use everything at her disposal to win him over.

'Ruairi, you've got it wrong; you've got me all wrong. Please . . .'

Sickeningly, she knew that no matter what they'd shared: the morning on the island, the snatched kisses in the kitchen and almost becoming lovers - he would always have the suspicion lurking at the back of his mind that she was too good to be true. That one day she'd run true to form and show her true colours.

She glanced up at his face in profile, at the almost dejected slump of his shoulders and wondered how the morning could have gone so spectacularly wrong; how she could have got *him* so spectacularly wrong.

'Will you listen to me for a moment,' she begged, desperate to turn the clock back. 'Maybe I didn't make myself clear.'

'Clear enough.' Plainly, he thought that in order to achieve her ends, she was prepared to sleep with him- turn him into play-doh in her hands. 'Can we go back to the Land Rover? I've got a plane to catch.' He glanced at his watch as if she hadn't spoken.

Defeated, Fliss knew the last thing she wanted was to sit by his side and be thrown against him as they negotiated the potholes all the way back to Tigh na Locha. Hurt turned to anger at his wrong-headedness and inflexibility - and she wanted to make him feel as wretched as she did.

'No.'

'No, what?'

'I don't want to ride back to Tigh na Locha with you. I want to walk back on my own. You're the Laird, as you're so keen to remind me. So, use your walkie-talkie and summon a member of staff to meet me at the bottom of the hill.'

'Now you're just being irrational. You'll get lost.' His lips were set in an annoyed line at what he patently regarded as a further example of her mulishness.

'That's not your problem. *I'm* not your problem. So if you wouldn't mind?' She squared up to him, hands on hips and stared him down.

'Don't be so pig-headed.'

'Pot and kettle . . .'

He moved towards her as if he meant to drag her down the hill. Then, apparently reading her determined expression, reached the conclusion that it was pointless arguing with her. He summoned Murdo on the walkie-talkie instead.

'*On my way. Ruairi - tell Fliss to stick to the well-trodden path and keep the sun on her right hand side. Is there a problem*?' Ruairi held the walkie-talkie at arm's length so she could hear Murdo's response but didn't answer.

'Over and out.' He put the two-way radio into his rucksack and shrugged it onto his shoulders. 'Is this how it's going to end? God help me, Fliss, I'm not even sure what we've argued about.'

'We've argued about differences. The difference between *asking* and *expecting;* of things staying the way they are - or changing. About you trusting me . . . Figure it out on your journey to Hong Kong.'

Last night, she'd believed they'd been on the brink of making love and starting a relationship. Now she realised that she'd read too much into it and they'd simply been about to have sex. Stung by his attitude, his inability to take advice and unwillingness to see the lifeline Angus was throwing to him, she cast around for caustic words to hurt and wound him.

Words that would make him feel wretched, too.

'I'm beginning to think . . .'

'Yes,' he clearly thought she was about to change her mind.

'. . . that Fiona had a lucky escape.'

'Is that how you see it?' His eyes were as cold and hard as dark sapphires.

'Isn't that how everyone sees it?' she shrugged, playing out her role.

He didn't respond. He tightened the straps on his rucksack and

269

started to make his way downhill. After two or three steps, he turned back. 'Here, you might need this.' He gave her the bottle of water they'd shared earlier and as she took it from him, their fingers touched, briefly and regret lingered, unspoken between them.

'Thanks.' He didn't reply but strode away from her and was soon lost behind a veil of her tears and the Brigadoon-like mist in the valley.

Chapter Thirty Two

Six weeks later, Angus helped Fliss to manoeuvre a new piece of therapy equipment into the drawing room of the Wee Hoose. Resembling a luxurious barber's chair with padded armrests and two independent legs which could be raised or lowered hydraulically, it was the answer to her prayers. Since opening the therapy centre to the public, appointments had flooded in - thanks to a combination of Isla's eye-catching flyers, the draw of the Urquhart name and the newspaper article about Iona's premature delivery on the night of the big storm.

'It's a great chair, Angus. Life's going to be a whole lot easier now Shona's found me a part time assistant. I'll be able to concentrate on holistic therapy, massages and spa treatments in the conservatory while my assistant gives pedicures and manicures in here. The drawing room with its view of the loch lends itself to the task, doesn't it? We're really on a roll, aren't we?'

She maintained an air of forced jollity whilst studiously ignoring the elephant in the room - the yellow brocade Knowle sofa with the cinnamon comforter folded neatly over one arm. She closed her mind to the loneliness and melancholy that had settled on her since Ruairi's departure. Her professional life was right on track but she was constantly drawn back to the ill-considered things she'd said on the hill top and the sight of him yomping into the swirling mist.

Pushing her fringe out of her eyes with the back of her hand, she sighed.

'That was a big sigh, Fliss - something you wanna share?' Angus angled the chair so it faced the windows. Fetching a matching bubble wrapped footstool from the hall he placed it by the side of the chair and patted it for her to sit down.

'Oh, it's just - you know . . .'

'You gotta spell things out for me, honey. I'm great at putting out wildcat fires in oil fields but when it comes to figuring out females I don't know Jack.'

'Well, to be blunt Angus. It's my contract.'

'Ah,' he sat down on the yellow sofa, clearly not trusting his six foot five frame to the newly acquired therapy chair. 'Go ahead.'

'It expires in two weeks' time right after the Highland Ball. I've started taking Christmas bookings, ordered new equipment. The therapy centre could really take off, if you and R-Ruairi were amenable. I - *we* could build a wooden gazebo outside near the rhododendrons and install a hot tub - then I'd be able to offer hydrotherapy alongside other holistic treatments. So - *please* tell me where I stand? Is my contract to be renewed or should I stop taking bookings after the last week in October and prepare to head back to London?'

Sitting on the bubble wrapped stool, she put a hand on Angus's khaki chinos and looked at him pleadingly.

'Fliss, I wish you hadn't brought this up. It's kinda awkward, you know?

'Awkward? Look, I *know* under the terms of the contract the position of manageress was temporary for six months, during which time we'd see if the therapy centre was a go-er, or not. Well, it is, isn't it? A go-er, I mean.'

'You've done a great job,' Angus started, but Fliss cut across him.

'And I know that part of my brief was to find a permanent manageress for the centre if necessary. Well, it isn't necessary, because . . . I - I'd like to stay on and manage the centre. If that's okay with you and Mitzi?'

'It isn't that simple, Fliss.' He shook his head sorrowfully.

'Not that simple? Angus, if you're about to close the centre because you and Mitzi are getting married or if I'm about to be *let* go, I think I have a right to know.'

'*Let go?* Never that, Fliss. It's just that Ruairi . . .' Unable to meet her eye, he fiddled with the large tassel on the end of the sofa.

'Ruairi - Yes?' She spoke sharply, already anticipating his answer.

'I spoke to him on the phone and he said . . .' Red faced, Angus ran his finger round his shirt collar. 'I wish you'd speak to Mitzi, honey.'

'Tell me what Ruairi said. I can take it; in fact I've been living in Kinloch Mara for so long now, I think I'm developing taibhsearachd - and can *guess* what he said.'

She thought back to a very different scenario on this sofa when Ruairi had tried to second-guess her reaction to him touching her. Then, in quick succession she recalled each of her well-aimed darts and his expression as they struck home - *it's time you thought outside the box. Stop thinking about what you can't do and concentrate instead on what you could achieve . . . . I'm not your problem.*

'Fliss honey,' Angus rubbed his finger across his upper lip, betraying his agitation. 'I don't know how to put this . . .'

'He doesn't want me to stay on, does he?'

'Yes and - no.'

'And he wants to shut down the therapy centre?'

'Er - kinda.' Angus looked like he was searching for the right words but they were proving elusive.

'If we're shutting down, why did you allow me to order all this new equipment? Am I a child to be pacified with new toys? Or bought off with expensive presents when life isn't going according to plan? What about the therapist Shona's just found for me? Do I sack her even before I've employed her?' Her skin felt tight, itchy and hives spread over her neckline and down her arms.

'Ruairi says he - he wants the therapy centre to continue. It's a money spinner and you've done a good job in setting it up.' Fliss glared at him, if he thought she could be placated with a few sweet words then he was mistaken.

'But how will that work? The therapy centre won't run itself and I can't see Mitzi breaking a fingernail to do it.' Anger made her speak more harshly than she'd intended. 'Sorry - I know I shouldn't shoot the messenger. But -'

273

'Ruairi's going to install a new manageress. In fact he's got someone lined up.' Angus retreated into the back of the sofa, as if hoping he could disappear down the sides of the cushions like loose change and avoid her wrath.

'A new *what?* Of all the dirty, rotten, underhand tricks.' Agitatedly, she picked at the bubble wrap, popping the blisters as she delivered each scathing word. 'He swans off to Hong Kong, loads the gun and leaves you to fire the bullets?' Angus looked like a man under siege so Fliss took pity on him, calmed down and asked: 'When's this - this *changeover* going to take place?'

'Soon after the Highland Ball, when he returns from the Far East in just over two weeks. But, Fliss,' Angus dragged himself out of the back of the deep sofa and took her hands in his large paws. 'Let Ruairi explain, honey. You'll see it all makes sense.' But she didn't hear a word of it, because her chest felt tight, her heart heavy and she was near to bursting into tears.

'But Angus - I thought you *liked* me,' she said with a catch in her voice. 'I thought I'd done a good job . . .'

'You have darlin'. It's just that Ruairi feels it's time for a change and -' He clammed up, as if he'd said too much. Fliss's lips twisted as she saw the irony in the situation. She'd told Ruairi to break free of the ties that bound him to Tigh na Locha and the past. When she'd exhorted him to move on with his life, she hadn't thought for one second that she'd be the first casualty of his reorganisation.

Thank God, they hadn't become lovers. How much worse would his rejection feel then? When she met Hugh Auchinloch she'd shake him by the hand . . . he'd saved her from making a complete fool of herself. She looked at Angus - he'd been so kind and considerate since their first meeting, almost avuncular. But at the end of the day, Ruairi was Laird of Kinloch Mara and his wishes were to be obeyed.

'OK, Angus, I'll play ball.' Resignedly, she stood up and ran her hand over the therapy chair she'd ordered with such optimism. 'I'll fill your appointment diary. And to show there are no hard feelings, I'll throw in the business plan I've drawn up for phase two of the therapy centre. And my ideas for expanding the business into a full-size spa - should you ever persuade Ruairi to swallow his pride, accept your loan and drag the estate into the twenty first century.'

'Sure, Fliss. I'd be glad to see them. You're a girl in a million. About Ruairi and the loan . . .' Fliss stopped him in mid-sentence by raising her hand.

'Nothing to do with me as Ruairi has made plain,' she said bitterly. Angus stood up and shuffled past, kissing her awkwardly on the cheek before leaving the house via the conservatory.

A girl in a million, she grimaced - and about to join the other two million or so seeking employment during a recession. She looked longingly at the telephone and thought how much she wanted to ring Becky and talk this over with her. But the pain was too raw, and besides she hadn't even told Becky the whole truth about her relationship with Ruairi. As far as she was aware, they were still at daggers drawn . . . which just about summed it up.

Two nights later, Fliss was cleaning her brushes and washing her sponges in the kitchen sink when Isla strolled in, took one look around and gave a so-this-is-what-you-get-up-to-down-here sniff. Having spent two days brooding over Angus's bombshell, Fliss was in no mood for Isla's game playing.

'Did you want something? If you've come for a treatment, you're out of luck. I've just hung the CLOSED sign over the door. Come back tomorrow, or better still - make an appointment like everyone else. I'm an employee of the Urquhart estate - not its slave. As of ten minutes ago I'm officially off duty.'

'Wow. That was quite a speech.' Isla wriggled her slim derriere onto a bar stool, helped herself to an apple from the fruit bowl and waved it in the general direction of the loch. 'I told you you'd get fed up living and working in this dump. Everyone does.'

'Like Fiona, you mean?' Fliss couldn't help asking. Now she'd been given the order of the boot she no longer felt the need to pretend she wasn't interested in Ruairi's disastrous engagement.

'*Princess* Fiona you mean,' Isla laughed. 'Such a lightweight. Two flakes of snow and a frozen pipe and she was off. That - and when I pointed out that her initials after marriage would be F.U. she lost interest in becoming Lady Urquhart of the Glen very quickly.' Somewhat surreally, it occurred to Fliss that if she were to substitute Urquhart for Bagshawe she'd have the same initials. Not that there was any chance of that happening!

'And doesn't it bother you that you chased away your brother's fiancée?'

'If she'd really loved him, nothing would have put her off. Now, would it? Actually, I think I did Ruairi a favour - she was totally self-obsessed and up herself,' Isla said, without a trace of irony. Restlessly, she got up and examined the contents of the fridge, read the notices fastened to the freezer with magnets, picked up Fliss's brushes and cast a cursory eye over them. She was really beginning to grate on Fliss's already shredded nerves and Fliss knew she had to get rid of her before she said something she'd later regret.

'Is there something I can help you with? Something specific, I mean?' She took the brushes away from Isla, threw dirty towels into the washing machine and banged the door shut to indicate how busy she was.

'Oh, yes. Thanks for mentioning my plans for Art School to Ruairi. He's arranged for me to have some private lessons with Malcolm Cameron, starting next week.' Fliss was about to remonstrate that she'd done no such thing, but then remembered their conversation on the morning of the Brocken Spectre. *Isla has a God-given talent, which you would see if you opened your eyes.* So he *had* been listening after all.

'Malcolm Cameron?' she queried.

'He paints iconic highland landscapes that sell for hundreds of thousands to ex-pats and the Japanese. Not quite my style but I might learn something from him. Why are you looking at me like that?' Isla's blue eyes narrowed suspiciously and the sharp angles of her face were thrown into relief by the westering sun.

'Because you've actually thanked me for something and admitted that someone might know more about a subject than you.'

'You've changed - know that?' Isla waggled a finger at Fliss. 'And not for the better - you used to be quite sweet, but now . . .' Ignoring the gibe, Fliss glanced at her watch and Isla took the hint. 'Anyhoo, I'd better be on my way, Cat wants to tell us all about her first week in the vet's practice, over dinner - urgh. Just hope she spares us the gruesome details of sticking thermometers up cats' bottoms.' Pulling a face, she tossed her half-eaten apple in the general direction of the waste disposal unit and missed.

Fliss wished she'd just go. She was expecting Murdo at any moment and wasn't in the mood for another of their strained silences followed by longing looks and heartfelt sighs.

'Expecting a visitor?' Isla asked, plainly not missing a trick.

'Murdo's coming down to teach me a few reels in time for the Highland Ball.'

'*Is* he now?'

'Don't start with me tonight, Isla. Murdo's a mate, nothing more. Stay and act as chaperone if it makes you happy. *Now* what have I said?' she asked as Isla's face crumpled.

'Murdo hasn't even *looked* in my direction since the YouTube viral. He's refusing to speak to me until he sees evidence that I've,' she gulped down some air, 'grown up. He's taken it all *way* too seriously - and strangely, Ruairi hasn't taken it seriously enough.' She forgot her self-pity long enough to shoot Fliss a suspicious look.

'Ever thought that maybe Ruairi has more to worry about than you and Cat making fools of yourself on the internet? Like, making the estate turn a profit and clearing his debts? As for Murdo, I thought you wanted him to leave you alone. Didn't you tell me there was no place for him in your life? Sounds to me like you've been - what's the saying - hoist by your own petard.'

That didn't please Isla, she jabbed the space in front of Fliss's face with her forefinger for emphasis. 'See? That's what I mean. You wouldn't have *dared* to speak to me like that, once.'

'Breaking news: Times - Have - Changed. Just telling it like it is, sister - it's an additional service I'm offering these days. Relationship counselling followed by a full body massage - shall I book you in?' Her days of treating Isla with kid gloves were over, Angus's bombshell and Ruairi's plans to replace her had changed all that.

Just as Isla was searching for some suitable retort, Murdo entered the kitchen with an ancient CD player under his arm and a stack of CDs in a carrier bag. Ignoring Isla, he spoke solely to Fliss.

'I think I'll set up in the hall - there's more room there. You might want to change out of your Birkenstocks, though; Scottish country dancing is pretty energetic.'

Leaving them behind, Fliss walked into the therapy centre and changed into a pair of Vans slip-ons. When she walked into the hall, Murdo was alone and loading a CD into the player.

'Everything okay, Murdo?'

'I might ask you the same,' he countered.

'Of course it is,' she said with forced jollity. She noticed, as he fiddled with the ancient machine, that he'd let his customary buzz cut grow out and his hair now curled round his ears and flopped into his eyes. Clearly, the Urquhart cousins' jibes of *ginger minger* no longer bothered him and he was comfortable with his strawberry blonde hair. And if that wasn't a signal to Isla - to everyone - that he'd moved on, then she didn't know what was.

'Ta dah.' She broke the heavy mood by extending her arms above her head and forming a circle with her thumb and forefinger.

Murdo shook his head. 'You're confusing *Highland dancing* - as performed in competitions at the highland gatherings - with Scottish country dancing. So no swords to dance over, I'm afraid.' His face clouded over and Fliss felt certain he was remembering Isla's performance over the two crossed pokers on YouTube.

'Look, Murdo. Do you want to do this some other time? Neither of us seems particularly in the mood and I'm not one hundred per cent certain that I'm going to the Ball.'

'Not going to the Ball? Why on earth not?' He looked so astonished that Fliss guessed he knew nothing of the proposed changes to the therapy centre. Although she liked Murdo and thought of him as a friend, she'd kept her own council and hadn't told him how things stood between her and Ruairi. She must have looked a bit dejected because he found *Mairi's Wedding* on the CD and played it - primarily, she suspected, to cheer them both up.

He bowed on the long first chord and held out his hand and she took it. If she *did* attend the Highland Ball, there was no way she was going to it as a Sassenach who didn't know the steps to the reels and had to sit on the sidelines like a drooping wallflower.

Like someone who had no place in Kinloch Mara.

Chapter Thirty Three

'Fliss - sweetie, is that you? Come on in,' Mitzi called, her voice muffled by the panelled door. Fliss hesitated; there was something intimate about entering someone's bedroom, especially when it was the Laird's Room and Ruairi's by right. Sensitive to Mitzi's grief, he hadn't claimed it back after Hamish's death but now it seemed that everything was changing - moving forward. After eight weeks in the Far East, Ruairi was returning home to announce Mitzi and Angus's engagement at the Highland Ball tomorrow evening. Mitzi and the girls were moving onto Angus's estate before the end of the month - and she was returning to Pimlico.

Changes all round it seemed.

Fliss pushed open the heavy door and family memories, ancient history, old sorrows and new beginnings met her at the threshold. To dispel the goose-stepped-over-my-grave shiver at the thought of Ruairi and his bride making love in the tapestry hung Laird's Bed, she cracked a feeble joke.

'Shouldn't we call the cops and report you've been burgled, Mitzi?' She gestured towards mahogany wardrobes that looked like they'd exploded and disgorged clothes everywhere.

Mitzi laughed. 'It may look like chaos, Fliss darling - but it's organised chaos. Now come and have a look as the evening dresses I've laid out for you.'

'Mitzi, I'm not - '

'Now don't start with all that nonsense about not attending the Ball. Ruairi will expect you to be there. Angus and I *want* you there; you're family for goodness sake.' Family? Fliss hardly thought so. But Mitzi, clearly unaware that she was smarting for being traded in for a new therapist, twittered on. 'Now, try on some of my dresses, one of them is bound to suit you. We're about the same size, although you are quite a bit taller. Cat will loan you a pair of dancing slippers - the Urquhart Ball is no place for killer heels, or sissies.'

Knowing when she was outgunned, Fliss selected an ankle-length kingfisher blue silk skirt and coordinating sequinned bustier knowing that the colour would suit her. Holding it in front of her with one hand, she piled her hair on top of her head and regarded her reflection in the cheval mirror.

Under different circumstances, she would have loved dressing up for the ball and the chance to show off the reels she'd learned. But all she could think of was meeting with Ruairi after an eight-week gap. The frank and honest exchange of views over her being *let go* that would take place - come hell or high water.

'It's a pity you're not entitled to wear a clan sash over your shoulder. But, never mind, I'll loan you the family tiara and a matching necklace. You'll look fabulous with your hair all pinned up.' Mitzi faltered, finally sensing that all was not well with Fliss and plainly anxious to please. Fliss winced at her innocent comment. There was nothing quite like being ineligible to wear tartan at a Highland Ball to underline that she was an outsider and her time here was coming to an end.

'*Such* a pity,' she agreed, having no desire to rain on Mitzi's parade.

'I was a Grant before marriage,' Mitzi burbled on, rooting in a mahogany tallboy and drawing out an orange-red tartan sash dissected by pale blue lines. 'I thought I'd wear *my* clan tartan tomorrow night - pinned to my right shoulder and tied over my left hip to show that it's not the colours of a clan chief's wife. That'll be fairer to Hamish's memory, my future with Angus *and* Ruairi's sensibilities.'

Mitzi's bright smile faded and Fliss felt ashamed that she'd allowed her own problems to blind her to Mitzi's feelings. She was abandoning her widowhood, turning her back on the home she'd lived in for over twenty years and taking a brave step into the future. Not to mention giving up the title of Lady Urquhart to become plain Mrs Angus Gordon. Fliss wondered briefly if Mitzi was marrying Angus the *man*, or Angus the *millionaire* who had it in his power to make her life a bed of thornless roses. Maybe, in Mitzi's eyes, they were one and the same.

She wriggled into the silk taffeta skirt, enjoying its cool kiss against her skin. Mitzi slid up the zip and handed her the boned bustier with its overlay of lace and ribbon. Fliss saw the Vivienne Westwood label sewn into it and shuddered to think how much it must have cost.

'A tip Fliss - take your bra off tonight and leave it off all day tomorrow. That way, you won't have any strap marks on your shoulders.' Fliss removed her bra and checked that the bustier fitted and she wasn't spilling out of the top. Scottish Country dancing was very energetic and she didn't want to embarrass herself by having her assets on show at the end of a strenuous reel.

'Thanks, Mitzi. I'd better get these things over to the Wee Hoose; I've promised to help Cat take some toys to the charity shop in Port Urquhart.'

'Thanks sweetie. I'll send Murdo over with the tiara and necklace tomorrow afternoon. For insurance purposes they have to remain in the safe when not being worn.' Fliss hung the bustier and skirt over her arm, stuffed her bra into her skirt pocket and picked up the three-quarter length white gloves Mitzi also pressed on her. Leaving Mitzi sorting through the disorder on her bed she left, closing the door softly behind her.

It looked like Cinderella was going to the Highland Ball after all.

Later that afternoon Fliss and Cat drew up by the back entrance to Tigh na Locha in a Land Rover. Cat switched off the engine and for a few moments they were lost in their thoughts. Fliss, planning what she was going to say when she met Ruairi again; and Cat, clearly wondering if she'd done the right thing by donating her collection of soft toys to the RSPCA.

Fliss sensed that Cat wanted to move on with her life. Her work experience at the veterinary practice in Port Urquhart had given structure to her days - and she loved every minute of it. Fliss felt justifiably proud that she'd played some part in removing Cat away from

Isla's corrosive influence.

'Thanks for coming with me today, Fliss. I know you're busy,' Cat turned in her seat to look at her.

'Not so busy I can turn down an offer to visit the teeming metropolis of Port Urquhart,' Fliss pulled a wry face and Cat laughed. 'The fish and chips on the quayside were delicious, as usual. You did the right thing giving away your old toys, you know? Although I'm guessing it was a bit of a wrench?'

'It was. Most of those toys were presents from Papa. But I work with real animals now and I'm too old for stuffed bears and the like. Besides, I don't know if I told you, when I passed my driving test two weeks ago, Ruairi asked Murdo to get this old Land Rover roadworthy - and now it's mine. Ruairi's offered to pay the insurance, road tax and to maintain it because I've saved him thousands of pounds in boarding school fees by not returning to take my A levels. Although I might think about taking them at some point, I want Ruairi to be proud of me.' Her eyes shone as she stroked the battered old steering wheel. Then she giggled, reminding Fliss that she was only seventeen years old. 'Murdo hung the fluffy dice over the driver's mirror. How kitsch is that?'

'Very.' Fliss thought what a great guy Murdo was. He'd kept the estate running while Ruairi was away, found time to help her master several reels, *and* taught Cat to coax the old Land Rover through its paces. But Cat wasn't laughing, she was regarding Fliss gravely. 'What is it, Cat?'

Cat reached over and squeezed Fliss's hands. 'Two things. First, I'm truly sorry that I didn't give you the heads-up over the viral - but Isla would have *killed* me and the thought scared the bejezus out of me. And then there's Murdo.'

'Murdo?'

'Isla's never been good at sharing her toys. Just be careful, that's all. You know?' she advised as Fliss got out of the Land Rover.

'Thanks for the warning, but there's nothing between us, I assure you. We're just good friends.' Fliss pulled a face at the cliché and retrieved her shopping from the back seat, acknowledging that Murdo *had* been her friend from start to finish. Deep in thought, she made her way past the permanently closed ornamental gates, through the rose gardens before finally skirting the rhododendrons and entering the Dower House.

Half an hour later Murdo arrived to give her a final dance lesson. He handed her a stiff card the colour of clotted cream. Attached to it, by a twisted cord in a darker shade of cream was a small pencil.

'It's your dance card, ma'am.' He laughed at her expression. 'I know what you're thinking - isn't this all just a bit too Jane Austen for words - but, believe me, you'll need it.'

Fliss opened the card and saw the dances listed in order, from the Dashing White Sergeant to something called 'Gallop/John Peel'. At number five there was a break for supper and something called 'flatties' which would take place - 'if time allowed'.

'Flatties?'

'Yes, other music, jazz or swing; and maybe a disco to keep the youngsters happy. The main thing to remember is: don't stop midway through any of the reels or you'll cause a motorway style pile-up on the dance floor. If you go wrong, don't worry - the more experienced dancers will steer you in the right direction.'

'No pressure then. And the pencil?'

'To write down who'll be partnering you for each dance so you can get into position quickly. May I?' He took the card and scribbled his name next to The Eightsome and Foursome Reels. 'I see that Mitzi's given you a pair of gloves,' he picked up the gloves which Fliss had discarded on the oak chest. 'They're considered a bit old-fashioned now, but Ruairi's a stickler for tradition. There's a little pocket in the glove - see? You keep the card in there.'

'Thanks, Murdo. You're a star.'

'Well, I wouldn't know about that.' Fliss was amused to see him flush and then he quickly changed the subject. 'By the way, thanks for helping Cat with the toys. It was quite a struggle for her to part with them. You see, after Hamish's death, Ruairi had to tuck the toys around her in a predetermined order each evening and read her a bedtime story before she'd let him switch off the light.'

Fliss absorbed this information in silence. She'd reverted to her original opinion of Ruairi as autocratic, unsentimental laird and had hardened her heart against him. Somehow, that image didn't sit easily with Murdo's story. Or, if she was being honest - the time she'd spent with him on the island and the frantic kisses they'd exchanged on the drawing room sofa. No - it had taken just five minutes and her unguarded tongue to ruin everything between them.

Nice work, Fliss, she congratulated herself.

'Guess we're all moving on?' She gave Murdo a penetrating look and wondered if he'd comment about the changes taking place in the therapy centre. Instead, he adeptly changed the subject.

'Talking of which - have you heard that Ruairi's put the Notting Hill house on the market? Isla's furious of course - she'd got some mad idea about attending art school in London and living in Elgin Crescent.' He gave Fliss time to digest this piece of breaking news before continuing. 'Ruairi thinks - and I agree with him, that the money will have more impact invested in the estate. Looks like he's been doing some hard thinking while he's been away.'

This time it was Murdo who gave Fliss a measuring look, as though he wondered what had taken place on the hills over Kinloch Mara the morning of the Brocken Spectre.

'What about the bench and the memories of his mother?' Momentarily, Fliss forgot that she was part of the rationalisation of the estate's debts. She had memories of Elgin Crescent too, even if they were concertinaed into twenty-four hours, like the TV series - 24. The disastrous party, the plaque on the bench, 'Klingon' phone call, the ride in the police wagon, visiting Cat and Isla the following morning to give them a piece of her mind.

Murdo broke into her reverie. 'I thought we'd give the Strathspey one last go.'

'Can I try it wearing Cat's dancing slippers?' She tried to slip one on as the music started but got in a bit of a tangle with the fastenings.

'What are you like?' Murdo said in a cod Sarf Lunnon accent. 'Come 'ere, darlin'.' Fliss sat on the third tread of the stairs while Murdo knelt in front of her, placed her foot on his thigh, and opened up the crisscross elastic for her to slip her foot through.

'Do you have this in suede, young man?' Fliss asked, haughty as a duchess. 'Or should that be each-uisge?' Murdo laughed as he helped her off the step and watched her prance around in her soft slippers, but then his mood changed and he regarded her soberly.

'Fliss, I don't know what's happened between you and Ruairi and I don't want to. But I had hoped - seeing how perfect you are for each other - that it'd be like Sleeping Beauty in reverse.' Catching Fliss's puzzled expression he went on to explain. 'With *you* as the princess who hacks through the garden of thorns and rescues the prince. Not from a hundred year sleep, in this case - but from years of sadness, duty and commitment to Kinloch Mara and his family.'

'Murdo Gordon, I'd say that you're an old romantic.' She stood before him with her hands on her hips to hide how moved she was by his concern for Ruairi. For her.

He put his hand on her shoulder and looked down at her. 'If I had just one piece of advice to give Fliss, it would be this: *Trust Ruairi.*'

She put her hand over his in appreciation for his thoughtfulness. At that moment two figures appeared in the open doorway, blocking the setting sun and casting shadows into the hall. Murdo removed his hand from Fliss's shoulder and looked towards the porch.

'*Ruairi,*' he greeted, love and affection in his voice. He walked over to his old friend and they embraced like brothers. 'Isla,' Murdo nodded towards her, she was standing behind Ruairi as though uncertain of her welcome. 'What do you want?' The contrast between the greetings was so pronounced that Fliss felt sorry for Isla.

'I've come to see what you two get up to down here,' she began with some of her old spirit. But there was a quaver in her voice, as though she was close to tears.

'And why would that be of any interest to you?' Murdo asked coolly, the highland inflection in his voice suddenly noticeable. Isla sent Fliss a look that would have intimidated a lesser woman and then exchanged some angry words in Gaelic with Murdo. 'I'll leave you in peace, Ruairi. I'm sure you and Fliss have lots to discuss. Catch you later?'

'Of course,' Ruairi shook hands with Murdo. Turning away, he headed for the conservatory and the short cut up to Tigh na Locha. Blatantly ignored, Isla stamped her feet like a stroppy teenager and went chasing after him - and they could be heard arguing all the way up the path to Tigh na Locha.

'Well,' Ruairi said. 'That's a first . . . Isla running after Murdo.'

'Indeed,' Fliss replied stony-faced, in case he also thought there was something going on between her and Murdo. Not that it was any of his business.

Although her face was expressionless, her eyes widened as she drank in every detail of him. From the crumpled business suit, tie at half-mast and six o'clock shadow - to his dark hair sticking up, all out of place. He looked so tired and downbeat that, in spite of everything that had happened, her heart squeezed with love for him. She wanted to take him in her arms and kiss away the lines of exhaustion radiating out from his tired, blue eyes.

But she resisted the urge and remembered instead the last time they'd met - the difference between *asking* and *expecting*; of things staying as they were or changing and her feeling that that he didn't trust her. And her last, cutting remark before he'd yomped away from her, *I'm beginning to think that maybe Fiona had a lucky escape.*

By asking Angus and Mitzi not to renew her contract he'd made his position very clear - he wanted her out of his life - and the sooner the better.

Chapter Thirty Four

'So,' Ruairi said, as the silence stretched out. 'Is this how it's going to be? A war of attrition?'

'I don't want to fight you. There's nothing left to fight *over*, is there? It's all been decided.' Ruairi looked at her questioningly and she stared back, unsmiling, waiting for him to fill in the gaps.

'Oh, you mean the therapy centre? I thought you would have been happy about the change in arrangements.' He stumbled slightly over the word *change*.

'Happy! Are you mad? The centre is my life - there *is* nothing else.' Her voice snagged and tears pricked her eyes.

'Nothing?' Looking disappointed, he was deep in thought for a few moments. Then he removed his jacket, hung it over the newel post, walked over to the CD player, checked the disc in the machine and pressed the play button. The late September dusk closed in and softened the edges of the distant hills visible through the open front door. The haunting strains of a Strathspey drifted out of the speakers and he held out his hand: 'Dance?'

'*Dance?* With *you?* You're the last man on earth I want to dance with' Fliss knew her voice sounded shrill and unattractive but was too put out with him to care. He certainly had some nerve, she fumed; but then, she already knew that - didn't she?

'Yes, show me what you've learned. Murdo has kept me up to date with your progress.'

'Has he now?' She viewed him with suspicion, trying to guess his motive in asking Murdo to report to him, like she was under surveillance or something. And why was he being so nice and conciliatory towards her when they'd parted on bad terms? Maybe *they* - Angus, Mitzi and himself - wanted her to stay on long enough to oversee the induction of the new therapist. Well, if they thought she'd be agreeable to that, they were whistling in the wind.

'A Strathspey, how can you resist?' He cocked his head on one side and held out both hands, a shadow of a smile playing on his lips. And then he pulled her into his arms - slowly, seductively, as though sensing her reluctance. For the first few minutes she held herself poker -stiff, only just managing to keep her treacherous body from moulding into his, in response to his nearness and the memory of the last time he'd held her.

'Oh, I can resist most things, believe me,' she said waspishly. *Especially men like you* her eyes flashed, though her heart sang a different song.

'Of that I have no doubt. But -' he weakened her resolve by sending her that sexy, beguiling, ghost of a smile again. The one which said he was weary and full of regret over how things had ended up between them, and acknowledged he'd made a hash of things that morning on the hillside. Although she found his show of regret dangerously attractive, she wasn't about to fall into his arms like a heroine in a romance prepared to settle for a happy ending at any price. As he was about to discover . . .

'Yes?' she asked, sharply.

'Look, I know you're smarting over the therapy centre. But believe me - it's for the best.'

'You think so?' At her sharp intake of breath, he stepped closer, as if realising that words weren't going to cut it. And, in fact, might actually be making things worse.

'I came straight over here when I arrived home, Fliss. I dropped my cases in the hall and came straight over,' he repeated, seemingly thinking she didn't get the message first time. 'I've missed you, know that?'

Concentrating on trying to work out how losing her job would benefit anyone - apart from him, and maybe Angus - it was a few seconds before she registered what he'd said: *I've missed you*. Completely caught off-guard, she tried to think of some caustic response but instead found it hard to breath as her heart swelled to fill her ribcage.

'I haven't missed you. Not for a second. Just so as you know,' she managed to gasp out as they stood poised to begin dancing on the downbeat.

'I'm sorry to hear that,' he said, his lips quirking, as though he sensed her surrender, in spite of her sharp words. 'Because I've missed you. More than I thought possible. More than I've missed anyone in my whole life. I couldn't wait to return to Kinloch Mara and to you.'

This time she didn't pull away from him, because the touch of his body against hers was too beguiling. He curled his forefinger into her palm, drew his fingernail along her heart line and brought a thousand nerve endings to attention. Fliss closed her eyes, the fight almost having gone out of her. She heard him take a step to bridge the infinitesimal gap between them.

They were standing so close, the heat and strength of his arousal seemed to scorch its way through the floaty material of her skirt. Her brain tried to remind her of their scathing adieu but her body recalled each teasing kiss. How it'd felt when he'd taken her nipple into his mouth and sucked, and when his hand had slid along her thigh. And it wanted to relive those sensuous, seismic moments over and over.

The three-four rhythm of the waltz went round several times but they made no attempt to dance. *This is wrong, this is very wrong,* she kept telling herself as her world contracted, and she could no longer deny how *right* it felt to be in his arms. Desire sizzled along her nerve endings, like a flame along a trail of gunpowder and Fliss knew she had to call a halt before she combusted. Or they ended up on the yellow Knowle sofa, making love with nothing resolved.

'You haven't missed me - not even for a second?' Ruairi prompted, his pupils dilating with desire until she could almost see her reflection in them.

'Not even for a nanosecond,' she lied, wondering why dancing with Murdo had never been this intimate, so charged with longing. The music forgotten, they stood tableau-still, each waiting for the other to take the first step. Then Ruairi moved his hand to span the space between Fliss's shoulder blades and pick up the beat and then discovered that she wasn't wearing a bra.

He seemed to find the fact that only a thin t-shirt stood between him and her nakedness very affecting. Bending closer, he whispered in her ear: 'Fliss-ss,'- drawing out the syllables so that, his breath along her jaw line became a pleasurable torment. A tremor rippled through her and she raised her shoulder to her ear to rub away the tingling sensation left in the wake of his whisper.

Swallowing hard, she looked up into his face and saw the shadows of fatigue underneath his indigo eyes and the desire he no longer bothered to hide. She wanted to tilt her head back, offer him her throat and beg him to cover it in soft, nibbling kisses that would drift downwards to her suddenly heavy breasts. And she wished she could take back the hasty words she'd spoken on the hilltop. Because instead of this awkwardness and a sense of unfinished business, there would be love, laughter and a joyous reconciliation. And she'd be able to admit just how much she'd missed him and lead him upstairs to her bedroom, close the curtains and pick up where they'd left off, eight weeks earlier.

She wanted to tell him that; but pride and self-respect wouldn't allow her to show how much she longed for him - cared for him - *loved him!*

The realisation was like a thunderbolt. But *how* she asked herself, could she love him when he'd turned her world upside down? Replacing her with another therapist, telling Angus not to renew her contract? Her struggle must have shown in her eyes - because Ruairi raised his hand to the nape of her neck and made her look up at him.

'Do you trust me?'

'Trust you?'

'There are things that need to slot into place. Things I can't reveal just yet, not until I'm sure.'

'Sure of what?'

'Of you.' His fingers curled round the nape of her neck, drawing her closer and his lips lightly touched hers. 'And me.' His questing fingers found their way under the bottom of her t-shirt and before she could utter a word of protest, had curled around her breast. In the same instant, his mouth came down upon hers, hard. She returned the fierce kiss, breath for shaky breath and as her tongue pushed into his mouth, her nipple hardened against his palm. 'God, Fliss - don't you know what you do to me?'

She knew exactly what she *wanted* to do to him. Her body had dreamed of little else for the last two months; it was what kept her awake at night and made her stare dreamily into the middle distance. Removing his hand with a show of reluctance, he sighed and took a distancing step away from her. The cold air blowing off the loch and through the open door covered her in goose bumps. She wrapped her arms protectively around herself to keep warm and to hide how readily her body had responded to his touch.

Clearly, the physical connection between them was as strong as ever - *that* part of their relationship had never been in question. But everything had undergone a sea change in his absence and she had to resist him with every fibre of her being.

But it was hard. God, it was hard.

'Am I forgiven?' He yawned, and looked so heartbreakingly jet lagged that she wanted nothing more than to close the gap between them, throw self-restraint away and make love to him. Then hold him in her arms and watch as he slept away the draining fatigue written on his face.

'Trust is one thing - forgiving might take a bit longer. By which time I'll be back in London and it'll all be academic, won't it?' She'd shown herself for a weak fool by falling too readily into his arms once before and she wouldn't do it again. She moved away, knowing she had to maintain the act, right up to the moment when Murdo drove her back to Inverness Airport.

Had to make him believe that she could dismiss him from her life with a so-what shrug and return to Pimlico with no regrets.

'At least let me -'

The CD track came to an end, and a cheesy version of 'Scotland the Brave' started up. Ruairi grimaced, moved over to the machine and pressed STOP. When he turned back, the dangerous moment had passed.

'Everything's ready for the ball,' Fliss said, moving the conversation adroitly onto safer ground. 'They've been erecting a large marquee over by the - what's it called - the Muster Ground? They've laid a duckboard path all the way from the back entrance of the house where guests will park their cars, right up to the door of the marquee. It's taken them the best part of two days and the mobile kitchens have just been installed.'

Ruairi's burning look said *this* wasn't the conversation they should be having, but he'd play along for now.

'The Highland Ball will be quite an event this year with Mitzi and Angus's engagement being announced,' he said in equally prosaic tones. 'That's why we've hired a marquee and outsourced everything to an event management team. The guest list is as long as my arm and beyond the capacity of Tigh na Locha staff; but what Mitzi wants - Mitzi gets.'

'Which is as it should be. A bride's wishes - even second time around - should be paramount.' She gave him a fierce look as if expecting him to contradict her. He didn't.

'I gather they want a Christmas wedding and a honeymoon in the West Indies, which means, come Hogmanay, I'll have Tigh na Locha to myself for the first time in years - unless I see it in with Murdo and his family.' Somehow, he didn't look as if this thought brought him much cheer.

Fliss had been looking forward to seeing in the New Year on a highland estate, perhaps snowed in - picturesquely, of course - shut off from the world, with Ruairi doing the first footing. Now she'd be getting drunk with Becky and the rest of the gang, teetering round the damp, cold streets of Pimlico on a pub crawl. Not wrapped in tartan and furs as she'd envisaged, but wearing a bum-freezing skirt, killer heels and a smile.

'Well, nothing stays the same for ever, does it?' she asked.

'I guess not.'

She removed his jacket from the newel post and handed it to him.

'You look all in. Go get some sleep. I'll see you tomorrow at the Highland Ball.'

With a heavy heart, she watched him turn on his heel with his jacket hooked over his thumb, and walk into the autumn gloaming.

Chapter Thirty Five

N ext evening, Fliss walked up to the Muster Ground where a huge marquee had been erected.

Pulling Mitzi's borrowed pashmina around her against the cutting wind, she looked up at the faint opalescence of the Milky Way streaking across the north-western sky. It saddened her to think that when she returned to Pimlico she'd never see the planets and constellations projected against a pitch-black sky so clearly again.

The Port Urquhart Ceilidh Band started playing a familiar tune and her stomach twisted into a Celtic knot. She was unsure how to react when she met Ruairi tonight. She longed to question him over his reasons for asking Angus not to renew her contract, but this need was tempered by Murdo's words of caution: *'If I had just one piece of advice to give Fliss, it would be this: Trust Ruairi.'*

Trouble was, by trusting him she was granting him the power to destroy her dreams, deprive her of her livelihood and break her heart. She'd been a complete pushover last night, falling into his arms and putting all her longing into one kiss. She should have kept him at arm's length and made her anger and disappointment clear. However, she did not intend to compound her folly by begging for her job in front of everyone tonight.

That particular conversation could wait until they were alone.

'Champagne, Madam?' A waitress looked at her expectantly.

'What? Oh, thank you.'

Fliss handed over her gilt-edged invitation and was escorted to a table. She sat down and tried to dismiss her troubles and concentrate instead on the scene before her. She'd probably never attend another event of this kind and she wasn't going to waste a moment of it stressing over Ruairi Urquhart.

But that was easier said than done. A quick glance round at the place names revealed that not only was she sitting on the Urquharts' table, she was sitting at Ruairi's right hand.

Was this his way of saying *sorry*, she wondered?

Or was it the beginning of a long goodbye?

Half an hour later, everyone got to their feet as Jaimsie entered the marquee playing his pipes and the band took up the refrain. Mitzi, Angus and the girls were escorted in with due ceremony, while their guests and clansmen clapped in time to the bagpipes and snare drum. Then Jaimsie played a different, more blood-stirring tune and Ruairi was escorted in between a phalanx of his clansmen. He looked handsome and dashing in his ancient Urquhart tartan, evening shirt and short, black velvet 'Bonnie Prince Charlie' jacket belted at the waist. He seemed in his element - masterful, in control and graciously accepting of his clansmen's homage. In contrast, Fliss was experiencing a complete physical meltdown - her traitorous heart leaping around in her ribcage and her legs unable to support her weight.

Ruairi addressed the gathering in Gaelic first, and then English.

'Thank you for attending this Clan Gathering but more importantly, Mitzi and Angus's engagement. *Thàinig Chlann Airchartdan* - the Urquharts are come!' This battle cry was taken up by his clansmen and repeated, accompanied by thunderous applause and much enthusiastic foot stomping.

Ruairi appeared to be in his element. The very epitome of noble highland manhood as he acknowledged their homage and the last cries of *Thàinig Chlann Airchartdan* faded away. Then, as the candlelight caught the silver buttons on the folded back cuffs of his velvet jacket, he scanned the room. Fliss raised a gloved hand to Mitzi's tiara which had taken a box of hair pins and half a can of Elnette to fix into place, anxious that the tiara/diamond and sapphire necklace combo looked rather OTT on a soon-to-be-redundant therapist. Apparently catching her tell-tale gesture, Ruairi glanced over at her and held her gaze. He appeared to lose his train of thought for a moment and then gained command of himself, and he was back in the room.

He nodded to the Master of Ceremonies to outline the night's events.

'The ball will commence with champagne and canapés to allow the ladies time to fill their dance cards. The reels will begin with the Dashing White Sergeant and we'll take a break after the Reel of the 51st Highland Division - number four on the dance card. At which point Mr Angus Gordon will say a few words and dinner will be served. The reels will continue until breakfast is served around 1am. The celebrations will draw to a close with *John Peel* at 3.30am, after which 'carriages' will be brought round.'

'*Thàinig Chlann Airchartdan,*' the assembled Urquharts repeated as Ruairi kissed Mitzi's hand and then gave Angus a fierce handshake and a man hug.

'I think - on this auspicious occasion - we should add YEE HAW, in Angus's honour!' Ruairi's announcement was followed by much laughter and rebel yells, after which Angus and Mitzi were surrounded by guests keen to offer their congratulations. Then he was called away and it was left to Murdo to escort Cat and Isla to the family table.

Isla marched straight up to Angus's place, picked up his name card and ripped it into tiny pieces which she then threw on the floor.

'Ruairi and Mumma have sold us down the river,' she began without preamble, her blue eyes shimmering with tears.

'How? I mean - why?' Fliss asked.

Isla threw herself into the nearest chair, plainly beyond speech and Cat offered up a whispered explanation.

'The trustees have agreed to wind up the fund we inherited on Papa's death. Ruairi, Mumma and Angus have spent the last half hour explaining all the ins and outs to us. The money in *our* trust fund will revert to the Kinloch Mara estate on Mumma's marriage and in its place, Angus - as our prospective step-father, will set up two new trust funds.'

'But we can only draw interest from the capital until we reach our twenty-fifth birthdays. We could be dead by then,' Isla protested.

Fliss made no comment, but she and Murdo exchanged a look over Isla's head which said they thought changing the terms of the trust was a good move. It would bring much needed funds back into the estate, *and* the new trust fund would establish Angus's authority over Cat and Isla by controlling their spending.

'Surely,' Fliss began, treading carefully in view of Isla's volatile mood, 'money is money. I don't quite see why you're so upset . . .'

'Because it's not *Urquhart* money. Duh. It's *Angus's* money. Not that I'd expect *you* to understand.'

'Luckily my landlord and utility companies aren't too bothered where the money comes from to pay the bills - as long as it's been obtained legally. Not that I'd expect *you* to understand,' Fliss snapped back. No way was Isla going to take her bad mood out on *her* this evening.

'One thing I *do* understand - ever since you arrived in Kinloch Mara, everything's been out of kilter. It's as if someone dropped a great boulder into our lives and the ripples have eddied out, touching us all. Everything's changing, and not for the better.' She shot Murdo a murderous look as though he was part of the conspiracy. Fliss didn't rise to the bait; and she shook her head when she sensed Murdo was about to spring to her defence, knowing that would only make matters worse.

'I like working at the vet's,' Cat said cheerfully, in an attempt to restore the party atmosphere. 'And maybe it's time things *did* change around here. I don't really mind moving onto Angus's estate - the plumbing works, the roof doesn't leak, he's upgrading the swimming pool and having the tennis courts resurfaced. Plus, he says I can decorate my suite of rooms just how I like. *And* his estate is closer to Port Urquhart so I won't have to worry about getting snowed-in come the winter months.'

'You and those bloody animals - you think of nothing else! You don't get it, do you? It won't be the same as living in Kinloch Mara, which is full of *our* history, *our* memories. Mumma won't be Lady Urquhart once she's married; she'll be boring old Mrs Angus *Pimp-My-Kilt*-Gordon,' Isla said huskily. Murdo seemed to have some sympathy for her because he laid a hand on her bony shoulder, but she shrugged him off. 'We won't be *Urquharts*, we'll be Aberdeen Angus's stepchildren,' she said, pulling a disdainful expression.

'Oh, I never thought of it like that,' Cat remarked.

'*This* is the shape of things to come.' Isla gestured at the triple-sized marquee, which was decked out as if for a country wedding - with tented roof, swags of flowers, electric chandeliers and fairy lights. Tables were set with china, glass and silverware and in a smaller tent, just visible through a curtained-off section, staff were busy preparing canapés and replenishing huge fridges with wine and champagne.

'What do you mean?' Fliss asked, puzzled.

'Mumma will go on a mad spending spree. There'll be disagreements over her maxing-out on her credit cards - it'll be like when Papa died and Ruairi had to curtail her extravagances . . . arguments, recriminations and fallings out. Angus will probably divorce her within eighteen months, by which time Ruairi will have married some frump from the glens and we'll be forced to come back to Tigh na Locha to live, like . . .'

'Like unwanted, impoverished rellies in a Jane Austen novel. Oh, I hope the family lawyers have made sure that Mumma's pre-nup is watertight,' Cat said, looking suddenly very anxious.

'Hardly impoverished,' Fliss couldn't help adding, deciding a reality check was well overdue for the Misses Urquhart.

'Okay, that's enough,' Murdo cut in. 'Calm down Isla, you're overreacting, as usual. You know Ruairi wouldn't do anything to hurt you or Cat.'

'Ever the faithful retainer,' she sneered, Murdo's intervention seemingly making her angrier than ever.

Picking up her name card, she ostentatiously crossed through *Urquhart* using the pencil attached to her dancing card and then removed her tartan sash and put it on the table along with her clan brooch. Getting to her feet, she scraped her chair back and walked away - the desire for revenge and retribution written all over her pinched face. Fliss, Cat and Murdo exchanged a worried look; in this mood, who knew what she was capable of?

Sometime later, as hot canapés were served and champagne glasses refilled, the serious business of filling in dance cards began. Young men, some wearing tartan trews and the distinctive red and black mess jackets of officers in the British Army, crowded round Fliss and requested that she put their names next to such reels as *The Duke and Duchess of Edinburgh* and *Hamilton House.* Within five minutes, her dance card was filled, leaving no room for Ruairi . . . should he deign to ask her to partner him in one of the set reels.

Perhaps, she thought darkly, that was his intention.

'My Lords, Ladies and Gentlemen, take your places for the Dashing White Sergeant,' the Master of Ceremonies announced and the band played the familiar chord. Fliss, desperate not to disgrace herself, concentrated on the steps Murdo had taught her and danced her way through the reel. The next two dances - the Eightsome and Foursome reels - were down to Murdo and she managed to exchange a few words with him between the changes.

'Have you seen Ruairi?' she asked, a little breathless from her exertions.

'The last time I saw him he was circulating amongst the guests, checking things out, making sure everyone's happy . . . the usual. Is there a problem?' Fliss showed Murdo her completed dance card as they waited for the Foursome Reel to begin.

'Ah - I should have explained - on these occasions, Ruairi doesn't dance.'

'Why ever not?'

'Because it sets up an *expectation* amongst the unmarried ladies - like a code? One dance means he's interested, two dances means he's *definitely* interested and after three dances, she's the next Lady Urquhart. He thinks it keeps things simple if he doesn't dance with anyone.'

'Oh, I see.'

'Ready?' Murdo bowed on the long chord, she bobbed a half curtsey and they were off.

After the two reels, Murdo escorted her back to the table and then excused himself. Mitzi was seated at the table, taking a breather, and wafting herself with a little wooden fan that looked like it had seen action at quite a few Highland Balls.

'Having fun, sweetie?' she asked, waving to various relatives and friends as they walked past.

'Yes,' Fliss replied, telling a half-truth. How could she enjoy herself when she had issues to resolve, with Ruairi? If she could find him. Was he avoiding her or was she being overly sensitive? 'I was looking for Ruairi,' she said as casually as she could, knowing that Mitzi never missed a nuance.

'He's had to sort out some problem with the event management team over the valet parking. Cars have been blocked in and - oh, I don't know - some business with the delivery vans not having enough room to manoeuvre.' She waved an airy hand as though it had nothing to do with her. 'Angus has gone out to help him - oh, look - there he is.'

Ruairi was standing next to a willowy blonde who was wearing a navy blue satin dress and had a diamond tiara on her upswept hair. Something about her body language, the way she insinuated herself into his side and her hold on his arm, made Fliss bristle.

'Oh that's Fiona,' Mitzi said, apparently reading her mind.

'*The* Fiona?' Fliss asked, her blood turning to ice.

'Yes - Ruairi's ex-fiancée, now Mrs Malcolm Balfour. That's him making his way towards them . . . terrified in case Ruairi runs away with her.' Mitzi laughed as a powerfully built man with a florid complexion and a straining tartan cummerbund barged his way through the tables, knocking chairs over in his haste to reach them. Fliss remembered Ruairi mentioning that his stepsisters called his ex-fiancée *Princess* Fiona and it did rather look as though she'd married SHREK.

'Why are they here tonight?' she asked, dismissing the nonsensical thought and concentrating instead on the way Fiona placed herself between Ruairi and her husband. Mitzi gave one of Isla's *whatever* shrugs before replying.

'As is the way with highland families, Malcolm is related to me in some vague fashion and Fiona's apparently been pestering him for weeks to ask for an invitation. They were married a couple of months back in one of those awful beach weddings in the West Indies and are still on extended honeymoon. She got a wealthy husband as part of the deal and he got his trophy wife. But if you ask me, she wouldn't say no to some extracurricular activity with Ruairi - *if* it came her way.'

'Mitzi - something tells me you're playing reverse cupid by inviting them here.' Fliss gave her a suspicious look and Mitzi laughed and looked straight back at her with canny blue eyes.

'Just making sure that she knows it's over and Ruairi isn't holding a torch for her. She had her chance with him and blew it. Besides - everyone knows it's *you* Ruairi wants.'

'He does? I mean, they do?' Fliss blushed to the roots of her hair.

'Everyone apart from the two of you, it appears . . .'

'Mitzi. I'm not in love with Ruairi . . .'

'Of course you are, darling. Now, go and do something about it.' She tapped Fliss on the cheek with her fan. 'Go on! Men can be so dim about these matters and often need a nudge in the right direction. Angus would still be searching for the right words if I hadn't cut to the chase and told him - of course, I'd love to be Mrs Angus Gordon.' Fliss wasn't sure the same went for Ruairi but she smiled at Mitzi, nonetheless.

There was a drum roll and a clash of the cymbals after which the Master of Ceremonies announced: 'My Lords, Ladies and Gentlemen, take your places for the *Reel of the 51st Highland Division.*' This was greeted with cheers and Fliss's partner claimed her before she had time to follow Mitzi's advice. During the reel, her attention was focused on the complicated steps, double handclasps and changes. But every time she whirled round, she saw Ruairi standing with his back to the band, arms folded across his chest, looking very serious and watching her intently. The reel ended and she removed her dance card from the pocket in her glove to check out her next dance partner.

Ruairi strode over, took the dance card from her and tucked it in his pocket. 'You don't need that,' he declared.

'I don't?'

'No, you're dancing with me. Then, afterwards - we have things to discuss. Ghosts to lay.' Fliss shivered at his use of *ghosts,* but was warmed by the passionate look he sent her. She knew their relationship couldn't progress with so many issues between them and welcomed the chance to finally say her piece, to put things straight.

'But - but, Murdo said you never dance.'

'Tonight, I do. With you, mo chridhe.'

He sent her another dark look - but this time it was full of promise and she knew she'd been right to put her trust in him. As he took her hand and kissed it, the burgeoning feelings she'd kept in check over the last months and the realisation that she loved him took wings. And when he escorted her onto the dance floor, all her reservations melted away and were replaced by a light- heartedness she hadn't felt since the morning on Shingly Beach, when they'd kissed and talked foolishly of the *each-uisge*.

Ruairi nodded at the Master of Ceremonies who announced that - in a change to the printed program, there would be a waltz, followed by the Gay Gordon in honour of the engaged couple and finally Marie's Wedding. (In honour of Ruairi's late mother, Mairi Urquhart, and a link with the past). A past they all seemed more than ready to leave behind.

Apart from Isla, that is.

Jaimsie touched the brim of his Glengarry with his pipe's chanter in salute to Ruairi and then blew air into the bag. Fliss immediately recognised the tune as the one he played when Ruairi and Murdo beat the bounds. Other couples joined them on the floor and, judging by their amazed expressions, Fliss knew that dancing with Ruairi was sending out a signal that everyone understood.

'F - Fiona?' She forced herself to ask the question.

'Gone home with her husband. It appears this evening hasn't quite worked out the way she planned,' he explained.

'I - well, I'm glad,' she said simply.

As he held her in his arms, the familiar scent of his aftershave mingled with the scent of her heather and lily of the valley corsage. She was glad she was wearing gloves; otherwise, he would have known her hands were slippery with nerves and her body was on fire from his touch. She tried to keep a sensible distance between them - but Ruairi was having none of it; he laughed as if seeing through her ploy and pulled her even closer into his body.

'Cat got your tongue? That's a first, for you. Now *that's* better, a smile. You look very - pink,' he observed delightedly. She looked away from him, using the pretence of concentrating on the steps as a way of avoiding his too-knowing blue eyes.

'That's because everyone's looking at us, as if . . .' She stopped herself from saying *as if this was our wedding breakfast and our first dance together.*

'I'm dancing with the most beautiful woman in the room. In the whole of Wester Ross. Why wouldn't they look at us?'

'Enough,' she whispered 'You know very well what I mean.'

'What *do* you mean?' he asked, giving her an amused look.

'I'm not - what you've just said. And this is -' she was about to say *all too much*, when the waltz ended and everyone got into position for the Gay Gordons - with Angus and Mitzi in poll position. The only thing in that particular reel's favour, Fliss decided, was that it precluded speech and kept Ruairi moving round the room. When the dance was over, however, Ruairi picked up the conversation where they'd left off.

'Tonight I'm going to say all the things I should have said that morning on the hillside before I sounded off at you like a fool.'

'Well,' she conceded, 'I shouldn't have interfered in your running of the estate - or said that Fiona had a narrow escape.'

'I rather think I'm the one who had the narrow escape, don't you?'

Luckily, the Master of Ceremonies announced Marie's Wedding and she didn't have to answer. A guest grabbed the microphone and sang along as they danced: *Step we gaily, on we go, Heel for heel and toe for toe, Arm in arm and row in row - All for Marie's wedding*. When the dance ended, Ruairi didn't bow as he had at the end of the other dances, he kissed her on the back of both hands - and then on the mouth, in full view of everyone.

It was a perfect moment and Fliss recalled Murdo's words: 'One dance means he's interested, two dances means he's *definitely* interested and after three dances . . .' Fliss wished she had Mitzi's fan because she was chilli-hot and burning up like she was incubating a fever.

She was granted a breathing space when the event coordinator presented Ruairi with another logistical problem to solve. Giving a resigned *nobless oblige* shrug and mouthing *later* at her, he walked off with Angus and Murdo. The band put their instruments on their stands and went off to the bar, the disco took over and the younger members of the party cut some shapes on the dance floor.

Fliss felt like an ancient dowager as she returned to her table and watched them gyrate like this was Ibiza, not Wester Ross. Cat flopped down beside her and poured out a long drink of water.

'Great party, eh Fliss. You and Ruairi - what's that all about?'

'I'm not sure myself - yet.' Cat grinned and dug Fliss in the ribs. As they watched the dancers, it occurred to Fliss that she hadn't seen Isla for quite some time. 'Where's your sister?' she asked Cat.

'Outside snorting coke off the back of a business card holder with Charlie and Freddy Gordon last time I saw her.' Cat sighed. 'Idiots! If Ruairi catches them . . .'

'I can imagine. Is she still upset over the trust fund?'

'What do you think? She wasn't too happy seeing you dancing with Ruairi either, even though she still believes it's Murdo you're after. Murdo, thank goodness, is at last showing signs of softening towards her, after the YouTube viral. Who'd have thought he'd get so upset over something as silly as that?' she asked, artlessly.

'Who'd have thought it,' Fliss agreed, dryly. Her attention was drawn towards a group of young Urquharts gathered round the DJ. At that moment, Isla walked into the marquee and as she was crossing the dance floor, *'Don't You Wish Your Girlfriend Was Hot Like Me'* blasted out at full volume.

'Go Isla.'

'Go Isla.'

The cousins positioned themselves at various poles around the marquee that supported its structure and replicated Cat and Isla's now infamous YouTube dance routine. This carried on until Murdo went over to the record deck, pulled the plug and tore a strip off them. Instead of looking pleased at his intervention, Isla gave him a murderous look, stuck a finger up at her cousins and then flounced out of the marquee. Despite their earlier set to, Fliss felt sorry for Isla - she knew how it felt to have to have your world turned upside down and forced to move on with your life before you were ready to do so.

Now that things were working out between her and Ruairi, she was filled with a generosity of spirit. A desire to help not just Isla, but the whole world. She got to her feet, intent on following Isla out of the marquee but was forestalled by the event coordinator.

'Excuse me, Madam, the lorry carrying the replacement generator has arrived. It needs to get as close to the Muster Ground as possible in order to keep the fridges working and prevent the ice sculptures from melting. Where should we park it?' The hopeless coordinator was looking at Fliss as if she was a fully paid up member of the Urquhart family and had all the answers.

'Oh, I'm not sure. Can't you find Lady Urquhart? Oh, wait, Miss Urquhart is just outside, we can ask her. Give me a moment?' Fliss left the marquee thinking that whatever Mitzi was paying the coordinator it was too much. She was clearly out of her depth and had spent most of the party getting Ruairi, Murdo and Angus to do her job for her.

When Fliss found Isla, she was standing alone overlooking the loch and smoking a spliff. The scent of cannabis was strong and Fliss fervently hoped that it would take the edge off Isla's unhappiness. As she moved closer, the cutting wind off the loch wafted the tiny lanterns strung along the edge of the canopy leading to the marquee and cast Isla's profile into relief.

She looked far from chilled; in fact, she appeared totally wired.

'Isla,' Fliss began, already regretting the impulse that'd brought her out here.

'Oh, it's you. What do you want?' Isla asked, but not quite as brusquely as before - maybe the cannabis *was* helping her to calm down. Suspecting that she wouldn't welcome a shoulder to cry on in this mood, Fliss used the pretext of looking for Ruairi as her reason for leaving the marquee.

'The event coordinator is looking for someone to advise her where to park the lorry with the backup generator. Have you seen Ruairi or Murdo lately?'

'They walked up to the Big Hoose with Angus a few minutes ago.'

'Oh, I wonder how long they'll be. She said something about fridges and . . . ice sculptures being ruined?'

Isla shrugged disinterestedly and Fliss decided to cut her losses and return to the party.

'Unless . . .' Isla began slowly.

Fliss turned around, 'Yes?'

'Tell her to open the gates that overlook the loch. You know which ones I mean?'

'The ornamental gates - with the gilded coat of arms and the Urquhart lion?'

'The very ones,' Isla smiled encouragingly. 'I'd tell her myself but . . .'

'You don't want to face your cousins just yet?' Fliss suggested sympathetically. 'Don't worry, I understand.'

'That's it, exactly.'

'Fine, I'll tell her.' She turned away and started back towards the marquee. On impulse, she turned back: 'Isla . . .'

'What now?' she asked with characteristic irritability.

'I know everything's changing - but it's for the best. It'll all work out in the end, you'll see.'

'You know, I think it just might.'

Isla gave a tight smile, took another long draw of her spliff, held onto the breath and then exhaled noisily over the loch.

Chapter Thirty Six

When Fliss returned to the marquee the Reel of the 51st Division was halfway through and managing quite well without her. She found Ruairi and when she asked for her dance card back, he refused to hand it over. His broad grin made it quite clear that she'd be spending the rest of the night with him, whether she liked it or not.

The look she sent him said that she liked it - a lot.

As the evening wore on, speeches were made, dinner was served and the programme of set reels danced through. By midnight, Fliss was feeling more than a little drunk, thanks to her champagne glass which had miraculous properties and appeared to refill itself. She wondered if she was capable of dancing the last reel - the *Duke and Duchess of Edinburgh* - before breakfast was served at one o'clock.

'This has to be the longest night of my life,' Ruairi said around twelve thirty, sitting at her side, stone-cold sober, despite having knocked back his fair share of uisge beatha. He seemed transformed, lit from within and when he leaned towards Fliss and whispered: 'I want to take you to my bed in Tigh na Locha, make love all night and watch the sun rise over the loch together,' his eyes shone.

'That's an - interesting proposition,' Fliss said in a professional tone, as though he'd just suggested some improvements for the therapy centre. 'Be assured I'll give it my fullest attention.' Heart singing, a thrill of anticipation fizzed through her although she gave no outward sign of it. Sitting straight backed at the table - the bustier didn't permit slouching - she watched the dancers and smiled at people she knew. Was it her imagination, or did the other guests keep glancing towards her and Ruairi as though they were the eighth wonder of the world? Teasingly, Ruairi tried to break her composure by detailing some of the pleasurable things he was going to do once they were alone

'Will you behave?' she begged, gasping as he traced circles in her palm underneath the cover of the linen tablecloth. Although she knew that if he *did* stop, she'd die from sheer frustration. She was glad that the rest of the family were dancing the *Duchess of Perth* and weren't witness to their passionate handholding. Even Isla seemed in a happier mood since Murdo had leapt to her defence over the cousins' improvised pole dance. She had joined in the dancing and was wearing her clan sash and brooch over her right shoulder, as was her birthright.

'Mitzi told me that a Highland Ball was no place for sissies - I can see what she means.' She yawned and leaned her head on Ruairi's shoulder, feeling suddenly sleepy - despite her aroused physical state. Ruairi gave her a gentle shake when she yawned again.

'Come on, Fliss. Hang on in there. They'll be serving breakfast in half an hour - kedgeree and more whisky. The reels will go round on another loop until *John Peel* is announced around about three fifteen, signalling the end of the ball. Once we're in Tigh na Locha, anyone who disturbs us - especially that idiot of an event coordinator - does so at their peril.'

Something deep inside Fliss tightened and released at his passionate words. She threw her head back in mock despair at the thought of waiting another three hours before they could be alone. She instantly regretted it because the room spun round in front of her before righting itself. To stay awake, she tried counting how many glasses of champagne she'd downed - and lost count after six. No wonder she had difficulty focusing on the dancers whirling around.

She frowned. There was something else - a little thought nibbling away at the edge of her happiness. Something she had to remember, whispered phrases about her contract . . . the new manageress . . . trusting Ruairi to make everything right. But she couldn't remember the detail, or why it had seemed so very important at the start of the evening and now didn't appear to matter. So she shook away the bothersome thoughts, surrendered to her inner hussy and trailed cool fingers along the inside of Ruairi's thigh - which was far more pleasurable. Although his expression never altered, he gave a start as if he'd received an electric shock and then placed his hand over hers under the table to still her questing fingers. Fliss calmly picked up her champagne glass with her free hand and took a sip, revelling in her power to make him respond to her touch.

Around about a quarter to four Ruairi checked his watch and cast an eye over the diehards who were being politely ushered to their cars by an exhausted Murdo. Then, patently considering he'd executed his duties as Laird, he led Fliss out of the marquee and into the night. As they walked up to Tigh na Locha, he removed his black velvet jacket and draped it round her shoulders. The silky lining retained his body heat and she snuggled in to it as he put his arm round her shoulders and pulled her into his side.

Except for the stars, the night was ink black. Fliss was glad of the darkness because it allowed her to school her features; and the cool night air helped to sober her up as they zigzagged between the cars parked at the rear of the house. She was in a pleasurable state of turmoil as they entered the house - happy that he'd made his intentions clear, but anxious over how the evening would pan out. They walked down the long corridor that led to the kitchen and went through into the hall. It was quiet and welcoming with a peat fire burning in the large grate and low carbon wall lights casting shadows into the corners.

'Everything okay?' Ruairi asked, removing his jacket from her shoulders and draping it over the newel post.

'Fine,' she lied, unconvincingly.

Fliss was dismayed to find that her teeth were chattering and her hands were shaking. By returning to the house with Ruairi she was sending out a clear signal that she was cool with the fact they would be lovers before the night was over. However, it had been some time since she'd slept with a man, maybe eighteen months or more - and then it hadn't been a great success. What if she was no good at *this*, what if she didn't come up to expectations. What if -

'That's enough.' Ruairi paused with one foot on the bottom tread of the cantilevered staircase, held her firmly by the shoulders and gave her a gentle shake.

'What is?'

'You're overthinking this. Let everything just *be* tonight, Fliss. We'll thrash out the problems and settle all the questions in the morning. Can you do that?'

'Yes,' she whispered. Her mouth was suddenly dry as his hands moved from her shoulders, framed her face and he kissed her once - gently.

'We'll go to my room, no one will dare disturb us there. Not if they value their head,' he joked to lighten the atmosphere. Taking her hand, he led her up the stairs with its tartan runner fraying at the edges, ancient, rusting claymores arranged in a circle round a targe on the wall - and generations of Urquharts looking down disapprovingly from dark family portraits.

Suddenly Fliss remembered something Isla had said in the conservatory and stopped half way up the stairs. 'Ruairi - I just want you to know, I,' she gulped and took in a breath. 'I know Isla made out that I knew all about Tantric sex - but I don't. Just in case you have expectations and are disappointed . . .'

'Don't worry, Tantric sex hasn't made its way this far north yet,' he said straight-faced, though he struggled to stop a smile quirking at the corner of his mouth. 'I put it down to a combination of the Free Church of Scotland keeping it secret, and our freezing cold winters. In Argyllshire, it's considered daringly risqué if you make love without keeping your hat and gloves on - and possibly a fetching, woollen scarf.' That made her giggle and they continued up the stairs. When they reached the wide landing, Ruairi paused. 'Know something, Fliss?'

'What?'

'You are priceless.' He drew her into his arms, leaned back against the carved mahogany bannister, and kissed her. Then he held her at arm's length and sent her a burning, totally honest look. 'You can say no at any time. You know that, don't you?'

311

'And why would I want to do that?' This time her grey-green eyes sent out a bold message telling him how much she wanted this to happen. She wasn't a shrinking virgin being dragged unwillingly to a marriage bed. She was nearly twenty-five years old for goodness sake. Women of her age normally needed a calculator to keep score of the lovers they'd had. In her case, the fingers of one hand would suffice.

'Good.' He led her past Mitzi's bedroom - *his* room by rights, and then stopped at a heavy oak door, which had a flowered chamber pot strategically positioned outside it.

'A chamber pot?' Fliss questioned and raised an eyebrow.

'Don't worry; I don't have an undisclosed medical condition - the chamber pot's for the leaks. When it rains or when the snow melts on the roof, saucepans, buckets and chamber pots are dragooned into service to catch the drips. One of the first things I'm going to do when Cat and Isla's money reverts to the estate, is have the roof replaced. I've already applied for a grant to help with the costs. Tigh na Locha is a listed building and we have to replace like for like, which works out expensive.

'No more chamber pots?'

'Unless you want to grow geraniums - isn't that what people used to do?

'I'm too young to remember the olden days,' she laughed and relaxed, thanks to this inconsequential banter and Ruairi's consideration for her feelings. He pushed his bedroom door open and waited for her to cross the threshold.

The room was much smaller than she'd expected and she deduced it had probably been the laird's dressing room in the days when the lord and lady of the house slept separately after producing the required heir and a spare. It held a three-quarter brass bed deigned for a different generation of highlander and which was clearly much too small for Ruairi. The wallpaper - a faded vintage Laura Ashley design, reminded her of the décor in the Elgin Crescent house. Was this one room in the house Mitzi hadn't been permitted to makeover, she wondered?

'My inner sanctum,' Ruairi announced, as if reading her mind. There was little furniture in the room apart from a small, prettily tiled fireplace, two crammed bookcases holding an array of battered sporting trophies, the obligatory mahogany tallboy and a heavily carved wardrobe.

'It's very Spartan,' Fliss laughed, 'almost monk-like, in fact.'

'Ah, but with all mod cons.' Pretending to be slighted by her comment, he proudly indicated a wall-mounted flat screen TV, iPad and docking system for an iPod. 'As for it being monk-like, you'll have to be the judge of that. Come here . . .' He removed his sporran, and settled comfortably on a wide window seat built over a cast iron radiator which resembled a coiled serpent. Fliss joined him and he caught her by the wrists and pulled her into the space between his thighs.

For several seconds he looked at her without speaking as though he couldn't quite believe that she was here - in his bedroom, at last. Then he gave a sexy smile, brought his knees together and held her there - running his hands from her wrists and along her forearms before coming to rest on her shoulders.

'Madam, will you dance?' he asked in a husky voice, sending her a look of such passionate intent that a frisson ran thought her and the room blurred round the edges.

'With you - yes,' she responded, eyes shining as he pulled her closer into his body. His kilt rucked up, and then there was nothing between them but a silk taffeta skirt and her underwear.

'Now I know what a Scotsman wears under his kilt,' she said huskily without taking her eyes off his face, as his penis rose up against her stomach. Her smoky look sent Ruairi an unambiguous message - she was ready to take this step forward, no matter where it led, no matter what the consequences.

'There's nothing worn under *this* kilt I can assure you, lady. It's all in perfect working order,' Ruairi quipped, laughing at the old joke. 'Now shut up *wumman* and kiss me,' he commanded in broad Scots. Fliss did as she was told, knowing he wanted her to make the first move and show him she had no second thoughts. Their first kiss was tentative – but as Ruairi slid the zip down on her skirt she pressed harder against him and deepened it. Vivienne Westwood's finest couture slithered onto the floor and pooled at her feet in a rustle of blue silk and she stepped out of it.

She felt the warmth of the ancient radiator against her knees and the cool air of the bedroom around her as she stood before him - wearing nothing but hold-up stockings, bustier and thin silk knickers. She drew out of the kiss and opened her eyes to find Ruairi looking at her as though all his Christmases had come at once - which was exactly how *she* felt.

'I won't be needing this,' he said and removed the ceremonial *sgian dubh* tucked inside his thick white sock. 'And you don't need this.' He took the tiara out of her updo. 'Or this,' he unfastened the sapphire and diamond necklace and placed it on the padded window seat. 'You don't need any adornment, Fliss - you are beautiful just as you are.' She made as if to say something but he placed his thumb on her lips. 'No, don't say a word, just stay there. Now it's my turn . . .'

Moving away from her, he walked over to his bedside table, rummaged in a drawer and found a condom. Turning his back towards her, he slipped it on and then rearranged his kilt. Pulling a tartan comforter off the bed, he draped it round her with a theatrical twirl and then reclaimed his place on the deep window ledge and drew her back between his thighs.

'Now, let's remove that dangerous flower - it's already speared me twice. And while I don't mind being pierced to the heart in a good cause, I can do without it.' As he said *pierced to the heart*, he turned her round and unfastened each tiny hook and eye of the bustier. He peeled it back, kissing her shoulders and then down the length of her spine. Fliss closed her eyes and leaned against him, holding the cashmere blanket in front of her for warmth and modesty. Although her innermost thoughts were neither chaste nor virtuous when her bustier joined the skirt on the floor, and his hands covered her breasts. She covered them with her own and enjoyed the delicious sensation of his thumbs caressing her nipples for several long, earth-shifting moments before she twisted round in his arms.

'I think,' she said softly, 'that you're slightly overdressed, Sir Ruairi.'

Standing in front of him, naked apart from stockings, dancing shoes and silk knickers, she pulled at one end of his bow tie to release the knot and then dragged it free of his winged collar. Next, she unfastened his shirt buttons one by one, discovered he was wearing an old-fashioned dress shirt and pulled it over his head. Without bothering to untie the laces of his brogues, Ruairi slipped them off and wrapped his stockinged feet round the back of her ankles, drawing her even closer - so that her breasts were pressed up against his chest.

She felt the hard planes of his body against her soft flesh, let out a sigh and tipped her head back. Ruairi lowered his head and, supporting her with both hands, bent her back as he suckled each nipple in turn. Fliss gasped and pressed his head closer, closer, as though she couldn't get enough of the rhythmic tease and pull of his lips and teeth. This went on for several pleasurable minutes during which she was dimly aware of calling out his name, as if she was in a waking dream. Then she stood upright and drew him into a kiss that took his breath away as her tongue touched and explored the warm, sensitive skin of his lips and mouth.

With a muttered imprecation, he span her round until she was facing away from him and could feel the urgent press of his penis against her buttocks. Then he slid his fingers inside her skimpy underwear and found her moist, secret place and she shuddered. He whispered some words in Gaelic, words she didn't understand. However, that was almost immaterial because his tone - deep, sexy and full of promise, spoke for him.

She gasped as he stroked the sensitive folds of skin with one finger and instinctively fell into a rocking rhythm as he teased the tip of her clitoris with his thumb. She reached one hand behind her, pressed his face into the nape of her neck - and as words failed her, she moaned. 'Yes?' He breathed in her perfume, his breath hot against her skin, his stubble rasping against her neck. 'Is this what you want, mo chridhe? And this?' One finger slid inside her and began to move rhythmically but with greater urgently. When she could bear it no longer she turned round and saw his eyes were closed - as though that kept him anchored in reality and delayed *his* reaction to the delightful things he was doing to her.

'And maybe *this*,' she replied.

Showing none of her earlier hesitation or caring what tomorrow might bring, she stepped out of her knickers and pushed up his kilt. Climbing onto the window seat, half-kneeling, half-sitting on his lap, she straddled and enfolded him in one fluid movement. This time, *he* was the one on the brink as she tightened her muscles around his penis and moved along the length of him, holding onto his shoulders for balance. And, as he took her nipple in his mouth once more and sucked, she called out.

'I want this. This. This. *This!*' Her voice reached a crescendo as she climaxed and almost stopped breathing as waves of pleasure rippled through her. Ruairi pushed deeper inside her and she moved with greater urgency until she heard his groan of release and felt him pulse inside her. Then all was still.

'God. Fliss. . . A chuisle mo chroí,' he said. She laid her forehead against his shoulder and he wrapped his arms around her, supporting her slight weight on his knees until, reluctantly, he slid out of her. With one swift movement, he gathered her into his arms, carried her over to the bed, removed her soft dancing slippers and covered her with the tartan blanket. Then he walked into the adjacent bathroom and when he returned, he was gloriously naked. Grinning, he registered her hungry appraisal of him, raised a corner of the blanket and climbed into the bed beside her.

'Spoons?' he asked, turning her onto her side and snuggling into her back. 'The bed won't allow for anything more than that, I'm afraid.'

'Spoons it is then,' she yawned and wriggled her bottom until she fitted in the hollow made by his knees, which were drawn up in the foetal position. He laid one arm across her as if to ensure she didn't fall out of bed or escape, and then he kissed between her shoulder blades as she squirmed with delight.

'Fliss, don't do that,' he murmured against her left ear. 'Especially as you're still wearing those sexy stockings. Give me some recovery time,' he nuzzled her neck again.

'I'll be as quiet as mouse and as still as . . .' before she finished the sentence, she was fast asleep.

'When Mitzi moves out and I get my room back,' Ruairi said some hours later as he fed her a ham sandwich he'd brought up from the kitchen, 'I'm going to invest in a new bed. The estate carpenter should be capable of dismantling The Laird's Bed and rebuilding it round a new divan. Shouldn't he?'

'I should think so,' Fliss replied.

The way she felt, *everything* seemed possible, especially after they'd made love for a second and then a third time. Giggling as the old brass bed moved in harmony with them, creaking with every thrust until they'd been forced to drag the mattress onto the floor and make love there. Or wake the whole house.

She didn't know if he'd made love to Fiona in that narrow brass bed and didn't want to. And in a way, it didn't matter, those days were over. She focused instead on the wild, unrestrained lovemaking they'd shared last night. Maybe it was the romantic setting, the champagne. Maybe it was because she knew for certain that she loved him - had known for weeks, really - that she'd felt able to lose her inhibitions and make love in such an unfettered manner. She'd never acted like that with any other man, but somehow - like the memory of Fiona and what they might have done in this room, in *that* bed, none of that mattered, either.

'Can I ask you what mo chridhe means? You said it several times last night.'

'It means *my love.*'

'And the other thing, *a chuisle mo chroí?*'

'Pulse of my heart,' he translated and continued tracing a leisurely line from her lips, between her breasts and much lower before his fingers came to rest in a soft, tantalising place.

317

'Mmmm - and what else did you say?' Fliss wriggled and pressed closer to his hand. 'Sentences, phrases?'

'Ah, that,' he looked slightly embarrassed.

'What?' she demanded, laughing up at him.

'I was reciting the periodic table in Gaelic, starting with alkali metals and working my way through to noble gases. I had to do something to slow myself down - *oof.*'

'That is *so* not romantic,' Fliss poked him none too gently in the diaphragm.

'I also thought about redesigning the central heating system - very good for the concentration. That's another job to be undertaken when Mitzi and the girls move out. Sorry. Plumbing, leaking roofs and ordering new bedroom furniture - it's not exactly romantic talk, you're right. It's simply that I haven't been able to make any plans for so long that . . .'

'It's, okay - I get it.'

'And what's the story behind your intriguing little tattoo. *Carpe Diem*?' He'd traced it with his fingers last night, and then his tongue before moving lower - much lower.

'What? You think we don't use Latin in Pimlico? Speak it all the time for your information.' She propped herself up on her elbows and looked at him, wonderingly. She still couldn't believe that she was here, in his bedroom and they were together at last. 'Becky, my best friend and I had them done when we were seventeen - after watching Dead Poets Society.' She zoned out temporarily, remembering the night in the Elgin Square Gardens and Cat's desire to have a tattoo.

She looked past his broad shoulders to where dawn was edging in through the half-open curtains. Should she creep back to the Wee Hoose, she wondered? Or would Ruairi install her at the breakfast table still wearing last night's clothes and dare anyone to comment? She remembered her first breakfast at Tigh na Locha, the arguments, *their* stand up row in the library, him confiscating her contract and the cheque he'd written. It all seemed so long ago.

Move out. Moving on.

That's what they'd come up here to discuss, wasn't it?

'Ruairi,' she began tentatively. 'Since we're on unromantic things like plumbing and carpentry, you promised you would explain your reasons for asking Angus not to renew my contract. It's nearly morning - so . . .'

'I have a different position to offer you.' He kissed her once on the lips, leapt off the mattress and strode over to the tallboy, completely at ease with his nakedness.

'A better one?' Fliss swallowed hard and made herself focus on her future. But she was distracted by the way his muscles moved under his skin, and how much she wanted him to make love to her - now!

'I think it is; but I'm not sure what your reaction will be.' He hunted around in the deep top drawer, eventually bringing out a tissue-wrapped parcel. 'Almost dawn. A new day - the first day of the rest of our lives.' He paused and looked out of the window and towards the loch. 'And I want to ask you if - *what the fuck?*' he exclaimed as something beyond the window caught his attention and made him lose his grip.

The tissue-wrapped parcel slipped out of his fingers and landed at his feet.

Chapter Thirty Seven

'What is it? What's happened?'

Struggling to her knees, Fliss dragged the crumpled sheet off the mattress and wrapped it around her. Ruairi, seemingly rendered speechless, knelt up on the window seat apparently not caring that he was naked and in full view of anyone in the gardens. Joining him, Fliss looked over the rose arches and towards the loch. The only difference as far as she could tell, was that the ornamental gates were open and a lorry was parked on the gravel drive between them and the house.

'What's wrong?'

'The gates - they're open,' he said in a stricken voice. Fliss wrapped the sheet round them and pressed herself into his back. A cold feeling settled on her when Ruairi distractedly pushed free of the sheet and away from her.

'Open? Is that a problem - I don't understand.' Her voice trembled and her post-coital, loved-up feeling evaporated. She was transported back to last night - Isla smoking the joint outside the marquee, the stressed-out event manager, the melting ice sculptures. Then, Isla's ever - so - helpful suggestion: *Tell her to open the gates . . . you know which ones I mean?* And her, trotting back into the marquee happy to carry out Isla's instructions to the letter.

'The gates,' Ruairi enunciated slowly, almost as if he was dragging the words out of his heart, 'are only opened when the Laird's funeral cortege passes through on its way to the church. They've remained closed since the day my father was laid to rest and should've remained closed until my -'

'No, don't say it; don't even think it.'

Wildly, she turned her back on the wretched gates and threw her arms around him, trying to keep him safe. Unable to bear the thought of losing him - just when they'd found each other. She'd lost everyone she'd ever loved and it had left her vulnerable and prey to everything life threw at her. She didn't want to go through that again, not for a long, long time. She glanced up at Ruairi, his face was shadowy in the grey light and his eyes had lost their spark. He looked beaten and she feared for his welfare and - more to the point, his reaction when he learned of *her* unwitting part in the gates' opening.

She said nothing for a few minutes as she tried to process the problem and come up with a solution. Even so, her heart was beating in her throat and she was filled with dread at his reaction. When she spoke, she weighed each word knowing she had to make it count.

'Can't the lorry be moved quietly and the gates closed before everyone realises what's happened? No harm done?' Ruairi's incredulous look told her that she'd seriously underestimated the significance of the gates in Kinloch Mara folklore.

He drew his dark eyebrows together, rubbed his hands over his stubble and took a deep breath.

'Fliss, last night someone wiped out eight hundred years of Urquhart history in a single stroke.' She could tell he was eager to leave, keen to find out exactly how this state of affairs had come about. Retrieving his kilt off the floor, he pulled on a sweatshirt, tied the laces on his brogues and slipped the sgian dubh down his sock. 'Whoever has done this, will be handed their P45 by the end of this morning and sent packing,' he said forcefully.

Sent packing? Fliss's stomach flipped over, not only at his clipped tone but at the way he thoughtfully fingered the sgian dubh's ornate hilt. Ruairi might look every inch a man of this century with his Bang and Olufsen flat screen TV, iPad and the rest, but ancient warrior DNA was in his bones and at times like this - blood will out.

'Ruairi . . .' Last night's tender, generous lover had vanished, replaced by the stern-faced Laird of Kinloch Mara who had woken up to find almost a thousand years of family obliterated. The colour drained from her face as she steeled herself for his inevitable reaction when he discovered the truth.

Plainly misreading the reason for her pallor, Ruairi tenderly brushed her tangled, bed-head hair out of her eyes. 'I'm sorry the day's been ruined, I'd planned it so differently. But don't worry; this has nothing to do with you. Murdo and I will sort it out and then you and I can spend time together.'

She moved away from him, gathered her clothes together from the four corners of the room and laid them on the bed frame. She tried hard to hold onto the feeling of being loved, cherished and *belonging* she'd woken up with, but the feeling was fading fast - leaving only coldness and anxiety.

'That's just it, Ruairi. It has *everything* to do with me,' she said quietly.

'Of course, mo chridhe - that was thoughtless of me, you're part of my life now and these events will impact on you, too.' Sending her a contrite look, he rummaged under the bed frame and retrieved the radio handset, which had fallen off the bedside table last night.

. . . *You're part of my life now.*

Fliss gulped, aware of the impact her next words would have on Ruairi - but knew she had to own up to her innocent mistake, even if that meant . . .

'No, I mean - Ruairi, please listen. *I* told the event team to open the gates and park the lorry there.'

Ruairi turned round slowly, and looked at her perplexedly. 'And why would you do that?'

'I did it in error,' she began, but he wasn't listening. She could tell that his brain was racing ahead, trying to make sense of what she'd just told him and rationalising it.

'It makes no sense. Unless,' he paused and gave her a significant look. Occupied with getting dressed and pulling on her lacy stockings and silk undies, Fliss didn't immediately register his change of tone or the inference in his unfinished sentence.

'I was trying to help the party planner,' she explained as she slipped on her shoes and made a mess of separating the crisscross laces. 'And then Isla suggested - Oh.'

At last, pennies began slotting into place. Last night, Isla had been beside herself because of the changes to her trust fund and had thrown a tantrum at the dinner table. It was now clear to Fliss that Isla had exploited her ignorance of Urquhart tradition as revenge for - as she believed - Fliss having brought unwanted change to Kinloch Mara. And also on *Ruairi* for depriving her of the status and respect she considered her due as sister of the Laird.

'Isla? What about her?' Judging by his expression he thought Fliss was trying to shift the blame off her shoulders and onto his stepsister. 'Why would she do such a thing? She's an Urquhart through and through. She knows the legend - that a *gheusaibh* will fall on the Urquharts and all who claim clanship with them if the gates are opened.'

Last night Isla had been high on drugs, humiliated by her cousins and furious at having her trust fund arrangements handed over to Angus. Ruairi hadn't seen her ripping up Angus's card, crossing *Urquhart* out on her place setting and removing her clan sash in a fit of pique An Urquhart through and through? Only when it suited her, Fliss thought acidly.

'A *gheusaibh*? What - is that like a *curse*?' Distracted by trying to rationalise Isla's behaviour last night, she raised a sceptical eyebrow without thinking.

'I suppose all this must appear quaint to you. A bit of tartan kitsch on a par with Loch Ness Monster t-shirts, choose your own clan on the internet and bottles of highland mist. But here in Kinloch Mara such things matter.' Her confidence to explain herself disappeared before a man whose upbringing gave credence to curses, and who plainly believed in second sight and doom- laden prophesies over eight hundred years old. In the eyes of this community, that was roughly about - *yesterday*.

She could see that Ruairi was visibly distressed by the gates being opened and she knew she should cut him some slack. However, his instinctive championing of Isla over her and his scathing words, made Fliss answer more rashly than she'd intended.

'Don't start with the flash Londoner versus noble Highlander routine, again. It didn't wash the first time and it won't wash now. Maybe you don't know your sister quite as well as you think.' She didn't stop to consider the picture she presented - hands on hips, wearing hold-up stockings and silk undies and with the sheet laying at her feet. Instead, she pressed on before she ran out of steam. 'And what did you mean earlier when you said my opening the gates made no sense unless . . . unless what?'

'Get dressed Fliss; I can't deal with you when you're half-naked.' He turned away, making it plain that while he was devastated by what had happened, he nevertheless found her nakedness highly distracting and arousing. It was evident from his expression that he was torn between listening to her version of the story, ejecting her from his bedroom - or closing the curtains, drawing her onto the mattress and making love to her, all over again.

The belligerent light in Fliss's eye soon squashed that particular train of thought!

'Deal with me - *how*, exactly? Come on, spit it out. *Why* do you think I opened the gates?' Then the scales fell from her eyes and she answered her question. 'You believe I did it out of spite to get back at you for asking Angus to cancel my contract, don't you? And that last night was my back-up plan, a way of hedging my bets? Know something? The Urquharts really are a piece of work,' she choked out as she began searching round for her things, 'and you're welcome to your curses and each other. You've made it pretty obvious on several occasions that there's no room for me in your life. I was a fool to think otherwise.'

Overwhelmed by hormones, emotion and with a champagne hangover, Fliss was finding it difficult to breathe. She had to get away from this room - from him – and as quickly as possible, too, before he saw her tears and put a cynical spin on those, too.

'Fliss, look - it's . . .'

Just then, the walkie-talkie on the bedside table came to life: '*Ruairi -*

It's Murdo; come in. I've got some bad news.'

'I know, Murdo. I've seen the gates.'

'But who gave permission for the lorry to park there? The event management team won't return until ten o'clock to start dismantling the marquee, so there's no one to ask.'

'Leave it for the moment, Murdo. I'll explain everything later. I'm just - dealing with it. Meet you down there in five. Over and out.' Carefully, Ruairi replaced the two-way radio back on the bedside table.

'Dealing with it?' Fliss asked. 'I'm guessing that means *me*?'

Ruairi rubbed a weary hand over his eye and didn't answer. He gave the impression he was exhausted and overwrought, too. But unlike Fliss, he clearly thought this wasn't the time or the place to discuss unwitting mistakes, scheming stepsisters and *gheusaibhs.*

'Look, I'll sort this out and discuss it with you later. For the moment, I'll have to concentrate on damage limitation and the fallout from the gates being open. Will you be able to make your way back to the Wee Hoose without -?'

'Being seen? Embarrassing you further?' she asked tartly, zipping up her skirt and wrapping the sheet around her like an oversized pashmina. The bubble of euphoria that had separated them from the rest of the world for the past few hours seemed to have burst. Knowing she wouldn't be able to fasten up the bustier without help, Fliss draped it over the bed frame and then placed the tiara and necklace on the window seat.

'Make sure you put *those* in the safe. Or I'll probably find Callum McDonald waiting for me down at the Wee Hoose with handcuffs and a warrant for my arrest, for unwittingly dissing yet another bloody Urquhart tradition.'

'Now you're just overreacting,' he said grim-faced.

'Coming from the King of Overreaction I'll take that as a compliment.'

Opening the bedroom door, she checked that the coast was clear and the corridor deserted. She had her reputation to think of. It was one thing for everyone to know she'd slept with the Laird, when there had at least been a chance of them forming a relationship. But quite another thing for it to become common knowledge that they'd had a one-night stand. And that she was responsible for opening the gates and bringing a curse down on the house - days before flying home to Pimlico.

'Fliss,' he called after her. 'Wait. Please.'

But he'd left it too late. Without a backward glance, she hurried down the stairs and out of the house. She walked across the gravel, which was usually kept raked to within an inch of its life, and made sure she left her footprints next to the lorry's tyre tracks. And when she glanced back at the house and Ruairi's bedroom window, it was deserted.

Once back in the Wee Hoose, she picked up the phone and dialled Becky's number. Now that she'd run out of anger and the adrenaline had stopped pumping she felt weary to her bones.

'Hello,' Becky's mum picked up.

'Hi, Sue - is Bex there?' Fliss asked, trying desperately to keep her voice from cracking.

'No, she's away on a Hen weekend, seems like everyone's getting married round 'ere, at the moment. You alright, babes? You don't sound it.'

Hearing Sue's familiar voice made Fliss long to lay her head in her surrogate mother's lap and howl away her misery. Instead, she swallowed hard to dislodge the great wedge of wretchedness clogging her throat and managed a bright: 'No probs, I'll catch her later.'

'Ok, babes. Take care. You're coming home soon, ain't cha?'

'Very soon,' Fliss replied, and a plan began to take shape in her mind.

'Bye, darlin'.'

She ended the call and then walked over to her dressing table where a business card was wedged in one corner of the mirror. Since Iona's birth she'd become friends with Shona McAlester and she recalled her words on the morning Ruairi had driven her back to the far side of Kinloch Mara where she and her husband Archie had their small hotel.

If there's ever anything I - or my family - can do for you, you have only to ask. If things don't work out here - Remember that you have friends on the other side of the loch . . . the bit where His Gorgeousness doesn't call all the shots.

His Gorgeousness - Fliss's body was still tender from their lovemaking and it took all of her concentration to forget his touch, his kisses, his tenderness. How could everything have changed so quickly and irrevocably? How could he believe that she'd opened the gates deliberately *and* be so blind to Isla's faults?

Never had the cliché *cool light of day* had more resonance than it did this morning. Hardening her heart against Ruairi, she dialled Shona's number.

'The Rowan Tree. Good morning, how can I help you?'

'Sh - Shona?' The tears, which she'd held in check, now threatened to swamp her.

'Fliss? Is that you?'

'Uh huh . . .'

'What's happened?' There was no reply for several seconds and then Shona intuitively picked up the vibe. 'His Gorgeousness causing you problems?'

'Oh, Shona . . .' was all Fliss could manage on a drawn-out sigh before scalding, salt tears overwhelmed her. 'You don't know the half of it.'

Chapter Thirty Eight

Shona poured a slug of brandy in Fliss's coffee and pushed a box of Kleenex towards her. Shutting the door to her private sitting room, she dusted off her hands and gave Fliss her full attention. 'Okay, tell Auntie Shona *everything*.'

As intended, Fliss smiled through her tears and blew her nose. Shona was like a capable, grown up version of Becky; the sensible older sister she'd always longed for. Perhaps that was why they'd become firm friends in such a short space of time. After her phone call, Shona had driven to the rescue like Tom Hanks in Saving Private Ryan, well before Ruairi was aware of her hasty departure and the rest of Tigh na Locha was awake. They'd then spent a tearful half hour in a layby between Kinloch Mara and Shona's hotel *The Rowan Tree*, while Fliss wept inconsolably.

The thought was enough to make Fliss's bottom lip quiver again, so she took another restorative slug of her brandy-laced coffee and blew her nose for a second time.

'Repeat everything sloooow-ly, and in some kind of order this time, please,' Shona commanded, as she sipped her coffee. 'What *exactly* has His Gorgeousness done to you? Something about contracts - gates - revenge - believing Isla, not you?' Fliss related the story as concisely as she could, but glossed over the fact she and Ruairi had become lovers last night.

'I had to get away, I simply had to. That's why I rang you, Shona.'

'And I'm glad you did, Fliss. My, my . . . what a pickle. And His Gorgeousness doesn't know you're here?'

'No. And I don't want him to, either. I'm getting the next plane h- home to London and saying goodbye to Kinloch Mara f- forever,' she stammered. The very thought was enough to start the tears falling again. She blotted them with the sleeve of her sweatshirt pulled over her knuckles.

'Well of course you don't - and I'm right there with you on that one, sister. But what about Mitzi, Angus and all the people on the other side of the loch who think the world of you? Cat - Murdo - and even the wee girl who cleans the Dower House and does your laundry? They'll be anxious to know where you are and that you're safe won't they.'

'The family won't be awake for hours, not after last night's shindig,' Fliss began, but Shona shook her head.

'If opening the gates is as big a deal as His Gorgeousness has made out, then my guess is they'll all be standing in their pj's with massive hangovers, knocking back hair of the dog and wondering what form the curse is going to take.'

'Don't you believe in the *gheusaibh*?' Fliss asked, smiling weakly at Shona's robust summing up of the situation.

'Fliss, I'm from the Borders, almost an Englishwoman, we're a more prosaic species altogether, and aren't prone to bouts of away-with-faeries like the highlanders. This isn't to say that the so-called curse isn't genuine. You must have read about sympathetic magic; if people believe a curse is real, then - to them - it *is* real.'

'Yes - to *them*,' Fliss emphasised, some of her old spirit returning. 'I thought R- Ruairi would have been above all that, that . . . mumbo jumbo.'

'Mumbo jumbo?'

'You know - superstition, rituals, and archaic beliefs.' Fliss's spirits took a dive as she recalled his look when she'd suggested they quietly moved the lorry, shut the gates and act like nothing had happened. How could *he* have been so unfeeling? How could *she* have been so crass and lacking in understanding?

'Don't you ever touch wood for luck, salute a magpie or check your horoscope?' Shona continued in her role as Devil's Advocate.

Fliss thought back to the party when she'd touched the brass Buddha in the Urquhart's hall for good karma and the horoscope she'd downloaded onto her phone that same morning. *Friends will make or break your weekend. Have an escape plan at the ready.* She was prepared to admit that maybe Shona had a point. But she wasn't ready - yet - to concede that Ruairi's reaction to the gates being opened had been perfectly understandable. Or that he'd been in shock, spoken to her in haste and was probably regretting every one of his hasty words.

'Of course. Everyone does. Becky even has lucky knickers she wears when she's out on the pull,' she tried to bring some humour to the conversation. 'But that doesn't excuse him.'

'There you are then. Only, with highlanders - it goes deeper than that. It isn't superstition - it's more like belief.' Shona pushed the tissue box across to her and Fliss took a fresh one.

'But, I said . . .' In retrospect, Fliss now realised that she should have given him time to cool down before she'd owned up to her innocent mistake.

'Well, never mind what you said. I'm guessing that you'd spent the night together and were both . . . tired and emotional. Not thinking straight. High on *lurve* and hungover on champagne,' Shona crossed her eyes and pulled a funny face. Fliss gave a watery smile. 'That's better! His Gorgeousness has probably had the lorry driven away, gravel raked, the blasted gates closed and is - even now - realising what an utter pillock he's been. The only curse is the one he's brought on himself by throwing away his chance of happiness with a girl like you. End of.' Shona's upbeat tone restored Fliss's equilibrium. She drank the last of her coffee and put her collection of crumpled tissues in the waste paper basket Shona held out to her.

'Think so?'

'Know so.'

Fliss gave Shona an *I'm not so sure* look. 'But there's still the issue of my contract being terminated and a replacement being brought in to run the therapy centre,' she pointed out. 'Ruairi said he had a different position in mind to offer me, a better one.'

'What do you think he meant?' In her mind's eye, Fliss saw him removing the tissue-wrapped parcel from the tallboy and bringing it over to her. What *was* in it?

'Stupid of me, I guess, but I hoped he was going to ask me to live at Tigh na Locha with him. See how things went before - possibly - making the arrangement more permanent?' The words felt liked like they'd been gouged out of her heart, because it was the first time she'd actually given voice to them. 'And when Mitzi and the girls moved out -'

'You'd move in permanently?'

'I guess,' Fliss said noncommittally, knowing that in her heart she'd hoped for more. Much more.

In the cold, dull light of the October afternoon, Fliss squirmed at how naive and ridiculous her dreams appeared. Of *course* she couldn't move in with him. How could a therapist from Pimlico become the next Lady Urquhart? She looked out of the bay window down the sloping gardens of the old Victorian property and towards the grey sheet of the loch. The same waters would be lapping the sands below the Dower House where she'd been so happy. Where she'd never wanted to leave.

Her position as manageress had only ever been temporary and she'd known that from the outset. And initially, she'd simply viewed the appointment as her passport out of Pimlico and her way out of trouble. She hadn't foreseen that the longer she stayed in Kinloch Mara the more she'd grow to love it and the harder it would be to leave.

And the same was true of Kinloch Mara's laird.

'Okay. Say you found out what Ruairi had in mind, and that he was asking you to move in with him. Would you accept?' Shona broke into Fliss's sombre thoughts.

'How could I, knowing that he thought me capable of such deception? That I'd actually opened the gates in a fit of pique because my replacement had been appointed? And in order to save my own skin, had put the blame on Isla?'

'Isla. Hmm . . . she really is a piece of work, isn't she?'

'Spoiled and screwed up,' Fliss agreed but then, ever soft hearted, added a coda. 'But she was really hurting last night, has been hurting for years if the truth be known - over her father's premature death, denying her love for Murdo, Ruairi's heavy-handedness and so on. Then I arrive in Kinloch Mara, bringing change she didn't want and hadn't expected . . . and for a finale, bring a curse down on their heads.'

'Fliss, you're a better person than I am. I don't think I'd feel quite so generously disposed towards Isla in the circumstances. Now then - shower and bed, after which you come down in time for tea and we'll talk some more. Then,' she gave Fliss a searching look, 'you can book your flight home for the day after tomorrow. If you're sure that's what you really want.'

'Shona, to be absolutely honest, I don't *know* what I really want.'

'One final thing - should His Gorgeousness ring up begging for forgiveness, what should I tell him?' Shona asked, quirking an eyebrow.

'In the unlikely event of that happening, tell him it will take more than *words* to get me back into his life.' Or his bed, Fliss thought distractedly, as Shona led the way to one of the guest bedrooms.

'A grand gesture is required, then?' Shona said almost to herself as she paused on the bottom step and scooped up some bed linen placed there. Then, in her usual businesslike manner, she ushered Fliss into the suite reserved for family and friends. 'It's yours for as long as you want. No hurry. To use a cliché, decisions made in haste are always repented at leisure.'

Shona pulled back the bedcovers, drew the heavy linen curtains on the distracting view of the loch and the hills towards Port Urquhart and then quietly left the room.

When Fliss woke some hours later, she thought she was still dreaming. She imagined that she could hear Murdo's voice downstairs and - even more incredibly - Isla speaking to Shona. She glanced at her watch and saw that it was five in the afternoon and almost dark. To satisfy her curiosity, she slipped on the dressing gown Shona had thoughtfully placed at the foot of the bed and then padded onto the landing.

No mistake. It was Murdo and Isla down below in the hall.

'I'm not sure she'd want to see either of you,' Shona was saying firmly in a tone that even made Fliss quake. 'Especially not Miss

Urquhart.'

'Oh, but she must. I promised Ruairi I'd apologise, put things right,' Isla began and then looked at Murdo for backup.

'You think *sorry* and an anguished expression will do that, do you? I'm not quite sure who you're most sorry for - yourself, or Fliss.'

'She deserves your censure, Shona, I know she does. But,' Murdo put his hand on Isla's shoulder, 'I think she should be given the chance to square things with Fliss, especially if - as you say, she's flying home tomorrow.' He spoke quietly and with a steady determination that Fliss recognised. 'Don't you?'

'Shona, it's okay,' Fliss called down. 'I'll listen to what she has to say.' They watched as she descended the stairs in the too large dressing gown, raking her fingers through hair still knotted and tangled from last night's lovemaking. Nodding, but giving Isla the benefit of a cold stare, Shona led them into the small office and left them to it.

Fliss sat in the office chair, forcing Isla and Murdo to stand by the desk. Her body language made it quite plain that as far as she was concerned the Kinloch Mara phase of her life was over. Murdo perched on the edge of the desk and Isla stood in front of him, pale-faced and red-eyed, leaning back against his kilted knees as if she drew courage from the physical contact.

'And?' she prompted. Isla looked like she'd spent most of the day shedding tears of regret - as well she should, Fliss thought, glaring at her.

'Fliss, I did an unforgivable thing and I'm sorry. Please come back to Kinloch Mara and let me - *us* - make it up to you.'

'And that's it? No explanation as to *why* you did it?' Fliss asked, although she already knew the reasons. However, she wasn't letting Isla off the hook that easily. 'Thanks for coming over but I think I deserve better than that.' Getting to her feet, she held the door open, a signal for them to leave. Isla took a step forward, hesitated, and then burst into noisy tears. Murdo closed the door quietly and motioned for Fliss to sit back down.

'Isla had the mistaken belief that -'

'That she can do whatever she wants and get away with it?' Fliss finished his sentence for him. 'Breaking News - *she can't.*'

'I think she knows that now.' Murdo put his arm round Isla who hid her face in his shoulder. Fliss was far from mollified by the sight of them cosying up to each other while she and Ruairi were at daggers drawn. In fact, if anything, Murdo's show of consideration towards Isla inflamed her anger even more.

'And that's it, is it? She gets a mild ticking off, you get the girl and - what do I get? I'll tell you - a one way ticket to Pimlico and a pull-out bed on my friend's bedroom floor.' Murdo leaned away from Isla as if finally realising not only the implications of what she'd done, but how furious Fliss was. 'I'm assuming that Ruairi knows the truth now?' she asked sharply.

'Yes. M - Murdo suspected almost straightaway I was behind telling you to pass the message on to open the gates.'

'Unlike your brother.'

'Unlike Ruairi,' she agreed. 'Murdo took me to him. Made me tell him the truth. But, instead of being angry as I thought he would be, Ruairi simply said, quite coldly: *Isla, you don't know what you've done.*'

That brought tears to Fliss's eyes, but she blinked them away furiously.

'Go on,' she urged, stony-faced.

'At first, I thought he was talking about tradition and the *gheusaibh*, but then I realised - now I know . . . he meant I'd ruined things between you.'

'Isn't that what you'd intended?' Fliss asked coldly.

'Fliss, last night - I was out of control. I thought merely to make things difficult for you so that you'd leave Kinloch Mara and never come back.'

'Thanks for that.'

'Stupidly, I thought that you and Murdo were - lovers.' Her voice went up several octaves and the word came out as a strangled cry. 'And had - somehow - conspired to encourage Ruairi to change the terms of the trust, get me out of the way on Angus's land and leave you free to -'

'You were wide of the mark,' Fliss said and gave her a caustic look. 'It's Ruairi I love. It's always been Ruairi. I don't give a fuck about you, your trust fund or your jealous imaginings about Murdo and me. Now, if you don't mind, I'd like you both to leave.'

Murdo moved Isla out of the way and walked over to Fliss. He enfolded her in a brotherly hug and kissed her on both cheeks. 'Fliss, I'm sorry. So very, very sorry.'

'Murdo, you've been a great friend to me, but I want nothing more to do with anything or anyone connected with Kinloch Mara. Can you understand that?'

'Yes, Fliss I can.' He held onto her hands and seemed reluctant to leave her. 'But, what shall I tell Ruairi?' Fliss took a deep breath before answering.

'Tell him . . .' She was about to say *that our timing's always been wrong*, but then she changed her mind. 'Tell him he made his choice this morning and we can't turn the clock back.'

'But, when you see what he's done for you . . .'

'Murdo,' she released his hands. 'You once advised me to trust Ruairi and look where it's brought me. I've run out of faith, from now on I'm only trusting my gut instincts and they're telling me take the first available flight home.'

Murdo looked at her sadly but nodded, evidently seeing that the lady was not for turning.

'In that case, let me do one last thing for you.'

'Yes?'

'I brought you from Inverness to Kinloch Mara so, please Fliss, let me be the one who drives you back to the airport.' Fliss's heart contracted and she dug her nails into her palm to stop herself from crying afresh at Murdo's last kindness to her.

'Very well, I'll book my ticket when you leave and phone you at the Factor's House with my flight details and times.' As she walked them over to the front door, Isla turned and tried to say something, but Fliss ignored her. As far as she was concerned, Isla had placed herself beyond the pale by her scheming and conniving - and she would have to live with the knowledge of what she'd done

Just as *she* would have to spend the rest of her life without Ruairi.

Chapter Thirty Nine

Murdo put the last of Fliss's bags in the back of the Land Rover.

As they drove away from Shona and Archie's hotel, the weather conspired with the scenery to turn Fliss's last morning in Kinloch Mara into a glittering jewel. However, the beauty of the loch and the autumn colours were seen through a sheen of Fliss's tears as she fastened her seat belt and waved Shona goodbye.

'Okay,' Murdo said slowly as they drove along in silence, 'you're not going to ask, so I'm going to tell you.'

'Tell me what?' Fliss choked out, dashing away a tear from her cheek with a forefinger.

'How cut up Ruairi is over everything that's happened between you.'

'So cut up he hasn't been in touch? So upset that he didn't turn up this morning to drive me to the airport?' she rounded on him, tears forgotten.

'Fliss -' Murdo let out a sigh a parent might use with an unreasonable child. 'Didn't you tell Shona that you wouldn't speak to him if he rang?'

'Yes. But . . .'

'Would you have got in the Land Rover if he'd turned up this morning?'

'Probably not,' she conceded. 'But, even so . . .'

'Even so - *nothing*. You are both as stubborn and pig-headed as each other, throwing away your chance of happiness because you won't dismount from your high horses and admit that you love each other.'

'Murdo, I don't! He doesn't . . .'

'See. There you go again. And for what it's worth, he does - and you do!' Murdo frowned, apparently at his use of bad grammar and their intransigence. 'Fliss, I've wasted *years* waiting for Isla to grow up and realise that we were meant to be together. Don't do the same.'

They drove along in silence after that.

The two-hour journey to Inverness gave Fliss plenty of time to think. She didn't need Murdo to tell her she'd been a fool, or that running away from Tigh na Locha had been a mistake. She realised that she'd shown herself to be no better than the faithless Fiona. How had Isla put it: *If she'd really loved him and not just the idea of him, she would have stayed and toughed it out.*

Her appointment had only ever been temporary, she was aware of that when she'd signed the contract. When a new contract hadn't been forthcoming she should have acted like a proper businesswoman and demanded to know what other position Ruairi had in mind. He'd been about to reveal it just before he'd seen that the gates were open. With the value of hindsight, she realised she should have given him time to calm down, come to his senses and then pressed home her advantage to demand the terms she wanted.

Instead, she'd flounced off like a stroppy teenager, and would probably never know what lay inside the tissue-wrapped parcel. Judging by its size and shape, it most definitely wasn't an engagement ring. She blushed, one-night stands didn't usually result in marriage proposals. One- night stand? No, it was much more than that. It had been the beginning of something wonderful, something perfect - but then . . .

She groaned and laid her head against the window, watching the miles disappearing underneath the Land Rover's chassis. Every mile took her nearer to the airport and further away from the man she loved.

'So, you and Isla - how's that going to work out?' she asked Murdo, thinking she'd dwelt on her own problems long enough.

'Ruairi's arranged art lessons for her, as you probably know. I believe she has you to thank for that? She's hoping to hold an exhibition next summer in Port Urquhart - maybe it'll even become an annual event like the Pittenweem Art Festival in Fife. Then art school, as close to Kinloch Mara as possible, and after her degree show - who knows? She's young and I don't want to stand in her way.'

'But you're an item?' Fliss asked, keeping things light.

'Yep. We're definitely an item,' Murdo grinned, as though he liked the sound of it. Then he changed the subject. 'Do you want to stop for a coffee en route or go straight to the airport? We're in no rush.'

'Straight there.'

'No second thoughts?'

'None,' she lied and returned to looking at the scenery.

Half an hour later, she retrieved her mobile phone out of her handbag and checked it for a signal. Three bars - a miracle - but when she rang Becky she was put straight through to voicemail.

'Bex. Where are you? I need to talk to you. Looks like I'm back on the floor in your bedroom for a couple of months at least. Ring me. Pleeeeeeease.'

Murdo glanced at her. 'Still no luck?'

'No. Don't know where she is. Probably found a hot bloke and imprisoned him in the stock room of my old salon. Not like her not to return my calls though.' She put her phone back in her bag and pulled the leather string tight.

As they journeyed on, the words of the old Stevie Wonder song *I Just called to Say I Love You* played through her brain like an earworm. Maybe, if she rang Ruairi and left a message on his voicemail everything would come right. However, she suspected that their relationship was beyond the stage of cheesy lyrics. Besides which, apart from endearments such as *chuisle mo chroí* and *mo chridhe,* their liaison had been too brief to fit in declarations of undying love.

No. Any message she had for Ruairi had to be delivered in person. *Delivered in person.*

'Murdo. *STOP!*' She grabbed his arm urgently. 'Turn the Land Rover around – we're going back to Kinloch Mara.'

'To Shona's? Have you left something behind?'

'No - to Tigh na Locha. And, *yes*, I have left something behind - Ruairi. The man I love.' Her voice snagged and the ever-present tears welled up. But she swallowed them down, she'd cried a river and now it was time to call a halt. She had some serious thinking to do.

'Fliss, thank God you've seen sense.' Murdo straightened in his seat and urged the Land Rover forward. 'Putting the pedal to the metal, Ma'am - and hoping the speed cameras don't catch us.'

'If they do, Ruairi pays the fine,' she said. She and Murdo high fived each other and her heart sang as the Land Rover bowled along. But this time, the tune running through her head was Steppenwolf's *Born to Be Wild* and she grinned as Murdo got the motor running and headed out on the highway.

After all, she was going home.

When Murdo pulled up at the back door of Tigh na Locha, Fliss leapt out of the Land Rover before he had time to switch the engine off. She ran through the kitchen, past surprised staff and into the hall where she took the stairs two at a time until she reached Ruairi's bedroom. It didn't look any different from the morning when he'd discovered that the gates were open and she'd bolted. The mattress was still on the floor, although it looked as though someone had tucked a tartan shawl round it in an attempt to make it - and the room, look presentable. The Vivienne Westwood bustier was where she'd left it - draped over the foot of the brass bed, as if waiting for her to slip back into it.

Purposefully, she walked over to the tallboy - quite prepared to rifle through the top drawer in search of the tissue-wrapped parcel, if the need arose. But she didn't need to. It was lying sad and forlorn on top of the chest of drawers where Ruairi had left it, next to a bottle of his aftershave, cufflinks, a stubby pencil and other masculine detritus.

Picking it up, she sat down on the window seat, trying hard not to get emotional or sidetracked into remembering how passionately they'd made love on the padded cushion. She peeled back the faded blue tissue paper to reveal a silk sash in Urquhart dress tartan with a heavy silver brooch fastened to it. She frowned and searched the room for more clues - she couldn't afford to get this wrong. Her gaze soon lit upon a large silver-framed photograph on the side table by the brass bed.

It held a photograph of a dark haired woman wearing a long white dress in a style that was nearly thirty years out of fashion. The tartan sash was fastened at her shoulder by the silver brooch Fliss held in her hands. She wore the sapphire and diamond necklace Mitzi had loaned Fliss for the ball at her throat and on her upswept hair was the matching Urquhart tiara. She wore both with becoming style and grace.

In a moment of epiphany, Fliss realised that in giving her Urquhart family jewels to wear at the ball, Mitzi had sent out a clear message to Ruairi. Go get the girl or lose her to someone else. Small wonder that he'd stalled briefly in delivering his welcome speech when he'd caught sight of her wearing the jewels. Heirlooms last worn by his mother.

Giving the photograph a more searching look, Fliss noticed that a handsome man in full highland dress was standing by Mairi Urquhart's side. A very young Ruairi was in front of them and each had a hand resting lightly on his shoulders, as though he was overexcited and needed a firm but loving hand to calm him down. She didn't need to learn any more. It was now plain that Ruairi had been about to offer her his mother's sash as a token of his feelings towards her, but the *bloody* gates had got in the way. She let out a cry of frustration and dismay and buried her face in the sash, breathing in the faint scent of lavender and Este Lauder Youth Dew that still clung to it.

'Oh, Ruairi,' she said, kissing the sash in lieu of kissing the man. 'I love you.'

Then she placed it back in its tissue paper and left it exactly as she'd found it. Turning away from the tallboy, she noticed a letter weighed down with a bottle of Chanel aftershave. There was something about the handwriting that caught her eye, something familiar.

'It couldn't be,' she said aloud and her solemn mood was broken as she gave an incredulous laugh.

Stealthy as a cat burglar, she moved the bottle of aftershave to one side and picked up the letter. Stifling her instinctive response that rifling through another person's possessions was wrong, she read the letter. This was her future she was fighting for . . . scruples and the difference between right and wrong could go hang.

'I *thought* so!' she exclaimed as she read to the end of the letter with its almost childish signature. 'But why would they be writing to each other without telling me?' Then she remembered what Murdo had said in Shona's hall yesterday: *when you see what he's done for you.*

She put the letter back under its paperweight. 'Oh, Ruairi,' she said again, with a catch in her voice. She knew she had to find him; explain how much she loved him. She was suddenly filled with the belief that everything would come right and they could have a future together. If only she could talk to him. If only he would listen.

Galloping down the stairs and jumping into the hall, she almost fell into Murdo's arms.

'Ruairi. Where is he?'

'Stalking on the hills. I can get him on the two-way radio,' he unclipped the handset from his belt but she forestalled him.

'No, just drive me to where he is - or as close as you can. I'll take it from there. What I have to say to Ruairi has to be said face to face.'

Murdo's worried expression vanished, replaced by a broad smile. 'Now you're talking, lassie. Come on, and take this spare radio, I'll show you how to use it - should you get lost.'

'I won't lose my way,' she said determinedly. 'Not this time.'

She found Ruairi standing by the triangulation point where he'd shown her the Brocken Spectre nine weeks earlier. He was viewing the valley through a telescopic sight unscrewed from the high-powered rifle propped up against the trig point's stone pillar. He looked like a very lonely monarch surveying his mist-shrouded glen and his body language seemed to reflect his mood. His shoulders were hunched, he was tapping his foot on the base of the stone pillar agitatedly and - even in profile - he looked dejected. As if he owned all these acres but had lost something much more precious.

Heart in mouth, Fliss tiptoed up to him. At first, she thought he hadn't heard her approach through the long grass because he remained with his back towards her. But then he spoke.

'If I turn around, will you melt away like a spectre in the mist?'

'No,' she said softly, her heart slamming into reverse at the sound of his voice.

'Only . . . if you did - I don't think I could . . . I mean, I wouldn't be able to . . .' His voice thickened. He lowered the telescopic sight but remained where he was, watching the light fading over the loch as the autumn twilight descended.

'I'll never go away again,' she vowed.

'Never's a long time, Fliss,' he replied, putting the sight in the pocket of his gilet and turning round. She stood stock-still, not sure what to say, all she'd known for certain was that she had to find him. Now that she had, the words simply wouldn't come. It felt as if years had passed since they'd last been together and they were strangers to each other.

'Ruairi . . . I,' she managed on a sort of strangled half-cry. Deciding that actions in this case spoke louder than words she flung herself into his arms, almost knocking him over and sending them both rolling down the hillside. 'Say it,' she begged, grabbing his gilet in both hands and giving him a rough shake.

'Say that I'm sorry, I've been an idiot? That the gates don't matter. The only curse is the one I've brought on myself by putting my obligations as laird before my needs as a man? I'll say it, and gladly - because that's what I did. And that's what everyone in Kinloch Mara from Mitzi down to Jaimsie the Piper thinks; if their accusatory looks are anything to go by.'

'No, not *that*,' she said impatiently, and stepped back from him. 'There'll be plenty of time for *that* later. Repeat what you said to me in the bedroom before we made love. I can hardly say it to myself, now can I?' she asked archly, standing with her hands on her hips. He frowned and then his face lightened as he remembered.

'Shut up *wumman* and kiss me,' he commanded.

'*Tha mo cridhe buin do Thu,*' she replied, hoping that her stilted – *Ha Mo Kree boon daw OO* - was enough to let him know her heart belonged to him. Then she kissed him and he pulled her into rib-crushing embrace, holding her like he'd never let her go. For a long moment they stood on the hillside with the purple gloaming settling round them. Then they kissed as if they drew their life's blood from the scorching touch of mouth on mouth. As if being together was the reason for their existence and nothing in this world - or the next, mattered.

'Where did you learn to say that?' he asked, when he finally broke off the kiss. He brushed away the tear on her cheek with his finger and Fliss's heart swelled when she saw tears misting his eyes, too.

'Shona. She taught me a few other phrases last night. Rude ones, too, in case I should have need of them. Do you think she has second sight?'

'Nothing about Shona would surprise me,' he laughed. Then he bent down, picked up his rifle and slung it over his shoulder. 'Come on, it's a long walk back to Tigh na Locha and we don't want to be out on the hills in the dark.'

'Don't worry, Murdo's waiting for us at the foot of the hill,' she explained, slipping her hand quite naturally into his and giving it a reassuring squeeze.

'Let's go home, mo chridhe. The old house is empty without you,' he said roughly. He delivered the words with such feeling, that Fliss stumbled on the path - her ability to walk seemingly affected by his passionate words. Determinedly, she righted herself and led the way back to Tigh na Locha - to the untidy bedroom with the tartan sash on the tallboy and the mattress on the floor.

And she knew it was the most wonderful place in the world and that it was waiting, just for them.

Chapter Forty

The bedroom smelled of tuber rose and fig from the candles Fliss had brought up from the sitting room and arranged on the mantelpiece of the Victorian fireplace. Ruairi had pulled the mattress up to the fire and was now kneeling on it, twisting a half-empty champagne bottle in an ice bucket to cool it down. The firelight softened his features and Fliss, standing in the shadows over by the window, felt her heart swell with love as she watched his deft movements. When he turned and smiled at her, she felt as if she'd won the Euro Millions on a double rollover week.

There were thirty rooms in Tigh na Locha but tonight she wanted nothing more than to be in this simple, almost Spartan room, with the man she loved. Mitzi and the girls were over on Angus's estate for a few days and Ruairi had dismissed the staff for the evening. Letting out a happy sigh, Fliss glanced behind her to where frost was riming the roof and turrets of Tigh na Locha, and smiled. Outside it was a freezing cold October night, but in her heart, it was high summer.

However, ever pragmatic, she knew that before she joined Ruairi on the mattress there were things they needed to talk through - sort out. So she applied the brakes to her runaway emotions, and broke the silence.

'Will we drink champagne every night?' she teased, as he topped up their glasses. 'Or only every other night?'

'Whatever your heart desires,' he replied seriously, as she joined him on the floor, tucking her legs beneath her. Then he stretched out along the mattress, laid his head in her lap and closed his eyes. 'You're very quiet, Fliss,' he said after some time. 'And that worries me.'

'There are matters which have to be settled before we can put this romantic fire and the rest of the champagne to good use,' she said.

'In that case,' he reached up and pulled her down so he could kiss her, 'you'd better talk fast. Otherwise, I can't guarantee my good behaviour.' Fliss pulled back from the kiss and pushed him away from her, pretending offence.

'Okay. I'll keep it brief. Although, I am quite tempted to find out what your definition of bad behaviour might be.' She laughed; pleased they could finally relax and enjoy each other's company after everything that had happened between them. Then she asked: 'Will you explain to me why you've sold the house in Elgin Crescent?'

'Simple, I came to the conclusion that, in spite of its history, it's only a house. Just so much bricks and mortar. It's surplus to requirements, is a source of temptation to Isla and holds unhappy memories for me. After our – ahem – frank and honest exchange of views the morning of the Brocken Spectre, I had time to think over what you said. During the long flight to Hong Kong, I reached the conclusion that you were right. I should consolidate my assets and realise my dream of building up the estate for ecotourism, not let the past hold me back. I needed a push and you gave it to me!'

'I was bang out of order on that occasion, sticking my nose in where it wasn't wanted,' Fliss freely admitted. 'But I could see all the stumbling blocks standing in the way of our happiness, and you were too close to the problem and couldn't. Am I forgiven?'

'Totally.' Ruairi reached out for her hand, caught it and kissed it. 'But only if you forgive me for saying that your grief over your parents' deaths was any less real than mine. That was unforgivably crass of me, but – in my defence – you touched a raw nerve that morning. Several, if we're being totally honest, and my reactions reflected that.'

'The house?' she reminded him, picking up her champagne glass.

'Grandfather bought it for a song in the early sixties when the slums were being cleared, leaving behind grand, dilapidated houses no one wanted. He liked the bohemian atmosphere I guess - maybe that's where Cat and Isla get it from,' he observed somewhat wryly. 'My parents renovated the property extensively in the seventies when Notting Hill was beginning to rival Chelsea as an uber cool address. They loved the house because it was the only place they could truly escape the demands of Kinloch Mara. I didn't realise *quite* how much it was worth until I had it valued nine weeks ago.' He mentioned a figure and Fliss let out a long, slow whistle.

'Wow. Maybe I can order two hot tubs for the Spa,' she joked, 'and a sauna.'

'You can have whatever you want, mo chridhe,' he grinned, kissing each of her knuckles in turn. Desire lanced through Fliss, but she kept a lid on her emotions. There would be time for that - later.

'Talking of which,' she blushed, glad that he was staring into the fire. 'I inadvertently saw a letter lying on the chest of drawers this afternoon when I came looking for you. I recognised the signature. Is Becky Casterton my replacement?'

'So much for my so-called surprise! It backfired spectacularly when you thought you'd been sacked. Poor Auld Angus, he'd been sworn to secrecy and was dying to tell you the truth.'

'I've never been any good at maths,' she admitted, raking her fingers through his thick, dark hair. 'Stupidly, I added two and two together and got five.' Ruairi levered himself upright, drew his knees up to his chest, crossed his bare feet at the ankles and regarded her, earnestly.

'Fliss, I have business to conclude, investors to bring up to speed with the changes taking place at Kinloch Mara. I'll have to leave you for long stretches of time until things are settled; wrapped up. I don't want you to feel neglected or lonely while I'm away.'

Like Fiona.

The thought hung in the air but Fliss wafted away the ghost of fiancées past and his concerns with a wave of her hand.

'I'm more resourceful than Fiona,' she said, straightly. 'Besides, I won't have time to feel lonely if I'm to build up the Spa. I'll have Angus and Mitzi to consult on an almost daily basis once plans are finalised and Becky and the new girl's induction to oversee. Becky's as mad as a box of frogs but a brilliant therapist and we're lucky to have her. But I warn you, we might hit the hot spots of Port Urquhart together on a

Saturday night when you're overseas . . .'

'Let me know if you find any,' he said dryly, 'and I'll inform the Scottish Tourist Board.'

'I will. But tell me something, how did you persuade Becky to leave London?'

'Well, for one thing, she's really missed you. And, I may have said there were,' he gave a mischievous smile that made her heart perform flick-flacks in her chest, 'wall-to-wall Hot Highlanders. Men in Kilts, forming an orderly queue awaiting her arrival.' Fliss pictured Becky running rings round the Urquhart cousins and bewitching all the males under forty who came within her orbit.

'She'd like that - and I've missed her, too. But I can't promise she won't punch Isla on the nose when she learns about the business of the gates.'

'It's a risk Isla will have to take,' he shrugged unconcernedly.

It would be a long time before Isla was welcome in Tigh na Locha, Fliss suspected.

'It's a mystery how Becky kept all this secret from me? Oh, wait - is that why I could never get through on her mobile? She'd switched it off to stop herself blabbing? Nice one, Bex.'

Evidently losing patience with her Q and A session, Ruairi started to unbutton the pearl buttons on her shirt.

'You promised that your questions would require brief answers. I suspect you of reneging on your deal, Miss Bagshawe. I think it's time you were taken in hand,' he declared, giving her a warm look.

'Not so fast, your Lairdship,' she re-fastened her blouse and regarded him sternly. 'If I remember correctly, you said you had a better position to offer me. What could possibly be better than manageress of Kinloch Mara's therapy centre and proposed Eco Spa?' Although she spoke lightly, she held her breath, consciously thinking of his mother's tartan sash and what it meant. At least what she *thought* it meant.

Ruairi was suddenly very pensive.

'Fliss,' he applied himself to unfastening the buttons she'd assiduously fastened just seconds before. 'You arrived in our lives like a force of nature - Hurricane Fliss. I couldn't resist you - and God knows I tried my best. Mo eudail,' he stopped playing with the buttons, 'my darling. I love you and want to spend the rest of my life with you; if you'll have me.' He reached under the brass bed frame and brought out the tissue-wrapped parcel. 'I should have given this to you straight after the ball. But,' he smiled at the remembrance, 'we were rather preoccupied. Then events overtook us.'

He placed the parcel in her trembling hands.

'It isn't an engagement ring - we can choose one of those later - it's more precious than that. It belonged to my mother and I want you to wear it, as my wife, at the Christmas celebrations following Mitzi and Angus's wedding.'

'But that's only,' she did a rapid calculation, 'ten weeks away.'

'I don't want to run the risk of losing you again.' Then he grinned, a wide, disarming smile that pushed her insistence on being business like to the limit. 'One of the advantages of having one's own church and a second cousin who's an ordained minister in the Free Presbyterian Church of Scotland is that, apart from gaining the necessary paperwork, there's no reason why we can't be married before Mitzi and Angus.'

'Always assuming I say "yes", of course,'

'Of course,' he said humbly.

'But, won't people talk? Start doing calculations on their fingers.'

'Let them. What do we care?' he asked haughtily, reminding her he was the Laird of Kinloch Mara.

'Everything the Laird wants - the Laird gets, is that it?' she asked, matching his imperious tone. But it was hard to maintain the pretence, when her heart was singing and joy was bubbling up inside her like champagne.

'In your case, Fliss, I take nothing for granted. I've learned my lesson the hard way.' Unable to hold out any longer, Fliss unwrapped the sash and was about to slip it over her head when she paused.

'Is it bad luck to try it on before we're married?'

'Curses, bad luck, karma - our lives are what we make them. I know that now.'

'In that case, yes. I will marry you, Ruairi Urquhart - and as soon as possible.' She recalled old Nurse McLeish's prophesy, *a baby within the year* and the searching look she'd been given on the night Iona was born. She felt goose bumps along the length of her arms. Despite Ruairi's rejection of curses, prophesies and omens she couldn't dismiss the old nurse's words.

But perhaps that was because she wanted them to be true?

'Here, let me. You wear it over your left shoulder and fasten it with the brooch to show that you're a chieftain's wife.' Obediently, she held up her arms and he slipped it over her head and fastened it. Then he got to his feet. 'Come here. There's something else I want to show you.'

Taking her hand, he led her over to the window.

'Another Broken Spectre?' she quizzed. Shaking his head, he turned her round so that she was facing the loch. Resting his chin on her head, he wrapped his arms around her and pointed to the ornamental gates. They were clearly visible under a bright hunters' moon which lit up the gardens like a searchlight, all the way to the beach and beyond.

They were wide open!

'The gates - I don't understand. What about the curse?'

'We have no fate, but what we make for ourselves,' Ruairi whispered in her ear.

'A Scottish proverb? Shakespeare?' she asked, leaning against him, relishing the way his breath teased the hair on the nape of her neck.

'Och, no. Auld Jaimsie the Piper.' He laughed and swung her round twice, so that he was sitting on the window seat with his back to the gates and she was facing him. 'Fliss, I've already said how you came into my life like a dangerous, beautiful whirlwind. How you've made me change, re-evaluate my life. By inadvertently opening those gates, you freed my family and me; forced us to relinquish the past and get on with our lives. They're staying open from now on. Come our wedding day, we'll walk up from the church and lead our guests through them. A new day, a new beginning. But in the meantime . . .'

'Yes?'

'You know that thing you did?'

'Thing?' she asked, puzzled but warmed by his passionate look.

'On this very window seat, the night of the Highland Ball,' he laid the flat of his hand on the padded cushion and patted it. Fliss blushed, remembering the moment only too clearly. She'd thought about it many times over the last few days.

'I *think* I do,' she said slowly, wondering where this was leading.

'Do you *think* you could do it again?'

'I'm not sure that I would be able to replicate it.' Giddy with happiness, she moved closer to him and he opened his knees to accommodate her. 'I mean, I might get it all wrong.'

'In which case you'd have to practice until you got it all right, wouldn't you?'

'Well I do have high standards,' she agreed poker-faced and started to untuck his shirt from his kilt. She ran her fingers round the waistband, started to unfasten the buckles at the side and then paused 'Only, I'm not wearing my hold up stockings. So accuracy might be compromised.'

'That's a risk I'm willing to take,' he said just as solemnly. 'We'll count this as a dry run and you can fetch your stockings from the Wee Hoose tomorrow.' A devil of mischief danced in his eyes as he slipped her blouse off her shoulders and started kissing the line of her collarbone.

'Very well - here beginneth the lesson,' she managed to recite with due solemnity.

'I'm sure my second cousin - and, indeed, most of the Church of Scotland - would heartily approve of your devotion.' He leaned back against the window and placed his hands on either side of him in a gesture of surrender. Mimicking a look of intense concentration, Fliss pushed the pleats of his kilt slowly upwards and trailed her fingers along the inside of his thighs.

She paused as Ruairi drew in a shaky breath.

'But first, mo chridhe - *An toir thu dhomh pog* - will you give me your kiss?' she asked in almost perfect Gaelic as she bent her head towards him.

And the Laird of Kinloch Mara was only too happy to oblige.

Lizzie Lamb

Acknowledgements

Where would we be without our friends?

I wouldn't have started on this journey if it hadn't have been for Jean Chapman (former Chair of the Romantic Novelists' Association), her writing class all those years ago in Countesthorpe and her encouragement ever since. I owe her an enormous debt of gratitude and respect. I have also had much encouragement and support from friends in the Romantic Novelists' Association, published and yet-to-be-published, the Leicester Chapter of the RNA, Leicester Writers Club and Peatling Magna Writers' Group.

My lovely, funny friends on Facebook have cheered me on every morning and made me laugh before I glue myself to the chair in my study and get down to the serious task of writing. You know who you are. Thanks also mega successful authors Trisha Ashley, Kate Hardy and Carole Matthews whose books have inspired me and whose friendship, tweets and posts on Facebook have spurred me onwards.

I can't forget my 'people' in Leicester who've put up with my sometimes incoherent ramblings, don't really get why I'm doing this but who have stuck with me nonetheless. They are Joan Davies-Bushby, Maisie Newman, Barbara James and Gill Chapman. Thanks also to my holistic therapist Hannah Chapman for her insights into the world of beauty/holistic therapy and for giving me "P.I.N.T.A".

I owe an enormous debt to my friend and writing buddy Jan Brigden - proof reader extraordinaire - who has a gimlet eye for typos, excessive use of dashes and awkward phrases. Your turn next, Calam. Contact Jan for help with proof reading your manuscript on: jbrigden10@virginmedia.com

And last, but by no means least, thanks to author Amanda Grange, Nonpareil, whose inspiring words over lunch set The New Romantics 4 on this path to publication. And for all her help along the way.

Finally, if you have a dream, go out there and make it a reality. That's what I've done.

ABOUT THE AUTHOR

After teaching her 1000th pupil, Lizzie decided it was time to leave the chalk face and pursue her first love: *writing*. She joined the Romantic Novelists' Association's New Writers Scheme, honed her craft and wrote *Tall, Dark and Kilted*. She's had enormous fun researching men in kilts, falling in love with brooding hero *Ruairi Urquhart,* and rooting for heroine *Fliss Bagshawe* - and hopes you will, too.

Lizzie is also a founding member of the indie publishing group: *The New Romantics 4*. Her fellow New Romantics are June Kearns, Mags Cullingford and Adrienne Vaughan. If they are Athos, Porthos and Aramis - that must make Lizzie D'Artagnan! The New Romantics 4's watch cry is, *all for one and one for all.*

Follow The New Romantics 4 on Twitter @newromantics4

**To learn more about Lizzie, go to her website:
http://www.lizzielamb.co.uk**

**She would love to hear from you so feel free to get in touch:
lizzielambwriter@gmail.com**

Look out for Lizzie's second novel *Sweet Little Lies* in 2013.

Check out these other romantic novels published by The New Romantics 4

A Hollow Heart by Adrienne Vaughan

An English Woman's Guide to the Cowboy by June Kearns

Last Bite of the Cherry by Mags Cullingford

Read the extract on the next page from
Sweet Little Lies by Lizzie Lamb

Sweet Little Lies
by
Lizzie Lamb

The sound of a motor bike pulled her attention towards the ribbon of track that led up from the bay. She shaded her eyes and frowned as it sped towards her, churning up the dusty red earth. For the first time since she'd arrived in Door County she was suddenly aware of how isolated her house was. Unhurriedly, giving no sign of how vulnerable she felt, India stooped and picked out a large monkey wrench from her toolbox. She slipped it into the deep pocket of her overalls and turned to meet her unexpected visitor, her heart hammering like a crazy thing.

'You India Stuart?' the rider demanded curtly, pulling up several feet in front of her.

'That rather depends on who wants to know.' As he gunned the engine menacingly, she took a deep breath and tried to slow down the frantic beating of her heart. Clearly, her answer didn't please him because he switched off the engine, rocked the bike back onto its rest, dismounted and came towards her.

Instinctively, India took several steps backwards. Then she stopped; it wouldn't do to let him know how frightened she was - in spite of her brave words. She glanced up for a split second to gauge the measure of him. But his face was shaded by a disreputable baseball cap and his eyes were hidden behind a pair of aviator sunglasses that gave no clue to his identity or his intentions.

'Just answer the question, lady,' he demanded brusquely, walking over to the fence and touching the still tacky paint. He glanced at her over his shoulder and she caught the suggestion of steeliness behind the firm jaw; obstinacy in the determined line of his mouth. Here was a man used to having his own way; a man not easily deflected from his chosen path.

'I - I,' India stammered, feeling increasingly anxious yet annoyed with herself for allowing this man - *any man* to intimidate her. She felt

357

surreptitiously for the reassuring solidity of the wrench in her pocket but it slid from her grasp, fell through the hole in her overalls and landed on the dusty red earth with a dull thud.

For a long moment, neither of them spoke as they looked down at the murder weapon lying at their feet.

'I think this belongs to you.' He picked it up and handed it back, one corner of his mouth quirking in a humorless smile.

'Thanks,' India snatched it back, feeling suddenly rather foolish. It was obvious that she'd been prepared to use the wrench as a weapon for her protection. Now the whole idea seemed preposterous. She was of average height and slightly built - whereas he was tall, athletic and looked capable of anything. She guessed that it would take more than an inexpertly wielded wrench to deflect him from his purpose.

Whatever it was.

Available for download and paperback on Amazon Summer 2013

Printed in Great Britain
by Amazon.co.uk, Ltd.,
Marston Gate.